HARMLESS

HARMLESS

A NOVEL

MIRANDA SHULMAN

DUTTON

DUTTON
An imprint of Penguin Random House LLC
1745 Broadway, New York, NY 10019
penguinrandomhouse.com

Title page and space break art by Sylfida/Shutterstock

LIBRARY OF CONGRESS CATALOGING-IN-PUBLICATION DATA
has been applied for.

ISBN 9798217046065 (hardcover)
ISBN 9798217046072 (ebook)

Printed in the United States of America
1st Printing

The authorized representative in the EU for product safety and compliance is Penguin Random House Ireland, Morrison Chambers, 32 Nassau Street, Dublin D02 YH68, Ireland, https://eu-contact.penguin.ie.

For Charlie and Burt, with love.
Kinderhook forever.

1

An hour before her twin sister's memorial, Bea was sprawled on the kitchen floor, crying over a jar of Kalamata olives. She should've been on the train already, not shivering by the open refrigerator, unable to move. But each time she closed her eyes, it played like a looped clip from a horror film: Rosalie's fingers rooting around in the jar, her lips as she chewed, lurid and wet, the pit on a used coffee filter or cupped by a discarded clementine rind in the trash like it was nothing. Like these were normal olives. The jar was still mostly full, so Rosalie had probably only stolen one: at least there was that. If not for a droplet of reddish brine the size of a dime on the countertop, Bea wouldn't have noticed a disturbance. But she had.

She brought the jar to her face. "I'm so sorry." Her lips brushed the glass, breath clouded by the cold refrigerator air that washed over her. "I promised I'd always keep you safe."

Rosalie would be confused if Bea admitted how precious these olives were and probably disgusted to learn the unsealed jar was nearly two years old. Did Bea care what Rosalie thought? It wasn't as if she had reason to impress her; in fact, it was the opposite. The apartment had belonged to Bea first. She'd given Rosalie the room over many others from Craigslist with more convincing smiles. Ironically, Rosalie's draw was that she'd seemed quiet and private enough to respect

Bea's space and things. From a roommate, Bea wasn't looking for a relationship of any kind. No one could replace her sister.

The olive jar was the only labeled item in the refrigerator and one of Bea's most prized possessions. Her sketchbook was also important, which she was always nose deep in, and so was the pair of identical quilts, stacked and neatly folded at the foot of her bed, each made up of white pinwheels, like galaxies, against a dark blue fabric collage. After Audrey's death, Bea had inherited hers. They were exact replicas of the vintage ones that decorated the twin beds in their room at the yellow house, where they'd spent their childhood summers, and had been offered as consolation prizes by their mother the year they stopped going. She remembered hers had smelled so strongly of plastic packaging at first, she couldn't stand to use it. Over time, the scent had mellowed. Now both quilts smelled like human skin—musty and warm, like the ones from her youth. And if she pressed her face into Audrey's—differentiated by a lopsided A, drawn in Sharpie—closed her eyes, and really focused, she could still faintly smell her perfume, a rich blend of jasmine and patchouli.

The more Bea thought about the betrayal—Rosalie boorishly ignoring the Post-it note on the olive jar that read "BEATRIX" in all caps—the angrier she grew. Finally, after being pinned to the floor by grief for what could have been hours, she felt herself rising, inflating like a hot-air balloon, floating to the bathroom where she stood, arm overhead, poised to hurl the jar into the shower, where it would explode brine and glass. She'd leave a few of the sharpest shards behind, clean up the juice and olives, make it look safe and normal. The next time Rosalie showered, glass would pierce her bare feet. Then she'd know the pain in Bea's heart.

What was she doing? How could she even think it?

Dazed, she lowered her arm and wandered back to the kitchen whispering more apologies, tears blurring her vision. She placed the jar on the countertop, then knelt by the white plastic trash bin and began rifling through its contents, carefully at first, then with increasing desperation.

"There you are," she said when she found it: the olive pit. She cradled it in her hand, almond-shaped and rough where the meat had been sucked off, then dropped it into her pocket.

That it was there, against her hip, through two layers of soft fabric, filled Bea with nostalgic warmth. She stood and secured the jar's lid, twisting until she was shaking, then pressed it deep into the corner of the fridge where it belonged, Post-it facing out.

With Rosalie's magnetized refrigerator pen, Bea scrawled a few words on the matching refrigerator notepad: *YOU'LL BE REALLY FUCKING SORRY IF YOU EVER TOUCH MY THINGS AGAIN.*

She considered what she'd written, then tore off the note, crushed it into a ball, and tossed it over her shoulder.

Rage guided her pen, carving angular capital letters into the page, as she wrote another message: *DON'T YOU DARE TOUCH MY THINGS.*

This was better. Less overtly threatening.

She underlined her words again and again until the tip of her pen cut through most of the pad. Rosalie would be back soon—on the rare occasions when she left the apartment, she was never gone for long. She would find the note and know she'd been caught, that she'd crossed a line that must never be crossed again.

When Bea finally made it outside, red-eyed and swollen, she walked briskly with her chin tucked, using the blinding afternoon sun and her head position to shield against unwanted conversations. Park Slope was infested with people she knew or had once known, and since her sister's death, she found it humiliating to be visibly upset in public. It made her too readable. She wanted privacy in her grief, to not be the object of people's assumptions. In general, privacy wasn't easily won in Park Slope, where everyone was at least vaguely familiar and so were their stories. When she glanced up to check for the subway's green orbs, she spotted Armando of Mando's Mangos smoking outside his deli and crossed the street to avoid their usual "Sup," "Sup," exchange. Audrey used to think he was hot, "in a grandfatherly way," and would bat her eyes at him, blow kisses when his back was turned. Bea hadn't found it amusing. In general, she wasn't easily amused.

She was on her way to Westchester, where her parents had decided to host Audrey's memorial, delayed two years by COVID-19. They'd recently sold the brownstone, Bea and Audrey's childhood home, and left Park Slope for Bronxville, terminating loyalties to their hairdresser of the past two decades, the old-school knife sharpener who cruised around the neighborhood in his red truck, ringing his bell, and to their only living daughter, who would've inherited the brownstone one day. Their loyalty to the Park Slope Food Coop, however, was apparently eternal. They commuted to and from it every other week for supplies, or for their shifts, which consisted of Bea's father bagging groceries while her mother did something—Bea didn't know what—in the membership office upstairs. They either relied on Metro-North to get them there or braved the Brooklyn Queens Expressway traffic and subsequently what was known, in Park Slope, as "the parking situation."

By the time Bea made it to the Bronxville station, people were already arriving, and her parents couldn't pick her up, so she power walked across pristine suburban pavement, past single-story homes, freshly shorn lawns, and sprinklers spitting rainbows into sunbeams. A stinging bubble formed on her heel, her hamstrings ached, but she did not slow her pace. As she streaked along, she gulped down crisp, clear air, hoping to ingest the pallidness of this place, like a low dose of quetiapine, which, for a while, had made everything in her world very quiet and her eyelids droop until she'd made the private, executive decision to stop taking it. Today, given the fizzy, crowded feeling in her brain—and where she was headed—a bit of vacancy might've served her well. She still had the pills; they rolled around in their orange cartridge like a little rain stick whenever she opened her desk drawer.

As she walked, she muttered to herself, "So, I have this idea . . ." again and again with a slightly different intonation each time. At some point she began adding an extra word for emphasis. "So, I have this *great* idea . . ." "So, I have this *brilliant* idea . . ."

To Bea, the notion of a two-year delayed memorial service was pointless, verging on embarrassing, and Audrey would've felt the same. Everyone had already said the obligatory "I'm sorry for your loss," though at the time the sentiment could only be relayed via Facebook Messenger or email and accessorized by either a broken heart or a crying emoji due to pandemic isolation. By now, Bea's grief was like her father's bad shoulder, which he'd injured playing football when he was seventeen. It made her life worse but was more like a nagging soreness than acute pain, most of the time at least. The morning's olive incident had added sting to the day, which would've been appropriate, convenient even, had it not made her so late. She touched her pocket which held the pit and felt a shade brighter.

Bea was there on a mission. Her primary reason for journeying to the memorial both did and didn't have to do with Audrey, which could be said about her whole life. An idea—a *brilliant* one, she was certain, or possibly an *amazing* one—had been percolating in her mind for weeks, trapped in her skull like a fly in a hot car, and one of the only living people to whom it would mean something would be there. Telling her would be like rolling the window down; the buzzing would finally end. And it was possible, if Bea played her cards just right, presented it using the perfect words, that Tatum would want to help.

Before entering the front yard, standing belly button to gate latch, miniaturized by the rampart-type hedges to her left and right, Bea paused to suck in a deep breath. "You can do this," she said, her voice rippling the unearthly suburban quiet like a stone skipping across a lake. She tugged open her pocket and spoke into its small darkness, to the pit she knew was there but couldn't see: "We can do this." As she pressed open the gate, she muttered, "So, Tatum, I've got this *marvelous* idea . . ."

The new house was sprawling; the gardens were frizzy and lush, confettied by pockets of cheerful flowers working overtime to brighten her parents' gloom. For the first time, she noticed silver was beginning to stain the fresh wood clapboard on the newly constructed wing which her parents had commissioned to include an enlarged primary bedroom, a walk-in closet the size of Bea's whole apartment, and a bathroom with a skylight and a claw-foot tub. Bea often wondered what her parents would do if she died. What they would or wouldn't build, where they would or wouldn't move, if they would or wouldn't cry.

When she entered the house the chalky, new-car smell of fresh plaster mixed unpleasantly with that of cheese and earthy perfume. In the center of the crowded living room, amidst a sea of suits, knee-length skirts, and elderly, swollen ankles, was her sister's urn. A bouquet of red roses stood behind it, and next to it, a smiling picture of Audrey. Bea was thankful her parents had selected that photo, taken by their father in their old living room, rather than one of the sterile, retouched campaign pictures printed on glossy paper that lived in the big leather scrapbook Audrey had brought to castings. She'd also been contractually obligated to post them on Instagram, making her profile a collage of vanity. Slightly blurry and flushed, nestled into their old couch, was how Bea preferred to remember her sister, though it was a far cry from what she'd looked like at the end of her life.

Bea's gaze focused next on the potbellied urn itself—her first order of business, she'd decided on the train. Once long and elegant at five-foot-ten, Audrey had been reduced by their mother to the size and stature of a garden gnome. The matte-black urn reminded Bea of Patricia's tear-soaked surgical mask, how it had stuck to her face, sucking in and out with her breath, as she'd stalked the long aisles of urns, repeating the words "We need something chic and unassuming," until they were as grating as a bleating alarm clock that couldn't be switched off. For a year, it had lived on the mantelpiece in their old brownstone, and now here it was in this new house in the suburbs, which Audrey had never known and where she never would've wanted to be. Patricia had demanded that Audrey be cremated, and no one had had the heart to fight her on it. She was the mother, after all.

"Homeless people pee on tombstones," was Patricia's unfortunate refrain in defense of her decision. "I want to keep my daughter safe and dry with me."

As she neared the urn, Bea felt nothing. Once, before her parents had left Brooklyn, she'd opened it. She'd let herself into the old brownstone uninvited, and ignored the racket Patricia was making upstairs, her incessant calls of, "Bea, is that you down there? Speak so I know it's not an intruder," as she ran her fingers through the dull ash. She'd drawn a lopsided smiley face in it, then replaced the lid before ducking into the cramped bathroom beneath the stairs and washing her hands slowly, watching dark, powdered remnants of her sister circle down the drain. When she'd finally greeted her hyperventilating mother on the landing, Patricia had scolded her for taking so long to respond and for not texting before stopping by. "I was about to start throwing things downstairs," she'd said, explaining why she was brandishing an unplugged table lamp. "I was going to try knocking you out—the intruder, I mean, not you of course."

Standing in front of the urn now, Bea felt eyes on her, like she was the unapproachable popular kid Audrey had once been. She lowered her head, pretending to pray or do whatever people did at these things. When a commotion erupted by the window—someone had dropped their drink—she was able to dig the olive pit out of her pocket, lift the urn's lid, and drop it inside before attention shifted back to her.

As waitstaff pushed paper towels around and everyone else in the room recovered, Bea closed her eyes and imagined the pit sprouting into an olive tree right there in the living room, destroying the urn, her parents' new roof, and their freshly stained floors. Audrey's leaves would glitter against the sky, as big and beautiful as she had been in human form. Bea would climb her sister toward the sun.

When she opened her eyes, people were watching her again, many of whom—judging by their thick makeup and pearls—were her parents' new Westchester neighbors. There was also her distant cousin whose name she couldn't remember from her family's Republican enclave. Notably, none of these people were Tatum.

The crowd parted as she walked toward the kitchen, which was bustling with ladies in white aprons and hairnets. Mirrored trays covered every inch of countertop, and the ladies fluttered over them like city pigeons—a comforting reminder of home.

"What's this?" Bea asked no one in particular, touching something brown and rectangular.

"Fried tofu stick," someone answered in a Slavic accent. Bea shuddered and left it where it was.

"Have any of you seen my mom?" she asked. "The woman who hired you?"

Someone gestured toward the back door.

Outside, the deck was more crowded than the living room. Bea pressed through the mob, avoiding people's attempts to speak to her, to apologize for Audrey's death as if it had anything to do with them, until she spotted Patricia tucked into a corner looking corpsier than ever and chatting with Vera, her best friend and Tatum's mother. Usually, Vera wore bright colors, but today she'd dressed in respectful deep greens and grays. She'd always been impressively hip, especially for a mom, especially-especially for a mom who lived in Park Slope, especially-especially-especially for a mom-friend of Patricia's, the least hip human to ever walk the planet. Their close relationship didn't make much sense, Bea had always thought, but it had stood the test of time, since before Bea, Audrey, and Tatum were born. She could remember the revealing bathing suits Vera used to wear while sunning herself on the boulders at the yellow house, with slits up the sides and crocheted cover-ups hanging off her shoulders. Hers was the first woman's body Bea had ever really seen, soft and strong. Patricia, on the other hand, swam in a long-sleeved rash guard, skort, and sunglasses, even when she ducked under the water. As she approached, Bea heard her mother say, "At least this house is all on one level. No stairs for me to break my hip on when I'm eighty."

When she spotted Bea, Patricia's tone turned chilly—"Beatrix, you're late." She opened her long arms, Audrey's arms, and Bea stepped into them. Her mother's shawl smelled of mothballs and Weleda Skin Food, which she slathered on her face every night so thickly, her hair was always plastered to her cheeks in the morning, like spidery brown cracks in her skin. The sight had nullified Bea's appetite for breakfast when she was young, which had caused daily tension. As they hugged, Patricia's body was sharp.

"Say hi to Vera."

"Hi, Vera," said Bea. If she was here, it meant Tatum was, too. At least Bea hoped it did. She couldn't imagine Tatum not coming, regardless of Vera, but there was always a chance. Her heartbeat thumped in her ears as she scanned the crowd. Some people waved, but Bea ignored them.

Patricia frowned, licked her thumb and dabbed at Bea's cheek while Vera said, "Hi there," and reached for Bea's moist hand. She allowed her fingers to be squeezed, then stuffed them into her pocket.

"Can you not?" she said to her mother when her cheek began to hurt under Patricia's determined rubbing. Patricia muttered something about Bea's face being streaked by makeup, then something else about impressing the new neighbors as she tucked her hand back into the folds of her shawl.

A cool wind picked up and Bea crossed her arms. She never wore a bra because she found them too constricting and was proud of her full breasts, which Audrey never had, but didn't want Patricia to comment on her nipples.

"Where's Tatum?" she asked, trying to seem nonchalant, probably failing.

"Oh, she stopped for a glass of wine on our way back here," said Vera. She rose onto her tiptoes and surveyed the deck in much the same way Bea had. A sudden smile warmed her face. "There she is now." Vera raised a hand. "My girl."

Bea looked away and quickly practiced, "So, I have a *fantastic* idea . . ." And then Tatum was there, balancing a plastic cup between long, elegant fingers with lavender-painted nails.

"Hi," she said, her voice as silver smooth as moonlight. "Wow, there are so many people here."

"Between family and our Park Slope and Westchester communities, it's certainly a lot of names to keep straight," Patricia said, as if she hadn't insisted on throwing such a big event.

"The house is beautiful," said Tatum, embracing Patricia. "Love you. And you know how much I loved—"

Patricia put up a hand. "Please don't," she said. "I know you loved her. Let's keep things light for now. Is Ed here, too?" She scrunched Tatum's blond curls affectionately, then arranged them behind her shoulder. At least Bea wasn't the only person left for her mother to adjust.

Tatum quickly hugged Bea. Could she feel her vibrating?

"No, Ed had a work thing. A meeting with some bigwig movie person his dad knows. Apparently he couldn't miss it."

Bea counted the beauty marks scattered across Tatum's neck—there were ten, just like always. Tatum's whispery voice, her uniform of a soft T-shirt and jeans, both of which were black today, the cushion of blond that surrounded her face like an aura, and her smell, as subtle and bright as a newborn's, combined to make her the perfect candidate for love. Audrey had once said, "Tatum is like a healthy, twenty-first-century Marilyn Monroe, if Marilyn Monroe didn't know she was Marilyn Monroe." It was true. Bea couldn't deny it. If Tatum were a flower, she'd be a variety that could be dried and kept forever in a vase, one that grew only more beautiful with time and dust, like the delicate white fan of Queen Anne's lace. The words *chic and unassuming* perfectly described her, not Audrey's squat, black urn. They lived together, Bea remembered, Tatum and Ed, while at twenty-seven, Bea had never even had a boyfriend before.

The four of them were silent for a moment, failing to fill the space that should've held Audrey's flurry of excitement over Tatum's arrival.

Bea's version of excitement was silent and painful. Soon, she would either blurt it out or explode. "Well, Tatum, good to see you. Wanna go over there, then?" she said, hopping from one foot to the other. She pointed at the roots of a tree a few yards from the deck.

Patricia shook her head. "You two can sneak off together later. Tatum just got here."

Bea frowned, crossing her arms, chewing the soft skin inside her mouth as Patricia asked Tatum questions about work, her apartment, her friends.

So, I have this idea, Bea thought. *This really exciting idea. This proposition. I have this idea. I have a good idea. An exciting opportunity.*

She watched Tatum laugh at her mother's quips and her brow furrow as she spoke about Ed and her boredom at work.

Finally, Tatum turned to Bea.

"And how're you doing?" she asked. "How was—god, sorry, I can't remember the name of the place."

"Arizona's Arabia," said Bea, certain her idea was seconds from tumbling out in front of her mother. It was like she desperately had to pee.

"Right," said Tatum. "I've always been curious about WWOOFing. Was it fun?"

"For sure," said Bea. She looked pleadingly at her mother, who rolled her eyes.

"Just go," said Patricia, gesturing toward the tree, and Bea was off. She heard her mother say, "I try to slow Beatrix down, you know, but it's just no use—" before her voice was eclipsed by distance and the murmur of other conversations.

The grass was wet against Bea's ankles and the temperature cooler off the deck.

"It smells so good out here," said Tatum from a few feet behind. "Fresh. Reminds me of the yellow house in a way."

Bea didn't reply. Everything *nature* reminded her of the yellow house, too. Fifteen years had passed since they were last there, but it remained a blinding white light in her mind. She replayed the best memories from those days often: all of them piling onto the lumpy sofa to watch and recite practically the entirety of *Finding Nemo* on the television mounted beneath a life-size model of a swordfish; the ice-cream shack in town; jumping off the dock into the lake holding hands with Audrey. The yellow house was like shared DNA between her family and Tatum's, though after they stopped going, Tatum had grown much closer to Audrey than she'd ever been to Bea.

When they reached the tree, Bea leaned against its trunk, balancing between two gnarled, exposed roots.

Tatum's eyes were like the dots of question marks. Bea could tell her smile was forced.

"What's up?" she asked, squeezing Bea's elbow. "I'm sure this is weird and stuff. Is that why you wanted to talk in private?"

Bea shook her head. "So, I have an *exquisite* idea," she said, relishing the release of these words, the satisfaction of finally watching Tatum process them.

"Oh?" said Tatum, cocking her head. "What's your idea?"

Just as Bea was about to tell her, Tatum said, "Oh, shit."

Bea blinked, mouth half open.

"Holy shit," said Tatum. "Dude, I think that's—"

Bea turned to where Tatum pointed and saw a woman with sheet-white skin, dark hair, and glossy, red lips walking toward them. Her dress was black with large pearl buttons down the front and a furry collar. She wore fishnet stockings and patent-leather stilettos, which kept sticking in the grass. And she was waving at them frantically.

"Holy shit," Tatum said again, and Bea realized she'd never heard her curse before.

"Hey," called the approaching woman. Then Bea recognized her. That voice. It was the same as when she was young—deep and womanly; puberty had come early for her. But she looked nothing like the mousy brunette child Bea had once considered yellow-house family, same as Tatum, all scabs and dirt stains. They'd been out of touch so long, she'd all but deleted her from her memories.

"Layla?" Tatum squeaked.

The woman pointed at her chest. "Layla," she said, nodding. Her face scrunched, then burst into a smile. "You guys."

Bea didn't move, didn't speak.

Tatum placed her cup on the ground, then staggered toward Layla over the roots. "Oh my god."

They spun around as they hugged.

"I can't believe it's you," they both said, touching each other's hair and hips, complimenting each other's shoes, which couldn't have been more different—Tatum's narrow canvas sneakers versus Layla's shiny heels.

And Bea stood, tree bark digging into her shoulder, waiting. It felt as if something was lodged in her throat. She swallowed as hard as she could, then again and again, but it wouldn't budge.

Eventually Tatum and Layla made their way over, hair tousled, cheeks pink from squealing.

Layla reached out an arm, welcoming Bea into their huddle, and Bea accepted reluctantly. They rubbed her back and pressed their foreheads to hers. While they were like that, knit together in a tight little dome, Layla whispered, "Audrey, we miss you. We miss you so much." And for the first time since arriving in Westchester, Bea felt a twist of pain deep in her belly.

When they broke apart, Tatum's and Layla's eyes were wet.

Tatum tipped back her head and dabbed her cheeks. "God," she said. "Sorry."

Layla pressed her fingers—made bulky by gem-encrusted rings—to the corners of her eyes.

A mosquito hovered around their faces, and Bea clapped her hands over it.

"Got it," she said, proudly showing them her palm.

"Bea," said Layla, then paused and cleared her throat. "Wait, do you still go by Bea?"

Bea nodded.

"Okay, cool," said Layla. "When I saw your mom over there, she called you Beatrix, so I wanted to make sure."

"She does that," said Bea. "Always has."

"Right," said Layla. "I should've remembered. How're you?" Her eyes were wide. She grabbed Bea's hand, the one without the mosquito imprinted on it. "How're you holding up?"

Layla was one of the only people Bea hadn't heard from after Audrey's death, including others she'd lost touch with. Her mother, Nancy, had sent a large flower arrangement to the brownstone and signed a small white card, *With love, Nancy and Layla*, but that was it. It had hurt Patricia that neither of them had called, she'd been very vocal about that, but not Bea. Now, however, she felt it gave her permission to ignore Layla's question.

"Actually, there's something else I'd like to talk about," she said. "I was just about to tell Tatum when you walked up."

"Oh," said Layla, "of course," and Bea felt powerful, until she opened her mouth and realized she didn't know where to start anymore. Tatum had more context for Bea's life, but it might be worth backtracking for Layla, who'd missed the past fifteen years.

Though it had caught her off guard, she realized this was the ideal moment for Layla to suddenly appear. It was like magic, like the idea itself had conjured her out of thin air.

"Audrey and I were living together when she died," Bea began. "So, afterward, I had to get out of the city for a while."

Her voice was shaky, not because she found this difficult to say but because things had fallen into such perfect alignment. Overwhelmingly perfect. She must get this right, and talking to people—conveying information clearly, commanding their attention—wasn't her strong suit.

Layla's face crumpled like that of a bad soap opera actress. "Totally," she said. "Of course."

"So, I decided to WWOOF."

Layla looked confused. "Woof?"

Didn't everyone know what WWOOFing was? So many of her sister's friends had done it the summer between high school and college. One had worked on a peach farm in Georgia, another on a dairy farm in Vermont, yet another on a vineyard in France. It was what teenage city kids did to experience nature.

"WWOOFing is, like, a farm exchange program thing," Tatum jumped in. "You get hired to help out and are given free room and board."

Bea wondered if only New Yorkers to whom the idea of "free room and board" even remotely appealed knew about WWOOFing. Layla was rich, and though a lot of people in New York were, including Bea's own parents by most people's standards, Layla was richer than most rich people. When they were kids, this hadn't been the case—her mother had always been successful, but not the way she was now. The day the flower arrangement had arrived, after quickly downing the contents of a wineglass, Patricia had used the word *billionaire* to describe Nancy Bernard. Later, Bea had Googled Nancy's net worth and found that Patricia wasn't exaggerating.

Normally, wealth wasn't the sort of thing Bea cared about. She found it difficult to hold on to a well-paying job, so her parents paid her rent plus a generous weekly allowance, rendering money a nonissue in her life. But it was surprisingly intimidating to be faced with a person she knew had access to a billion dollars, which meant she had access to everything, which meant she could easily turn Bea's idea into reality.

"Sure," said Layla. "Okay, cool. So, you spent a few months harvesting veggies or something?"

"No," said Bea. "Mostly, I milked camels."

Now Layla looked utterly perplexed. She glanced at Tatum.

"Who knew camels could be milked, right?" said Tatum. "I was shocked when I first heard about this."

Bea continued: "I WWOOFed on a camel rescue in Arizona. The only camel sanctuary in the country. They take them away from people who own them illegally and stuff. Like, people who keep them in their backyards—you'd be surprised to know how many camels are in Queens. Anyway, I spent a long time there and discovered my passion. Or rediscovered it." She hoped they'd catch on now.

They didn't. Bea pulled a leaf off a branch and shredded it in four swift folds and tears, letting the pieces flutter down.

"Your passion is camel milk?" Layla asked.

"My passion is taking care of living things. So . . ." She took a deep breath. "My idea is—"

"No," said Tatum. She was getting it. Layla was smiling now, too. "Are you about to say what I think you're about to say?"

"I want to open a dog kennel."

Layla shrieked and clapped a hand over her mouth. The people on the crowded deck looked over, concerned, and Tatum gave a thumbs-up.

Layla whispered, "Okay, it was between that and you announcing you're going to medical school. Wait, Bea, are you serious?"

Bea nodded. She was as serious as could be, given she had no idea how to actually do it.

"Oh my god," said Layla.

"Bea." Tatum pressed a hand to her heart.

"Yeah, I just wanted to tell you since, you know, our history and stuff."

"Audrey would love that so much," said Tatum.

Layla was nodding. "I can't believe I almost didn't come today."

The whole thing had started with Audrey when they were very young, as so much had. There was nothing exceptional about the moment of inception itself. One upstate summer, they'd been on a walk with their parents along a dirt road and had run into a neighbor. While the adults chatted and Patricia flinched at each passing car, the four girls, Audrey, Bea, Tatum, and Layla, had huddled around the small dog attached to the neighbor's wrist by a muddy leash. They'd met this dog before and could sometimes hear her barks echoing off the cliffs surrounding the lake their families' yellow rental house shared with a few others.

As they stroked her curly fur and eagerly positioned their cheeks to catch warm, smelly swipes of her tongue, Audrey had said, "When we grow up, we should start a dog kennel and play with dogs all day and walk them and clip their toenails and pet them. They make me so happy."

Audrey's indelible cool-girl-ness, even then, coupled with the thrilling reminder that adulthood would find them eventually, that someday they'd be able to do whatever they wanted, had turned the kennel into their collective childhood-defining dream. It had inspired lemonade stands to raise money, battles for allowances, piggy banks tucked under beds as if their parents might rob them in the night, and countless aspirational pretend games in which Bea and Tatum played puppies and Audrey and Layla—as kennel employees—held on to locks of their hair and walked them outside to pretend to pee on flowers.

Tatum was smiling now, nodding her approval, but Bea wasn't sure it was true that Audrey would've endorsed this, let alone *loved it so much*. As an adult, she'd always tried to push Bea toward pursuing a practical career, anything that would make her self-sufficient—like accounting, she'd often suggested, since Bea was good at math. Perhaps Tatum hadn't known Audrey as well as she seemed to think.

Layla was biting her lip. "You're really doing this, then?"

Bea nodded. She'd asked Meghan, the owner of Arizona's Arabia, a lot of questions before she left, and yet starting a camel sanctuary in the Arizona desert and opening a dog kennel in New York City were two very different things. She would also need money, as this probably wasn't something her parents would agree to fund. But, yes, she was doing it. Especially if she had help.

Layla nodded back. "Right. Well, I'll think about it."

"Think about—" Tatum looked confused.

"Great," said Bea. She hadn't even had to ask.

Tatum's mouth opened again, but instead of her soft voice, Patricia's rang out from the deck, as it had at the end of every yellow house summer—"Girls, time to get in the car, please"—as it had at the most unwelcome moments throughout Bea's whole life.

"Everyone," Patricia called, tapping her cheeks with a crumpled tissue in apparent anticipation of future tears. "Time to head inside for speeches, please."

2

When tatum returned home that evening, Ed was asleep on the couch, his arm curled around an empty water glass like a child's around a teddy bear.

The apartment was in disarray, as she often found it after leaving him for any length of time: dining chairs at odd angles, dishes stacked in the sink next to a drain clogged with bloated pasta, everything marinating in blue light from the old box TV set Ed used for gaming.

Tatum switched on a lamp and collapsed into a rocking chair. Usually, she got right to noisy cleaning so he'd wake to the sound of her disappointment, though he never registered it as that. Not today. After traveling to Westchester, making small talk for hours, unexpectedly seeing Layla and mining herself for notable life events from the past decade and a half to share, Tatum was tired. She leaned back, eyes following a jagged crack in the ceiling paint. When she'd first noticed it, she'd been surprised to find that luxury buildings had ceiling cracks, too. She'd discovered the difference was that when landlords of luxury buildings were contacted by email about issues, they did nothing to help, whereas Matilda, the sweet landlord who lived just above Tatum's childhood ground-floor apartment, was always responsive.

Cracks aside, her apartment now had little in common with the one she'd grown up in, where her parents still lived, which was cramped and dark, blurred by dust and cluttered with tchotchkes and dog-eared books, with old nails protruding from warped floorboards, and which she hadn't expected to miss once she'd left. But her current apartment was about as homey as a hospital waiting room. It had tall white walls, shiny cabinets, and silver L-shaped doorknobs that bruised her hips in the night. It was the sort of place she'd always imagined living in one day when she could afford to, a place where everything was clean, and faucets didn't drip, but apparently ceilings still cracked. Ed's parents paid for most of their rent, though, which had facilitated her being there sooner and less contentedly than anticipated.

There was nothing nostalgic about this place, or comforting. The furniture didn't help. It was from Ikea and purchased on Ed's parents' dime, was gray to match the cabinets and stiff to match their relationship. A few items were hers: the vintage bedside table softened by many layers of paint, the pink floor lamp with the pleated shade beside the sofa, and the rocking chair she was sitting in that had once belonged to her great-aunt. These items alone weren't enough to breathe warmth into the white box that held them.

Such complaints made her seem ungrateful, which was why she never spoke of them. The apartment was larger than most of her friends', the windows were tall, and there was even a washer and dryer. It wasn't the apartment itself that she found unsatisfying, or the weapon doorknobs, or Ed's parents' blah taste. The simple fact was that this apartment didn't possess the quirkiness of her parents' or, more important, of the yellow house. Though Tatum viewed herself as cosmopolitan, not one to settle in the country, she'd always longed for that house, for the lake, and for large rooms packed with things she'd never encountered anywhere else, such as a massive bronzed chicken, different-themed chess sets on coffee tables, silk scarves draped over dusty chandeliers, and ceramic figurines acting out scenes within glass enclosures. That place had been her one true home, and she'd always hoped to evoke at least some of its personality wherever she landed as an adult.

"You're going to have to make a lot of money if you want a house like that someday," Vera had said when Tatum vocalized this goal.

In response, Tatum had rolled her eyes. "Vera, don't worry about that. I will."

She'd been in high school at the time.

Tatum called Vera by her name rather than "Mom" and had for as long as she could remember. It was a tradition that, like many others, had actually started at the yellow house when they were young, though she couldn't remember how. She'd noticed Layla upholding it at the memorial when they'd spoken briefly about Nancy. Audrey had done the same with Patricia when she was alive, and Bea did, too, for the most part. In her own case, it was so entrenched that when she called Vera "Mom," they both made disgusted expressions and shook their heads no.

The yellow house was magic, so was everything that had happened there, and Tatum treasured the rare traces she'd managed to carry into her adult life, yet she also knew she'd left some of herself there that last summer. Whenever Ed asked where she wanted to go on vacation, it was the first place she thought of. She didn't say so, because he was looking for offers of "Europe," "Panama," or "Bora-Bora," which sounded great, too, but it was always on her mind, that missing part of herself that, she liked to imagine, was strong willed and honest, the way kids tended to be.

Sitting in her bland living room, picturing that house, bright against the dark pines that framed it, its edges softened by imperfect memory and the romanticization of her youth, hurt. Especially today.

She took a shuddery breath. In Westchester, she'd felt like George Bailey in *It's a Wonderful Life*, watching a nightmarish version of her life play out, wishing she could slip back in time and fix whichever cosmic wires had been crossed to cause the death of her best friend. She'd spent the last two years ignoring it, made possible by pandemic isolation and the fact that she'd seen much less of Audrey in the months before the world shut down. Even at the memorial, she'd leaned away from her grief like she would a bad smell. Now that she was home, there were no more convenient distractions.

Layla's presence at the memorial was thrilling but had also emphasized Audrey's absence. If she hadn't come, it would've been easier to pretend that Audrey herself had voluntarily—rudely, even—skipped her parents' event, which, in this comfortable state of denial, had been held to commemorate something other than her death. Perhaps Tatum could've ignored the urn, the red roses, even the smiling picture of her printed on canvas. But Layla, who'd been MIA for so long, couldn't be ignored. Suddenly, there she was, and yet there was still no Audrey.

Tatum had been visiting her parents when Vera accepted a seemingly innocuous call from Patricia and returned with news that Audrey had died. At first, no one cried. They'd watched *10 Things I Hate About You* without smiling, then gone to bed. In the darkness of her childhood room, after telling Ed she wouldn't be home, Tatum had sobbed openmouthed into her pillow as the sound of her mother's wails drifted through the old, thin walls.

Tatum closed her eyes. The chair rocked, grinding against the floor, and when Ed stirred, she moved quickly to the bedroom, holding her breath, hoping he would sleep awhile longer. Head between her knees, she sat at the foot of the bed and let herself be heavy. Her spine lengthened vertebra by vertebra, her arms arched toward the floor like willow bows. *Be a willow tree*, she thought. *Willow trees have no troubles*. She was suddenly tense as she considered wildfires and deforestation. *Okay, maybe be something other than a willow tree.* She breathed deeply in through her nose, out through her mouth.

"Hey."

Tatum bolted upright, wiping her cheeks and tweaking her back in the process. "Hey," she said, trying to conceal her disappointment as Ed climbed into bed behind her and nuzzled her neck with his mouth. "Ow," she said as he pressed against the newly sore spot on her back.

"You okay, baby?"

"I'm okay," she said. "Today was harder than anticipated, that's all." She didn't want to talk about it, wanted to watch a crappy reality show in a dark room until she'd forgotten the rules of grammar and could speak only in bleep-outs and incoherent sentences.

"Tell me?" He tugged his fingers through her hair.

He was loving, yet every nice thing he did made her feel like she owed him something back: compliments, affection.

"I have to pee," she said.

In the bathroom, she sat on the closed toilet seat and turned on the water. Her mind raced, recalling everything at once: how it had felt to be there, how Vera had cried on the way home and spoken about Nancy, Layla's mother, marking the first time Tatum had heard her utter the word "cunt."

As far as she knew, none of the children had ever been told why the yellow house tradition ended. For a while, Tatum had been curious, but it was so foggy and distant now and still caused her mother so much pain that it didn't seem worth it to pry. Perhaps Layla knew, but Tatum wasn't sure she wanted to ask.

Over the sound of trickling water, Tatum sighed. The notion of starting a dog kennel was ridiculous. There was no more random career path, especially for her. At one point, she'd imagined herself a writer because she'd always wanted to be famous—important in some way. And she definitely couldn't sing or dance or act. Sure, she could type words into a document, but was she good? She still did not know for sure.

Straight out of college, she'd pursued a job in publishing, thinking it was the first step to literary stardom. Straight out of college, she'd been an idiot. First of all, the only publishing job she could get was in the children's department, and second, she was paid an embarrassingly low salary. How well did dog-kennel-starting pay? She'd always been more of a cat person, had gone along with the whole childhood dog kennel plot because the others were so excited about it, but awkward-looking dogs on the street didn't make her smile, not even little ones with underbites and wrinkles, and they never had. As a very young child, when she'd seen them coming, she'd burst into tears and hopped, arms raised, until someone lifted her to safety.

She flushed the toilet and faced the mirror.

Earlier, as they were saying goodbye, Layla had said, "Bea, give me your number. I'll let you know exactly what I can offer once I've thought about it and talked to some people."

Bea had eagerly given her number to Layla. Then Tatum had offered hers, saying, "I'm interested in talking more as well." She hadn't planned on saying it, couldn't tell for sure why she had. Out of a desire to impress or just stay in touch with Layla, or maybe because, with Layla's help, it could actually be something and she didn't want to miss the boat? Or maybe it was deeper than she knew yet. Probably. Most things were, she'd learned from her days in therapy. Did it matter why she'd said it? Did anything matter? Was she depressed? She smiled into the mirror unconvincingly. She should go back to therapy.

Ed's knuckles rapped against the door, startling her.

"You all right?"

"Mm-hmm." *Leave me alone*, she thought. *Can't you take care of yourself for three minutes?* This wasn't entirely fair. For a man in his late twenties he was relatively self-sufficient, or maybe just far more reliant on his parents than he was on her.

"Tate?"

"I said, 'Yes.'"

"I didn't hear you."

She pushed her hair off her face and exhaled.

"Sorry," she said when she opened the door. His hair looked like he'd rubbed it against a balloon. "I'm having a weird day." She pressed her forehead into his chest. "I just need to lie down."

"Sure," he said, massaging her shoulders.

He guided her back to the bed, lifting her onto it in a display of clumsy, half-baked strength signaled by an unsexy grunt and a sudden rush of blood to his face. Her face reddened, too, from swallowing her laughter as he tucked her in, pressing the covers around her so tightly her arms were stuck to her sides.

"Your phone was going off." He fished it out of his shorts.

Tatum freed a hand to receive it.

What would he think if she opened a dog kennel?

He'd love it because he loved everything she did, which wasn't a bad thing except that Tatum wished she could criticize him without feeling shitty about it. She wanted to say, "Pick up after yourself," when she came home to find the place a mess. When he farted under the covers before bed, she wanted to say, "Ew," instead of generously giggling at his childish declaration of "whoopsie." And whenever he made his "famous Bolognese," roughly every other week, she wanted to tell him it was always under-salted. It wouldn't hurt his feelings; he'd smile, tap a finger against his temple, and say, "Brilliant," in the made-up, Eastern European–adjacent accent he used sometimes, and eagerly correct his mistake. Yet she kept quiet, ate the bland Bolognese without adding salt herself, and resented him.

In college, when they'd first met, he was so certain about what he wanted to be: a movie director. So confident. He was always making things, holding auditions, renting out heavy equipment from the film department, blocking out weeks at a time to shoot, and editing for months afterward in a windowless basement room, shadowed by his friend Herb and the thick smoke from Herb's joints.

One of his short films was about a woman who compulsively cheated on her husband with her therapist. The sex in it was graphic. He'd been forced to cast Tatum's friend as the female lead because she was a sex worker—had Zoom-sex from her dorm room for money she used to pay for school—and therefore was comfortable with everything the film required. Even back then it should've bothered Tatum, at least a little, that he'd spent days watching her close friend's bare chest bounce madly as a football player named Saul fake-humped her against a mountain of pillows, two of which were borrowed from Tatum's own bed. And maybe it should've bothered her, too, that this was the sort of film Ed wanted to make in the first place—borderline pornography. But it didn't. She hadn't cared at all.

Since college, he'd made some other shorts he'd sent off to festivals across the country. A few were accepted by places Tatum had never heard of in states she had no interest in visiting. Thankfully, all their travel expenses were covered by his parents. She used to watch Ed on "red carpets" that weren't red or maybe had no carpet at all. He spoke about his work with a careful balance of pride and humility, and, in those moments, Tatum had felt proud to be with him.

One of his films, *Joey's Left Iris,* about a man divorcing a woman named Iris, was written up in the *New York Times*. Tatum had the clipping framed as a gift—a very large frame for a very small clipping, which had made him laugh. It hung above their couch. The review was mixed but its existence was thrilling, and its mixed-ness only added to the humor of it being on their wall. For months afterward, whenever they had friends over, he'd say, "Have you seen my mediocre review yet?" and point at it.

He hadn't made anything in the past year—told her he was working on a script for a feature, but she hadn't been allowed to read it. The last time she'd asked about his progress, he'd responded by asking about her writing, which was rude yet effective at shutting her up. Tatum had begun to worry that he'd lost his drive, which was her favorite thing about him.

Rain pecked at the windowpane. The light from her phone was harsh against her face in the dark. Ed was making tea—she could hear the pot hissing.

Hey it's Layla.

The text had been delivered while Tatum was in the bathroom.

So what're your actual thoughts
about the kennel?

Tatum sat up.

In the early days she'd felt closer to Layla than the others, probably because they shared a bedroom. Every night, they'd giggled into the dark long after they were supposed to be asleep. They'd also spent entire afternoons lounging in the hammock together—which Patricia never let Audrey and Bea do because it was "too much sun"—as sweat pooled behind their knees and macramé imprinted their skin, losing track of time, never running out of things to say.

These days, Tatum lamented that her adult friendships lacked that special ease. There were stricter boundaries, time constraints, lower energy levels. While some had come close to the comfort level she'd once achieved with Layla, Audrey, and even Bea, none had matched their four-way sisterliness, which, as an only child, was what she'd always craved.

Then suddenly Layla and her mother were gone, along with all of it—the yellow house, the promise of the dog kennel, and everything they'd cherished most about their lives and relationships. They were twelve years old, and without cell phones to keep in touch, so soon Tatum didn't even know where Layla's family lived anymore—still in Park Slope or had they moved away?

At the age when people were first creating Instagram accounts, Tatum had searched for Layla's and found that it was private. Her follow request had never been accepted. Neither was Audrey's.

A heartbroken, rejected Tatum had kept up with Bea and Audrey as a unit for a while, seeing them for an hour here, an hour there, in their high-ceilinged Park Slope living room, inventing explanations for Layla and Nancy's mysterious disappearance while their mothers chatted in the kitchen. They hadn't gone to the same school—Bea and Audrey had attended Berkeley Carroll, while Vera's entire teaching salary was less than the cost of one year there—and somehow they rarely ran into each other in the neighborhood. That was just how Park Slope worked: some people you never saw, some people—usually the ones who talked your ear off as your full shopping bag kept digging into your shoulder—you saw often.

Once they were granted cell phones, Tatum and Audrey had begun to text. She remembered finding a grainy photograph of the two of them with jam all over their faces in a pile of her mother's papers and summoning the courage to send a picture of it to Audrey, accompanied by a pathetic little "<3." Audrey had replied, OMG STOP, then added a few minutes later, miss u how r u? in the ultra-abbreviated text-speak that was used before cell phones had full keyboards.

At first, the revitalization of their friendship was thrilling. Had an official award existed for "Park Slope preteen IT girl," it would've gone to Audrey. Even people at Tatum's public school knew her name. When she went to friends' houses, their mothers sometimes asked, "You know Audrey Ellis, don't you? How's she doing?" with worry in their eyes. "She looks awfully adult for someone so young."

Despite Tatum's awe, her friendship with Audrey had grown until it was rooted in pure love, not intimidation, and they were closer than ever, and closer than they'd ever been with anyone else. They saw each other at least once a week, though, to avoid their families, rarely at each other's houses. And when they left for college, they'd relied on constant texts and calls. Their only rough patch occurred just after Audrey moved in with her sister, which had caused some strange problems. They'd worked through them, though, and afterward were even more bonded by having overcome tension—until Audrey began doing heroin.

Tatum couldn't help but mourn her lost friendships, traditions, desires, dreams. For the most part, these losses was part of growing up somewhere like Park Slope. Still, they were painful. She wondered if Layla felt this way, too. How could she, really? She could become anything, and anything could become hers. Nancy was a permanent fixture on *Forbes*'s list of "Television's Richest Women"; Tatum checked on it from time to time. The *Post* had named her "The Female Larry David." The show she'd created, *Tammy Rose*, was about a single mother living in New York City. It broke records and could still be found airing at any time of day, along with Layla's last name, BERNARD, in gold block letters at the beginning and end of each episode. Since then, Nancy had created more shows, most of them hits, though none with as much cultural impact as *Tammy Rose*.

At the memorial, Tatum had noticed Chanel emblems dangling

from Layla's earlobes, as religious a symbol as the cross, and the unnatural bubble of her lips. The prospect of opening a dog kennel with her was not like opening a dog kennel with anyone else Tatum knew. Opening a dog kennel with Layla had the potential to change her life, or to revive her, depending on how she looked at it. If she committed to it, she'd be *in it for the wrong reasons*, the cardinal sin people were always being accused of on reality dating shows, but it might be worth it.

A dog kennel. Tatum, dog kennel founder. Tatum, Layla Bernard's business partner. She began typing.

Hey. I don't really know yet. I'm
definitely intrigued by the idea.

Layla responded immediately.

Wanna get din tm?

Tatum looked at her window, which was black except for raindrops running down the screen in iridescent slug-trails. The outside world was still crying for Audrey, while inside she was starting to feel better.

She pulled her turtleneck over her mouth. The goal was to hit the perfect chord of composure and enthusiasm in her texts, and after years of communicating with her boss, Tatum knew how to convey just that. In the next room, metal clinked against ceramic. She typed carefully, then, to test them, whispered her words aloud: "Dinner tomorrow sounds great. Let me know where and when." Nothing fancy. Cool, calm, and collected.

Ed shuffled in and placed a steaming mug on the bedside table. Tatum moved her phone out of sight when he kissed her. His mouth was warm and familiar, despite his sour breath, and for a moment she was comforted by it.

"You all right?" he asked, settling into a catlike pose across the foot of their bed. She nodded as he began stroking her toes and shielded her phone from his view with a strategic fold in the blanket. She should ask how his meeting went—the one with the hotshot producer or director or something, which had kept him from the memorial. She didn't. Had it amounted to anything real, he would've already told her.

Tatum glanced down.

La Olivia. In Fort Greene. Seven thirty?

Tatum sent back a thumbs-up emoji.

What's your email? My assistant will send a Google Cal invite.

Important people had assistants, and people with money were important. Even relatively unimportant people sometimes had assistants, like Tatum's boss, who was only important on the twentieth floor of 1673 Broadway. Layla had a Wikipedia page, so of course she had an assistant, and of course her assistant had to send Tatum a Google Cal invitation to dinner.

t.kaplan@goldenpress.com. Will look out for an email.

No big deal. Friends' assistants emailed her Google Cal invites to meals all the time.

Layla responded with a shooting star emoji and Tatum slid her phone under the covers and reached for her mug. Steam rose in a perfect curl until Ed accidentally tickled her foot, causing hot, brown water to splash across her chest and the white sheets.

3

ROSALIE'S LIGHT WAS off when Bea opened the door. The olive jar, Bea checked, was still exactly where she'd left it in the refrigerator. A short apology had been added to the bottom of her angry note, which was now pinned against the counter by the oily stump of a cupcake.

Bea ate in the dark, red velvet crumbs sticking to her fingers, then crumpled the note with the pleated cupcake wrapper and clapped her hands to clean them. When she opened the garbage, she saw that the first note she'd written, which she'd left in a ball on the kitchen floor, had been flattened out. It rested neatly atop a limp banana peel as if waiting to be seen by her. *YOU'LL BE REALLY FUCKING SORRY IF YOU EVER TOUCH MY THINGS AGAIN.* She felt bad. The note made her seem scary, like she was going to do something to Rosalie, which she wasn't. She'd been angry, that was all, and it had passed.

The walls of Bea's room were covered in doodles: skeletons wrapped in flowering vines, vicious-looking serpent species she'd dreamed up, dogs with bared fangs and yellow eyes, dog bodies with long human legs and skulls for heads, human skeletons with flesh-and-blood hands and feet. She'd always had an artistic streak—that was one of Patricia's rare yet most repeated compliments—and her drawings were good, inspired by the kinds of books she read, movies she watched, and her outlook on the world. Dogs appeared in her work often and had even before the resurgence of the kennel dream. Probably because Audrey had always loved dogs, especially ones that looked like they belonged on the Arctic tundra, not tied up outside New York City delis where they were often found.

Audrey had plans to adopt a puppy with ice-blue eyes and a dense gray coat when she died. The puppy, Bea had thought at the time, looked sort of like her sister when she was healthy—something about the intensity of the eyes and the dog's big, floppy paws, which were suggestive of its massive potential. Audrey had been approved by the rescue agency, shocking since she was an addict then, which couldn't really be hidden. The dog was going to be spayed, and they would've picked it up the week after Audrey died. When they were informed of what happened, the agency had tried to convince Bea to take it home anyway, their emailed plea sandwiched between the words "I'm sorry for your loss" and three pictures of the animal surrounded by plush, vegetable-shaped toys, meant to tempt her with cuteness.

Even if Audrey had survived, Bea would've been the one taking care of the dog—there was no question. The last few months of her life were spent either unconscious or lying on the couch mumbling nonsense through cracked lips or sipping soup off a spoon Bea held for her. She was not exactly capable of walking a dog every few hours, picking up poop, or diligently topping off food and water bowls. All that would've been Bea's job, an extension of caring for her sister, and she would've done it—she would've done anything, and gladly. But tending to a cheerful, bouncing puppy in the immediate aftermath of Audrey's death was different. She wasn't ready for it and had declined. In some ways, now she wished she'd done it. It would've given her experience with dogs, and something to love, but it also would've kept her in New York, away from the camels. Who would she be then? What would she want?

They'd lived together in the same apartment where Bea currently lived with Rosalie. Audrey had died on the couch, inherited from their parents' basement, that was still in their living room. Bea had considered getting rid of it, but sometimes when she looked at it, for a split second she saw her sister there, openmouthed and lifeless, her complexion an inhuman lavender, the way she'd looked when the paramedics came to take her away. Those split-second-long illusions were very precious to Bea. Any time she got with her sister was.

Though Audrey had been their parents' perfect child for so long, even before heroin she hadn't avoided all trouble. The twists and turns of her life, all the mischief she'd gotten into, had given her a captivating depth. She'd been a smoker since age fourteen, had developed a shield consisting of Listerine plus gourmand Victoria's Secret perfume to prevent Patricia from noticing, and had even checked herself into rehab her sophomore year in college for drinking, a decision Patricia had celebrated as Audrey assured her it was precautionary. "Everyone drinks so much at college, and I just want to make sure I know how to do it responsibly," she'd said, followed by a toothy smile. "Trying to make you proud is all." It was the perfect thing to say, especially given that Patricia's father had died of liver failure due to alcohol abuse when she was young. Also, by default, Patricia loved anything and everything precautionary. She loved doctors and supervision. She'd been thrilled.

Even when their mother wasn't around, Audrey had pretended she was fine, that rehab was just a fun learning experience. But Bea knew her better than anyone and could tell she was scared.

Once, while Audrey was away, Bea had pointed out the obvious parallel between the two weeks she'd spent in the children's psych ward when she was nine—which no one outside their immediate family knew about because Patricia was so ashamed—and Audrey going to rehab: both places were for people who lacked control over their harmful impulses. Patricia had replied, without looking up from her book, that the first major difference was that Audrey had elected to go, while Bea had to be forced, kicking and screaming. The second, she'd said, was that Audrey wasn't going because she'd hurt another living thing. And so nothing changed about the way they were treated relative to each other. At dinner parties, Bea endured Patricia's whispers, judgmental glances across the table, and pained smiles whenever they made eye contact as if she was an uninvited guest in her own home, in her own family. And Audrey, as always, was asked questions and complimented for her looks—the way the faux-candlelight danced in her eyes, "like distant boats at sea," someone's creepy father had once said—while Patricia looked on proudly, as if no rehab stay had even occurred, though it was not a secret that she'd gone.

Audrey had claimed to be sober for a couple years afterward, asking for lemon seltzer or Earl Grey tea wherever she went in a charming, chirpy tone. She was beautiful, filled with life and promise, booking modeling jobs, paying for family dinners at fancy restaurants, rose-cheeked and effortlessly lovable. That was the confusing thing: it was as if Bea had two sisters, except that she was the only person who'd really known the sick one. Healthy Audrey, or Seemingly Healthy Audrey, was who their mother mourned, but that Audrey had died much earlier than most people knew: in the throes of her heroin addiction, she'd confessed to Bea that she'd been using drugs regularly since a month after returning from rehab.

She'd said it was easy to get Adderall from college friends—hadn't seemed like anything since people used it to write papers, not just recreationally. What had started as Adderall on long workdays and select nights out to stave off drowsiness had turned seamlessly into cocaine on nights out, which was fine until she needed it the mornings after, too, then on cozy nights in, and before and after dinner, and, and, and. Bea had seen her do it off a key that she hooked inside her nostril. She'd inhale sharply, bat her eyes and smile as if a new part of her consciousness was suddenly awake. Bea had believed her when she said it was "just a little," that it was "nothing to worry about." She'd thought it seemed reasonable when Audrey said, "It keeps me alert, that's all," as Bea herself had lived most of her life in a sleepy, depressed, antipsychotic-meds-induced haze. Plus, Audrey had things together, far more so than Bea. She was making money, had good friends, and seemed happy.

But then she started drinking again, a few weeks after they'd moved into their shared apartment. She'd started out slowly, like she had with Adderall: a beer at dinner, half a glass of wine while out with a friend. Before long, she was stumbling down dark streets in sky-high heels with a miniature liquor nip in one hand, a cigarette in the other, and Tatum following close behind with outstretched arms, like a mother spotting her unstable toddler. One morning, while Audrey slept on the couch in her clothes from the night before, Bea had looked through her purse and found eleven empty glass bottles in it. She'd watched her vomit into a trash can on the Chambers Street subway platform. She'd watched her talk to a lamppost she'd mistaken for a man. During the week, she was her normal self, bringing her laptop to coffee shops, sautéing vegetables while listening to music, jogging off to Pilates in matching sports bra and leggings sets, but when the clock struck nine on Friday or Saturday night, a wild light glowed in her eyes, nothing at all like distant boats bobbing peacefully at sea. Of course, much later it became clear she'd been on drugs the whole time; her normal, weekday self was who she was on drugs. On the weekends, she just let loose.

Bea remembered the day Audrey tried heroin for the first time. It had felt apocalyptic for multiple reasons, including a rare blizzard that knocked down trees and made the windows rattle, but that was the night Audrey had become a zombie and the shock of seeing her that way was unlike anything else. The next morning, she'd risen and seemed mostly herself. They'd gone for a walk together as sunlight glistened on snow, helped each other over waist-high piles created by plows at every intersection. At one point, Audrey whispered, "Trix, that was *everything*. You can't even imagine." Bea had looked at her sister and seen that she was different. From then on, it was Bea's job to keep her alive and comfortable.

She'd loved tending to her. It was all she'd thought about, cared about, and she'd been irrevocably shaped by the experience. It had given her purpose. A reason to rise in the morning. And life without it, without Audrey, was empty.

Having quickly shaken off the guilt over her angry words to Rosalie, Bea was feeling great, the best she had since returning from Arizona. She was glad to be home, and to have accomplished her goal for the memorial; the outcome was even better than she'd hoped for. Layla and Tatum wanted to help with the kennel—probably; soon, she'd know for sure. She lay on the floor, stretched out across her scraggly rug, which was a spiderweb for eraser shavings, charcoal dust, and coffee stains, wiggling her fingers and toes.

When her phone pinged, she fished it out of her back pocket with one hand while unbuttoning her pants with the other. Could it be Layla already? No, it was Tinder. She clicked on the pink-and-white icon.

1 new message.

Bea enjoyed Tinder, and more generally, talking to people online. She felt she could be someone slightly other than herself there. Over a messaging app, she wasn't as obviously odd as she was in person. She didn't know what about herself it was exactly that made her weird. She'd asked this of her former therapist, and he'd just turned it around: "Well, what do you think makes you weird?" which he'd done far too often, which was the reason she'd stopped seeing him. One helpful takeaway from their sessions was that he'd taught her to use the word *rage* to describe her fits, which she'd done ever since. It was good to give the rabid feeling a name. The fits didn't happen often, and she tried to sequester herself when they did, yet people still avoided her as if they sensed she could snap at any moment. What gave her away?

When Bea asked Audrey the same question she'd asked her therapist, *What's so weird about me?* Audrey had said she couldn't put her finger on it: "Generally, you're just kind of intense."

"So are you," said Bea.

"It's different."

"How?"

"You do things that make people uncomfortable."

"I make you uncomfortable?"

"Not me."

Even at the time, Bea had guessed she was talking about Tatum.

The Tinder message was from Dennis Sweeney, son of Rod and Mary Sweeney, and brother of Lane Sweeney, who'd been the talk of Park Slope when he was accepted to Yale at age sixteen after skipping two grades.

As for Dennis, he'd been in Bea's pre-K, third-grade, and seventh-grade classes before he was caught smoking weed in the faculty bathroom and sent away.

His opening Tinder message was: Long time no see.

"Long time no see," was a common refrain on Park Slope–Tinder since practically everyone in the neighborhood had seen practically everyone else at least once before. Either they'd taken the same pottery class or were assigned delivery duty at the Coop together or they'd gone to the same school in different grades or they'd gone to different schools but knew many of the same people or their parents knew one another or, in Bea's case, they knew her notoriously gorgeous sister.

Adult Dennis was cute enough, which was why Bea had decided to swipe right while on the toilet two nights earlier. His hair was spiky like grass, his shoulders were broad and flat, and the shape of his wallet was well worn into the pocket of his jeans, which Bea found appealing for some reason. A blurry tattooed snake was coiled around his neck, the kind of blurry tattoos became after a while, which she also liked. How old was he when he'd gotten it?

Still, it was Dennis who'd shot spitballs across classrooms and fake-jizzed all over the pages of her notebooks in an encouragingly flirtatious display, then asked what Audrey was doing after school. That she remembered this about Dennis—and similarly unappealing, ancient details about many others she saw on Tinder—was the problem with dating in Park Slope.

Indeed, she typed back.

To her surprise, his response came quickly.

How are things with you? Do you still live in the neighborhood?

Things are things.

The rug was painful against her elbows. She adjusted her position.

And yeah. Still in PS. What's up with you?

I'm between jobs so I'm back for a few weeks. I live in LA now.

How are Rod and Mary?

Lol. Good. Thanks for asking. How's Patricia?

Bea smiled. Along with everyone knowing everyone in Park Slope, everyone also knew everyone's parents, except for her father, who was always holed up in his office "working late" and had never been around for school pickup. Still, she appreciated him more than she did her mom. When she really needed him, he was there. When she didn't, he left her alone. He didn't judge her, or ask annoying questions, or micromanage her to the brink of suffocation, though it was also true that, since Audrey's death, depression had cured at least some of Patricia's OCD. Bea no longer received flurries of frantic texts from her every day.

She's living in Westchester now. White picket fence, pretty yard, waspy neighbors, the whole shebang.

Bea climbed into bed and sat, legs pretzeled, facing the window.

Sounds . . . pleasant?

Does it?

Lol, well is it?

In some ways, I guess. Minus the waspy neighbors and monotony.

Bea flipped onto her back as she waited for him to reply.

Fair. Park Slope is like a never-ending K-hole. It's always so weird to come back.

Bea smiled. The statement seemed true from what she could tell, having never done ketamine or any other drug. Dennis had probably experienced a real K-hole if his expulsion for smoking weed in seventh grade was any indication.

Is your sister still in town, too?

No, she isn't.

For a moment, Bea considered leaving it at that.

She's dead.

Dots that indicated typing appeared, then disappeared, then appeared again. She clicked out of their conversation, giving him privacy, and began searching for someone new.

Carson stood shirtless and proud in front of a tower of red cups—no. Paul was one of her least favorite names—no. Sydney was impossibly tanned, with thighs as thick as tree trunks; he was positioned in front of a row of treadmills and was holding a svelte woman over his head with two large weights balanced on her back—fuck no. Simon had brown, shoulder-length hair and was posed beside a Scrabble board—sure, why not? Keen wore his baseball cap backward and had so many freckles, Bea knew all she'd want to do was count them if they met—no. Thomas had marijuana leaves as his bio, and was barely visible behind a wall of smoke in his picture—no.

I didn't realize, I'm so sorry.

Bea felt for Dennis. It was distressing to learn that someone you'd once known was dead.

Thanks. It was two years ago so I'm okay. Anyway, to answer your question, I'm the only one from my family who's still living in Park Slope.

She knew that if he'd been thinking about asking her out, he wasn't anymore. And if he'd been thinking about using her to get to Audrey, he wasn't anymore, which left them with zero reasons to keep talking. Even from beyond the grave, Audrey made dating difficult and Bea insecure.

Wow, I just can't believe my mom didn't mention it.

Bea slid her phone away. She felt for Dennis and agreed that his mother must've known, as it seemed the whole neighborhood did, but wasn't going to comfort him. It was late and she was tired. Technically, she had work tomorrow.

Since returning from Arizona, she'd been the sole employee of a paint-your-own-ceramics studio. Her responsibilities included watching little kids jab brushes into the bulging eyeballs of sports-themed animal figurines, washing paintbrushes, placing ceramics in the kiln and then pressing start, sweeping when she felt like it, showing up when she felt like it, and swiping people's credit cards. Her boss went by the name Savage and either had a raging cocaine addiction or severe ADHD. The studio was probably a front for something because the register was always filled with hundreds and fifties though customers spent, on average, thirty dollars at a time and never used cash, and because of the scar that ran down the length of Savage's neck like a zipper. Also, when she'd started, Bea had to google everything she needed to know about the kiln and hope for the best, since Savage couldn't answer any of her questions.

In many ways, though, Bea was perfect for the role, and vice versa; she didn't have a college degree or any use for money besides food since her parents subsidized her rent, and Savage offered a salary well below minimum wage and circumstances that would make a more responsible person nervous. Park Slope parents were too afraid to let their kids work for Savage since she looked like she ate kids for breakfast. Though she'd only been there a few weeks and exclusively because Patricia had insisted on her finding something to do, Bea had already surmised that she was virtually unfireable, which was a good thing. Unfireable was exactly what she needed to be to keep a job. Plus, it seemed like Savage's investment in the business was on par with Bea's investment in it—another good thing.

At various times in her life, she'd tried to be normal: go to college, start a career, date with the goal of finding love, but she'd always lost interest quickly, and once she did, there was no faking it. As an employee, she was unreliable, often calling out at the last minute, and her short attention span made it hard to learn the ropes of a new role.

Before Audrey died, Bea had had a gig filling out surveys about movie previews in exchange for a weekly stipend—another good fit for her limitations which also allowed her to stay home with her sister—until they fired her. The termination email read:

> In every case, your emotional responses to the previews in question are in direct contrast with what we'd expect, and with

others' responses, which leads us to believe you aren't taking this seriously.

Though she had taken it seriously, she didn't care enough to plead her case, and let the message go unanswered.

Since she'd burned most bridges with past employers and couldn't risk them being called for references, the only job other than "Ceramics Store Manager" listed on Bea's current résumé was her role on the camel farm in Arizona. Her position there had been amorphous, always changing. On her résumé, she was called a "Livestock Assistant." Her father, who'd helped with formatting and wording, had vetoed her offerings of "Camel hand," or "Camel nurse," or just "Milker," which he felt were "too specific" and ultimately inapplicable to any job in Park Slope.

"We want to work the word 'assistant' into it somehow," he'd said, scratching his head.

She'd certainly been invested in her role as "livestock assistant" and, to her own happy surprise, had excelled at it. For months she'd shoveled camel shit, which looked like enlarged deer shit, milked the females, picked dirt from hooves, brushed them, and distributed grain. Sometimes she just sat with them, stroked their coarse flanks, and watched them chew their cud. If they were sick, she helped administer medicine, apply poultices to wounds, do whatever else was needed. All the camels were rescues, brought to the farm from zoos when they were old or after they were confiscated from owners who'd unlawfully purchased them off the black market. Most weren't in good shape when they came. The fulfillment she'd gotten from caring for them was immense. The most magical moment of all was when their eyes fell shut for the final time and their incessant pain turned to nothing as a lethal dose of pentobarbital worked its way through their systems. Memories of those quiet evenings still brought tears to her eyes, for she'd come away with an improved outlook on death and life at a time when she really needed it.

She'd found the place—Arizona's Arabia—through WWOOF USA, after scouring the results of her googled query, "Get me out of NYC ASAP," and turning one hyperlink after the next purple in a tearful search. Most of the articles she skimmed were about breakups—long-winded recommendations of the book *Eat, Pray, Love,* followed by even longer-winded recommendations of *Eat, Pray, Love*–inspired trips to Bali, including where to stay, where to eat, which shamans to visit. At the time, she'd been sitting in her living room, on the couch where Audrey died, which shared a wall with Audrey's old bedroom, which was practically a mausoleum, filled with Audrey's unmade bed, makeup, posters, her corkboard collaged by pushpinned photos of herself and friends—including many shots of Tatum—and her clothes, piled in a heap on the floor of her closet.

Arizona's Arabia was the very last hyperlink she'd clicked on. She'd chosen it in part because "Arabia" made it seem far, as far as could be within the bounds of America, since, at the time, there were strict pandemic regulations for international travel. From the moment she'd sent off her application, breathing had come easier. In the end, it was the best thing she could've done. The place itself had healed her: that shivering horizon line, those doe-eyed, long-legged camels moving in slow motion, and the sweltering heat.

Even just thinking about her time there relaxed her. Eyeing her hazy reflection in the window, she stood and lifted the hem of her shirt up over her head. She imagined that someone out there in the world could see her, that she was putting on a show.

Bea's fingers found her nipples and twisted. Just enough light filtered in from the hall through the crack in the door to illuminate her shape in the rain-spattered glass. She threw back her shoulders.

"Agh," she moaned as she collapsed against her bed, fingers hooked inside her slippery vagina, tapping out a slow, deep rhythm. When she thought of the imaginary person watching from outside—Dennis, she'd decided at the very last minute, standing beneath her window like a very horny Romeo—she came quickly in a crescendo of shrieks and stiff toes.

Panting, she pulled her shirt back on, along with a fresh pair of underwear, and settled into her desk chair, feeling wonderfully unwound. She switched on the lamp and drew for a while: an olive jar.

Her phone pinged.

Tinder again.

1 new match.

She clicked. It was Simon the Scrabble boy who'd seemed uninteresting but "whatever" enough to make her swipe right.

Hey, what's up? he'd written. You're hot.

He's not cute, Bea could practically hear Audrey say. She had only been attracted to tall, waifish boys with dark hair, lots of piercings, and jutting cheekbones, who were often proudly bisexual and either in rock bands with tens of thousands of followers on Instagram, or models. It had always seemed unfair that she would judge the dating profiles of Bea's prospects so harshly. Rarely, if ever, had Bea sought out her sister's brutal honesty—just her excitement and encouragement—yet so often it was what she'd received.

You're hotter than him.

He kind of looks like an incel.

You can do better.

Maybe Audrey's harsh judgment was why Bea had never been in love before—because she'd been holding out for Audrey's approval. The truth was, Bea didn't have her pick of the litter the way Audrey did. Perhaps she'd passed over someone due to Audrey's advice who would've been kind and embraced—even valued—her quirks, which was all she'd ever wanted.

"Shut up," she said to her empty room.

Hey, she typed. Hit me with your go-to Scrabble word.

She waited.

I've never met a two-letter I didn't like. Za and Qi are my all-time faves. You play?

Bea typed quickly:

I've played before but I wouldn't say that I play.

She was bored, stalling. Would Dennis message again? Would Layla text? If she didn't, could Bea start the kennel herself? When she really thought about it, it seemed impossible. Suddenly, everything hinged on Layla, who, before that afternoon, she hadn't thought about in years. There was nothing worse than feeling out of control, beholden to someone else. It made her resentful, which wasn't ideal since resentment made it that much harder to be nice. Her momentary, self-pleasure-induced calm had already evaporated.

Bea's whole life was shaped by waves of obsession; she knew this about herself. The kennel had come to her like a mirage while sitting around the campfire in the desert listening to the farmhands sing songs she didn't know. Having been up for two days straight tending to a sick camel, she'd deliriously eyed a smoldering marshmallow suspended over the fire. One of its bubbling, black burn marks vaguely resembled the shape of a dog, which had instantly reminded her of Audrey, her old life, and the dog kennel of her childhood dreams. And then she was no longer tired. It was perfect. The perfect answer to her uncertainty about the future since she couldn't stay in Arizona forever. The idea itself, to start a kennel, was like a homecoming, like a comfortable reversion to the past, like playing pretend, but somehow it would become real.

The morning after her epiphany, she told her supervisor she was leaving and her parents she was returning. She'd already decided to tell Tatum about her plan at the upcoming memorial, too. Ironically, her obsessions were often cagelike. Inescapable. Her own type of kennel. The fact that she didn't especially care for dogs? It didn't matter. The fact that she had no knowledge of how to start a business? Irrelevant. And the fact that she had no money of her own didn't occur to her until much later.

When she'd finally returned, her Park Slope apartment was as she'd left it, albeit dustier—in their grief about Audrey, her parents had paid the rent in full while she was gone without a second thought—and the refrigerator was empty except for an unsealed jar of olives. Soon, Patricia would call and tell her to find a job and a roommate, and the search for Rosalie would begin via Craigslist; the memorial would take place a few short weeks after Rosalie moved in.

Now, alone in her room without any sense of what should happen next, the inconvenient truths she'd previously ignored were undeniable—her inexperience with dogs and lack of business knowledge and savings—and suddenly everything hinged on Layla. All Bea could do was sit still and wait, either for Layla to officially sign on or for the next whirlwind obsession to strike and redirect her interest as had happened many times before. It was hard to imagine—she'd been daydreaming about the kennel for weeks—but she knew herself well enough to admit it was always a possibility, especially when she reached an impasse like this one. She knew herself well enough to admit she couldn't really know herself at all.

4

TATUM TEXTED ED: I won't be home for dinner.

The 2 train roared as she sat beneath a canopy of arms on her way to meet Layla. Though eating out was expensive, especially at the place Layla had suggested, it was nice to have dinner plans after work. Atmospheric restaurants reminded her that she was a real adult, in a good way. A New York City woman. Too much of her time was spent in bed, since Ed usually claimed the living room, or at work staring into a computer screen like it was a hypnotic spiral. She was wasting her twenties, wasting her city. She welcomed all reminders that it was special to be twenty-seven, a youngish yet fully formed metropolitan woman. Plus, she hoped Layla would insist on paying.

Ed didn't have many friends in Park Slope. And since he'd followed her there after college, she often felt responsible for his lack of plans, which became pressure to invite him along to hers. A few people they knew from college had moved to the city, too, and occasionally he saw them, but most of the time when he wasn't with her, he was at home alone, lacing the ringlets of his headphones cord through his fingers or mashing controller buttons. He was charming, though he could be pretentious, and kept to himself by choice, which was worse than if it was by default. At least if no one liked him, Tatum could've pitied him. But since he always chose to be at home, she was hardly ever alone, which was exhausting.

He used to claim his isolation was a function of his work, by which he meant his self-appointed creative projects. In the past, Tatum had no reason to doubt this since he was always editing at his desk, knee vibrating from excitement and caffeine. Now, though, the excuse had shifted to sleep: he wasn't sleeping well due to the stress of his unfinished screenplay—of writer's block. This would've been more believable if Tatum didn't sleep beside him every night with a pillow clamped over her ear to dull the sound of his thunderous snores, which lasted from the moment his head hit the pillow until late morning.

About a year after college, over drinks, a friend had playfully asked how they'd ended up living together, clearly hoping for a romantic story, one to learn from and aspire to. Unfortunately, theirs wasn't that. A few months before college graduation, Ed had announced over dining hall chicken cutlets that he'd be moving to Brooklyn with her; when she'd leaned in to kiss him, he'd leaned away, because there was spinach stuck in her teeth. Once she'd fished it out with the prong of a plastic fork and the help of his phone camera, they'd finally kissed under fluorescent lights, then headed back to her dorm to smoke weed and watch a movie until they were both asleep. The end. Utterly heartwarming.

Soon thereafter, he'd begun sharing links to expensive apartments. "Do you like this neighborhood?" "Is outdoor space important to you?" And then they were discussing their finances, he was offering to pay for a place while she looked for a job because he could, and she was asking if they could look in Park Slope.

To convince him, she spoke rapturously about Hanco's passion fruit bubble tea, the perfect marriage of tart and sweet, and about all the quirky characters from her past. It was clear that Ed, though he wouldn't admit it for respectable reasons, was heavily inspired by Woody Allen as a filmmaker, so the stories Tatum chose to tell about Park Slope capitalized on that specific brand of New York City romanticism.

She told him about Neil, the father of an elementary school acquaintance, who seemed to be everywhere at once, waiting with open arms to pull her into a sweaty hug and a long, boring conversation. "When I'm home I see him about once a week," she said, "usually when I'm in a rush. It's insane."

There was Mando's deli, of course, which sold alcohol to underage kids without even asking to see IDs. In high school, she and Audrey had been frequent patrons, and had struck up quite the rapport with Mando himself. Once, Audrey had offered to kiss him on the cheek as payment for two Corona tallboys. He'd gladly accepted. Ed winced, and Tatum nodded before moving on to her next Park Slope selling point.

"Also, in Park Slope, you're weird if you've never seen a therapist before," she said, which Ed hadn't. Again, he winced but was clearly amused. Most Park Slope residents were *in conversation with their trauma*. Everyone was confronting their id. Everyone knew the term *limerence*. And most people their age had been diagnosed with anxiety, ADD, ADHD, or a nondescript "learning disability," during preschool or kindergarten, which granted them extra time on standardized tests.

And finally, the organic cherry on top of the flourless, dairy-free, Park Slope–themed cake, was the notorious Park Slope Food Coop. After years of mentioning it offhandedly, Tatum chose to end her rant by telling Ed everything. She explained that the Coop—a glorified members-only grocery store on Union Street, to which both her parents and the Ellis parents proudly belonged—was like the White House of Park Slope, complete with all the same ridiculousness, fearmongering, and the equivalent of Secret Service agents guarding the doors; in many ways, it really was the neighborhood's governing body.

Coop members, while unsuspecting behind their hemp aprons and labels of "middle-aged," "stay-at-home mom," "dad," "lawyer," "teacher," and the façade of their reasonable passion for organic food, were a bloodthirsty, tyrannical mob, always hunting for the freeloaders and defectors among them. Sometimes disobedient, overextended, or just plain rich-and-lazy members paid their nannies to work their shifts as cashiers or restockers or delivery people. On more than one occasion, Tatum had overheard her middle school friends' parents describe occurrences of this as "betrayals of the community," as if they'd been taught to use this exact language by the food Coop cult leader.

"Lilian should've known better," she could remember one mother tsking about another. "I won't be speaking to her again anytime soon."

Offenders of the Coop rules were unceremoniously kicked out of the hearts of many Park Slope parents, in addition to the Coop itself, and thus forced to buy slightly less high-quality food from a slightly less cutesy store for slightly more money. The biggest loss was the clout. It was like a neighborhood social death sentence to be a Coop reject. Everyone knew who was on the outs and why; even the children gossiped about it. One of the most important responsibilities of Coop members, it seemed, was to keep the neighborhood rumor mill well-oiled. They took every aspect of their duties seriously.

Of course, Tatum loved that the Coop existed, for she loved—or at least appreciated—every DNA strand that made Park Slope itself, even those that made her life difficult. Plus, theirs was the best peanut butter she'd ever tasted.

Tears glinted in the corners of Ed's eyes by the time Tatum was done, and he was wheezing from laughter. She'd won, not that he'd put up much of a fight in the first place. There was so much comedic whimsy to her life in Park Slope, also true of her life at college and presumably true of lives in other New York City neighborhoods, but she liked to think that Park Slope was special.

On a more serious note she mentioned that the neighborhood was predominantly white. This felt necessary to call out, though it put a damper on their excitement. They nodded at each other's regurgitated points about gentrification—how real estate developers were mostly to blame, but so were the college grads with rich parents who moved to lower-income neighborhoods claiming they couldn't afford anywhere else. Tatum's final argument for Park Slope was that living there wouldn't mean actively displacing others or changing the culture, because it was already so far gone. They'd lamented the failures of society for a while until the air in the room had grown stale, and a few months later moved into the high-ceilinged apartment where they still lived.

Back then, Ed was her hope. He was motivated and well-connected. He was a pair of warm arms. He made life easier.

Things were different now. The luster had worn off him like cheap silver plating thanks to his career not developing fast enough and the pandemic having shrink-wrapped them together for months without respite. Though the pandemic was over, she was still stuck: terrified to be alone after almost ten years together, terrified of ending up with this version of him, terrified that any version of him wouldn't be enough for her forever.

The restaurant, La Olivia, was in Fort Greene, a few neighborhoods over from Park Slope. The closer Tatum catapulted toward her stop at Atlantic Terminal, the more anxious she grew. When socializing, she always felt an unshakable responsibility to entertain: if there were silences or awkward moments, she'd let herself and her audience down. She'd once been told by a therapist this might have to do with her upbringing, the feeling that she didn't quite belong that had permeated her childhood as a non-ultra-wealthy person in New York City, as well as her college years at Morristown, the small liberal arts school where she'd met Ed, which she'd only been able to attend thanks to a large scholarship. But when it came to Layla, there was more to her anxiety than just that.

Layla had grown up to be beautiful, Tatum had discovered at the memorial—the sort of beautiful that made her stomach lurch. She was also clean, the cleanest person Tatum had ever seen. No lint flecks blemished her black dress, no mascara bubbles clung to the corners of her eyes. She was impeccably designed and maintained. Before Nancy had become so successful, Layla had worn frayed Bermuda shorts and pit-stained T-shirts in the summertime.

To Tatum, Layla was an old friend, a beautiful woman, and an aspirational conquest—Audrey had been all the above, too, before their friendship found its easy stride. Over the years, she'd kept vague tabs on Layla, clicking on articles that popped up about her or that she thought might mention her. In 2016, Layla's "style" had been deemed "iconic" by the *New York Times*. She'd been crowned *Teen Vogue*'s guest editor for June 2018 and was a guest judge on *Project Runway* a few months later. Tatum had even seen paparazzi shots: real, honest-to-goodness blurry, watermarked candid pictures of Layla in sunglasses, brandishing a sweating cup of iced coffee.

She'd attended the Met Gala on her mother's arm in 2019; a clip had briefly circulated of Elle Fanning accidentally stepping on the train of her dress, grimacing in a way that became a meme and profusely apologizing before embracing Layla as if they were old friends. Audrey had texted it to Tatum, who sent back a million hahas in a row, then changed the subject. But, that night, jealousy had given her a terrible cramp. So, Tatum's nerves over meeting Layla at La Olivia were the product of many years of built-up wonder and envy, and only a filthy martini would help soothe them.

At the next stop, Tatum pushed off the train through throngs of people, fussing with the back of her pencil skirt, tucking thick curls behind her ears. Sweat dripped down the small of her back and dissolved into the elastic band of her underpants. Temperature was tricky to plan for in New York in early spring. While it was stuffy and hot inside subway cars and on subway platforms, the air outside was cool and clear.

It was a joy to walk the streets of Brooklyn at dusk, especially in Fort Greene, with its stately double-wide brownstones and double-wide windows begging to be glanced through. The air held a touch of humidity beneath the breeze, a whisper of the summer that was coming, and Tatum shrugged her light jacket off her shoulders. La Olivia was across the street from Fort Greene Park, its outdoor seating area illuminated by garlands of lights, making it look like a pot of gold against the deep blue atmosphere. When she arrived, she gave Layla's assistant's name and was seated at an outdoor table set slightly apart from the rest.

"Is tap all right?" the waiter asked.

She smiled and nodded, feeling the last embers of sunset in her eyes. When her phone pinged, it was Layla announcing she would be late. The waiter returned and took her martini order: filthy, with vodka. When it came, its consistency was like soup, thick and perfect, and the skewered olives were bright blue-green, her favorite type. A recurring argument she'd had with Audrey for years was over which olive variety was best, Audrey's Kalamatas or Tatum's Castelvetranos, though they'd agreed Tatum's were better for drinks, of course—no contest there. She smiled as she bit one off the skewer, still feeling residual smugness.

"So sorry," Layla said, touching the back of Tatum's shoulder seventeen minutes later.

Her breasts spilled out the corseted bodice of a black gown, spaghetti straps cutting into her shoulders. Quickly, Tatum looked away from her old friend's cleavage.

Layla listed off excuses for her tardiness as Tatum admired her eyes inside their dark liner. Wisps of hair floated around her face like butterflies. A silver charm attached to the velvet choker she wore rested neatly in the hollow of her neck, as if it were custom fit for that space. The booze, Tatum reasoned, must be to blame for her incestuous thoughts, but then wouldn't this be any bisexual woman's natural reaction to Layla? And they were adults now. Tatum would acclimate, just as she had with Audrey, who'd never shown any sexual interest in her, but for whom—if she was painfully honest—Tatum would've left Ed in a heartbeat.

Surveying the menu, Layla bit the tip of her finger. "I think I'll have a Dirty Shirley. Most places can make that for me."

Tatum laughed easily, thanks to her martini. "That's your drink? A Dirty Shirley?"

Layla nodded, grinning, batting her thick lashes. "I like wet, pink things," she said. "Sue me."

Embarrassingly, Tatum's mouth filled with saliva. Dressed in work clothes, hair frizzy despite her early-morning decision to double the amount of mousse she usually applied, Tatum sipped her martini, grateful for the rumble of other dinner conversations from afar as theirs stalled for a charged moment. Layla was watching her.

"This is weird," she said. "Isn't it? It's been so long, and here we are with alcohol and adult bodies"—she grabbed her breasts—"and apartments and lives and secrets." She spoke with overwrought passion, but Tatum hung on her every word, utterly convinced.

"Before yesterday, we hadn't seen each other since we were sobbing at the end of summer. Flash forward fifteen years and here we are." Tatum shook her head. "We must've been twelve then. Now we're—what—sixty?"

"Something like that," said Layla. "I don't know about you, but my brain is short-circuiting."

The waiter arrived to take her drink order and soon Layla was sipping a Dirty Shirley, their food orders had been placed, and their conversation had begun to flow, though Tatum was still overthinking everything. Thankfully, the more she drank, the smoother it got.

"I work in publishing now," said Tatum.

"Oh, yeah? My mom's writing a book."

Tatum held up a finger as she chewed on the end of a tuna crostini Layla had ordered as an appetizer to share. "Don't I know it," she said when she'd swallowed. "Industry people are freaking out."

Layla laughed. "I'm happy for her. Will you two ever interact?"

Tatum shook her head. "Not more than me possibly transferring her call to someone a million times more important than I am. I'm probably not even important enough for that, though." She'd wanted to keep her most humiliating cards close to her chest for now, but apparently that wasn't happening.

Again, Layla laughed. "Oh, honey."

Their entrées arrived. Parmesan was grated over carefully arranged pasta, black pepper was ground, and they were left alone again.

"So, what brought you to the memorial after so long?" Tatum asked as she watched Layla prepare a mouthful using both a fork and spoon, employing more sophisticated dining choreography than Tatum knew.

Layla's brow furrowed at Tatum's question, and she abandoned her dance before any food reached her mouth, laying both utensils against her dish, and leaning far forward. Across the table, Tatum caught a whiff of perfume—a leathery vanilla scent—and inhaled it reverently but subtly, she hoped.

"I don't know," said Layla. "I mean, I guess I was really glad Patricia included my mom on the email." She was drawing circles on the tablecloth with her finger, wet from her drink's condensation. "And I've just sort of been in a rut." She squinted at Tatum and pouted, an expression that said, *You know what that's like I'm sure*, which Tatum did. "And, I don't know, and I just didn't want to wait any longer since I'd already waited far too long. I couldn't risk anything else happening." Layla leaned back. "It's so horrible. The person I remember was so young. For me, it's like a child died. Like, a child I loved so much."

The rock-solid dam protecting Tatum from an ocean of tears was made up of alcohol and lustful intimidation. She nodded, dry eyed, and said, "I can't imagine," though of course she could.

"I've always loved her, just like I've always loved you, and Bea, too, but I never got to tell her."

Again, Tatum nodded. It was all she could do. "Back at you." *Back at you?* She scolded herself by twisting a pinch of skin on the back of her arm.

"It's such a shame how things happened," said Layla. "That we were separated for so long."

Tatum said, "Yes, and I've never known why."

"Really?"

Tatum shook her head.

Layla seemed to relax. Her shoulders fell away from her ears slightly, and she smiled sadly as she reached for Tatum's hand. "I think it was complicated."

It was clear she was avoiding saying more, but Tatum's focus was on her touch. "Right." Layla was stroking her knuckles.

"Anyway," said Layla, "For whatever reason, I really felt like I should be there. And I'm so glad I was." She bit her lip. Was she flirting? It seemed increasingly possible as they were still holding hands. The thought was almost too much for Tatum. She had a boyfriend and this was her estranged childhood best friend. She wasn't about to uproot the only life she'd known for more than nine years at this dinner, wasn't about to cheat, and what would it mean for the relationship she hoped to build with Layla? But her skin was so soft. And her eyes were so pretty.

Slowly, perhaps even reluctantly, Layla reclaimed her hand.

Tatum cleared her throat, twirling her fork through her noodles, momentarily feeling more like a child Layla was babysitting than her friend.

Layla said, "Do you think I'm crazy for wanting to help Bea with the kennel?"

"No," said Tatum quickly, though she kind of did. Not crazy, because Layla could never be crazy, not even if she jumped onto their table, squatted, and peed into Tatum's bucatini. Tatum would probably slurp the noodles up even faster if she did that, the thought of consuming any part of her was so painfully enticing. No, not crazy, but it was true she didn't understand why Layla wanted to help Bea open a dog kennel when she could do anything else. Layla didn't know Bea as an adult yet, but she was, well, strange.

"I think you should do it with me, then," Layla said, and finally took a bite of pasta.

Tatum nodded. What else was there to do but agree? "Okay," she said.

Layla's lips moved in tight, mechanical circles. "Just hear me out." She swallowed. "And don't agree to anything tonight."

Again, Tatum nodded.

"I know people with a lot of business experience. And I can finance it." Layla rolled her eyes. "I've certainly got the means. Basically, I can make this thing big, and I'd really like to do something to commemorate Audrey and our friendship and stuff, since—" She paused. Suddenly, her eyes shone. "Since I missed out on it for so many years." She dabbed at her nose with her napkin. "So, I'm seriously considering getting involved, but I'll only do it if we're in it together. At the end of the day, that's what matters most to me."

Tatum stared at the warped reflection in her water glass. Her. She was what mattered most.

"So, why this exactly?" Tatum wasn't trying to talk Layla out of it, but was curious. If it was about honoring Audrey's life and doing something together, they could start a fashion brand in her name since she'd been a model. Or they could create something that didn't have to do with her, but could be named after her: Audrey's Housewares, Audrey's Nail Polish, Audrey's Salads. The truth was, though Audrey was a dog person, Tatum knew she wouldn't have really cared about any of this; she'd never been very sentimental. She was practical and driven. At the memorial, she'd only said Audrey would've loved it because that had seemed like the thing to say to Bea, but it wasn't true. Still, Layla's intentions—and Bea's, for that matter—were sweet.

"I guess I just want to do something totally different," said Layla. "I've tried to start businesses before, most recently one called Band It." She smirked, clearly still proud of the idea. Tatum could feel her face being studied, so she nodded enthusiastically. Layla pointed at her forehead. "Like, headbands."

"Oh, very cool," said Tatum. Somehow, the prospect of starting a headband company was even less appealing to her than starting a dog kennel, and for a moment she was grateful.

"Well, it never happened. My mom's business manager thought it was stupid; so did my mom, for that matter. I don't know, I don't really have a brain for that kind of thing—idea generating or whatever. Apparently, I didn't inherit my mom's creativity."

With as much feeling as possible, Tatum said, "I think headbands are a great idea, though." She was an expert at this kind of lying.

"Right?" said Layla. "I thought we could make thick ones and thin ones. Ones to match any hair color, and neon ones. I pitched it as the Skims of headbands."

"Sure," said Tatum, nodding stoically. "I can totally see that."

"Well, they couldn't," said Layla. "So it didn't happen. And, honestly, I look like shit in a headband." She sipped her drink. When she spoke again, her lips were shiny, grenadine red. "She's actually said that to me before, by the way."

"What?"

"My mom has said she wishes I inherited her creativity. Too bad she didn't account for that when picking a sperm donor, huh." Layla laughed and rolled her eyes again as if this wasn't the deep wound it clearly was. Nancy had never had a romantic partner—at least not in the time their families had known each other, and not since, according to the internet. It wasn't something they'd spoken of often when they were young, though sometimes Layla had asked off-the-cuff questions about what it was like having two parents: if there were twice as many rules; if Tatum loved one more than the other; if each parent got her a birthday present, or if they bought her a big one together; if one stayed home while the other was away on work trips. Tatum's parents never traveled for work, which, she remembered, Layla had found truly shocking.

"Anyway, rescuing dogs isn't just a business—that's what I like about it," Layla continued. "It's doing something good for the world. I might as well do something good while making money, you know? And I came up with a name for it, too."

Tatum raised an eyebrow.

"The Bennel Kennel." Layla beamed.

"That's great," said Tatum automatically, straining to keep her expression neutral.

"Get it?"

"It rhymes?" This was all she "got" about it.

"It's a mixture of our last names: Bernard, Ellis, and Kaplan. But yeah, it also rhymes with kennel. The word 'kennel' technically just means the enclosure where a dog is kept, and what we thought was a kennel as kids was actually a dog rescue or a shelter—my assistant did some research—but I don't see why we can't call it whatever we want. And 'kennel' is so much cuter than 'shelter.'"

"Totally," said Tatum. "That's a pretty *creative* name, if you ask me." Layla smiled. "And maybe we can make headbands for the dogs," Tatum added, hoping Layla would take this as a joke, not mockery.

Layla laughed. "That's great," she said. "Headbands to keep their bangs out of their eyes." She fingered the lip of her glass and suddenly her stare was intense again. "I mean, this thing is ours. It's always been ours. Obviously, I won't open a kennel with Bea alone. And Audrey will be with us every step." Layla looked at the night sky, marooned by pollution, giving Tatum a moment to catch her breath and wipe sweat from her upper lip. "And it's been too damn long since we've known each other. I'm just ready to do something with my life. I've never really done anything cool."

The image of Layla standing beside *Project Runway*'s Tim Gunn materialized in Tatum's mind. If Layla hadn't done anything cool with her life, what did that say about Tatum?

"What will I bring to it exactly?" she asked.

"Don't undersell yourself. You're smart, and you've always been super loyal. You'll bring your work ethic, and your heart."

"Okay," said Tatum, robotically. "I'll do it, then."

But Layla shook her head, still smiling. "No, just think about it. That way, when you say yes, I'll know it's for real." She winked. "No pressure, though." Another wink.

Tatum wasn't hungry anymore. Her fork slipped through her fingers and clattered against her plate. She was captivated but also conflicted.

Did Layla like dogs or—better yet—love them? It occurred to Tatum that hadn't been part of her spiel. Was that part of it for any of them? Did it have to be? The Bennel Kennel. God, it was such a bad name.

"And just to sweeten the deal," said Layla in an extra-low voice, as if she were about to confess something. Automatically, Tatum leaned forward. "I can promise you this: I'll take you somewhere amazing as a company retreat."

"Where?" Was she drooling? Tatum touched her lips to make sure she wasn't.

"For now, that'll have to stay secret," said Layla. She raised her eyebrows. "But I'll tell you when the time is right. And you'll love it. You'll really, really love it." Again, she reached for Tatum's hand.

Where? Tatum wanted to ask. *Come on, where?* But she didn't.

Her answer would be yes whether she said so now or in a few days—whether she wanted anything to do with a dog kennel or not—but she'd wait, because Layla had asked her to. Nothing mattered except the boat of Layla's hand and the promise of the amazing places it would take her.

5

BEA HADN'T BEEN able to remember his house number, only his street, but she didn't have to because his door was still painted neon green. There were snowflakes cut from faded construction paper taped to the first-floor windows, which had probably been there since Dennis was little, too, but were less memorable than the color of his door. The garden was tidy and low, all clovers and ground cover except for a flowering rosebush in the dead center.

Holding a sketchbook, Bea stood a few feet away from their yard to ensure she couldn't be seen from inside. The lights were on and every so often she watched the top of someone's head move in, then quickly out, of view. These fleeting moments were enough to keep her there.

She hadn't ventured to his house for any reason other than the nagging curiosity she'd felt since their brief Tinder exchange.

His mother wore her blond hair in a short pixie cut like Dennis's own—Bea saw her around the neighborhood every so often—and she remembered that his father had a similar hairstyle, too. Three spiky blond humans, and one jet-black, smooth-haired, genius little brother, Lane, whose head she definitely hadn't seen cross the bottom pane of a window yet.

The plight of the imperfect sibling was one she knew well, which wasn't to say that Audrey had always been perfect, but at least she'd gone to college. At least she'd seemed perfect for a while. Immediately after graduating, she'd been signed by a modeling agency, booked a campaign for the Gap, and walked in a fashion show for a brand Bea had never heard of—despite the agency's warnings that it usually took a while for new clients to get any work.

At the fashion show, Patricia had filmed Audrey's strut, asking Bea, "Am I getting it? Am I really getting it?" during. And, "Did I get it? Did I really get it? Make sure I got it!" afterward. They were seated directly above a galaxy of professional photographers and videographers, but yes, she had gotten it, though the video was shaky and had picked up her barrage of anxious questions.

The clothes were too skimpy, according to Patricia, and it was too loud, but she'd enjoyed watching her daughter shine—Bea could tell because a proud smile had flickered across her face as she'd lowered her phone before the next wave of anxiety set in.

Never once had Bea inspired a smile like that from her mother. Especially not when Patricia was called by a concerned high school principal stating that Bea was staring at classmates too much and drawing them instead of taking notes. Or when the only college she'd been accepted to was Audrey's safety school. Or when she'd failed every class but math her first semester there and been asked to leave the institution despite her parents paying full tuition. And not when Bea had lovingly cared for her sister throughout the final months of her addiction while the rest of their family only tried to throw money and doctors at the problem.

Bea adjusted the sketchbook she was supporting with her forearm. What had it been like for Dennis? For her, the shame of being a disappointment had dulled over time and, for the most part, she'd grown comfortable in Audrey's shadow. She'd learned how to use the shadows, which had become a point of pride. There was a lot she was proud of, including—even if no one else acknowledged or knew the full extent of it—the way she'd helped her sister. She'd stepped up and taken control. It spoke to an impressive depth of compassion, she'd decided, and the unique ability to innately sense and provide what was needed. Once, in the middle of the night in Arizona, Bea had found herself on a grief-themed Reddit board and someone had used similar language to describe caring for their ailing mother. They'd ended their post by writing: *I have no regrets and love myself more today than ever for having done all I could.* That part she remembered verbatim. With Audrey, Bea had almost no regrets.

When a breeze lifted the hair off the back of her neck, she shivered. She'd have to go soon. It was getting cold and it was usually good to leave these things before she was ready.

Hopping from one foot to the other, she pulled out her phone and rested it atop her drawing. Still no text from Layla about the kennel. At home, she'd wait and sketch and sketch and sketch to pass the time without any real inspiration. She'd masturbate, as she did most nights, out of terrible, loathsome boredom, stare at the ceiling, count the seconds as she held her breath, and eventually go to bed.

Rising onto her tiptoes, Bea took one last long look through Dennis's living room window before lumbering off, hands heavy in her pockets, sketchbook tucked under her arm.

The streets were emptying, which always happened as darkness crept across the Slope, with people either heading home or to neighborhoods with more popular bars. Three years ago, come the weekend, Audrey would've been one of those people, teetering in dangerously high, pointy heels over uneven pavement, then picking her way down the subway steps. Bea used to watch her, too, from safe distances, wearing all black and a downturned baseball cap. She'd admired her sister's graceful gait, the way her hair blew up around her face, and how European she'd seemed passing a cigarette back and forth between her dry knuckles and lips.

Because they sensed things about each other, the way some twins could, Bea had always assumed Audrey knew she was there, though she'd still kept a low profile out of respect; if so, it hadn't seemed to bother her. Watching Audrey was harmless fun, and when she ventured out to purchase drugs from hulking men, it became an important measure of protection. Besides, she was used to being watched. Everywhere Audrey went, strangers' heads turned.

Bea took her time unlocking the front door. Would Rosalie be there? Did she want her to be? Sometimes her quiet company was nice, but Rosalie wasn't exactly an uplifting presence. She wore big, dark clothes and shuffled around the apartment barefoot in pants long enough that only the fleshy rims of her big toes poked out from below the cuffs. Right off the bat, Bea had liked that she was strange: her silver barbed-wire necklace, which pinched the skin around it, her hunched posture, and the mask of hair she wore across her face.

"Rosalie?" Bea called as the heavy front door fell shut. They hadn't seen each other since before the memorial.

The apartment was dark. It wasn't fully dark outside yet, but the window in the living room was small and faced a brick wall, so the apartment was always dark if the light wasn't on. "Rosalie?" Bea tried again. Prior to the olive incident, things between them had been fine. Sterile and polite—so different from her near-boundaryless relationship with Audrey. At their peak, they'd fought bitterly over dirty dishes, dust accumulation, and toilet-bowl stains. With Rosalie, everything was clean and quiet. Ultimately, Bea was glad her mother had told her to find a roommate. It was nice to have life around. Comforting to hear movement: cheap kitchen cabinets smacking shut, old floorboards buckling beneath human weight.

Rosalie had migrated to the city from Long Island. Clichéd as it was, Bea had a special, elitist prejudice against people from there—they seemed small to her—but Rosalie wasn't at all who she pictured when she thought of Long Islanders. She was more what Bea pictured when she thought of white people who moved to Bushwick straight out of college. She didn't wear leggings, baby pink lipstick, or pearl earrings. Rosalie was the personification of a storm cloud, or maybe an exhaust cloud from the back of a noisy truck, or a dark, urine-scented subway tunnel, and Bea was convinced she would fit in well in New York if she tried, but Rosalie seemed to keep mostly to herself.

The toilet flushed. So, she was home.

Bea sat on the couch, fingers laced over her stomach as she waited.

When the bathroom door opened, she said, "Hello," to Rosalie's silhouette, which yelped and dropped the towel it held. Steam curled into the living room; so did the familiar smell of Rosalie's shampoo, which Bea sometimes used.

"Shit," she said, scrambling to cover herself.

Bea reached for the lamp beside the couch. "Sorry," she said, blinking as her eyes adjusted to the sudden light.

All Bea wanted was to talk, to fill the hours with something—anything but nothing.

Rosalie hovered in the doorway, wet hair twisted in a loose bun, arms much thinner outside her sweatshirt than Bea had imagined, and face far more symmetrical. "Uh—" she started.

"Wanna hang?" asked Bea. "Chat or something?"

Rosalie still seemed cautious. "Sure."

"I'm not going to hurt you." Bea laughed. "You look scared."

Rosalie moved to sit in the chair opposite the couch, goose bumped and cautious, hiding as much of herself as possible with her towel. Her smile was unconvincing.

"You can put on clothes first, if you want."

Rosalie flushed. "Oh, cool." She pulled her towel even tighter as she stood.

When she returned, she settled back into the chair and began picking at her black nail polish. Her hair, released from its short-lived bun, dangled in front of her face like dark tentacles, her eyes wide behind it.

"So, what's up?" she said.

What was up? Nothing much that Bea knew how to talk about. She didn't want to mention the kennel, because that would mean talking about Audrey, which would mean talking about the olives, which would mean getting into stuff she didn't want to explain. The point of conversing with Rosalie was easy distraction from her anxiety and boredom, so she said quickly, "I went to a boy's house today," which seemed numb enough and light enough, and was true, though also tantalizingly not.

Rosalie's head cocked, exposing a sliver of pale cheek. "Damn," she said. "I was kind of expecting you to yell at me about the olives in person or something."

Bea shook her head—so they were going to address it after all. "Oh, I'm over that," she said. "Like, obviously don't do it again, but it's in the past."

"Sure."

Silence.

"So, what's up with the olives, anyway?" Rosalie asked, still refusing the less complicated conversation bait Bea had laid. "Like, are they special or something?"

Yes, very. "My sister loved Kalamata olives." It was all Bea would say on the subject.

Rosalie brushed the hair out of her eyes. They were a rich chestnut brown. "Damn. Sorry I fucking did that then." Bea watched as her stubby fingernails dug into her wrist.

"Hey," she said, "really, it's okay," hoping her words would stop Rosalie from hurting herself. When they didn't, she fought the desire to slap her hand away.

"Sorry," said Rosalie again, following Bea's disturbed stare to her wrist, though she did not release it.

Bea was quiet.

"My boyfriend loved Twizzlers," said Rosalie. "I keep a bag of them in my underwear drawer."

An ex-boyfriend? So even Rosalie, depressing as she was, had earned someone's love.

"Travis. He killed himself a few months ago."

Bea's mouth dropped open. Rosalie nodded in agreement with Bea's surprise, as if she still couldn't believe it herself.

"Jumped off the Tappan Zee Bridge." She held up her index finger, which wore a hammered silver ring. "This was his. It's too big, so it slides off really easily, but it's everything to me. He wore it all the time, but left it on the kitchen table for me to keep with a note that day. We'd just moved in together. Picked a fucking dining table up off the street and lugged it upstairs three fucking days before he did it."

Bea didn't know what to say at first. The sporadic sound of Rosalie's sniffles perforated the silence.

"Shit," she said eventually, as Rosalie pressed her fists into her eye sockets. "He must've been in a lot of pain." She couldn't help but think of Audrey.

Rosalie nodded. "He was." She was violently kneading her eyes with her knuckles, reddening the skin around them.

"I'm sorry."

"You've been there, I know. Not that, like, your sister did it to herself, or maybe she did, I don't really know what happened." Her hands fell away from her eyes, but she did not look up. "So, anyway, I'll never touch your olives again. Fucking idiot—I thought you'd forgotten about them or something because they'd been in there for so long. I don't even like olives, I was just hungry. I only ate one."

This was not shaping up to be the easy time suck Bea had in mind. No, it was much, much—*better* wasn't the right word. She tucked her hair behind her ears and adjusted her position on the couch, folding her legs beneath her, resting her elbows on her knees. Softly, in a voice she hadn't used in a long time, she said, "It's really okay about the olives. I'm just sorry about your boyfriend." Her heart was beating fast. It was happening; her focus was shifting, like it had around the campfire in Arizona, and many other times, too. There was nothing to do but surrender, she knew this by now.

Rosalie's whole face was bloodshot, and she was crying big, glistening tears that darkened her sweatshirt where they dropped off her chin. "It's been hard. I'm, like, always fucking crying these days."

Bea nodded. "I get it." She tried to remain composed.

"Fuck," said Rosalie. "Goddammit." She punched her thigh.

Before tonight, Bea had hardly considered what Rosalie might be hiding beneath all her dark layers. Since moving in, she'd existed on the periphery of Bea's life. Now she was the center of it.

Bea asked if she could move closer.

Rosalie nodded, still pawing at her eyes.

She was like a wounded animal, a rescue camel, but Bea knew humans were far more complex when it came to building trust. Handfuls of treats wouldn't suffice. When things first changed with Audrey, it had taken a lot of trial and error. If Bea said anything remotely accusatory, Audrey had become defensive. The first time she'd noticed her sister's groceries growing mold in the fridge, for instance, she'd asked, "When's the last time you ate?" To which Audrey replied: "It's none of your business." Instead, Bea had learned to say, "Can I make you some food?"

Now, rather than, "You really shouldn't punch yourself," she said to Rosalie, "I know how good the pain feels."

Rosalie looked up, blinking through her tears and hair. "You do?"

Bea nodded. "Of course I do. It's the best distraction in the world. Everything else melts away for a moment." She lifted the hem of her shirt to expose a row of purple scars on her side. "See?"

Rosalie sniffed and wiped her nose, then stood and pulled down her pants to expose organized bloody gashes on her upper thighs.

Bea stifled a gasp. She touched Rosalie's arm. "Do you want some ice to put on those?"

Rosalie sat back down and nodded. "Thank you."

When Bea returned from the freezer with a little parcel of paper towel–wrapped ice, Rosalie pulled her pants back down and moaned with gratitude as she pressed the cold to her skin.

"Feels almost as good as the cutting itself, huh?" said Bea, and Rosalie almost cracked a smile.

"Sometimes," Bea continued, "I punch my pillow or yell into it when I'm upset—or overwhelmed or whatever."

Rosalie was nodding. "I just—" she started. Bea waited for Rosalie to catch her breath, allowing only her finger, which tapped rapidly against her kneecap, to betray her calm façade. "I just don't know why I shouldn't cut if I want to. If I don't care, why is it a bad thing to do, you know?"

Bea knew what she was saying. It was her body to destroy if she chose to; the same was true of both Travis and Audrey. But Audrey's body had become Bea's, too, in a way. In the last year of her life, she ate only what Bea prepared, wore only what Bea dressed her in, went to the bathroom when Bea reminded her it was time, the same way a young child's body belonged mostly to her parents.

"I get it," Bea said. "I really do." It hadn't always been easy with Audrey, of course. There was a learning curve. At the start, it was torture to watch her sister slowly killing herself. Bea was angry and devastated by it. Their parents had tried to send her away again and again, to no avail, and when it first got bad, Bea had done what she could, too, screaming at her sister, begging her to go. Nothing worked. It was her choice, after all, her body, until it wasn't.

Over time, Bea's relationship with Audrey's addiction changed. She'd discovered her role within it, which had grown increasingly important as the disease progressed. She lifted water to her sister's lips, brushed and braided her once-thick-and-lustrous hair, washed her body with a soft towel and soap, cooing, "Doesn't that feel lovely? One arm up; now, second arm up; spread your toes." She'd given Audrey everything, and she'd never felt closer to her, or more self-respect, like that woman had written on Reddit. She was something to someone, finally—something good. There was power in that, and so much love.

Rosalie was drying her eyes; her breath was less choppy. "Thank you. I'm sorry again about the—"

"Don't. It's fine. Can I make you some food?"

Hours later, as Bea tucked her into bed, Rosalie said, "Why're you suddenly doing all this for me?"

Bea sat by the lumps of her feet under the covers. "I know how to," she said, "and I don't want you to be in pain. I like you."

Did she?

"Well, that's nice. You're really good at it. You're, like, gentle and stuff."

Bea looked down, trying to seem humble, though she knew she was good. "In high school, I took a weekly babysitting class after school where they taught us all the basics: the Heimlich maneuver, how to use an oven, how to bathe a kid, how to make a simple meal."

"Damn," said Rosalie, sleepily. "Bougie."

"Sure," said Bea, though she'd never thought of it that way. "My mom made me do it. Said she didn't want me to end up in prison for involuntary manslaughter though she also never let me babysit anyone."

Rosalie turned onto her side. "Well, thanks again."

"Before you drift off"—Bea pulled a little orange tube out of her back pocket—"I was wondering if you'd like to take one of these."

She held up the pill cartridge for Rosalie to inspect. "They were prescribed to me a while back and made me pretty numb."

Rosalie squinted at the label, "Quetiapine," she sounded out. "What are they?"

Bea shrugged. She didn't want to say they were antipsychotics, because of what that suggested about herself. "You could just try one for now. They'll be on the counter in case you want another tomorrow."

Rosalie opened her hand. "Why not?"

Bea spilled a pill out into her palm and said, "In the morning, I'll make breakfast for you."

"You really don't have to."

Bea shushed her. "I want to. Take that." She pointed at the pill, then at the glass of water on Rosalie's nightstand. "Sleep well."

In her own room, Bea stood with her back against her door. Her heart was still pounding against her ribs, but she'd kept her cool around Rosalie. Through the dark, she strode quickly to her bed, lifted her pillow, and screamed into it as loud and for as long as she could. And when she finally surfaced, she was loopy and smiling.

6

From: Bernard, Layla (layla@bernard.com) April 11, 11:33 a.m.
To: Sachs, Anita (anita@bernard.com)

Subject line: Kennel Project

Anita,

I want to commit to the dog kennel thing we spoke about. I'm sure you're like, "Here we go again," but this is different. Think of it as a nonprofit. But a nonprofit we make money from. That's how we should pitch it to Jeb, anyway. I mean, not in those words because it sounds stupid, but you know what I mean. Let's talk more about it soon because he has to say yes this time.

I'm going to email the girls with you cc'd so you can handle logistics. And for now, I'm not going to explain that my mom's business manager has to approve it, blah, blah, blah. I really don't want to get into the stipulations of my trust. We'll just be sure to get his approval so it's a nonissue, unlike before. I think we'll be okay—this really is super different than anything else we've pitched!

xx
L

From: Bernard, Layla (layla@bernard.com) April 11, 11:47 a.m.
To: Ellis, Beatrix (beatrix.ellis003@gmail.com); Kaplan, Tatum (t.kaplan@goldenpress.com)
Cc: Sachs, Anita (anita@bernard.com)

Subject line: The Kennel

Hi babes,

This is Layla (remember me? Your long-lost friend? lol). Tatum gave me your email address, Bea. I know we exchanged numbers, but I feel like email is a little more professional. Plus, it's easier for my assistant, Anita, to keep track of things (she's cc'd).

After mulling it over, I've officially decided to join forces. I'm so excited!!! It's obviously also bittersweet (miss Audrey so much, ugh).

Anita will set up some meetings. Lmk if you have any other thoughts. We're gonna make this shit HAPPEN.

Would also love to meet just us to chat and celebrate IRL?? Maybe sometime in the next few days??

Lmk, lmk, lmk!!
Layla

From: Kaplan, Tatum (t.kaplan@goldenpress.com) April 11, 11:52 a.m.
To: Ellis, Beatrix (beatrix.ellis003@gmail.com); Bernard, Layla (layla@bernard.com)
Cc: Sachs, Anita (anita@bernard.com)

Subject line: RE: The Kennel

Hi!!!

I'M IN, TOO, AND I'M EXCITED. Keeping this brief because I'm at the office. I'm around to meet up this week, just say when. Also, hi, Anita!

Lots of love,
Tatum

From: Ellis, Beatrix (beatrix.ellis003@gmail.com) April 11, 12:07 p.m.
To: Kaplan, Tatum (t.kaplan@goldenpress.com); Bernard, Layla (layla@bernard.com)
Cc: Sachs, Anita (anita@bernard.com)

Subject line: RE: The Kennel

Hey.

Cool. When and where should we meet?

From: Sachs, Anita (anita@bernard.com) April 11, 12:28 p.m.
To: Ellis, Beatrix (beatrix.ellis003@gmail.com); Kaplan, Tatum (t.kaplan@goldenpress.com); Bernard, Layla (layla@bernard.com)

Subject line: RE: The Kennel

Hi,

Regarding the meeting Layla requested between the three of you, I'd like to suggest 6:30 tomorrow at the South Slope Dog Run. See attached map.

Warmly,
Anita Sachs

From: Ellis, Beatrix (beatrix.ellis003@gmail.com) April 11, 12:53 p.m.
To: Sachs, Anita (anita@bernard.com)
Cc: Kaplan, Tatum (t.kaplan@goldenpress.com); Bernard, Layla (layla@bernard.com)

Subject line: RE: The Kennel

Will be there.

From: Kaplan, Tatum (t.kaplan@goldenpress.com) April 11, 1:04 p.m.
To: Sachs, Anita (anita@bernard.com)
Cc: Bernard, Layla (layla@bernard.com); Ellis, Beatrix (beatrix.ellis003@gmail.com)

Subject line: RE: The Kennel

Aw, cute idea to meet at a dog run. I'll be there, too!

From: Bernard, Layla (layla@bernard.com) April 11, 12:53 p.m.
To: Kaplan, Tatum (t.kaplan@goldenpress.com); Ellis, Beatrix (beatrix.ellis003@gmail.com)
Cc: Sachs, Anita (anita@bernard.com)

Subject line: Re: The Kennel

RIGHT?! Anita's the best, guys. See y'all tomorrow!

7

TATUM PINCHED HER eyelid, cursing under her breath. A dog with a tongue too long for its mouth had kicked up a cloud of dust as it sped by. A piss-soaked dog run dust particle was now scratching the back of her eyeball.

She staggered to a bench, also dust-coated, and blinked and rubbed until something small appeared on her finger. When she blinked again, tears ran down her cheek.

"I'm not crying," she promised a nearby blurry octopus that was actually a dog walker with a tangle of leashes hooked onto his belt. She smiled at him as her vision cleared, hoping to appear friendly, especially since she was there dogless, which she worried made her creepy, like a childless adult at a playground. "I just have something in my eye."

He nodded and shrugged, looking stoned.

She'd come straight from work, dressed in her typical starched button-down, slacks, and flats outfit, the components of which she owned in a few different colors and wore most weekdays. She rooted around in her work bag for a cloth or a tissue or anything she might use on her shoes, which, usually polished leather, were now frosted by a fine layer of silt. A dog that looked like a stuffed animal, with shocks of oily hair growing from inside perky ears, raced up fast as if it were spring-loaded, planted its weightless front paws on her leg, and barked, making mean eye contact.

"No," she said. "Down." She shook the dog off, then rubbed at the marks left by its paws. "Bad boy," she said bitterly as it trotted off. When she inspected her pants, the marks were already gone.

Dogs were everywhere. Ones with feet the size of her big toe, ones with muscled shoulders and haunches that reminded her of rotisserie chickens, ones with prominent puckered buttholes; one was in a diaper, another in a wheelchair. The sound of their synchronized pants was like a heartbeat, and the dog run itself: one giant, dirty organism.

Where the dogs all looked different, their handlers were like clones. There was a dog-lover uniform, it seemed: faded baseball cap, toned arms, jeans with dirt caked into the knees, autumnal-hued suede sneakers, reusable coffee cup, and white-cast skin from poorly applied mineral sunblock. They chatted amongst themselves, nodding, gesticulating, every so often rising onto their toes in search of their dog or pausing to break up some nearby roughhousing. Tatum stuck out like a sore thumb in her lipstick. She could feel dirt seeping in between her toes, liquified by her sweat into a gritty paste.

At first, when she arrived, she'd worried about seeing someone she knew. But these dog run people were older than her by a few years, much younger than her parents, and that was the sweet spot of Park Slope anonymity. They were in their early thirties, she guessed from the shallow parentheses around their mouths, married according to most ring fingers—gearing up for parenthood, indicated by them choosing to live in Park Slope where children were practically the neighborhood currency, and also by the seriousness with which they took their dog ownership: the silicone collapsible water bowls, bags of treats, the Frisbees, and rubber balls. They were practicing parenthood first on dogs, whereas she was practicing entrepreneurship on dogs. She still couldn't wrap her mind around the whole thing. Couldn't quite get herself to believe it was really happening, but here she was.

A calm one jogged up to her, as casually as if it already knew her, and sat by her leg. At first Tatum shied away from it, but when the dog caught her eye, it seemed to smile. Its mouth opened slightly to expose rows of sharp, yellowed teeth, which normally would've scared her, but there was something distinctly goofy about its expression, and almost familiar. Cautiously, Tatum reached out and the dog sniffed, then licked her fingers. It was large. The kind of dog one might see attached to the wrist of a model in a magazine. Its eyes were misted blue, and its coat was gray. As she ran her hand along its flank, its eyes closed blissfully, and she felt a spark of warmth.

"Sorry about that." A pair of long, thin arms reached for the dog's collar. "Willow, it's time to go home." The owner's voice was soft, and oddly familiar, too, but by the time Tatum looked away from the animal, she'd missed the opportunity to glimpse the woman's face. As she watched them walk away together, Tatum saw that she was tall and slight, with a thick, gleaming mane of dark hair. Her outfit reminded Tatum of something Audrey would've worn—low-rise baggy jeans, a thin gray tank top haphazardly arranged to expose some skin despite the chilly weather. Tatum was glad this gentle animal belonged to someone who seemed kind and gentle, too. She leaned back against the bench, uncrossed her ankles, and was comfortable. The dog's visit held the same drug-like power as an affirming word from a strict professor. On her cheek she felt a "phantom tingle," the term she used for formication, which was the dictionary's name for the strange, tickly sensation that something imaginary was crawling on her.

Tatum had asked her mother about this phenomenon when she was quite young and Vera had replied, matter-of-factly, "That just means you've been brushed by an angel's wing"—surprising, given she was such a staunch atheist. Tatum had never forgotten it, and since Audrey's death, she took comfort in these fleeting occurrences.

Layla was late again. It was part of her rich person shtick and Tatum didn't mind. The sunlight was golden and warmed her face. She tipped her head back and let her eyes close. She was tired. It had been a long day of all the usual things such as delivering palm-scorching coffees to people too busy to thank her, breathing wilted office building air, trying not to seem aimless.

"Hey," said Bea suddenly. She was standing over Tatum, blocking out the setting sun. Her bangs were cut in a blunt line across her forehead, high enough to expose her raised eyebrow. Standing that way, ignited from behind by fiery light, she was pretty. Her eyes were a vibrant honey brown, and the rest of her features, cast mostly in blue shadow, were soft and delicate.

Tatum squinted up at her. "Hey," she croaked, straightening out her shirt as Bea sat down. She was wearing a paint-stained sweatshirt over pink spandex shorts. She looked, as always, like a quirky Greta Gerwig character. Tatum, on the other hand, resembled a bowl of dry oatmeal.

Bea kicked at a lump of dirt that rose in little puffs like winter breath. If Tatum was someone else, she would've asked Bea to stop since the dirt was getting on her, but she was Tatum, so she kept her mouth shut.

They were quiet as Tatum eyed Bea, whose straight hair rode the breeze around her face. Her expression was impenetrable. Tatum wished they could be closer. Wished she could tell her how conflicted she was about the kennel, how much she'd been thinking about Audrey, and about old times, specifically the yellow house days, and wished she could ask what Bea thought about fancy, adult Layla. Despite her strangeness and lack of friends, Bea had always struck Tatum as a mental health wizard. The fact that she was so unbothered could make her seem antagonistic, but it was also awesome. Plus, she'd maintained closeness with her sister despite Audrey's astonishing beauty and social genius, and had even been there, unwaveringly, throughout her addiction; she wished she could talk to Bea about that, too. Apologize for not having been there at all.

But there was something that stood between them. Actually, many things, but one that made Tatum especially uneasy. Years ago, she'd caught Bea following her and Audrey on a night out. Though it may have been irrational—it was just Bea, after all—she'd been rocked by it. It had made her uncomfortable enough that she'd voiced it to

Audrey the next day in a sharp, scolding tone typically reserved for disputes with her parents.

As a result, Audrey had sworn it would never happen again. "I've taken care of it," were her exact words. What if, when talking to Bea, Audrey had made it seem like Tatum overreacted—and, in fact, what if she had overreacted? Or maybe Bea thought Tatum was intentionally driving a wedge between sisters? That was probably Tatum's guilt talking, but also, wasn't there some truth to it? She'd always wanted to be as close to Audrey as possible.

Ever since, Tatum had wondered what Audrey might've said while *taking care of it*, and what Bea might think of her as a result. Someday, she'd address it. If they ended up working together, eventually she'd lay it all out there. Mostly, she'd apologize and explain.

The silence made her nervous even though Bea seemed totally comfortable in it, leaning back, face tilted toward the rosy sky.

Tatum followed suit. They waited that way for Layla.

When she arrived, Tatum was even groggier, but she sat up straight and smiled with every muscle in her face. Her mouth was dry, and her head ached. She blinked as Layla fluttered above them, speaking quickly. Tatum tried to match her energy in nods and "yays" wherever they could be inserted. She was talking about how excited her "team" was to get started, that this meeting was for brainstorming and aligning their "wants." She went on and on, hip cocked, abs bared and taut.

Her hair was slicked back in a ponytail. Even without her usual dark makeup to enhance them, her eyes lit up the dusk. Sweat glinted off her shoulders and brow. Seeing her this way, in leggings and a sports bra, Tatum was startled by how small most of her was. The circumference of her upper arm couldn't have been much larger than Tatum's wrist. Her legs looked easily snappable, which made Tatum think about how, when they'd left La Olivia the other night, Layla's plate was still mostly full. Judging by her sweat and the data displayed on her illuminated Apple Watch, she'd run there at the pace of a five-and-a-half-minute mile, which was concerningly impressive since the neighborhood was, true to its name, sloped, which meant she'd probably been running mostly uphill.

"So," said Layla when she finally sat down on Bea's far side. She began slapping her thighs, which barely jiggled, loosening tight muscles. "What're we all thinking?"

Tatum waited to see if Bea would respond. When it seemed likely that she would not, Tatum said, "I think everything sounds great."

Layla seemed satisfied by this. "Nice." She bounced excitedly and clapped. "Any thoughts about, like, what vibe you want for the space?" Without a martini in Tatum's hand, and with all the exercise endorphins coursing through Layla, she found that she was still attracted to her, but less so, which was good. Layla's smallness, her innocent, eager glow, her hyperactivity, made her seem childlike, despite her assistant, large silicon breasts, and the very millennial-coded Apple Watch strapped to her wrist. Her expression was open; she looked hopeful yet cautious, as if waiting to be shut down. Tatum remembered Nancy had always been strict and quite pretentious, never hesitating to correct Layla's grammar, her pronunciation, always quizzing her on things, like which author wrote what great literary work, which actor starred in what black-and-white film, then turning to the other moms, after Layla answered right, like *ta-da!* as if Layla were a robot she'd built. This was clearly still their dynamic, judging by the insights Layla had shared at La Olivia. Though Tatum had been tipsy, she could remember most of what was said.

On top of all her other feelings, suddenly Tatum felt bad for her, too. She pressed a finger to her lip. "Hm," she said. Of course, she didn't have thoughts about what "vibe" kennel they should open, only hesitations about the whole thing. At this point, she couldn't tell what was happening: if she and Bea were humoring Layla, or if she and Layla were humoring Bea, or if this was the right moment for all three of them to agree to set this idea aside and work on something else. They were children when they'd taken it seriously; now they were adults and knew how the world worked—what constituted a childhood dream versus a realistic, fulfilling career path—but she wouldn't be the first to say so.

"Maybe the vibe should be—" She squinted, unsure how she'd finish the sentence. "Happy? Since dog shelters can be depressing?"

Layla nodded emphatically. "No, totally," she said. "Totally, totally. That's also why I want to call it a kennel: less depressing. Wait, Bea, I haven't told you what I want to name it yet."

"What?" asked Bea.

"The Bennel Kennel." Layla wiggled her fingers excitedly. "A mixture of our last names, and it rhymes."

"Sure," Bea said absently. Tatum was confused by her lack of engagement when only a few days ago she'd been chomping at the bit to tell them her "exquisite idea," as she'd put it. Now she was more focused on the swirly design she was creating in the dirt with her shoe and was even humming to herself while they spoke. Tatum knew to expect inadvertent rudeness from Bea, but she wanted Layla to feel appreciated.

"I can see it working in some, like, really catchy commercial jingle. Nothing like Sarah McLachlan's 'Angel.'" Layla pretended to gag. "To your point about 'happy,' Tatum." She gestured at Tatum's work bag. "Hey, got a notebook in there? Wanna write this stuff down?"

"Oh, of course." Tatum rooted around for a moment, locating her materials.

When she was ready, Layla said, "Okay, great. So, what else?"

No one spoke.

"I mean, I guess the point here," said Layla as she smoothed the top of her already perfectly smooth hair, "is that we're gonna take this thing pretty fucking big. And I want to make sure we're aligned about that. Like, I want us to be the ASPCA for people who don't cry themselves to sleep every night."

She looked from Tatum to Bea, who was looking at the ground, then back at Tatum and raised her eyebrows, which reminded Tatum to begin taking notes. *TAKE THIS BIG,* she wrote in all caps. *ASPCA FOR PEOPLE WHO DON'T CRY.*

"To be extremely clear," Layla continued, "I'm not fucking around." She twirled the end of her ponytail, running it between her fingers. "I want to help dogs and stuff, and I want us to be important. Like, *the* dog kennel. Like, *the* one."

Tatum wrote, *THE dog kennel.*

Now she actually liked what she was hearing. Important was all she'd ever wanted to be, after all. She said, honestly, "That sounds pretty amazing."

When she caught Layla's eye, they both smiled.

"Can you believe we're really doing this?" Layla tapped Bea's knee to get her attention. "Hey, you—can you believe this?"

There was no emotion behind Bea's eyes when she looked up. "Nope," she said. "Can't."

"I really can't, either," said Tatum quickly. "Also, how did we manage to go so long without running into each other in Park Slope, where I'm always bumping into people I *don't* want to see?" Neil had trapped her in a conversation, yet again, on her way to the dog run that evening. She'd dissociated her way through the exchange, but it had dragged on as usual.

When Bea suddenly looked up from the dirt, it was a rare moment when Tatum could read her perfectly: she knew she was someone in the neighborhood Tatum hoped to avoid. And, though Tatum had been referring to Neil, Bea was right. Tatum felt bad, knowing it was a comment they'd each think about from time to time when they were together, an unfortunate echo that would never be addressed because it was too vague—would be too presumptuous—to apologize for, and if Tatum started apologizing to Bea, she wasn't sure she'd ever stop.

Oblivious to what had silently passed between Bea and Tatum, Layla said, "Yeah, well, my life is mostly outside of Park Slope. I jog in the park and stuff, but aside from that, I live between my apartment and Manhattan. This guy, Stanley, drives me everywhere. It's been this way since I left boarding school—all throughout college." Tatum had learned Layla was an NYU alum through Wikipedia. "I can't bring myself to move anywhere else, though I don't really feel like I even live here. Not like I used to, anyway."

"Is your mom still here, too?" Tatum asked, trying to ignore the pit in her stomach over Bea. This was a question she hadn't asked the other night.

Layla shook her head. "She lives in Brooklyn Heights now, on Henry Street. It's such a crazy place. You have to come over sometime." She smiled and raised an eyebrow. "It's, like, really nice."

Tatum nodded. She could only imagine. "I'd love to."

Layla stretched her arms overhead, craned her neck to the right, then the left. "She's still a Coop member, though. Says it's good for her to work with her hands, and apparently the produce and cheese just can't be beat."

Tatum wondered if her mother and Nancy had ever crossed paths there, over the years. No. Vera would've mentioned it if they had. But if not, how was that possible? It wasn't entirely surprising Nancy was a member, as many wealthy celebrities were, yet Tatum hadn't considered it before.

"So, all our moms are still at the Coop," said Bea. She'd stopped humming; though she wasn't looking at them, apparently she was listening.

"I guess so."

"Interesting."

The streetlights switched on, bathing everything in sudden acid yellow. Layla gasped, then laughed. "Shit, that scared me," she said, glancing at her watch. It was seven-thirty. People were gathering their dogs now, shouting for them, hooking leashes onto their collars—a chorus of metallic *clicks*—and dragging them toward the exit.

"We should probably go," said Layla as they watched a single-file line form by the narrow gate. "That was enough for now. I think we're on the same page, which is the most important thing."

Once they made it out of the dog run, Layla hip checked Tatum. "I'm excited," she said, biting her lip the same way she had at dinner.

When they glanced over at Bea, it seemed like she was mouthing the words to a song—maybe the same one she'd been humming earlier. Or maybe she was speaking to herself, or an imaginary friend; it was impossible to know.

"Oh, yeah, same," Bea said when she realized they were waiting to hear from her.

"Okay, epic," said Layla. "Glad we're all with it."

"Just let us know what you need," Tatum said, and she meant it.

"'Kay." Layla placed a strip of gum on her tongue. "Anita will set up meetings this week, as she said over email. I'll keep you posted, and you should come if you can, but Anita will take notes if you can't."

She was jogging in place now, beachball breasts bouncing up to her chin, ponytail bouncing, too, lips smacking. Her hair was very thick and, suddenly it dawned on Tatum, much longer than it had been the last time they'd seen each other. Extensions—it had to be. God, Layla's world was so different from hers now.

"Does email work for kennel stuff?" Layla asked. Tatum nodded and so did Bea. "Great," she continued. "That way I can cc Anita on things. She's my eyes and ears. I'm, like, helpless without her." She was still jogging, her breath sharpening. "Okay, it's getting chilly and I'm gonna run home, so I've gotta get going. See you two very soon." She winked at Tatum, spat her barely chewed gum on the pavement, and said, "It's compostable," before bounding toward what Tatum assumed was the second-most beautiful home in the city, after Nancy's.

When she realized that she and Bea were still standing together, watching Layla, she waved quickly and started toward home herself, taking a roundabout route that led her away from Bea's apartment and forced her to walk along the Prospect Expressway for a few blocks. She was too tired to make polite, one-sided conversation with Bea even if the alternative meant inhaling exhaust fumes. She just wanted to be in bed, within the fleecy folds of an oversized sweatshirt, under the covers, scrolling on her phone until her brain was mush.

A few minutes later, though, she found that her route had changed; all the feelings from their meeting were steering her away from home.

Scenes from her youth played like old stock footage, flashing images: the dock, the yellow house glowing atop the rocky bluff, Audrey's smile, her long legs, the pink birthmark on her inner knee, the room Tatum and Layla had shared, the disgusting buckwheat pancakes Patricia used to make; everything was strobed and sickening. Her breath chapped her throat. The air was cold, and she was sweating, which only made her colder. Where was she going? Would she ever stop walking? What was happening to her? It felt as though she was being pushed from behind. Her legs could hardly keep up.

Sometimes it was a relief to be alone in Park Slope at night. The typical anxiety of *Who am I about to run into?* wasn't so prevalent then. Sometimes it was eerie. At any time of night or day it could be nostalgic and sad; tonight, especially having just seen Bea, it was both eerie and nostalgic. Apart from the sound of her own breath and the slaps of her shoes, the quiet reminded Tatum of death.

Audrey had walked along this very street—the observation was both totally obvious and totally surreal and occurred to her a few times a week at random intervals. Already, after only two years, Audrey was more myth than memory. For Tatum, Park Slope was tainted by her absence in subtle, inconsistent ways. What used to evoke comfort, in the right mood Tatum now found depressing: Mando's deli, which stayed empty for hours through the night; children bouncing around their cozy, illuminated first-floor bedrooms; bicycle skeletons stripped of their wheels, chained to parking meters; hungry rats rummaging through garbage bags. Audrey would never be here again. Life's in-between moments held a different significance now, because Audrey was missing them. She'd left and Park Slope had moved on without her, and it would do the same when Tatum left someday.

As she walked, she could see Audrey, sturdy with baby-pudge, toddling over uneven bluestone, catching colorful leaves in her dimpled fists as they drifted to earth. When she passed the bus stop, she could see a taller, leaner version of her old friend, thumbs hooked onto loose backpack straps on her way to school, cheeks crisped by winter. And then there she was, at Joe's Pizza, which was closed now, its windows haunted black, but which was crowded with teens in the daylight. She could see Audrey leaning against the front window, her spaghetti strap dangling off her shoulder, requesting "the usual," then dripping hot cheese and orange oil into her mouth, down her chin—the very best pizza commercial Joe's could ask for: "Joe's pizza can make you look like this!" That life-filled person, who'd been very young, then only slightly less young, would die a month after her twenty-fifth birthday. She wouldn't get married, as they used to talk about, or have children of her own, or grow old with Tatum. It still seemed impossible when she thought about it. And yet, Tatum wondered, had the signs always been there, even when they were young? Was Audrey just a figment of her imagination? Had she ever existed?

Finally, her pace began to slow, and there it was: the old Ellis house. It looked like every other house on the block, in the neighborhood, yet the sight of it turned her stomach. The stoop railing was metal, and the front yard was paved with cobblestones that glittered in the night. This, plus the plants in the yard, the placement of the number, painted onto the stoop rather than next to the door, were what made their house individual to Tatum. For all the sameness in Park Slope, there were always subtle differences that Tatum knew how to spot.

The curtains were drawn on the parlor floor, though the fabric glowed, telling her the new family was home. Tatum was grateful she couldn't see inside because this way she could pretend the living room was the same as always: the low-hanging Noguchi lantern suspended in the center; a life-size painting of two women reaching for each other over the mantel, which Patricia used to call her "feminist Creation of Adam"; the cluster of thick, battery-operated candles arranged in the fireplace; and Audrey, curled into the velvet armchair, awash in the peachy light from Patricia's fancy Edison bulbs.

Now Tatum was crying. She'd cried more in the past week than she had in the two years before it. Sometimes Ed called her "unflappable," typically after watching movies that left him dripping tears into her hair and startling her by blowing his nose as she dozed off. She couldn't tell if he was generally disappointed that she wasn't more sentimental, the way women were supposed to be, or if she was disappointed that he wasn't tougher, the way men were supposed to be, or if the specifics of their disappointment even mattered anymore.

Tatum touched the iron fence that bordered the front yard and wondered if somehow it remembered her. Brownstones had always seemed sort of alive. A square inch of black paint flaked off in her hand, revealing a copper color, like blood beneath skin. She'd seen this color before on other peeling Park Slope fences. Park Slope, with its historic landmark designation, was so specific; for instance, the very fact that there were people trained in the art of brownstone restoration, who handled all the residential exterior construction in the neighborhood, including fence painting, who couldn't transfer their skill set to anywhere outside the city, said it all.

Each very special Park Slope fence was painted copper first, for whatever reason, then glossy black. Park Slope's very special trees belonged inside dirt wells of a very specific size, which were to be decorated with flowers in the spring and lined with evergreen sprigs after Christmas. Teenagers belonged at Joe's Pizza after school but not at Pizza Plus or Ottava, where adults went for casual date nights. Readers belonged at the Community Bookstore, not at Barnes & Noble, and coffee drinkers at Connecticut Muffin, never Starbucks. There were the right places to summer, such as Fire Island, the Hudson Valley, or the Hamptons, and the wrong places, such as Park Slope itself. Anyone who stepped outside these parameters, who shopped at the Goodwill on Atlantic Avenue rather than in SoHo, who couldn't afford Ugg boots like their friends, or lived in a ground-floor apartment rather than a three-story home, who were carted off to rehab, whose complexion wasn't white as snow, was either wrong or radical. Tatum, whose family had money relative to most of Earth's population but not a lot for here, was wrong, while Audrey, beautiful, mysterious, and troubled, was radical.

Standing there, she felt a phantom tingle, same as earlier, and her breath caught.

She whispered into the night, "Is it you?"

"Chh."

She gasped. Behind her, the street was as still as a painting. Amber pooled beneath streetlights like urine. She could've sworn the sound was Audrey's unique sneeze, short and swift, though this was obviously impossible. Searching the shadows, she was tense until she'd convinced herself that missing her so much hadn't brought her back. Still, she felt a chill. The silence was too perfect, as if she was the only human alive.

Tatum turned back toward the fence and tore off another flake of paint. She let it go and watched it soar over invisible hills of air, lower and lower until it landed on the pavement, daring herself to linger, to be brave, instead of fleeing like her instincts urged her to.

8

FROM HER CROUCHED position behind the Stieglitzes' garbage can, Bea could hear Tatum's jagged breath, like the ignition of an old car. Why was she there, at the brownstone?

Bea had waited a few seconds after they said goodbye outside the park, then began her pursuit. A long time had passed since she'd done this—followed anyone, but especially Tatum. It came back easily, like muscle memory.

The rats were out, scurrying as fast as their toothpick toes could carry them, their movements as instinctual and witchy as Bea's own. It hadn't occurred to her where Tatum was heading until they'd turned down her old block, and even then, she hadn't known for sure until Tatum stopped short in front of the house, standing on the slab of cement into which Bea and Audrey had once carved their initials.

Tatum was stroking the craggy fence. The streetlamps cast long shadows across the brownstone's façade. In the daylight, it was different: cheerful. This block had been the winner, two years in a row, of the "Greenest Block in Brooklyn" competition—a testament to how lush and lovely it was in summer—which her parents had advertised on the Corcoran listing and which, according to their real estate agent, had increased its value by at least fifty "gees."

Bea would always think of this house as hers. She'd been back a few times since it sold, watched a long moving truck cinch itself into the tight space out front, kept permanently open by a fire hydrant, which her own family had used every summer to pack and unpack the car on their way to and from the yellow house, blinkers ticking like a clock. She'd watched a new little girl drag her teddy bear up the steps by its barely attached arm, then returned another time to watch the same little girl playing on the stoop with her friends, a gaggle of parents nearby pinching goblets large enough to hold their children's brains, wet with a puddle of red wine. These children played with their Barbies the same way Bea and Audrey had, sliding them down the metal stoop railing in what they'd always called "The Barbie Amusement Park Game."

Watching those girls play with her house had filled Bea with the same rage she now felt watching Tatum cry over her dead sister. Bea remembered peering out the upstairs window when Audrey left to meet her, watching them embrace in the front yard as if they hadn't seen each other in years when it had only been a day. They were the first people she'd ever followed. The ritual had sprung from a desire to be included, and though she'd apologized once—the only time they'd caught her—she hadn't meant it.

When they were still quite young, Audrey had asked if she felt bad when they did things without her.

"No," Bea responded convincingly, "I don't care." When they moved in together years later, Audrey had asked her the same question using adult, more sensitive words: "Since we're living together again, I want to make sure you're still feeling okay about my friendship with Tatum. Please tell me if you're not and I can talk to her."

"I don't care," Bea repeated. By then, it was almost true.

But at that very moment, as she watched Tatum's shoulders shake from across the dark street, she'd never cared more. Palms sweating, Bea gulped down big mouthfuls of air, scrambling to resist the overwhelming impulse to pick up the rock that lay in the tree well beside her and hurl it across the street as hard as she could. She imagined Tatum's shriek if she managed to hit her old living room window, and the clatter of broken glass. The people inside the house would think it was Tatum, perhaps, who'd thrown it. Bea was placated by the image of Tatum's fear rising into the night like steam as she desperately claimed her innocence over screaming sirens. She took one last deep breath to make sure the impulse had passed—that picturing it was enough—but air scratched her throat. She was able to stifle her cough, but it boiled in her nose.

"Chh."

Tatum whipped around. Bea was very still, breathing silently through parted lips, letting liquid mucus from her sneeze run into her mouth. She couldn't see Tatum anymore; her head was tucked to fit entirely behind the three-foot garbage can. She waited until her knees were about to give way and it felt like the vertebrae in her neck had rusted over, then lifted her head slowly, painfully, to find herself alone. Tatum was gone. She breathed out a sigh and stood on stiff legs.

At first, she turned to go, then turned back and crossed the street. Her fingers found the gate latch, as habitually as ever, and pressed it open. The hinge made the old familiar *clink*. Chalk drawings covered the front yard pavement: rainbows, tic-tac-toe boards, what was probably a poorly drawn unicorn.

Bea stepped on the drawings, leaving faint footprints behind, as she ran her hands through the shrubs her mother had planted years ago. Cold twigs nipped her palms.

She looked around for something to mark her territory beyond the footprints, which could easily be missed, to remind the house and its new family they weren't the first and would never be the only. Something tame, she told herself, and less illicit than breaking a window.

She was still standing there, chewing on her lip, searching for inspiration, as if she had all the time in the world, when the lock on the door at the top of the stoop clicked.

"Shit," she whispered, and leapt behind one of her mother's bushes, crushing a ring of pansies in the process. Seconds later, through brambles, she watched a tall man thump down the steps with a trash bag hooked over his shoulder. She held her breath as he lugged it out to the street.

On his way back into the yard, the man paused where she'd stood only seconds earlier—and Tatum had before her—yawned, stretched, farted loudly, then latched the gate behind him and started back up the steps at an achy pace. Bea allowed herself to breathe only after she'd heard the lock again.

A few minutes later, she was on her way home, dirt caked under her fingernails. While crouched in the garden waiting for the man to disappear, she'd eyed the remaining uncrushed pansies and been taunted by their happy, near-human faces. In a sort of frenzy, when he was gone, she'd pulled them out of the earth and left them in a heap at the bottom of the stoop where she used to leave her leggy dolls between games with Audrey.

There's something wrong with you.

Audrey had often said this—usually playfully though not always. When Bea knew exactly what she would say, she could hear her sister's voice in her mind, clear as if they were next to each other.

Once the house was out of sight, she stopped, pulled out her phone, and clicked past a missed call from her mother.

With muddy fingers, she hit Tinder, and typed: What're you up to tonight? Wanna do something? She slipped the phone back into her pocket and broke into a run. It felt so good to release, to ignore traffic lights and the resulting car horns that cut through the quiet night. There weren't many drivers out, but she managed to anger everyone she encountered. She even flipped off a man whose car screeched to a stop just before hitting her. He pounded his steering wheel with the heel of his palm, then screamed, "Moron," out his window. He had no idea who he was dealing with.

When she reached their front door—hers and Rosalie's now, but forever hers and Audrey's—she stood with her nose inches from it, panting, certain she looked like she'd been zapped by lightning. Rosalie couldn't see her like this. She reached into her pocket and fished out her phone first, then her keys, as she read Dennis's response.

Oh hey. Can't tonight but another
time.

It was good that he couldn't. He shouldn't see her like this, either, though it would've felt so good to tear off his clothes, to let herself be wild with him in that way.

She'd also received a few texts from Layla and Tatum proclaiming their excitement about the kennel, which made her wish she could flip them off, too. She keeled over, scraping her forehead against the door, yelping from pain as she sank to the ground. "Relax," she said through gritted teeth. Blood trickled into her mouth from her forehead. "Relax, Beatrix. You can't go inside until you relax." Sometimes she was flooded with venom and could do nothing but wait for the rush to pass—why her mother had forced medication upon her at a young age and why she'd been banished to the white-walled psychiatric children's hospital in the first place. When she was thirteen, she'd beheaded Clyde, the family gerbil, in a rage fit like this one. She hadn't intended to. She'd loved Clyde very much, and afterward felt terrible about what she'd done; it had been her job to hunt down his severed head, the size of a cotton ball, which she'd thrown in the heat of anger. And when she found it, behind the armchair in the living room, she'd cried.

When she raged, she flew out of control, yet control and attention were also what she blindly sought—this was one of the helpful things she'd learned from therapy. In the moments before her mother found her, she'd squeezed and squeezed Clyde's little body and relished the reckless abandon, the power she wielded over life and death. The impact of her thirteen-year-old, too-often-ignored self. Patricia had sworn the family to secrecy over the incident. "People will think terrible things about her," she'd said. "We'll never speak of it again." The only people they told were the doctors at the psychiatric hospital, where Bea was sent the following week. Her mother had even lied to her school; she'd told them Bea needed time to rest after an emergency appendectomy.

Most often, it was manifestations of injustice that set Bea off, the likes of which she'd faced all her life for not being Audrey. Even back at the yellow house when she was so small, her mother had scolded her through many ragefits while the others looked on: "Beatrix, stop growling at me, for god's sake. Beatrix, use your words, do not scratch or hit me. Your words, Beatrix." The heat from their normal-person stares—Audrey's, Tatum's, and Layla's—had only made it worse. At the hospital, she'd been prescribed meds that had evened her out for a while, too much, until she'd felt almost nothing. Under Patricia's watchful eye, she'd taken them every day, but she was her own boss now.

How dare strangers live in her brownstone? How dare they be happy there?

Relax. She was an adult. She could manage her emotions. She punched up against her chin, biting her tongue in the process, and blood, salty as brine, filled her mouth from two wounds. It helped distract her—in that moment, she felt close to Rosalie

Buzz, buzz. There was her phone again. The repetitive vibration helped, too. *Focus on the buzz*, she thought. *Just focus on the buzz*. By the time it stopped, she was breathing more normally.

When she was strong enough, she stood and let herself inside. In the bathroom upstairs, her fingers shook as she dabbed the cut on her forehead with damp toilet paper, then the one on her tongue with a Q-tip.

Rosalie was in her room, door shut, which was for the best. Around her, Bea hoped to seem even keeled. Trustworthy. Dependable. Before heading to her room, she made a quesadilla and left it sizzling on the counter beside the pill container. When she was safely away, she texted Rosalie: Left some food out for you <3

Rosalie responded with two crying emojis and: Thank you so much. I haven't eaten dinner.

Bea smiled.

She stripped off all her clothes and lay on the floor making stinging angels against the rug, letting it burn her, proud she hadn't done anything worse than rip apart a flower bed and injure herself during the frenzy.

Buzz, buzz.

Patricia would keep calling until she answered.

Buzz, buzz. Bea's phone was still tucked into her balled-up pants. She rooted around for it, enjoying the tightness of her raw skin.

"Beatrix?" Her mother's voice was suddenly loud in her ear. She winced and moved the phone a few inches away.

"Beatrix?" she said again. "Are you there?"

Bea was quiet.

"Beatrix?" said Patricia, her voice even more elevated.

"Hi," Bea finally grumbled. "What's up?"

Whoosh: the powerful sound of Patricia's sigh.

"Beatrix, I was starting to think you'd been kidnapped because all I could hear was loud breathing, so I was about to use the landline to call nine-one-one. Speak to me next time when you answer the phone if you don't want me to call the police."

Her parents were the last people on earth with a landline, Bea was certain. They'd even gotten a new one when they moved.

"Sorry," she said. "What's up?"

"I just called to say good night." Her mother sounded tired as usual.

"Okay," said Bea. "Good night."

"How was your day?"

Sometimes, every now and then, her mother called to say good night. On the nights when she did, she pretended she did so every night, that Bea should've expected it.

"Fine," said Bea.

"You're taking your meds, yes?"

"Yes," Bea lied, thinking of Rosalie swallowing them with a gulp of water.

"Good," said Patricia.

"I saw Layla and Tatum today."

She shouldn't have said it, wanted to keep their conversation short but also wanted to talk to someone.

Her mother cooed into the phone, suddenly a different person. "Oh, you did? Well, isn't that something."

Bea said, "I guess."

"What were the three of you up to?"

"We went to a dog run."

"Oh," said her mother. "A dog run?"

"Yes."

"Dog runs are dangerous, Beatrix. Not all dogs are friendly. You must be careful. It's not safe. Cynthia's daughter's girlfriend had her throat ripped out by a pitbull and died at a dog run. I'm not kidding."

Bea sighed and said, "I'm careful."

Patricia scoffed. "That's not good enough. Promise me you won't go back there."

"Sure."

"Beazie!" her mother half shrieked, the nickname Bea only heard when her mother was in crisis. "Please. You're giving me a migraine. Never go back there."

Bea's resentment flared. Suddenly, she was in the mood to mess with her.

"We're actually starting a dog kennel."

"What?" her mother howled. Bea wondered if her father was there. If they were in bed together, he'd probably just clamped a pillow over his ear. "Haha, very funny. Like the old days. I get it."

"I'm not kidding," said Bea. "Layla's setting up meetings with her mom's team this week. We're going to rescue stray dogs. I'm really excited about it." In truth, Bea wasn't anymore. But saying she was would be like twisting the knife in her mother's back.

Instead of being hit with the usual hailstorm of horror stories, threats, and bribes, all she heard were gasps. Patricia did not carry her own dog-related trauma. No, she was simply disturbed in general. Anything under the sun could spark the fear of death in her—nail salons, which she considered "cesspools," biking through the park, sunbathing, soft-serve from ice-cream trucks.

"Mom?" said Bea as her mother's sounds grew more worrying.

"You're gonna leave me now, too? You're gonna—" As Patricia was saying this, her voice drifted away, and Bea was no longer worried. She rolled her eyes.

Sure, Patricia was a mother who'd lost a daughter, but before that, she was a mother who'd abandoned Bea countless times throughout her life, sending her away, forcing mood-altering medication down her throat instead of gently asking what was wrong. And she was a mother who'd thought she'd known what was best for Audrey at the end of her life but hadn't. She'd had no authority then, because she wasn't there every day, preparing warm food, dressing her in soft clothes, laying her down on the couch. Throwing money and doctors at the problem wasn't always the best way, but it was certainly the easiest.

There was a rustling before Bea's father's muffled voice asked, "Where are your pills, Pat? Did you forget to take them?" Into the phone, he said, "Hey, Bea. Your mom's tired. She says good night and that she loves you."

Bea flipped onto her back.

"Good night," she said, and hung up.

Now it was Patricia's turn to calm down. Maybe Patricia's mother, who Bea had never met, should've sent her daughter off to a psych ward for her "episodes" when she was young, what Patricia politely called her own mental breaks when apologizing for them. Her apologies also always included the caveat that, while her reaction was "admittedly a little over the top," her fears were "undeniably rational." On the other hand, she liked to call Bea's mental breaks "psychotic rampages" or "dangerous tantrums." Bea was always "flying off the handle."

After a while, Bea rose from the floor, naked, forehead throbbing, and tiptoed to the kitchen, tapping her fingers along the walls. When she opened the refrigerator door, the cold was shocking against her bare skin. She reached all the way to the back and pulled out the olive jar, holding down the Post-it with her name on it.

"Hello," she said to the jar. "Our mother's a freak."

With it in hand, she pressed open the door to Audrey's room, where Rosalie lay in bed with the lights off. The plate Bea had used for the quesadilla was on the dresser. For a moment, Bea held her breath to hear Rosalie's. Satisfied that Rosalie was peacefully asleep, she returned to her own room and arranged the jar on her pillow so that, she imagined, they were lying eye to eye.

"I had a big night," she said, clamping the blanket in her armpit. "I went back home, tore up the yard. You wouldn't have liked it."

She imagined the jar spontaneously combusting to symbolize Audrey's anger, glass shooting into her eye. But it didn't. Nothing happened.

"Now Layla and Tatum are super into the dog kennel thing." Bea sighed. "It's not that I'm not anymore, it's just that, I don't know." But she did know, she just didn't know how to say it. So, instead, she whispered, "Good night. Love you."

Eventually, she slept.

9

TATUM WAS FINALLY in bed after another long workday and then a long, unexpected fight with Ed.

It was over food. Specifically, the waterlogged particles he always left in the sink drain instead of cleaning them out. She hadn't meant for it to escalate; at first, she had thought she was voicing something small, yet it had grown, billowing up like thick smoke until they were both yelling, and he was saying, "I've gotta get out of here," and the front door was slamming shut. Then there was silence except for the gurgle of the refrigerator making ice.

Tension between them usually was defused quietly over time—or never. In the moment, it had been exhilarating to unleash some of the emotion she usually kept to herself, but now she felt guilty, ashamed, and unsatisfied, as always. There was no relief no matter what she did or didn't do.

Tatum sneered at the lopsided pile of printed children's books manuscripts that sat on the nightstand for her to review by morning. Books about sharing, caring, and friendship. What did those authors know? Behind their pens, colored pencils, keyboards, they were just like everyone else. Flawed. Depressed. She was certain they'd done bad things. Where were the children's books about that? About betrayal? About falling out of love? About hurled insults and disappointment and the big lie of childhood? It was irresponsible to teach children to be good people, Tatum thought. Or that if they were good, they would be rewarded. The important lesson was that if you did bad things, had bad thoughts, you were normal. The lesson should be that adult life required leveraging others, brutal honesty, and tears—this was what they had to look forward to.

Obviously, their fight wasn't really about food or cleaning or about him not listening to her or even about respect. At its core, it was about something even more vital to a healthy relationship than respect.

She still hadn't told him about the kennel, or about Layla, and wasn't planning on it. Keeping this separate felt right for now—texting Layla from positions where her body shielded her phone, slipping it into her pocket when he reached for her hand, sneaking out of their bedroom on work mornings knowing the day would hold something extra, beyond what he knew.

Layla's friendship was a golden ticket, both in the literal sense—she still thought of the promise Layla had made at their first dinner, to take her somewhere amazing—but also a ticket to a different life. It was hers to protect or lose, and hers to decide not to share.

The stress of trying to match Layla's confidence and ease, of trying desperately to be liked by her, contributed to Tatum's shortened fuse with Ed, she was certain. It threw off the careful balance that had allowed her to exist in apathy for so long. Her capacity for pretend games was lower now than when she was young. Somehow, she found it self-centered he hadn't asked about the kennel, as if it was his fault he hadn't. Lately, it had become nearly impossible to differentiate between rational and irrational irritants, so she stewed, and had even begun snapping at him when she could get away with it—when he was distracted enough to not really hear her by video games or by staring at the wall above his computer screen, nibbling his lower lip as he "worked."

This wouldn't last forever. The balance would be restored when Tatum felt more comfortable with Layla. Their relationship ran deep. Layla had seen her cry, sleep, retch, pimpled and in braces, not to mention her bald, prepubescent vagina, and had loved her before she'd mastered the art of people-pleasing. And Layla wasn't always so perfectly maintained, either; she used to be scraggly and wild. Once things neutralized there, Tatum's relationship with Ed would return to normal, too.

She checked her phone to see if he'd texted since storming out—nope—so she clicked on her latest messages with Layla. The last one she'd sent was, lol I hate stink bugs, in response to Layla finding one in her Jacuzzi. The last message she'd sent Ed was, u 2, in response to him sending I miss you earlier that day. Both of her responses were stupid. The one she'd sent Ed was also evil. He was a good guy, good at expressing his feelings and being devoted. He deserved to be told that he was missed, too, in real, spelled-out words. Sure, his breath whistled through his nostrils and the corners of his mouth semi-permanently glowed red from chip powder, but he was nice and well-intentioned and always went straight to the bathroom to clean his face when asked, no offense taken. Now that he was gone and hadn't texted her, she felt vulnerable. Now she actually did miss him more than just "u 2."

Hi, she typed. Where'd u go?

She wasn't sure she owed him an apology on principle—he should be an adult and clean out the drain—but wanted to give him one anyway so he'd come back and because she was used to apologizing for things that weren't her fault. Without him in it, the apartment suddenly felt bigger than usual. Or maybe she was smaller without him to fluff her up. She wanted to be hugged and babied the way Ed did when she was sad, even though, in the moment, she often found it annoying and unsexy when he spoke in falsetto.

She picked up her phone again.

On a walk, he'd replied. Sorry I am the way I am.

Come home, she typed. I'm sorry, too. And she was, for making him feel that way.

Love you, he sent. Be there soon.

Love you. The tendons in her neck went rigid. The longing for him drained from the tips of her fingers as they typed the words love you too.

The tape was rewound, and she was back where she'd been when she first arrived home from work that evening: overwhelmed and tense and lying. She navigated away from her conversation with Ed and pressed the green "phone" icon. Tatum had never saved a contact for Vera in her phone, rather she preferred to dial the number manually. Something about the antiquity of it, the familiar way her finger moved across the numbers and their little beeps. Despite her phone's high-definition touch screen, it brought her back to the past.

"Vera?" she said when she heard a noise on the other end of the line.

"Sorry, one second." It sounded like Vera was standing inside a washing machine.

Tatum waited.

"Sweetie?" Vera's voice was clearer now, the wind sound was greatly subdued.

"Hi, hi," said Tatum. She extracted herself from her pillow cocoon, so she was sitting upright, pressed the speakerphone button, and set her mother's voice down on the comforter. "What's up with you this evening?"

Another loud sound.

"Oh," said Vera. "Making some pea soup."

Tatum smiled. Her mother loved soup. "Everything's better liquified," she always said, which, as Tatum had pointed out many times, wasn't true at all. The washing machine sound was coming from an immersion blender; she should've assumed.

"Cool," said Tatum. "Fought with Ed tonight."

She hadn't told her mother about the kennel yet, either. Her reasons for that included something about the sentimentality of it—how difficult they still found it to talk about Audrey together—but mostly it was that Vera would see right through her. She'd know instantly why Tatum was involved and would give good advice about not being blinded by money and power—advice Tatum wouldn't take. Vera didn't understand why Tatum wanted more than she'd had growing up, because Vera had never wanted more than that. And, without meaning to, she made Tatum feel ashamed at times. It was for similar reasons that

Tatum chose not to share her many Ed-related doubts. Her mother knew her better than anyone, but clearly that wasn't saying much.

Vera sighed. "No fun," she said. "Wanna meet for a walk?"

Ed would be home soon, expecting her to run, then jump, into his arms, for them to fall onto the couch, knotted together, crying into each other's hair and kissing. This had never happened before, but he was a brain-fogged romantic, except when he was playing video games.

Though Ed would be confused and disappointed by her absence, yes, Tatum did want to meet her mother.

"Sure. The park in ten?"

Mom just asked me to go for a walk, she typed. Is it okay if I meet her for a bit?

She was already out of the house, a block away from their meeting spot, by the time she checked his reply: I guess. Tell her hi.

Vera was wearing red leggings and her favorite threadbare sweater. She always dressed in outfits made up of bright, clashing colors, oversized, comfortable silhouettes, and usually accessorized with the same slouchy leather bag. She looked at least a decade younger than her age, which was sixty-two. Her skin was smooth and springy, and her long hair was always tucked into the perfect tousled shape. She was staring down at her phone through thick bifocal lenses, the flesh beneath her chin bunching adorably.

"Vera," called Tatum.

Slowly, reluctantly, she looked up from what she was typing.

"Just pressing send," she said.

Vera was a teacher at Little Wings, a private preschool, which meant that her after-work hours were filled with anxious email exchanges with young Park Slope parents.

Her finger hovered over the send button as she mouthed the words she'd written and Tatum waited patiently. Suddenly, she exclaimed, "Done," and dropped her phone into her bag. "For now, anyway," she added with a shrug and opened her arms to her daughter. "C'mere."

Tatum groaned.

Vera groaned back. "I know," she said. "It's so hard. It's all so hard."

Arm in arm, they strolled along the gravel path that lined the perimeter of the park.

Tatum didn't want to talk about the fight. The fight itself wasn't why she was upset; it was the chill she'd felt after he left, which was probably loneliness. It had frightened her, like a bad omen. Her mother's voice and company were warm, so she listened as Vera spoke about her work drama: one child had accidentally scratched another's cornea.

"Of course, Blanchard didn't mean to do it," she said. "She was dancing to 'Mary Had a Little Lamb,' her favorite song, and her limbs just got away from her."

Tatum nodded, speaking up only to agree with her mother, to curse the parents who were making her life difficult, ignoring the fact that a scratched cornea did sound pretty bad.

Eventually, Vera said, "So, a little birdie told me something the other day."

Tatum sighed, knowing exactly what this meant. "Patricia told you about the kennel," she guessed. Whenever there was a "little birdie," it was Patricia.

Vera nodded, smiling innocently.

Tatum shrugged. "I was going to tell you. I just didn't want to make it a whole thing."

"Yeah," said Vera. "I was surprised that Bea told Patricia before you told me. Not offended but . . ." She winked. "Okay, maybe a little offended."

Tatum smiled and hugged her mother's arm tighter. "You know I love you, Vera-mama," she said.

Vera kissed Tatum on the head. "Okay, please fill me in."

Tatum told her what she could about it, which wasn't much. And soon, though she hadn't planned on it, she was speaking about the inadequacy she felt around Layla, and her worry that her only dream was to achieve success and wealth and had nothing to do with a specific passion. Maybe she was just an icky, greedy person, one of the bad ones. Or maybe there were only bad ones.

"So, yeah," she said glumly when she was finished. "Basically, I'm pathetic."

Vera kissed her cheek. "Unsurprisingly, I disagree."

Tatum pretended to wipe her forehead. "Okay, good."

Vera said, "It's awful to be in your twenties. My least favorite decade of life, by far."

Tatum sighed, leaning her head against her mother's shoulder.

"Your twenties are for making yourself miserable." Vera glanced at an imaginary watch. "Give it three years and you'll be happy again."

Tatum laughed. "Jesus," she said. "That's not fair. Too far away."

Vera raised her hands. "I don't make the rules." She pressed her cheek against Tatum's. "Patricia's been hilarious about the whole kennel thing, as you can imagine."

What Vera found hilarious about Patricia, most other people found insufferable.

"Beneath all the anxiety, I think she's really moved like I am. I mean, we both remember how seriously you girls took it when you were kids, all the money you raised, how you'd walk each other around by the hair 'practicing'"—she used air quotes—"for walking dogs one day." She placed a hand over her heart. "It was so charming. Those little girls would be so touched by what you're doing now, whether it actually happens or not. And, god, I loved those girls so much. But, yes, naturally she's opposed to the idea of you three being anywhere near stray dogs." Vera rolled her eyes yet maintained her smile. "Because she's obsessed with making something out of nothing."

Patricia had always driven Tatum insane. Thanks to more than thirty years of working with four-year-olds, Vera had the patience to spend a lot of time with her. When they were together, of course, Tatum feigned patience, too—she was never rude—but she couldn't be around her for long.

"Well," said Tatum. "I am unsurprised by this."

Vera laughed. "I told her to lighten up. She's got high blood pressure, you know. Stress is no good."

"I'm sure that effectively stressed her out more than anything else you could've said, and she immediately scheduled, like, twelve doctor's appointments and cut out salt and red meat and sugar from her diet."

Again, Vera laughed, then said, "You know her well. And no, she cut all that out years ago." She looked up at the bruising sky. "She tries her best. It isn't easy. The worst thing imaginable happened to her."

What was the worst imaginable thing? It didn't seem right that anyone who'd lived in Park Slope for decades, then moved to a large home in Westchester, could've possibly experienced the worst. However, they were talking about losing Audrey, who was definitely the best.

"It's just extra funny to me," Vera continued, "because you've always been afraid of dogs. Even when you were a kid."

"I've gotten a bit better," Tatum said defensively. Then she remembered this was her mother, who wasn't trying to take the kennel or anything else away from her by acknowledging the truth. "No, I mean, it's ridiculous for me to be part of this, but I guess the point is I don't know what's going to happen. We've bonded over the kennel, which has been nice, and the Layla Bernard of it all certainly makes things interesting, but . . ." She stopped.

"Right," said Vera. "Well, I love that you're bonding. And I love that Layla's back in the picture, even if she's a little intimidating. You'll get over that, I think. Speaking of Layla's great return, I have some news of my own."

"Oh?"

"I think we're going to try to track down her mom. Force her to return, too."

Tatum perked up. "Really?"

Vera nodded. "You girls are reconnecting and, I don't know." She paused. "I guess it just feels like time for us to do the same with Nancy. Not that we expect to be close with her again, but maybe we'll at least get to know each other."

Tatum nodded. "Okay," she said, then added, "But, like, remember when you called her a 'cunt' pretty recently?"

Vera cocked her head and smiled. "Hm," she said. "Nope, don't remember that, actually."

It had become a strange version of tradition for Tatum to not know what broke the mothers up. When they were children, the four of them were shielded from every adult thing, including fights. Sometimes heated whispers could be heard from the kitchen at the yellow house, like sharp gusts of wind—usually shooting from Patricia's lips—but whenever she'd noticed it, Tatum had quickly, in either an act of self-protection or because she knew she wasn't supposed to be listening, tuned it out or moved away until it was gone. Childhood innocence was protected not only by parents, but also by children. Even all these years later, knowing exactly what tore the mothers apart would feel wrong, like hearing her parents have sex.

"You think it's a good idea?" Vera asked. "Us reaching out?"

"I think you might as well try if you want to," said Tatum. "My only words of caution are that she might be really different now—maybe even cuntier than before, if that's possible."

Vera laughed.

"Layla's a trip." Tatum locked eyes with her mom and raised her eyebrows. "She's very fancy."

Again, Vera laughed. "Eh," she said. "Nancy was always kind of that way. She didn't dress fancy, but fanciness was in her."

Tatum squeezed her mother's arm even tighter. "Who knew."

People were jogging away from the park in fluorescent sneakers; dogs were out for their final walks. A beagle—which Tatum could identify because she'd spent some time at a bookstore the other day reading about dog breeds—sniffed at her ankle as it trotted past. Involuntarily, Tatum flinched.

Vera snickered.

"The other thing I was going to say"—Tatum spoke over her mother's laughter—"is that Nancy apparently still works at the Coop for some reason."

"I've actually known this," said Vera, "thanks to Patricia's role in the membership office."

"Ah—so, that's why I've never heard about a run-in."

Vera shrugged. "What can I say, we're wimps. Patricia always lets me know when Nancy's scheduled to work, and we avoid those time slots. I've never seen her shopping, either. Sometimes I wonder if the VIP Coop members get special allowances in terms of personal shoppers or other things. I've never heard anything about that, but I just can't believe we haven't accidentally seen each other after all these years. And it's suspicious that I've never run into the other big movie star members, either."

"Is that very disappointing for you?"

"I mean, would I like to watch George Clooney squeeze-test some grapefruits? Yes."

Tatum winced. "Ew, let's not forget you're my mother. Is he a member?"

"No, but I can never remember the names of the bigwigs who are: Maggie Something and her husband with a Scandinavian last name. And then there's that guy from *The Devil Wears Prada*."

"God, the Park Slope Food Coop is truly one of one," said Tatum.

They walked together, giggling as they dreamed up "worst-case scenarios" for reconnecting with Nancy, and other hypotheticals involving George Clooney and different varieties of produce, until Tatum's dad called to ask where Vera was.

After dropping her mother off at home, Tatum texted Layla.

What's up

Casual. Off the cuff.

Of course, she read it over twice before pressing send—What's up; What's up—her eyes tracing each letter as if it was an important work email. Wasn't it?

Hey hey. Just getting kennel things
in order.

Tatum smiled because it was nice to hear back so fast. Layla had yet to realize, somehow, that Tatum was utterly superfluous to the endeavor.

Or maybe she had realized and wanted Tatum around for other reasons. The thought was thrilling but also sickening. It made Tatum nervous and felt wrong on some level, the same way her own attraction to Layla did. They were family. Sisters. Or they had been, once.

Another text bloomed: I'm thinking 50k will get the ball rolling. To blow this thing up I'll have to invest a lot more over time ofc but that's a start.

Fifty thousand dollars as if it was nothing. Fifty thousand dollars, which was five times what Tatum had in her bank account after years and years of diligent saving.

Thank you sooooo much. She typed out each "o" individually, until the word looked long enough, but not so long it seemed overly effusive or—god forbid—disingenuous.

Woohoo, Layla replied.

Tatum chewed on her nail. If the conversation ended there it would feel like a failure because it was so brief, but what else was there to say?

Suddenly: Ok wait so what's the deal with Bea . . . Layla had added the emoji with spirals for eyes, then the blushing one with a yellow hand covering its mouth.

Of course, Tatum was familiar with "the deal" to which Layla was referring. Even for someone who wasn't used to first-class treatment the way Layla was, Bea was off-putting. She wasn't warm, didn't smile easily, didn't dish out compliments to make others feel good, and didn't overtalk. In fact, she often didn't talk at all.

Tatum responded, Say more to avoid saying bad things about Bea herself. How could she, when she knew from Audrey that so many others had over the years. In high school, Bea was bullied and isolated. Tatum was painfully aware of how alone she'd always been, but especially so now that Audrey was gone.

She paused in front of her building, waiting to head inside, knowing that another conversation awaited her upstairs.

Idk, Layla sent back. I guess it's nothing, she's just pretty cold??? And isn't very enthusiastic and doesn't make any effort to be in touch though this whole thing was her idea??

This was all true, and yet Tatum's investment in the kennel was far less than Layla's, so none of it really mattered to her beyond how it affected Layla's investment.

Totally. Bea can def come off a lil apathetic. Is it something you're wanting to talk to her about?

She dipped her chin into her turtleneck as, Ed had once pointed out, she often did when she was anxious.

Maybe at some point. Not now tho.

Well, you should feel appreciated since you're the one making this happen.

Layla responded with a shrugging emoji, then, It's obv my pleasure it would just be nice to feel like she cares. At our dog run meeting she was so low energy or something.

Ya that makes sense.

NBD just like slightly disappointing.

I hear ya. That's fair.

No response. This seemed like a fine place to leave it for now, especially given how chilly it suddenly was. She dropped her phone into her pocket, pressed her key fob to the box, then yanked open the heavy glass door.

Upstairs, Ed was lying on the couch, one leg thrown over the arm, fingers erotically flicking a game controller.

"Hey," he said, glancing up, then quickly back at the screen. "There you are."

"Here I am," said Tatum, sitting down next to him, pushing his foot away to make room for herself. When she was settled, he slid it into her lap.

"Sorry," he said. "Just a sec."

Tatum waited without checking her phone. The buzzy blue light burned her eyes.

Eventually there was a muted explosion and a muttered, "Fuck." He tossed the controller aside and arranged himself so that his head was in her lap instead of his foot.

She placed a hand over his ear, absently stroking the tough cartilage down to the fuzzy lobe, thinking about the kennel, but more than that, about how much of herself she could afford to give Layla, for whom her feelings were conflicted and layered, like a Russian doll with massive fake tits and Chanel earrings. She opened her mouth to tell Ed about the kennel and about Layla, because she might as well now that she could blame them for her heightened stress, use them as excuses for her behavior—

"Mmm," he moaned.

Whoops. She'd forgotten that ear stuff turned him on.

Immediately hungry-eyed, he sat up and kissed her. His upper lip was salty. His tongue drew slow, sweeping circles inside her mouth, across her teeth. He was a filmmaker, an artist, and this was how he believed artists kissed: wetly, deeply, imbued with, from Tatum's perspective, excessive passion. She could feel his heart beating against hers.

So, there would be no conversation about their fight, or anything else, after all. Maybe this wasn't the worst thing. Sex would be much faster and require less effort to fake than heartfelt apologies or declarations of undying devotion. Already, her mind was pleasantly emptying.

"I'm sorry," she said when he finally drew back for a moment to gaze lovingly at her. If she said this now, she wouldn't have to say it later when there was more time to elaborate. Her lips were slippery from his spit.

"I am, too," he whispered, breath hot against her cheeks, eyes glazed by desire. He leaned in again. His lips found her neck, and despite herself, she bloomed, arching her back and gasping when she felt his teeth.

The issue between them wasn't that she found him unattractive. No, he was tall with thick, floppy hair, defined shoulders, long arms, and big fingers. Ed resembled Timothée Chalamet, sort of, as much as any pale, mop-haired man did, though he was much sturdier.

Soon, she was sighing, her eyes closed, her body coiled like a live wire.

"Yeah," she breathed as his fingers pressed inside her underwear. She reached for her pants, tugging them off, eyes still closed, and lay back against the couch. Her shirt came off clumsily over her head, knocking her elbows together. Behind her closed eyelids, there was only sound and breath and sensation.

Lips were against hers. Stubble chafed her chin. Fingers massaged her breasts, tugging fiercely at her nipple, rolling and pinching, like they were forming it, then pinching so hard she shrieked. From the void of her empty consciousness emerged an image, two women entangled on a slipcovered couch in a room that looked like her living room, one pinning the other's arms overhead, the way Tatum's were, one crouching over the other, the way she could feel that Ed was. One of the women had babyish blond curls, the other's hair was pin-straight and dyed black. Both bodies were swollen from heat and desire. Tatum knew that she was imagining Layla on top of her, fucking her. She knew it and couldn't stop it and didn't want to. She imagined Layla's full, parted lips hovering just above hers, Layla's fingers against her clit. She gripped Ed's butt cheeks, but they were Layla's. As Layla fucked her, she whimpered like a desperate puppy until she was screaming and atoms were zipping across the backs of her eyes like water bugs across the yellow house lake.

When it was over for her, Ed was still ramming himself against her so fast their skin squeaked. He braced against the sofa arm behind her head. Her nostrils stung from her own hot breath. She watched the veins in his neck bulge and his mouth open. His cheeks were the color of lox as he came—a placid, orange pink. Still, she kissed him. He gasped as he removed himself, cradling his dick like a newborn and waddling with it in his hand to the bathroom. She stayed on the couch until she heard the toilet flush, semen leaking out of her, darkening the Ikea slipcover she'd purchased in response to Ed's messy Dorito obsession.

Her whole body fizzed. She closed her eyes again. It was safer in the dark.

"All you." His voice cut through her peace. He stroked her arm with wet fingers as he sat by her feet.

She shrugged him off and stood. Semen dripped down her leg as she made her way to the bathroom. Inside, she sat on the toilet, cleaning herself with rough paper until she was dry, then running a hand under the faucet, rinsing until every trace of him was washed away. When she returned, he was sprawled across the couch again, same as when she'd returned home, though now he was naked and his dick was shriveled like dehydrated fruit. He opened his arms to her, and more than anything she wanted to run away. But, naked, she crossed the room and fit her body into his damp folds.

She used to only have sex in the dark—jumping up with a naughty smile and turning off the lights as if it was all part of the fun. Only then would she remove her shirt and bra and climb into bed to be partially seen through the haze. The shift from that to this, fucking under unflattering overhead lights, bathed in TV blue, on the couch—even lying the way they were so that her relaxed stomach bulged over her thighs—was either the mark of hard-earned trust or because she didn't care what he thought of her anymore, or about impressing him, or about him. She cradled her belly, enjoying how the soft skin felt in her hand.

Usually, he didn't last long cuddling after sex, and this time was no exception. It used to make her sad; she'd curl herself into the warm shape he left behind, feeling abandoned until he returned to kiss her nose. Now, the instant he stirred she untangled herself and sat up, complaining that something or other ached—her neck, her shoulder, her hip. He often recommended she see his deep-tissue masseuse, Angelika, whom it didn't occur to him she couldn't afford, or he'd offer to give her shoulder rubs himself thanks to her lie that he was brilliant at them. Fortunately, the aches were usually lies, too.

"That was nice," he said, standing, dick flapping. He stretched one way, and it bounced right in front of her face, then stretched the other way, so that she was nose to his hair, which smelled distinctly like scalp and was thinning slightly at the crown.

"Yeah," she said. This wasn't a lie. She did feel better now, loosened, ready to be twisted back into her usual, uncomfortable knot, but first, ready to sleep for a long time. "It was."

He started toward their bedroom. "Do you feel resolved, though?" he asked over his shoulder, before disappearing.

She didn't bother answering him aloud until he returned in pajama pants. Still naked, she sat cross-legged, her stomach round, breasts now small and unimportant.

"It was just a stupid fight. I'm having an off week," she said, and licked her raw lips.

He nodded, leaning against the stove. She imagined him switching a burner on accidentally, bursting into flame, then disintegrating to ash, which she'd sweep into a dustbin. God, he'd turned her into a monster. Their relationship had. Life had.

"What?" he asked.

She touched her lips and found them pursed. "Just icked by my behavior, I guess."

"It's not all you," he said. "I wasn't my best, either, though afterward I guess I was." He wiggled his eyebrows. "At least judging by those sounds you were making."

"Right." She smiled charitably, then rose and took her turn in the bedroom, where she rummaged around until she found fresh clothes. When she returned, he said, "Your phone must've gotten lost in the couch during fornication." If she wasn't so worried about him having it, she would've cringed for longer at the word *fornication*. He balanced the phone against his palm, and she snatched it off, nails grazing his skin.

"Thanks," she said casually, as if she hadn't just lunged at him.

"Whoa." He laughed. "What was that?"

"What?" she asked. She wouldn't tell him about Layla or the kennel—about this, she felt a renewed resolve. Her strength had wavered momentarily, but it was back. She must protect this boundary that separated him from her future.

If he wasn't so oblivious, he might've worried that she was cheating (was she?). Thankfully, he moved on by inserting a fingernail between two teeth and saying, "Jeez, do we have any floss?"

Tatum sat next to the semen mark on the couch wondering what food remnant was wedged between the teeth she'd just spent the past twenty minutes exploring with her tongue.

"I've got some in the medicine cabinet," she said, and off he went.

She listened to the creak of the hinged mirror, the sound of him knocking over pill bottles, humming to himself. Eventually, he was back with a long white thread.

Later that night, while Ed slept, she and Layla texted more.

BTW, keep this weekend free.

Okay!! replied Tatum. I'm free this weekend, next weekend, and every weekend forever. (: This was the type of self-depreciation that had always amused Layla, Tatum remembered.

lololol, Layla replied. Oh c'mon, you've got FRIENDS. But anyway, stay tuned. With any luck, you'll be hearing from me!!

Tatum stifled a yawn. She had to be up for work in five and a half hours, but she'd stay awake until Layla said good night. Tatum imagined her tucked into the shiny lips of satin sheets. She imagined the room around her was made from gold and that her bed was the size of a pond and that she wore a matching silk pajama set and that, in her bed, as they texted, she was more comfortable than Tatum had ever been in her life.

Yayyyyy!!! Tatum sent.

Phone propped against her knee, she pressed her eyelids open with her fingers, fighting her brain's undulating desire to shut off for the night as new messages from Layla populated the bright screen.

10

From: Bernard, Layla (layla@bernard.com) April 21, 2:03 p.m.
To: Sachs, Anita (anita@bernard.com)

Subject line: RE: Kennel Project

Okay, honestly, fuck Jeb.

So, there's really nothing we can do? I still can't believe he gets the final say every fucking time . . . what's the point of a trust fund if you can't spend it the way you want to!!?! We're only talking about an initial investment of $50k. I mean, granted, I kind of made up that number because I thought it was small enough for him to go for, but still. Makes me want to sue my mom for making this stupid rule, but then Jeb would have to approve the money for legal fees, and something tells me he wouldn't . . . anyway, it just sucks. I called her to talk about it, and she wouldn't budge. Even after I explained everything. I'm at a loss. She lets me buy my fucking house, renovate it, buy cars, all on her dime, but not create a fucking business of my own so I can start my life. I don't want to be controlled by her and her henchman, Jeb, forever.

Also, I told Tatum and Bea to expect something this weekend . . . I just really thought we'd get approval . . . or at least that my mom would be chill this once because she knows all the history and stuff. I guess that was naïve. Anyway, I have to think about what I'll tell them. Fuck, I really don't want to tell them.

From: Bernard, Layla (layla@bernard.com) April 21, 2:08 p.m.
To: Sachs, Anita (anita@bernard.com)

Subject line: RE: Kennel Project

Okay, wait. Actually, I'd still like you to set something up for this weekend. I just want to prolong the fantasy for a little while. Maybe we could tour a rental space or an existing kennel for "research" on Saturday or something easy like that? We could even tour a rental space? I don't know. I'll probably have you join us to make it seem legit. That'll give me a few more days to figure out how to break the news. Anyway, thanks. I know this is a weird request. You're the best.

BTW: please don't mention anything about transportation when you reach out to them about date/time. The three of us will figure that part out on the side.

From: Sachs, Anita (anita@bernard.com) April 21, 5:27 p.m.
To: Bernard, Layla (layla@bernard.com); Ellis, Beatrix (beatrix.ellis003@gmail.com); Kaplan, Tatum (t.kaplan@goldenpress.com)

Subject line: RE: The Kennel

Good evening.

I've scheduled two appointments for this weekend. On Saturday morning, you're all set to tour a large rental space in Long Island

City. I've included the link below. The listing agent will meet you outside at 10am.

Afterward, you'll tour a dog shelter called "Bestest Friends" located in Bushwick. Please confirm your attendance.

Warmly,
Anita

From: Kaplan, Tatum (t.kaplan@goldenpress.com) April 21, 6:11 p.m.
To: Ellis, Beatrix (beatrix.ellis003@gmail.com); Bernard, Layla (layla@bernard.com); Sachs, Anita (anita@bernard.com)

Subject line: RE: The Kennel

Hi!

This is so great. YAY!! IT'S REALLY HAPPENING!!

The listing looks fantastic. I'll be at both appointments on Saturday. Thank you so much for setting this up, Layla and Anita!!

Tatum

From: Ellis, Beatrix (beatrix.ellis003@gmail.com) April 21, 8:46 p.m.
To: Bernard, Layla (layla@bernard.com); Kaplan, Tatum (t.kaplan@goldenpress.com); Sachs, Anita (anita@bernard.com)

Subject line: RE: The Kennel

I'm pretty busy this weekend. Not sure I'll make it to either.

From: Bernard, Layla (layla@bernard.com) April 21, 8:49 p.m.
To: Kaplan, Tatum (t.kaplan@goldenpress.com)

Subject line: RE: *******PRIVATE LAYLA AND TATUM*********** The Kennel

I'M. . . . . ANNOYED. Does her lack of enthusiasm ever get to you??? She's always killing the vibe. Wait, sidenote: do you want to hang out after the kennel tour? We could do some shopping in the area, or you could come to my place.

From: Kaplan, Tatum (t.kaplan@goldenpress.com) April 21, 8:56 p.m.
To: Bernard, Layla (layla@bernard.com)

Subject line: RE: *******PRIVATE LAYLA AND TATUM*********** The Kennel

I totally hear you about Bea. And yeah, would love to hang after!

From: Ellis, Beatrix (beatrix.ellis003@gmail.com) April 21, 9:12 p.m.
To: Bernard, Layla (layla@bernard.com); Kaplan, Tatum (t.kaplan@goldenpress.com)
Cc: Sachs, Anita (anita@bernard.com)

Subject line: RE: The Kennel

Actually, I'll be at the second thing. The Bushwick thing.

From: Bernard, Layla (layla@bernard.com) April 21, 9:19 p.m.
To: Ellis, Beatrix (beatrix.ellis003@gmail.com); Kaplan, Tatum (t.kaplan@goldenpress.com)
Cc: Sachs, Anita (anita@bernard.com)

Subject line: RE: The Kennel

I mean, only come if you want to be there.

From: Ellis, Beatrix (beatrix.ellis003@gmail.com) April 21, 9:22 p.m.
To: Bernard, Layla (layla@bernard.com); Kaplan, Tatum (t.kaplan@goldenpress.com)
Cc: Sachs, Anita (anita@bernard.com)

Subject line: RE: The Kennel

That's why I said I'll be there.

From: Bernard, Layla (layla@bernard.com) April 21, 9:27 p.m.
To: Ellis, Beatrix (beatrix.ellis003@gmail.com); Kaplan, Tatum (t.kaplan@goldenpress.com)
Cc: Sachs, Anita (anita@bernard.com)

Subject line: RE: The Kennel

I feel like Bea's making me seem like such a shithead lol. Grrrrr. She's like The Grinch. The Grinch that stole the dog kennel—a new picture book. Now I'm picturing The Grinch with Bea's bangs. I think I'm onto something here. Maybe you should take this idea to your boss . . . LET'S GET THIS THING ON BOOKSHELVES. THAT'LL BE OUR NEXT BUSINESS VENTURE. Also, I'M DEFINITELY NOT inviting her to hang out with us after, so don't mention it to her.

From: Kaplan, Tatum (t.kaplan@goldenpress.com) April 21, 9:29 p.m.
To: Bernard, Layla (layla@bernard.com)

Subject line: RE: *******PRIVATE LAYLA AND TATUM*********** The Kennel

Wait, Layla—I'm so sorry—you sent that to Bea, too.

From: Bernard, Layla (layla@bernard.com) April 21, 9:33 p.m.
To: Kaplan, Tatum (t.kaplan@goldenpress.com)

Subject line: RE: *******PRIVATE LAYLA AND TATUM*********** The Kennel

Fuuuuuckkkkk . . . fuck fuck fuck. Too many email chains about the same fucking thingggggg. I'm gonna email her privately and apologize ughhhhhh. Shit.

From: Bernard, Layla (layla@bernard.com) April 21, 10:05 p.m.
To: Ellis, Beatrix (beatrix.ellis003@gmail.com)

Subject line: So sorry

Well, it's probably clear I didn't mean to send that to you. I'd love to have you there this weekend, I just wanted to give you an out if you're looking for one. I know the kennel has a lot of sentimental value, to all of us but especially you, and I'm just really sorry. No pressure to go on Saturday. And you can totally hang with us after, if you want. I'm sorry again.

11

ON SATURDAY AT eleven-thirty, Bea was settling into her seat on the bus. She'd be just over forty minutes late to their appointment if there were no delays, but at least she was going. The kennel in Bushwick was more than an hour's travel from Park Slope by public transit. She'd decided to take the bus there and the train back to keep things interesting.

Trees and spring jackets streaked past outside. She was furiously sketching everything she saw, blurry people, blurry houses, blurry cars. It all blended on the page to create one streaky smudge.

The driver mumbled the same words over the intercom as they pulled into every stop. To Bea, it sounded like he was speaking gibberish: "Blee-gee-do-da-do." But she knew he was actually saying, "Please exit through the back door," because she knew Brooklyn by heart. Beside and above her, people swayed, casting dirty looks down at the luxurious two-seat configuration she protected with her backpack.

Bea's nose was inches from the page that buckled beneath her pencil tip. She wore a pair of gaucho pants she'd had since middle school. They were so small on her from years of dryer cycles and normal adult weight gain, they showed the top of her butt crack if she wasn't vigilant. Her shirt was small, too, uncomfortably tight around her arms and the hump of her lower stomach. The discomfort of this outfit matched her feelings about the day.

When she glanced up again, she caught the judgmental eye of a standing, white-haired woman, her skin-and-bone fingers clenched around a pole as she rocked with the bus's movements. At that moment, amidst Bea's own irritability, the woman's judgment of her was delicious. She could stare all she wanted, Bea would never give her a seat.

She'd spent the morning caring for Rosalie, as had quickly become the norm. Made her Patricia's buckwheat-blueberry pancake recipe drizzled with syrup and powdered sugar; washed the dishes Rosalie had left out the night before; wiped the bottom of the tub with bleach and paper towels, then ran the water for a while so Rosalie could safely bathe if she chose to—all this before Rosalie was even awake. She'd done the same with Audrey most days: prepped the house for her. Bea loved the sense of accomplishment and the way their sleepy eyes showed gratitude as she listed off the things she'd done.

After the pancakes were rewarmed, Rosalie had sat down to eat while Bea watched.

"Yum," she said, between bites. "There's something different about these, I—"

"They're buckwheat," Bea said. "Very healthy."

As a child, she'd begged her mother for normal pancakes to no avail. Now she could understand the pride Patricia must've felt watching her children wolf down food she'd made that was good for them.

"Cool," said Rosalie. "Thanks a lot."

Bea sat with her hands folded in her lap.

"Will you have any?"

Bea shook her head. "They're all for you."

This pleasant memory from earlier did not sooth the rage that tightened the back of Bea's throat as the bus finally shuddered against the curb at her stop. She was a mere ten-minute walk from Layla and Tatum now. It would require self-control not to say anything, do anything, to them she might regret. When she pictured Rosalie's face, mouth stained by blueberries and powdered sugar, satiated because of Bea's efforts, she felt a little better. Stronger. She got off the bus, knocking people's shoulders as she made her way, and found herself alone on the street, loose backpack strap slung over one shoulder, the bus's taillights winking red.

No one was forcing her to be there—Layla had made this clear—yet there she was. In Bushwick. Far from home. She was there because she'd said she would be, and because she was genuinely curious about the inner workings of a kennel and what similarities she might find to the camel farm and even to her work with Rosalie. Everything would be okay so long as she kept her cool. The maps app told her which direction to walk in, where she'd eventually turn left, which she memorized, then started shuffling along, her shoes scraping the pavement.

The stab of pain she'd felt upon receiving Layla's insulting email was acute, though not foreign. In high school, people had been mean. It didn't matter who her sister was, she was laughed at, left alone in the cafeteria, and sent cruel messages from fake Facebook accounts. What set Layla's message calling her "The Grinch" apart from all the others in her past was that it had further polluted Bea's yellow house memories. She should've seen it coming. Tatum and Audrey's close friendship had started the job, now it was Layla's turn to finish it. The yellow house was just a house, Tatum and Layla were just people, no better or more special to Bea than anyone else. She was better than they were, in fact, they just didn't know it.

When she arrived at the kennel, she lingered outside, staring up at the sign, which featured a line drawing of a spotted dog suspiciously identical to Snoopy. The windows were large and reflective. In them, she could see her own torn-up forehead from when she'd scraped it against the door a few nights earlier.

Don't be immature, her sister's stern voice rang in her ears as she stalled. *Go inside and apologize for being late like you should.*

"Fuck off," Bea said aloud. She was angry. It wasn't a good headspace to be in given the circumstances. Rosalie—she was what really mattered. Bea took a deep breath and pushed inside.

The kennel's walls were beige, the waiting room chairs upholstered in vinyl. There was a curved desk and a receptionist behind it in a bulky sweater. Framed pictures of dogs hung on the walls. Bea assumed they were of boarders or fosters or charges or inmates or whatever the fuck they were considered, but they also could've been stock photos.

Layla and Tatum filled two of the chairs. They were pitched forward, thighs supporting their elbows, faces very close together. When she saw them notice her, Bea nodded a curt hello and sat down next to Tatum. On Layla's far side was a woman furiously typing on her cell phone; the only sound in the room were her nails against the screen.

Tatum said, "Hi," softly. Bea could hear pity in her voice.

"Hey," said Layla. "Glad you made it."

They sat silently.

Eventually, Layla said, "This is Anita."

Bea didn't look up.

"We waited for you."

Bea didn't react.

"Anita will see if they still have time for us."

Bea peered through her bangs as Anita stood. Her hips were wide, and due to the sheeny material of her pants, it sounded like her crotch was breathing as she crossed the room. She leaned over the reception desk and whispered something to the woman behind it.

I shouldn't have come, Bea thought. She wasn't projecting cool confidence but rather bitterness and hurt.

By the time Anita returned, Layla had sighed twice, and Tatum's foot had begun to bounce.

"They'll take you back in a few minutes," said Anita. "No problem."

Layla frowned as if Anita had said, "Big problem," then replied, "You're the best."

Again, they were quiet until Layla began fiddling with a tangle of gold bracelets on her wrist. The sound was grating. Bea bit her lip to keep calm. *Shut up,* she wanted to scream. *Shut the fuck up, you piece of shit. You coward. You bully.* But she wouldn't let her rage win this time. She must stay calm, or as calm as she could. Through her teeth, she said, "Can you please stop doing that?"

And Layla did. And there was silence once more.

Bea could feel Tatum looking at her, imagined popping her pale, doleful eyes out of their shallow sockets, mashing them into a blue-gray paste with her fists, slurping them down, then vomiting onto the kennel's wall-to-wall carpeting. Those stupid fucking eyes, always filled with sadness and worry when they focused on Bea, since long before Audrey died. Bea was fine. She was fine and, anyway, Tatum's concern was empty, just like the two bloody, gouged-out sockets Bea now saw when she looked at her.

"You okay?" Tatum's voice was barely audible as she gestured at Bea's forehead. "That looks painful."

Bea nodded curtly and looked away.

More silence.

Layla shifted position on her vinyl seat, creating what could only be described as a fart sound. "That obviously wasn't—"

Bea scoffed.

"It wasn't," Layla said again. "It was the chair."

At that moment, a woman swirled into the waiting room dressed in a white doctor's coat.

"Layla?" The woman's wide eyes bounced between Layla's and Tatum's faces, never reaching Bea.

Layla raised her hand. "That's me," she said cheerfully. The metal bar that pierced the cartilage of her left ear in two places glinted under the fluorescent lights as she stood. Bea wanted to hook her fingers behind it and yank it out. Her appearance, complete with studded heels and dark brown lipstick, did not match her sunny tone and smile, both of which had emerged so suddenly.

The woman looked on the brink of happy tears.

"It's such a pleasure to meet you," she said, grabbing Layla's hands. "I couldn't believe it when they told me you were stopping by. Tammy Rose's real-life daughter."

"Aw." Layla laughed. "Well, it's a pleasure to meet you, too." Her tone was cloying. It turned Bea's stomach. "Thank you so much for your flexibility today." Layla made that terrible apologetic expression again and heat spread across Bea's body. Her hands balled into fists.

No matter how hard Layla tried to make her, she would not feel guilty for her lateness.

"Oh my god, don't worry about it." The woman shook her head. "Thanks for taking an interest in our mission. We're super excited to show you around."

As they walked, the kennel woman said, "Your mother." She kept looking back at Layla and almost bumping into things: a person, an empty animal-carrying case, the wall, a tall plant. "I'm sure it's weird of me to say so, but she's brilliant. *Tammy Rose* changed my life. I'm a single mom now and I still watch the show on difficult nights."

They were moving down a long hallway, footsteps echoing off stark white walls. No cheerful framed photographs here. It greatly resembled the children's psychiatric hospital.

She remembered Patricia's words to the doctor as they'd dragged Bea along, past locked doors: "I just want to know what's wrong with her. That's really all I want." What it was, though, no one could say. Once Patricia was gone, Bea had been on her best behavior at the facility, and when it was time to go, at the end of two weeks, the doctor had concluded, "We don't have a diagnosis," to Patricia's great dismay. Still, based on Patricia's anecdotes, and not on Bea's observed behavior, she'd left there with a prescription for strong antipsychotics.

Up ahead, Layla was saying, "Oh wonderful, how many kids do you have?" She and the kennel woman small-talked while Tatum and Bea were quiet and Anita took notes on her phone, thumbs blurring, pants whispering. Bea couldn't imagine what sort of information these notes included. Probably:

- Kennel manager has a four-year-old, Pete, named after her dead grandfather
- Layla to let mother know that kennel manager says hi
- Kennel manager named Ella
- Kennel not actually a kennel but a rescue, according to kennel manager

Eventually, they crowded around a closed door with a tight rectangular window reinforced by thin chicken wire.

"So, here's where we give our dogs baths when they first come in," said Ella. Bea could hear rushing water from inside but couldn't see into the room from where she was.

"Usually, the dogs we admit have fleas, or they're malnourished, or there's something wrong with them that led to their surrender, whether that's a behavioral issue, incontinence, or otherwise. Each rescued pooch gets a bath immediately no matter what because fleas spread like wildfire."

"Right," said Layla, whose face sagged slightly at the mention of fleas. Anita was nodding as she typed. Tatum's round eyes reflected the bright room.

"So, we give them a nice rubdown with this special shampoo, as you can see Georgia doing." Ella pointed at the window, and Bea rose onto her tiptoes for the chance at a view. From that height, she could see the top of a mangy gray coat. The hands working soap through it were cased in blue rubber.

"This one is a real sweetheart; about two years old. Owner died suddenly. Her name is Willow."

Tatum placed a hand on the door. "That's so strange," she said, stepping closer.

"What is?" asked Layla.

"I think I recognize her from the dog run. And I even remember her name was Willow."

Layla squinted into the room. Bea was careful to seem disinterested. She yawned, shifted to stand with her back against the wall.

"Really?" said Layla. "It's so pretty and big."

Tatum seemed dazed. "Yeah," she said. "I don't know. That's so weird."

Layla touched her shoulder. "You okay?"

Tatum smiled, though she looked ill. "I'm okay. It's just—you said the owner died?"

Ella nodded. "I don't have more details than that, but yes. Willow was surrendered early this morning."

Bea was growing impatient. "What's next?" she asked sharply.

Layla shook her head and sighed. "You're really okay, Tatum?"

"I am," said Tatum. "I can't explain why, it's just weird to see her here."

"I mean," said Layla as Ella began guiding them away, "it's definitely an odd coincidence. And you probably saw the owner, and now you know she's dead."

"Yeah," said Tatum, as she looped her arm through Layla's and Bea walked behind them.

"The dog was really sweet and sat beside me for a while. Then the owner came and got her. I don't know, something about her was—" Tatum laughed darkly. "Whatever, it's fine."

Layla rubbed her back. Bea found the whole display obnoxious. It was so dramatic. Tatum didn't know this dog or its dead owner; she might've seen them once for a few seconds, but they couldn't even be sure it was the same dog. Willow seemed like a common enough name.

"This, right in here, is where we quarantine sick rescues," Ella said when they reached the next door.

Now Bea was curious. She peered eagerly through the little window, not bothering to make room for anyone else. Inside were cages stacked all the way to the ceiling. The dogs in them looked either agitated or tired. Gliding about were two hazmat suits, presumably inhabited by people, though they looked more like ghosts. They waved with blue-gloved hands.

"That's Berry and Candace," said Ella. "They're our vets. They wear those suits out of an abundance of caution so that nothing spreads to the healthy dogs."

Bea asked brightly, "How many of these will get put to sleep?"

Everyone looked at her, their expressions ranging from surprise to embarrassment.

"Oh," Ella stammered. "We try to save as many as we can, but of course we can't save them all. I don't have the statistic offhand."

"Let's move on," said Layla, who was still nervously eyeing Tatum.

Ella obliged, beckoning them along, but Bea wasn't quite ready. She couldn't break away from their wide eyes, crusted over in some cases, bright and scared in others; big paws were hooked up to IVs; little rib cages fluttered from labored breath. They reminded her of the camels and of her sister and of—

"Coming?" Ella called over her shoulder, and reluctantly Bea shuffled away.

It was for them, those pained, tortured animals, that she'd wanted to do all this in the first place. She had many more questions for Ella than she knew how to ask, so she was quiet for the rest of the tour, which was fine. Mostly boring. Eventually, they left with a lot of what Layla called "helpful information," after promising to send Ella a *Tammy Rose* poster signed by Nancy and a donation. Bea was exhausted, and the trek home would be long. More than anything, she wanted to get away from these people.

Outside, Layla said, "Well, that was nice," which had not been Bea's experience nor anyone else's as far as she could tell.

Tatum, still slightly green, nodded. "It was."

Bea continued not speaking.

"So," said Anita, whom Bea had forgotten was there. "I'll spend this evening typing up my notes, then send them over to you girls." The way she said it made Bea aware of their age difference. Anita had to be in her mid-forties. Biologically speaking, she was probably old enough to be their mother. Her forehead was debossed by wrinkles; so were the corners of her eyes. *You girls*, she'd said. Bea wondered just how much she hated her job, how much she hated Layla and all of them, and their stupid kennel. Bea wondered how Anita channeled her anger. What she did behind closed doors to survive.

"Sounds great," said Layla. "Thanks a bunch for coming today."

Anita waved. "Good to meet you girls," she said—there it was again. It might as well have been *you little girls*.

When she was gone, Layla immediately turned to Bea.

"You never responded to my email," she said, "So, I wanted to tell you I'm sorry in person, too."

Great way to apologize, Bea wanted to say. *Always good to start with criticism.* But she wouldn't. It didn't matter. She didn't want anything from Layla anymore, apology or otherwise.

Tatum reached for Bea's hand, but Bea moved it away. Suddenly, she felt like crying. She turned her back to them.

"Hey." Tatum's voice was kind. "Bea."

But Bea could not speak.

"I really am sorry," said Layla. Her voice was gentler now.

Bea croaked, "It's fine." She wanted to want nothing from them, to be strong on her own or at least numb, but the sadness felt good in a way, too. It wasn't anger, which burned so hot. Suddenly, her fingers and toes were very far, as if she'd been stretched tall and thin to the point of almost breaking. It was an out-of-body feeling. A feeling with no cure since Audrey was gone. She needed her sister to pull her back down to earth. Whenever Bea felt sad, Audrey was the reason why and the only antidote.

When Bea was certain her tears wouldn't fall, she turned back to find that Layla and Tatum looked two different kinds of worried.

"I'm going to go," she said.

Layla said, "We decided to go thrifting before heading home. I know I said otherwise in that email—I'm sorry again, by the way—but you're welcome to hang out if you want."

Tatum flinched. "Or we could skip shopping."

"Sure," said Layla. "Or that."

"No," said Bea.

She appreciated Layla's lack of façade. Tatum wore a mask. Her guilt was palpable. Maybe Tatum's charms worked on Layla, but not Bea. The anger was flowing back into her, warm like blood. Soon, it would be scalding.

"Okay," said Tatum. "Well, we'll see you, then."

Layla repeated, "I'm sorry again," as Bea walked away.

12

TATUM COULDN'T HELP but wonder what the people they passed might be thinking as they walked along. Layla wore an oiled bun pulled so tight the sun glinted off it like a mirror, and baggy, low-riding, too-long jeans that dragged across the ground with her every step. A bedazzled bikini top hugged her torso with strings criss-crossing her narrow rib cage, and a stiff leather jacket seemed to hover in the air above her shoulders.

The aura of wealth and power that surrounded her must be unmissable, Tatum thought. If she saw Layla on the street, she would certainly wonder about her. And if people were wondering about Layla, they were also probably wondering about Tatum, the plebeian to her right—insulting things like, *What's so special about her?* Still, Tatum was proud to be noticeable.

When she saw a teenager turn to her friend and whisper something, hand blocking her mouth, wide eyes flitting between her friend's ear, Layla's bare abdomen, and Tatum's Converse sneakers, she was satisfied. Even after the heartrending events of the day—staring into Bea's sad eyes, learning what had happened to that gorgeous dog from the park—there was room for Tatum to be dazzled by Layla's glamorous existence. She closed her eyes against a wave of self-loathing-induced nausea. Layla grabbed her hand when she swayed.

"Whoa," she said. "You okay?"

Dazed, Tatum squinted into the bright sun. "I think so."

"Why don't I call the car?"

They hadn't made it far from the kennel.

"You wanted to shop, though." Tatum's mouth was very dry. She was beginning to suspect what she felt was more than pure emotion.

Layla laughed. "Yeah, right. Like I'm going to force you to shop with me like this. I can come back anytime." She was already typing on her phone. "Besides, I was just trying to get some—" She paused. "Alone time, I guess." Suddenly, her cheeks were pink.

Tatum nodded. "Okay, cool. Maybe I'll sit down."

Layla guided her to a step, and she sank onto it.

"God, I'm so sorry about this," said Tatum. It was embarrassing. What was embarrassing? What exactly was happening to her? Layla crouched so they were eye to eye.

"Hey," she said. "Stop apologizing. I want to take care of you."

Why can't you be like this with Bea, too? Tatum thought, *Warm and nurturing.* Though Bea wasn't innocent in everything, Tatum wished they'd parted ways on a better note.

She'd never seen Bea like that before: vulnerable. And though she wanted to blame Layla alone for the tears in Bea's eyes, she blamed herself just as much for all the things she should've done differently over so many years.

At the very least, it wouldn't have killed her to ask Bea to coffee every once in a blue moon. Their coffee dates would've been quiet—an hour of awkwardness—but so what? It would've meant something to Bea. Instead, she'd done nothing. And now she should speak up on her behalf to Layla: *Bea's obviously really hurt. You should be nicer to her.* But she wouldn't, despite her regrets. She'd choose the easy thing again, knowing it was wrong. Was anything easy for a self-absorbed empath?

"The car will be here any second," said Layla, still crouched. Her hand cupped Tatum's knee. The heat was comforting. Tatum could smell her minty breath. "Will someone be there when you get home? I could come over, if you want."

They'd talked around Ed's existence before—*Will "someone" be there*, for example. Tatum had never spoken the words "I have a boyfriend." Instead, she'd said things like, "*We're* usually out of town for the holidays," or "*Our* apartment," or "Video games are a big thing in my house."

"I'll be fine. Thanks, though," Tatum said, covering Layla's hand with her own. She might not have made such a move if she wasn't so delirious and confused. It was the kind of gesture she normally would've made a mental pro-con list about before performing. But Layla pressed her thumb against Tatum's knuckle, pinning her hand there.

A black car appeared and slunk down the street, right blinker flashing.

"There's Stanley," said Layla, helping Tatum to her feet.

The car was low to the ground and wide. Now, having ridden around in it all morning, she was familiar with how to enter, though stooping so low was uncomfortable given her stomachache. Stanley held her arm as she got into a near-squat position. Just before ducking into the cool darkness, her eyes flicked up at the storefronts across the street, and there, leaning against a tree, head cocked, was Bea. Her eyes were focused squarely on Tatum. Her long, severe face, constellated by freckles, was always unmistakable. Today, it was made even more so by the gash on her forehead framed by her bangs.

Tatum gasped.

A moment later, when she looked out the car window from inside, Bea was gone. Had she been there, or was her image a delusion? Tatum was panting as Layla settled in beside her.

"You okay?" she asked.

"Yes," said Tatum, though her voice told a different story.

"We'll get you home quickly," said Layla. "Don't worry." She pulled down a buttress as wide as the seat between them with two cup holders in it, then gestured toward the glowing refrigerator at Tatum's feet. "Take a water."

Tatum did as instructed. Her hands were too weak to unscrew the lid, so Layla did it for her.

It was nothing, Tatum thought as icy water stung the back of her throat. *It wasn't her. It was in your head.*

Through the navy-tinted car window, people outside were like silent film stars: the woman selling sliced mango; the plump child hand in hand with his mother; the construction worker smoking beneath a scaffold. Viewing the world from just outside it made her homesick. Every Brooklyn neighborhood was unique, though as upper-middle-class white people spread across the borough, this was becoming tragically less true. Tatum had spent enough time in Bushwick to appreciate the neighborhood's specific vibrancy but not enough to find it unspecial. Suddenly, she missed her own normal, the noise and grit of real life, the camaraderie of it. And she was afraid—of Layla's world and of Bea. She wanted to open the door and flee.

"Oh, by the way, do you like the Medusas?" asked Layla, who was scrolling on her phone.

Tatum had only heard their music at rave-y dance parties before, the likes of which she hadn't attended in years. She didn't particularly enjoy electronic music, rather she preferred a soft, folky vibe, but nodded, of course, and said, "They're great."

Layla pressed play on her phone and a deep bassline pounded up through the floor like the end of a disgruntled neighbor's broomstick. As Layla began nodding in time with the beat, Tatum said, "Love it," with as much feeling as she could muster, though the vibration made her nausea worse.

"Can I crack this a bit?" She pointed at the window.

Layla nodded.

Tatum wanted out, though she wasn't sure where she'd rather be. Maybe her parents' house, behind the thick iron bars that protected the windows of their apartment.

"Just a little motion sickness," she said as she closed her eyes.

Layla patted her shoulder. "Open the window as much as you like and let Stanley know if you need us to pull over."

Bea's face was all Tatum could see, painted in neon across the backs of her eyelids. Had she really been there? It wasn't the first time she'd asked herself this question. Though Tatum had only definitely been on the receiving end of her stalking once, the thought of it happening again was always in her mind.

A few months after the sisters had moved in together, Tatum and Audrey had enjoyed a night of raucous fun, lovesick bartenders offering up free drinks, and random men teaching them to shoot pool. Well after three a.m., they'd stumbled out of a bar onto East Sixth Street.

"Cab or subway?" Audrey had cooed, eyes flashing. "Cab or subway, cab or subway, cab or subway?" She shook Tatum gently by the shoulders.

Tatum threw back her head and groaned, privately delighting in Audrey's touch. "Should we just cab?" She watched as Audrey lit up a cigarette. "I don't wanna wait for the train. I just wanna be in bed."

Audrey laughed a cloud of smoke into Tatum's face. "I don't wanna wait for the train," she mimicked.

Tatum stuck out her tongue and Audrey pinched it between her sour pointer finger and thumb. She should've been disgusted that Audrey was touching her tongue with dirty fingers she'd used to hold the subway pole, wipe herself in the graffitied dive bar bathroom, and fish white powder out of a Ziplock with the tip of a silver key, but she wasn't. So, she faked it.

"Ugh." She swatted Audrey's hand. "Get away from me."

"Wait," Audrey said, looping her arms around Tatum's neck. "Love me, goddammit."

Tatum had struggled against her playfully, knowing better than to take Audrey's words seriously; she was an affectionate drunk.

"Get off," Tatum said. "Off." They tussled, giggling into each other's ears, until Tatum's eyes fell on a shadowy figure who appeared to be watching them. She hissed, "Audrey."

"What?" Audrey's arms were still around Tatum's neck.

"Look." When she pointed, the figure ducked behind a tree. The dark street was desolate so late at night, except for the occasional speeding taxi. She assumed the avenue would be busier—brighter—and Tatum wished she was there.

"Oh, shit," said Audrey, detaching herself. She walked clumsily toward the tree, calling out, "Hey," again and again. The figure had nowhere to go, contained by a parked car on one side and the bright light of a streetlamp on the other.

Tatum stuck close to Audrey, unwilling to let her go alone but wishing they were running in the opposite direction. When Audrey reached the tree, she singsonged, "I see you."

"Hi," said a familiar voice.

"Seriously?" Audrey crossed her arms. "Tatum, relax. It's just Trix."

Unlike Audrey, who'd seemed only minorly peeved, Tatum had felt momentary relief that it was Bea and not a murderer, then confusion, then anger, then crippling shame. The same shame she always felt when it came to Bea.

Instead of waiting for the sisters to hash it out, drunk and stupid, Tatum had turned and walked to Avenue A, hailed a cab of her own, and left Manhattan.

The next morning, she'd called Audrey. "What happened in the end?"

"Well," she said, voice hoarse from sleep, cigarettes, and hangover. "Apparently, Bea followed us around last night." Audrey cackled, which turned into a raspy cough. When she recovered, she said, "I mean, you just have to laugh because it's so classic and, like, ultimately harmless."

But Tatum hadn't felt like laughing. "We should be inviting her out with us since you guys live together now. I feel terrible."

"Oh my god," said Audrey. "We're still allowed to hang out without her. Don't worry about it. This is just something she does. She likes following me around. She's really good at it; when I'm out, I never know if she's with me or not. It's been this way since long before we moved in together. Somehow, she always knows how to find me."

Tatum didn't know how to respond. She felt violated.

"Tatum? Did the connection drop?"

Tatum said, "We need to talk about this in person," and hung up.

Later that day, they'd met for the first and only contentious conversation in their long friendship. Tatum asked Audrey to make sure Bea never did this again.

"It's just not okay," she said when they were settled at a table in their favorite coffee shop, Otto's. It seemed reasonable to not want to be stalked. "Guilt aside, it makes me super uncomfortable. Especially since this might've happened before without my knowledge."

"I get it," said Audrey. "But you have to understand where it comes from. She doesn't mean to creep you out, she's just lonely."

"Right," said Tatum. "Well, now I feel bad again."

Audrey threw up her hands. "Dude, I kind of think you have a guilt problem! I don't know what to tell you!" She glanced around the way they often did in Park Slope to make sure no one they recognized was within earshot. More quietly, she added, "She's *my* sister. I'm the one who should feel bad."

Then Tatum softened and joined Audrey on her side of the table, draping an arm across her shoulders. "I know. I'm sorry. I'm making this about me."

"It's not like I want to live with her," Audrey said, dabbing her nose with a crumpled napkin, facing the wall for privacy. "I have to take care of her. She's got no one else to live with besides our psycho mom."

"You're a great sister," Tatum said, combing her fingers through Audrey's long hair, watching it fall against her shoulder, as fluid and healthy as water. "You really are." *But Bea isn't the same to you,* she wanted to add. *Great sisters aren't stalkers.*

The next time they saw each other, Audrey had assured her it wouldn't happen again, and that was that, though Audrey was right—Tatum did have a guilt problem, and the worry over what Audrey might've said to Bea lingered.

Soon after, Audrey's addiction had taken over and Bea was there and Tatum wasn't. It turned out Bea was a great sister, after all. Tatum was the bad one. She used COVID quarantine to justify not visiting, when really, she couldn't stand to see her friend that way, especially knowing she was partly to blame. Somehow, Tatum had missed the signs that should've been so obvious, trusted that Audrey was in control of her substance usage because she was Audrey, and she'd checked herself into rehab for drinking when she didn't even have a problem. Maybe Tatum's biggest mistake was not questioning that more. But it wasn't their relationship to lie to each other. Audrey had talked about her fears, her issues with Patricia, worries about Bea, insecurities, sex life, even her digestive problems in graphic detail. But not about this. Or maybe Audrey had been in denial. It was comforting and devastating to think that might've been the case. Comforting, because it meant Tatum had missed just as much as Audrey herself had. Devastating, because it meant Audrey had marched into her own grave without realizing it. But that just wasn't her. It was more likely she'd known and been afraid, and Tatum hadn't noticed. Maybe investing in Tatum's friendship was Audrey's biggest mistake.

When she finally showed up to their apartment after Audrey's addiction was in full swing—once—it was worse than she'd imagined.

"Is there anything I can do?" she'd asked Bea over Audrey's slumped body, positioned on the couch between them like a doll. "I could try to convince her to get help."

Bea said coolly, "She's got help."

"I mean like a doctor or a rehab center or something."

"Sure." Bea crossed her arms. "Just try."

"Hey," Tatum said, touching Audrey's cold shoulder. "Aud?"

Audrey opened and closed her mouth. Her dull eyeballs searched the room for Tatum's face.

"Hi there," Tatum said when they found her. "I think you should get some help. Can I find you a program?"

Audrey's eyes closed again.

"Maybe I should come back when she's more lucid."

Bea said, "She's rarely more lucid."

"We could cut off her supply. Confiscate her phone?"

"I do the best I can."

Tatum had left shortly after and never returned. Selfish, selfish, selfish. Bea was odd, but she was a better person than Tatum—stronger and more generous. Tatum would carry the weight forever, of not having sounded the alarm when Audrey's addiction was laid out in front of her like a map to her death, of not having been there when things got bad because it was too painful. If anyone was responsible, it was the one person Audrey had spent the most time with, who'd seen her do the very things that would end up killing her and done nothing to stop it. In this case, Tatum's guilt was well-earned.

The car swerved around a pothole and Tatum swallowed hard.

"She's not feeling well," Layla reminded Stanley over the blaring music. "Drive carefully, please."

The water bottle in Tatum's lap wasn't helping her queasiness, but she held it there, its condensation bleeding into her clothes. Was it food poisoning? A virus?

Tatum pressed her fingers to her mouth.

Layla was rocking in her seat, jabbing the air with her elbows in an awkward performance. Her stomach barely folded over the waistband of her pants. Her bare shoulders were decorated with delicate line drawings: a cactus, a lily, a tiny hand making a peace sign. The hump of her collarbone cradled a longer tattoo, a sentence written in illegible cursive. She was very, very thin, while her breasts threatened to slip out of their skimpy bra cups as she moved.

In Tatum's stripped-down, uncomfortable state, she felt nothing but longing for the little girl she'd once felt so close to. For the moment, the awe and admiration she usually felt in Layla's presence was gone.

Searching for distraction, Tatum said, "This is so good," about the song that played. She spoke through gritted teeth.

"Funny you should say that," said Layla. "This song has always reminded me of us."

Sure enough, the singer, in a heavily auto-tuned drawl, was repeating the words *just like skipping stones* again and again. Then added:

You've gotta find the one, the right one. Find the right one, the one that takes you far. Tatum hadn't been paying attention to the lyrics at all.

Layla sang along, bobbing her head.

When the song ended, she said, "You know, 'cause Audrey was always so good at skipping stones."

"She was," said Tatum. She hadn't thought about that in a while, how they used to huddle on the pebble beach at the lake, clutching their coin-shaped stones. One by one, Audrey would stand behind them, guiding their arms in quick snapping motions, then step back to admire the arcs across the water. Tatum could remember the sound of pebbles shifting beneath their feet, like ice in a water glass. It was still one of her favorite sounds in the world.

"That time it was all you," Audrey would say charitably after a successful skip, though none of them had ever been able to do it without her.

Layla laughed. "We were so annoying, I bet. Couldn't just let her do it, we all had to, too."

For Tatum, this was a pure, happy memory. She didn't see her young self as annoying.

"We really admired her. She was so good at everything."

Layla nodded. "Back then, sure she was."

Was Layla Bernard competitive with the memory of a twelve-year-old?

"I mean, as an adult, she was a successful model," Tatum said. "Totally gorgeous. So fun, hilarious, smart. You didn't know her then, but she was really amazing."

"Right," said Layla. "Don't doubt it."

When they drove over a speed bump, Tatum's stomach twisted that much more.

"God, I'm really, really not feeling well," she said. It was overwhelming. She folded over in her seat and Layla shut off the music.

"Okay, just breathe. Do you want to get out?"

Tatum managed to shake her head.

Minutes later, they drifted to a stop and Layla touched her back. "We're here," she said.

Painfully, slowly, Tatum straightened.

Layla peered out her window at Tatum's building. "Nice," she said. "Cute."

"I'll see you soon," said Tatum as Stanley helped her out of the car. She thanked him, then waved weakly from the curb.

Layla blew her a kiss through the window. "Get into bed or go vom or something."

As Tatum crossed the sidewalk, she fished for her keys in her overstuffed bag. When she reached the door, she stopped. Where were they? She dug and dug, brow furrowed, pushing aside crumpled receipts, rogue ChapSticks, the notebook and pen she'd brought to the kennel in case Layla asked her to take notes.

Finally, she hooked the key ring with her finger and slapped the plastic fob against the electronic box so hard it made a cracking sound.

"Fuck," she said as she pushed through the door. Such relief.

Behind her was the street she knew well; the familiar Park Slope faces; happy shrieks spiraling up from the nearby playground. Yet when she turned back to face it all from inside, again she saw Bea's face reflected in the glass like a lingering camera flash.

She scoured the block, her nausea on momentary pause. All was calm apart from her own frantic heartbeat.

When she heard a noise behind her, she screamed.

It was Bill from down the hall with a cigarette behind his ear.

After apologizing for her reaction, Tatum stood alone in the mirrored elevator rubbing away the goose bumps on her arms, then slapping color back into her cheeks.

"You're fine," she said to her reflection. "Get a fucking grip."

13

Bea's trek back from Bushwick took even longer than the way there since the G train was delayed. She let her body slam into the people near her, not holding on to anything as the train bounced her around, apologizing as if the collisions weren't her fault until people caught on and moved away, shooting her looks from safe distances.

By the time she was aboveground in Park Slope, she was underdressed for the much cooler early evening. She walked quickly for warmth and to distract herself, and dug her phone out of her back pocket, checking all the usual apps, which rarely amounted to anything exciting: Instagram, iMessage, Tinder. Nothing from Dennis. It would be good to see him. She hesitated for a moment before crossing the street—should she visit his house again? No, she decided, she should go home.

Her shoes slapped against the pavement, a different kind of angry sound from the slow, scrapy one they'd made as she dragged herself to the kennel. The kennel. Layla. Tatum. She felt something like ravenous hunger brewing inside her, but food would not solve it. Her legs catapulted her toward home, skin soft from sweat, hair streaming behind her like a dark flag. When she reached her door, her hands shook as she pressed the key into the lock. Though she didn't want to be seen by Rosalie like this, she had no choice. Her heart was about to explode.

Upstairs, Rosalie was folded into the couch, black yarn wrapped around her fingers as ominous music played from her laptop. She glanced up, then quickly back at her work.

"Hi," she said.

Bea was panting. She bounded to the kitchen sink and gulped down mouthfuls of stale tap. When she pulled back, a viscous mixture of water and saliva laminated her chin.

Rosalie looked up at her for longer this time, still unconcerned.

Bea dabbed her stinging forehead with a wet paper towel, then opened the fridge and removed the olive jar from her bag. She placed it back in its spot, twisting it so the label faced out, as usual. She'd brought the olives with her to keep her company and keep her calm. Their muted splashing, especially on the train ride home, had been helpful, though she couldn't say her plan had totally worked. Regardless, the jar was becoming a sort of security blanket that she needed around constantly.

Staring into the fridge, she decided to make food for Rosalie. That always made her feel better. What might she want?

But as Bea scanned the contents of the fridge, she realized something was different. Usually, her side of the shelves, the left, was crowded, while Rosalie's side was barren except for a row of Cozy Shack pudding cups and a dense log of plastic-wrapped spelt bread that had appeared shortly after she'd moved in and was still unopened. Before Bea started feeding her, Rosalie had subsisted mostly on cereal from a box she kept in her room, and granola bars. Now, though, on the right side of the fridge were two stacked containers of hummus, a bag of baby carrots, a tub of vanilla yogurt, and a plastic carton of berries. Blocking the fridge with her body, Bea touched the yogurt lid. It came off easily, and the plastic film had been removed. She could see scoop marks through the clumpy white. She exhaled and resecured the lid.

"Hey," she said, closing the fridge. "Did you get groceries?"

Rosalie smiled—a sight Bea found disquieting—and nodded. "I did." She seemed proud. "You've been so generous, and it's been helpful for my energy and brain and stuff." Rosalie lifted her hands. "I haven't finger knit in a really long time, but I stopped at a yarn store on my way home from the supermarket. I got you something, too."

She dug in her sweatshirt pocket and produced a crushed box of large Band-Aids.

"We didn't have any of the big ones in the medicine cabinet, so I got some for your head."

This kind of shift in behavior was not something Bea had encountered before with Audrey. There had never been any improvements, only further and further descent. There were moments, however, when she'd expressed the desire to leave, to find a different kind of help—how had Bea managed those?

As soon as she remembered, she slipped seamlessly into character.

She opened the fridge once more and grabbed a peeled, hard-boiled egg from a Tupperware container. When she'd made it, she'd envisioned slicing it, arranging it carefully across a slab of buttered toast she'd serve to Rosalie in the morning—another of Audrey's favorite meals. Instead, she bit into it. Beheading it, in her own mind. She stared at the mushy yellow innards and felt a spark of pleasure.

As she chewed, she crossed her arms, eyebrow raised.

"Okay," she said coolly. "In that case, you don't need me to cook for you anymore."

"I mean, only if you want to." Rosalie was still smiling, though her lip was bloodied in the spot where Bea had noticed she liked to pick it. There was still evidence of her depression. It was there, beneath this new, thin layer of competence.

Bea took another messy bite of egg. Yolk crumbs shot from her mouth as she said, "I'll just stop, if you think you can do it all by yourself."

Rosalie's forehead wrinkled. "Or you can keep doing it if you want." She'd begun rubbing her silver ring with her thumb, which seemed like a nervous tic rather than a conscious action. The ring was so big, it spun around and around her index finger.

Bea placed the egg roughly on the counter. It rolled a few inches, leaving a yellow smear on the white quartz.

Slowly, she approached Rosalie. "If you think you're better and you don't need me, I'll stop."

Bea sat on the couch so their kneecaps touched, and she began stroking the end of Rosalie's knit cord with wet, yolky fingers.

Rosalie stammered, "It's not that I think I'm all better, but what you're doing means a lot, and I just want you to know that I'm trying, too."

"Okay." Bea pressed her fingers through the holes in the knots, enlarging them. "Well, you either want my help or you don't. But if you don't, you're on your own entirely. In fact, if you don't want my help, you can leave." Bea smiled. "You're not on the lease."

Rosalie was quiet, watching Bea mutilate her knitting.

"I don't have to cook for myself," she said eventually. "I just didn't want you to feel taken advantage of, or whatever." Her shoulders were rounded again, like before, and her head hung so her hair was back in front of her face. No more smile.

"It's not about what I want," Bea said, trying to sound like a therapist—clinically calm. "It's about what you need." She'd spoken the same words to Audrey, though she'd been talking about something else, threatening to withhold what was far more important to her than their apartment or even food.

Rosalie said softly, "I definitely still need support."

Bea asked, "How're your thighs?"

"They're not great. Pretty slashed up."

Bea tsked. "Well, that's no good, is it?"

Behind her hair, Rosalie sniffed. "I just want to be okay," she said. "Whenever I miss him, I cut and I feel better, or I take a quetiapine and feel better. Today, I thought I was good on my own, but then I just . . ." She glanced at the drug canister on the counter. "Ended up taking one."

Bea picked up the box of Band-Aids in Rosalie's lap.

"Stand," she commanded, and Rosalie did.

Bea tugged down her elasticated pants to reveal her bloody thighs.

The gashes were angry, puckered, red. They glistened. There were squiggly pants-fibers stuck in them. They were untreated, unhealed.

She tore open the box and began gingerly applying the bandages to Rosalie's skin.

Rosalie gasped.

"Some of these, we'll have to clean," Bea said, looking up.

A cloudy tear dangled off the tip of Rosalie's nose and fell onto Bea's forehead when she nodded.

"Sorry," Rosalie whispered.

"Do you want me to draw you a bath?" Bea asked, ignoring the sting of Rosalie's salty tear against her own wound.

"Sure. Thank you."

"And while you bathe, I'll make you soup."

Once Rosalie was cleaned and fed, and her cuts had been treated, Bea finally felt better herself. Things were as they should be again and where they should be; she'd slid the yogurt, berries, and hummus over to her side of the fridge after Rosalie had gone to her room.

When the dishes were done, Bea checked on Rosalie and found the light was off, her breath was slow and even. For what could have been minutes or hours, she sat on the floor of what had once been her sister's room, her back against the foot of the bed, feet against the wall, listening, reveling in the rhythmic sound of Rosalie's life. Eventually, she left.

Before retiring to her own room, Bea dumped the remaining quetiapine tablets in the toilet. No more of those. They had made Rosalie think she was stronger, better than she was. Bea left the empty canister in the bathroom trash bin so she would see it there.

In bed, Bea pulled out her phone and saw that Patricia had texted.

I'll be in the city tomorrow. Would
like to catch up.

Though it was late, and her mother was definitely asleep, Bea wrote back, sounds good. I'll be working so come by.

Patricia ventured into the city often to shop, work a Coop shift, or visit Vera—never, ever just to see her daughter. Usually, Patricia waited until the very last minute to tell her, too, which provided the perfect, somewhat believable excuse of, "I'm busy." Tonight, though, Bea was open, felt powerful.

She migrated to Tinder, to her last exchange with Dennis. Lately, she hadn't been swiping much, instead finding herself closely examining his profile a few times a day, zooming in on his pictures, his face: stubbly cheeks, the reflections in his eyes, trying to make out who was holding the camera. In at least one picture, she could tell that it was his own hand. Did he have friends? How much of his life resembled hers?

She pressed the messages icon. The most recent one was his rejection of her manic invitation to hang out. She typed the words sorry about the other night, and thought, *Why not*, as she pressed send.

He responded quickly.

No need to apologize. We should
still meet up sometime.

Of course he was awake.

Bea squirmed happily. First, she sent back a simple blushing emoji, then added, taking full advantage of her bold mood:

I kinda wanna see you naked.

Dennis was tall and lanky, with yellowed smoker's teeth. Though he wouldn't have been Audrey's type, Bea was definitely attracted to him

Hahaha. Oh, you do, do you?

It was noncommittal and unfun. She wanted to push him to play. She bent one leg and crossed the other over it, so the seam of her pants pressed against her clit, noncommittal masturbation until she knew which way this was heading.

Ya, I do. What do you think about that?

She was rocking back and forth against the floor, clit throbbing.

We might be able to arrange it.

She could sense his intimidation. He wasn't going to play. She stopped rolling around and typed out a simple question:

Tomorrow?

Sure I'm around.

Tomorrow, Bea realized, would be busy.

She pulled her laptop onto her bed and opened it. First iCloud, then photos. She scrolled through them so quickly they blurred. Past the mosaic of desert pictures—red dust, sprawling skies, cleft camel hooves—to the scans of childhood photographs she'd sent her mother for the collage they'd used to announce Audrey's death. Tearfully, Bea had combed through the thick rubber-banded stacks taken on disposable cameras that had lived in wicker baskets, labeled by year, in their Park Slope basement.

When she spotted one of her favorites, she paused. It was a picture of herself and Audrey, arm in arm, in matching bathing suits at the yellow house, smiling. Audrey's cheeks were pink. She wore goggles on her forehead. In the picture, they were the same height and looked very similar, which was true for the first four or so years of their lives. Why had only one of them become so tall and striking if they'd started out the same? There were a precious few photographs from those years, and Bea treasured them.

She started scrolling again, more slowly this time. The next picture to catch her eye was of herself and Audrey, Layla and Tatum, as babies, rolled up like sausages and arranged on the wooden dock in a line; next to that was another of the four of them, asleep on their sides beneath a quilt identical to the one that covered Bea's legs now. She pulled it over her head and the computer.

There was the series of Audrey posing in a pair of stained sweatpants and a tank top, her face bright and joyful. Suddenly, Bea was pinned against the mattress by grief. How impossible everything else seemed when she looked at that face. How she wished she could slip into that photograph and never return.

Finally, the grainy era of disposable camera scans ended and a less nostalgic one began: pictures of Audrey's pencil-thin limbs and gray skin. Shots of her nodding off and drooling, which Bea had taken on her phone and now served as reminders of the pain she was no longer in.

Audrey's physical transformation in the last year of her life was breathtaking. She'd resembled a corpse well before she died. Her once-shiny hair had turned brittle and frizzy, wiring the air around her emaciated face. Loose skin hung off her thighs and arms and stomach—Bea was familiar with every inch of her since she'd helped with showers, then baths—no matter how much Bea fed her. Though her mental decline was equally quick once she tried heroin, there were still moments when her personality had shone through, and Bea had cherished the times when they could laugh together—Audrey was the only person who could make her laugh—just as much as the times when Audrey needed her.

What had always baffled Bea most was how differently they had responded to the same mother who'd threatened to send them to what she called "a boarding school" in Alaska if she ever smelled weed on their clothes. She'd printed out images of grimacing teenagers lugging plows across broad fields, their faces caked in mud, which had looked photoshopped. It worked on Bea, just as intended, who had never so much as touched her lips to the orange butt of a cigarette but had the opposite effect on Audrey. Why? And why had Bea been treated like the bad one, and Audrey like the good one, when the opposite was true in the end? It wasn't fair.

In high school, several of Audrey's friends had wound up in strange, inhumane juvenile rehabilitation programs that stole weed-smoking teenagers from their childhood beds in the night, packed them into unmarked vans, scared and alone, and shipped them off to work camps. The kidnapping experience itself was enough to fuck a person up to the point where they needed drugs, but in Park Slope, it was not uncommon—it had happened to Dennis. Though Audrey hadn't ended up there herself, her choices had ruined their family, as promised, but, unexpectedly, had also bonded them as sisters.

Bea was about to close her computer when she noticed a picture of a puppy. It was gray with piercing, human eyes and a nose that gleamed like a lump of onyx. So innocent and beautiful, like Audrey when she was young, before everything. "Isn't she cute?" she could remember Audrey saying of the puppy, pressing her finger to the phone screen. "She's all mine."

Blinking back tears, Bea placed her laptop on the floor, then pulled the quilt over her face again, bathing herself in musk and memories.

Just before she drifted off, Tatum entered her mind: her surprise when she'd spotted Bea across the street as she climbed into Layla's car. Bea had followed them, allowed herself to be seen by Tatum, as punishment, and it was clear she'd achieved the desired effect. Dried tears crusting her cheeks, Bea fell asleep smiling.

14

IN THE RISING elevator, still on her seemingly endless trek upstairs from the kennel tour, Tatum had made the mistake of dropping her keys in her bag, which was deep, but usually well organized.

Typically, there was a pouch for toiletries—facial and hand lotions, a few makeup products, a wide-tooth comb meant for dividing wet curls—her wallet, which was long and green, a pair of socks to combat the office air-conditioning, a baseball cap, a ChapStick, a thin binder filled with whatever manuscripts she was reading for work, and a few other miscellaneous necessities: a Tide to Go pen, a writing pen, a few stubby tampons, and a packet of birth control to match. Nothing more than this, and nothing less.

Over the past few weeks, the contents of her bag had grown more chaotic with the rest of her life. Now, as she searched for the keys she'd just held, her hand moved like it was part of a rigged arcade claw machine, sifting through undesirable prizes; her fingers grazed crinkled receipts, loose change, a gum wrapper, a paperclip, a second, superfluous pen, the notebook she brought whenever she saw Layla, and a dirty, un-balled pair of socks.

She was spreading herself thin, no longer making time for friends the way she'd been so careful about doing since college. As a result, she'd received a few disgruntled texts, to which she'd responded with gushy words, vague promises of being better, and honest excuses. But on top of everything, she didn't have time or strength to "be better," and didn't know when she would.

One bag strap dangled off her arm as the other inched closer to the slope of her shoulder, threatening to—

The contents of her bag spilled out across the welcome mat.

She felt like crying. She was exhausted and sick, her feet hurt from walking all day, and so did her cheeks from hours of forced smiles. There were her keys, at least. Quickly, she gathered the rest of her belongings until her fingers rolled across a bullet-shaped tampon. She sat back on her heels and brought it to her face, then lifted the packet of birth control.

Each row of pills was labeled with the days of the week. The packet indicated that she should've been taking Friday's pill that night, which was white, which made it one of the placebos. She closed her eyes. It was Sunday, not Friday, and she was not on her period, which she should've been; this meant she'd missed two pills over the past month. Two pills. And the fact that she hadn't gotten her period when she always did either meant that she'd fucked up her hormones by skipping them or something else.

Her period was never late. Never. She was also unusually diligent about taking her birth control—had only missed a few pills before in her life. The first time it happened, she'd accidentally dropped it down the bathroom sink drain and called Audrey from college, inconsolable.

"Worst-case scenario," Audrey said, "and I mean absolute worst-case, abortions aren't painful." She'd had one the year before.

When Tatum admitted she hadn't even had sex that month, Audrey didn't mock her for being anxious anyway.

"It's not the biggest deal. I don't know why I'm so upset," Tatum had said through tears. But she did. In that moment, she just couldn't find the right words. Her stress had to do with the relatively new pressures of being an adult woman, of needing to take a medication every day at exactly the same time, the injustice of it.

"I understand," said Audrey. "Anxiety is as anxiety does," which was enough.

The elevator dinged at the end of the hall and Tatum remembered she was still in semipublic. Going inside would mean Ed, but going anywhere else would mean walking, either to her parents' or to a park and being in real public. At least inside there was a bathroom with a lock on the door. She could take a long bath. She could finally throw up. She could take a pregnancy test. She slapped a hand over her eyes and groaned.

Bill, whom she'd run into downstairs on his way out for a smoke, emerged from the elevator and waved before heading into his apartment.

She had to go somewhere, so she unlocked the door.

"Hey, there," said Ed. He lay on the couch, eyes glued to the violence unfolding on the television, like always.

Tatum didn't answer. Instead, she removed her shoes and headed straight for the bathroom.

"Taking a bath," she called over her shoulder.

"Ooo," said Ed, half-heartedly. "Want some compan—"

She interrupted him. "Nope."

In the bathroom, she rummaged through the disorganized space beneath the sink. This was Ed's domain. He kept various shaving accoutrements there, sex toys, too: flavored condoms, a battery-operated cock ring, dildos he'd given her that she'd never used, fuzzy handcuffs, even nipple clamps he'd purchased for himself. "I'm just curious," he'd said when she teased him about it. She shouldn't have teased him. Maybe this was karma for every mistake she'd made in her life.

In the back of the dungeon, as she called this liminal cabinet space, was a box labeled *Clear Blue*. She'd purchased the pregnancy tests for a friend. One from inside this box had told her friend she wasn't pregnant, which gave Tatum hope as she removed the plastic wrap.

She yanked off her underwear and squatted over the toilet, carefully holding the test between her legs until she thought enough urine had ricocheted off the tip. Then she removed it, fastened its cap back on, and continued peeing while setting a timer on her phone. Two minutes. The little screen blinked while it thought.

There was no question what she would do if she was pregnant, which she almost definitely wasn't. She definitely wasn't. She wasn't. She'd only had sex once, maybe twice, over the past month. People tried hard to get pregnant. In fact, she'd recently learned that people could only get pregnant a few days out of their menstrual cycle. She'd grown up believing that she could get pregnant any day, at any time, from as little as the decision to wear a short skirt on the subway, because essentially this was what she'd been taught. The health teachers she'd had and trusted, even in progressive New York City, had lied to her about her body. And it wasn't fair to be told an untruth intended to make her fear herself and the world. And, as she flushed the toilet and craned over her still-blinking test, she thought about how this wouldn't be fair, either.

"Please," she prayed to no one in particular. "Please be negative, please be negative."

But something told her it wouldn't be. She tried her best to ignore it, to remind herself how unlikely it was, but when the test finally stopped blinking and revealed the word "Pregnant," written in a casual font, Tatum wasn't surprised. She was, however, weak.

She lay on the bathroom floor, staring into the blinding recessed bulbs in the ceiling, letting her eyes burn. Would her life ever stop moving too fast? Would she ever catch up to it? Would it ever just, well, stop altogether?

A fetus was growing inside her now. She pressed a hand to her pelvis. It was convex and warm. A fetus that she didn't want was in there, protected from her by her own flesh. God, she wasn't old enough for this. And yet people younger than her were mothers. People younger than her were married. People younger than her were millionaires, authors, hit television show creators—probably even founders of big, successful dog kennels. What would Layla think?

More than anything, Tatum wished she could call Audrey. Since she couldn't, she was grateful for the call they'd shared all those years ago when she was so naïve.

"Abortions aren't painful," Audrey had said, then paused before elaborating. "It feels like nothing. The worst is when you try to have sex again afterward, but that just feels like tightness and then it passes."

How would Ed respond? Tatum was horrified by the thought. She didn't want to tell him, wanted to deal with it herself in secret, felt that it would be her right to do just that if she so chose. However, the idea of facing this alone was too much. If she didn't tell anyone, she worried it would paralyze her. And if she was paralyzed, unable to arrange for it to be vacuumed out, then by default she'd end up giving birth to it. The word *baby* made her nauseous. Or maybe it wasn't just the word. She sat up, pressed the toilet seat back, and wretched into the gleaming white bowl, knowing Ed would hear.

A few seconds later there was a knock.

"Babe?" he called. "You all right?"

Tatum slid across the floor and unlocked the door, then slid back.

Ed poked his face inside the room and turned on the bathroom fan.

"Damn," he said, at the sight of her, bare-bottomed and spiny, hunched over the toilet. "What's up?"

Tatum felt him crouch behind her, his knee bounce against her back. She didn't speak. He'd notice the test soon enough on the counter.

"Was it something you ate?" he asked. "Are you sick?"

She shook her head.

"No?"

She shook her head again.

"Okay," he said. "Can I get you some water?"

She shook her head.

"Is there anything I can do?"

She gestured at the counter.

"What?" he said, rising up. His voice strained. "What're you—" Then suddenly he was standing. She could hear crinkling plastic, his crinkling dry mouth when he spoke: "Oh my god," he said. "Are you fucking serious?"

Tatum said nothing but wretched again. It was as if she'd only become pregnant after seeing the word appear. Now, immediately, she was symptomatic. But she'd also been nauseous in the car with Layla, and overwhelmed, and breathless. Still, everything was different now.

Ed did not touch her, just repeated, "Oh my god," over her sounds.

This time, when she finished, she finally felt empty. Ed sat on the wall of the tub. "Babe."

She noticed tears in his eyes. "This is fucking—" He ran a hand through his hair. "This is fucking amazing. How did this happen?"

Tatum squinted at him.

He was holding the test gently in both hands as if it, itself, was a baby. Their baby. "I-I-" He stammered as tears streamed down his face. His mouth hung open. His breath washed over her, the smell of it making her sick again.

"Can you close your mouth?" she asked. "Your breath." She pinched her nose.

Ed did as she asked, lips making a *thwoop* as they quickly connected. "Babe," he said again, lowering himself onto the floor next to her, shielding his mouth with one hand, and wrapping an arm around her. It felt good to be hugged. To feel warmth. She realized that she was shaking; the tile was cold against her skin; the effort of vomiting had left her frail. It was nice to feel his strength.

He sniffed. The sound was loud in her ear.

"Oh my god," he said. "Should I—" He leaned back and grabbed her shoulders. "I mean, do you want to marry me? Like, do you want to get married? Should we do that or something? I don't even know—"

"What?"

"I don't know what to say right now." He was smiling, laughing, crying. He was incredulous. Had he always wanted kids so young? He'd never said so before.

Tatum was incredulous, too, except not so joyfully. Two hours ago, she'd been touring a dog kennel with Layla and Bea, and now she was a mother. And Ed was proposing? On the bathroom floor, next to a toilet filled with bile?

"We're not doing that," she said, her fatigue and depression allowing for pure honesty.

"Okay," he said. He was stroking her kneecap, drawing hearts on it with his finger. She moved her leg out of his reach to prevent herself from puking again.

"Please," she said. "I just need space."

He scooted backward, eyes still leaking, lips pulled tight by a smile. "Sure," he said. "Sure, sure. Want some water now?"

Tatum shook her head. "I want you to be quiet." She'd never spoken to him like this before. It wasn't the same as picking a silly fight. Her voice now was barbed, not by annoyance or even anger, but disgust. He was making her sick. Her nausea canceled out her inhibitions. She was raw, exposed, her underwear in a pile somewhere, torso folded over her legs because that was most comfortable.

"Sure," he said, unfazed though he should've been. If he really knew her, he would've been. "Sure, sure, sure."

They sat quietly for a moment, as she'd requested, listening to the HVAC humming in the walls.

"I still can't believe this," he said eventually, reaching for her foot, guiding it into his lap.

"I need you," she said, jerking her stolen leg at him as if to kick him, then crossing it over her other leg, "to not touch me."

For the first time Ed began to look concerned. "Okay," he said. "Did I do something to upset you or—"

Tatum lifted her head. "Yes." *For starters, you got me pregnant.*

"Oh," said Ed. "I mean, I know I probably shouldn't have asked you to marry me like that. If you're pissed off, I get it. I was just trying to do the right thing because we're, like, pregnant. But I can wait, and put more time into it and also thought, and get a ring and stuff. I'm really sorry. The words just kinda came out, you know?"

Now he was nervous. He was never nervous. *He should be nervous*, Tatum thought. She felt eerily mad. Like she could do something horrible, something bloody and totally out of character for the agreeable girl next door she usually played.

"*We*'re not pregnant," she said. "And I'm not having a baby."

Finally, his eyes dulled; his face fell. "Oh," he said. "So, you're not—"

"No," she said. Shamefully, she was enjoying this part, the pain in his voice. "I'm going to get an abortion."

His smile continued to wilt. "You've already decided?"

Tatum nodded, still fueled by unjustified vitriol. Or maybe it was justified. Or maybe that wasn't how emotion worked. It wasn't either justified or not.

"There's nothing I can say or do?" he asked.

Tatum shook her head. Acid rose into her throat again. She swallowed hard.

"Can you tell me why?"

Tatum shook her head. "I don't have to." Breathing made her nauseous.

"Okay," he said. "You don't have to, but I'd really like to understand your thinking here." His shoulders were slumped. He was sitting with his hands on his knees, head cocked, looking at her the way a dog stares helplessly at its stationary ball, waiting for it to be tossed.

Tatum turned back to the toilet and wretched again. Panting, she pressed down the flusher. Was she really going to do this? Now? On the bathroom floor? Beneath a positive pregnancy test? During a category-five mental spiral, after putting it off for more than a year, hoping Ed would finish his screenplay and revert back to the driven, inspiring person he'd been when they first met, which hopefully would revive her appreciation of him? Yes. Yes, she was doing this now. Where would she go when it was done? His parents paid for their apartment and her parents' apartment was too small for her to live in comfortably now that she was an adult with things and a need for privacy. She squared her shoulders and wiped the corners of her mouth with toilet paper. Still, yes. This was happening. It was now or never.

"Because I don't think our relationship is working," she said. "I don't think we've been happy for a while."

Ed's face twisted in disbelief. "You haven't been happy?"

Tatum tried to swallow a laugh. This heartless monster lived inside her always. There were few opportunities for her to release it.

"Why are you smiling?" he asked, chin dimpled like a shrunken brain.

"I should've said all this to you a long time ago."

Ed dropped his head into his hands. "Are you—" He stopped.

Tatum waited for him to look at her, then nodded. "I am."

He yelped as if she'd stepped on his tail. "You're telling me you're pregnant and breaking up with me?"

Tatum considered this, then said, "I guess." She placed a hand on her stomach again, wishing she could remove the intruder and give it to him. He could have it. She wanted it gone. Once she finally said goodbye to him, she wanted him totally and completely gone.

"Do you suddenly hate me or something?" he spat through his tears. "You seem to really fucking hate me, the way you're talking right now."

Did she hate him? There was a time when she definitely hadn't, when she'd probably loved him. And no, even now what she hated was how long they'd been together while she was miserable, the fact that he'd never noticed. She felt numb, cold, bitter, completely at odds with the person she'd learned how to be, the person she'd been told she was since birth, the one who was always polite, caring, compassionate.

"No," she said. "I don't hate you." She was doing her best to soften, but it wasn't easy. This strange other-her was armored. "We spent many important years together. But I'm going to move out and get an abortion." She still sounded mechanical—heartless. There was nothing she could do about it. Slowly, she drew herself up to standing, steadying herself on the vanity. Standing over him, her vagina was at his eye level. She felt no shame. No doubt. She felt, as she strode out of the bathroom—leaving him alone to cry—the way she imagined Bea felt all the time: brave.

That night, she quickly gathered her necessities, crammed them into bags, and called Vera to tell her the news: she was coming home.

Every few minutes, she had to run to the bathroom to vomit, over Ed, who was still crumpled like a wet towel on the floor. The total chaos was making everything possible, she knew, stopping her from thinking too hard about what was happening, what it would mean. Somehow, she managed to remember her cell phone charger, laptop, toothbrush, contact lenses, socks and underwear, some pajama-like items, work pants, work shirts. She secured her leather tote to her suitcase, filled a plastic take-out bag with two pairs of shoes, slung her coat over her shoulder, and left, weighted by suitcases. She called, "I'm leaving," as the door swung shut. This wouldn't be the last time she saw him. There would be more conversations, less charged ones, more emotional ones, to come. But for now, she wasn't in the headspace for anything more than "I'm leaving."

Balled up in her pocket was a vomit bag, though her nausea had subsided for the moment as she descended in the elevator. The last time she'd ridden this elevator, a few hours earlier, she never could've imagined this was about to happen. She hated this elevator. This building. This whole sterile, industrial aesthetic that was slowly but surely transforming Brooklyn for the worse. Finally, when she thought of her childhood bedroom, cramped and dingy—which her mother had turned into a makeshift gym but had never removed her bed from, "just in case," she'd always said—Tatum began to weep. Not guttural, heartbroken sobs but soft gasps. Her bags were heavy, straps cutting into her shoulders, and bulky, and they were difficult to maneuver onto the street, which was surprisingly slick from rain she hadn't realized was falling. She'd have to call a car. Feeling afraid, uncomfortable, wet, she longed for childhood, when she was never alone or scared of anything but the dark—it glowed before her, bright and yellow through the gloom, but she knew better than to run toward it into traffic. With every passing second, the fetus grew. And if she lived somewhere else in the world, in the country, she'd have no choice but to deliver it.

The car she'd called was one minute away. She strained against her bags, staring up at the thick, matte sky, until she heard the rush of wheels against rain. Bea might be out there, somewhere, watching, but Tatum no longer cared.

The driver got out and helped load her bags.

"Thanks," Tatum said as she climbed in after them. She clicked her seat belt and lay down, stretching out across the back seat, resting her head on the take-out bag of shoes. If the driver mistook her depression for intoxication, she didn't care. For a moment, she didn't care about anything except rest.

In her pocket, her cell phone buzzed.

It took all her strength to extract it and hold it to her face. Of course, it was a text from Layla.

> Hey. I promised you a special trip
> back when we started this whole
> thing. I think we could all use it now.
> Call me.

Tatum lifted the phone to her ear with trembling fingers. A retreat, somewhere beautiful and luxurious, maybe with palm trees and five-star accommodations, was just what the doctor ordered.

15

THAT'LL BE FORTY-SIX dollars," said Bea.

It was late afternoon; outside, the sun painted the pavement in rapidly shifting patterns. Apparently, it was windy. People held on to their baseball caps as they passed the window.

The woman Bea was speaking to towered over two identical tots, their little heads capped by thick black curls, their pants sagging to fit their diapers. They had just finished painting identical ceramic frog statues in baseball uniforms with so many thickly applied colors, Bea knew they would emerge from the kiln in disappointing shades of brown.

"Great," said the woman. "So, if I come back in a week, they'll be ready?"

"Mm-hmm."

The machine buzzed, then beeped when she tapped her card, and Bea shook her head.

"I'll try swiping, then."

As they waited for the machine to process, Bea asked, "Are they twins?" The woman, whose name was Ada, according to her card, smiled.

"What gave it away? Everything about them?"

Bea nodded. "I had a twin," she said, and Ada's face fell instantly.

In the end, she paid in cash—the machine had stopped working. Bea called Savage to let her know the card reader was "being a little bitch again," while, toward the front of the studio, Ada muscled her kids into their stroller seats. Savage said she'd be right there. Patricia was due to arrive at any minute, too.

After helping squeak the double-wide stroller out the front door, Bea watched Ada face the wind. She wished she could drop everything and follow her down the street, learn her ways. This was the sort of woman who made motherhood seem appealing. The sort of woman who embraced the havoc of one son dragging a paint-soaked brush across the other's shirt. When she'd noticed, she'd said, "Whoops. Well, it looks cooler now anyway."

Patricia would've lost her mind. She'd always spoken to her daughters as if they were dogs—"Bad Bea"—as if they were misbehaving when they were just being kids.

Instead of following her, Bea busied herself by picking thick glaze droplets off tables. She hoped Savage would be in and out quickly before Patricia arrived, not because she'd resent Bea for having a visitor, but because Patricia was conspicuously disgusted by Savage's piercings and tattoos. Alas, her mother barreled into the studio, prompt as ever, jacket thicker and more tightly fastened than the spring temperature necessitated. *Overreacting, as usual*, Audrey would've said under her breath.

"My commute was a mess," said Patricia first thing, mouth barely escaping the high neck of her coat. "Don't even ask." She began disrobing, walking straight into the back area, past the EMPLOYEES ONLY sign. "To make matters worse, we're practically in the eye of a hurricane."

Bea looked at her skeptically.

"You haven't been out there," she said. "Don't be fooled by the sun. The sun doesn't knock trees over."

"Nice to see you, too," said Bea as Patricia noisily dragged a metal stool across the floor.

"Oh, stop," she said.

Her face was skeletal, which was how she liked to keep it. She had a treadmill at home and walked on it for forty-five minutes a day at an incline of twelve percent and an impressive pace, with weights strapped to her ankles. In pictures from her youth, she was beautiful, though not quite Audrey's degree of striking—her face was extra-long like Bea's and the tip of her nose swung to the left—but more beautiful than Bea, who'd inherited her father's small eyes and adolescent acne, which had left permanent craters in her cheeks. Patricia was addicted to "wellness" and health, except when it came to consuming enough food, "I'm too stressed out to eat," she was always saying.

"What brings you to Park Slope today?" asked Bea. She stretched and her mother frowned at the hairs under her arms and the roll of flesh above her waistband.

"Groceries," she said. "Making my biweekly Coop pilgrimage with Vera in"—she checked her watch—"about forty-five minutes."

She never left much time for Bea, which was fine, as they didn't have much to talk about.

"Cool," said Bea. "My boss is supposed to arrive any second to fix something."

"Oy," said Patricia.

"Get it out now."

"I just don't understand why anyone would want to do that to their body."

Bea said, "That's right, get it out."

"I'm entitled to my opinion."

"No one said you weren't."

Absently, Bea brushed her bangs out of her eyes, forgetting the gash on her forehead. Patricia grabbed her arm. "What have you done to your face?"

"Nothing," said Bea. "It's a scrape."

"That looks bad, Beatrix. Really, you must go to urgent care as soon as you're done here. Will you text me when you're on your way and immediately after your appointment? I can make one for you now."

She began digging for her phone. "People think they're walk-in only, but they're not if you call and insist."

"Stop," said Bea.

Patricia's eyes pleaded. When Bea shook her head, she dropped her phone and folded her hands in her lap.

"So, aside from the grisly untreated wound in the middle of your head, how're things?"

Bea said, "Fine."

"Right," said Patricia. "Well, I have some articles to send you about safety around canines and some statistics, too, and now I'll have to send you something about the risks of infection from open cuts."

Bea was quiet.

"Sepsis—ever heard of it?"

"How about instead of sending me articles, you don't, because I'll never read them."

"Oh, hush. It's important. You'll see what I mean."

"I won't," said Bea, picking at an especially stubborn paint blob beside the register. "Because I won't even open your email."

"Beatrix, why don't you do me a favor and take care of yourself? If you won't do it for yourself, then do it for me."

This should've registered as love—at least in part—but it didn't. It was love without the good, the trust, and the respect, which left only the annoying and the nagging.

Bea shrugged. Though she'd all but moved on from the kennel, she wouldn't say so to her mother. Partly because, if she did, Vera would know, and then Tatum would know, and partly because, when Patricia worried, at least it meant she was thinking of Bea. Even in her absence, Audrey took up nearly all the space inside their mother's brain. It wasn't fair and never had been.

Sometimes Bea wondered if Patricia was to blame for her social problems; maybe she was shaped—deformed, othered—by the very words her mother had often used to describe her long before it was fair: *stunted, different*. Audrey was the perfect beauty, her pride, whereas Bea was, well, different; "on a different path," or sometimes, when asked about Bea, Patricia's only response was to wince and shrug.

"I can only send them," said Patricia—a surprisingly unforceful conclusion.

Bea's phone buzzed.

It was a text from Layla sent only to her.

> Hey. I know things are weird right now so I thought it might be a good time for some bonding. I'm not sure you'll be open to this, and I understand why you wouldn't be, but I had the idea of taking you and Tatum to the yellow house for a weekend. Let me know your thoughts. We can talk more before you commit if you'd like.

"What?" Bea said aloud.

Patricia took a long look at her own phone before placing it face-down on the desk and saying, "Put away your phone, sweetie, it's rude."

"Layla just—" Bea stopped and reread the message.

"Close your mouth."

Bea looked up.

"Layla just invited me to the yellow house."

Patricia's jaw dropped.

Bea looked back at the message, blinking hard to make sure it was real, while Patricia shielded her eyes with quivering fingers. Eventually, she produced an unconvincing smile, and her hand fell away. "Oh, how nice," she said, as if she wasn't recovering from what had seemed like a miniature panic attack.

Bea shook her head. "I mean, how can she do that? I guess the house is still for rent or something?"

She could tell that Patricia knew the answer.

"Mom?"

Patricia stood up as if to leave, reached for her coat, then sat back down empty-handed and said, "Well, it's her house. Or Nancy's, at least."

Before now, Bea had never even considered that the house still existed. Her longing for it was akin to her shimmery, nostalgic longing for her paternal grandmother, who'd died when she was ten.

"So, what about the Jeans, then?" she asked, the simplest of the million questions racing through her mind.

The Jeans—a lesbian couple, both named Jean—used to own the yellow house. Patricia was always terrified of upsetting them: "Don't you dare break the Jeans' dishes," she'd say when Bea carried too many bowls to the dining table at once. They were constantly calling the Jeans to make sure this or that was allowed, for instance, to check if they could use the dusty Frisbees in the garage.

Patricia's face darkened. "Nancy bought it from them."

Bea was about to ask more questions when Savage shouldered her way through the door.

"Hello, there," said Patricia, merrily, as if nothing had just been revealed. "Lovely place you've got here. I'm Bea's mother."

Savage grunted, then said, "I remember you."

The two of them had met many times and it was embarrassing that Patricia continued to reintroduce herself.

Savage ducked beneath Bea's knees, stroking the cords that ran from the computer into the wall.

"Bea," hissed Patricia. "Get over here by me."

But Bea stayed where she was, still dumbstruck.

Eventually, Savage emerged, the scent of tobacco stinging the air around her. Metal clinked with her every movement.

"Should be good now," she said, running a hand through her dark hair. Without another word, she clomped out of the studio.

Patricia breathed a deep sigh when she was gone. "I hate cigarettes," she said. "Consider yourself disowned if you ever pick up that nasty habit." Little did she know that Audrey had smoked until her last day on Earth. There was so much Patricia didn't know or pretended not to.

"When did Nancy buy the house?" asked Bea.

Again, Patricia sighed. "What do you want me to say?" Her eyes were misty. Maybe it was in their shared best interest to stop, at least for now. It was getting late. Bea had plans to meet Dennis when the studio closed, which meant she had things to do before then. Not that anyone would care if she didn't sweep or wash brushes, but if she didn't do it now, then future-her would have to. Plus, she wasn't sure yet how much she wanted to know from her mother. She was hardened in so many ways, but somehow this topic made her feel like a little girl.

"So, will you go back?" Patricia broke the silence.

Bea wasn't certain, but why wouldn't she? It would be challenging, things were tense with Layla and Tatum, but wasn't everything hard? If she went, she'd bring Rosalie, which would make it easier. It would be good to see it again. Maybe it would help somehow.

"I guess," said Bea.

"Oh." Patricia covered her face with her hands. Through her fingers, she whispered, "Won't you miss her too much, being there?" She shifted to face the back of the studio, away from the street.

Bea was uncomfortable showing emotion to her mother. Patricia often made unfair assumptions. If Bea let her guard down and cried, even if Patricia was supportive in the moment, later on she might spontaneously decide she was unfit to live alone and stop paying rent for the apartment, forcing Bea to rot in Westchester under her watchful eye.

"I guess," said Bea. "But I miss her here, too."

Patricia scoffed. "And you think I don't?"

"Is that what I said?"

Patricia pulled a handkerchief from her bag.

When she was young, Bea remembered how rare and nauseating it was to catch her mother crying. Now she'd seen her cry countless times. The boundaries of their relationship had warped and changed, which happened in any parent-child relationship, but in their case, the process had been accelerated.

While Patricia took some deep breaths, Bea began tidying up. Eventually, her mother said, "Okay, I'm off." Bea could hear the zip of her bag without looking, the shift of her metal stool as she stood.

"Do you remember Dennis?" asked Bea. She was arranging wet brushes in the plastic carton she'd brought in after ordering wonton soup one night. "Dennis Sweeney. His parents are—"

"Rod and Mary," Patricia finished. "Of course I do. He certainly caused them a lot of grief back in the day."

And what about the grief Audrey caused, infinitely worse than what Dennis had ever done to his mother? Whenever Patricia spoke haughtily like this, Bea felt like knocking her back down to earth.

"I'm supposed to meet up with him soon."

Patricia sneered. "Oh, great," she said. "Fantastic."

"He's different now," said Bea, because it felt like the thing to say. Realistically, Dennis had never done anything worse than smoke pot when he was young, as far as Bea knew. Patricia could act holier than thou, but she took pills—drugs—to settle her nerves as needed. Just because they'd been prescribed by a doctor didn't mean they were safer or better.

"I hope so," said Patricia. She sounded tired. "At any rate, I better get going."

"Me too," said Bea.

"Apparently Tatum moved home last night." This was always how they gossiped: hastily, as if it was a chore.

"Interesting," said Bea, though she didn't really care.

Patricia brushed her hair behind her ears and inspected her face in a little ceramic mirror available for painting, though no one ever chose it.

"I didn't have long to speak to Vera this morning, but I'll get more information presently, I assume. Bye, darling."

Patricia kissed Bea on the cheek.

"See ya."

The door opened and a gust of wind rushed into the studio.

This time, Bea couldn't help herself. Instead of completing the outstanding tasks before closing, she yanked her own jacket off the hook, dimmed the studio lights, flipped over the OPEN sign, and left.

Patricia walked in the irritable way most New Yorkers did, huffing at people who accidentally stepped in her path or were moving too slow, even at a man using a cane. She tapped her foot at red lights, checked her watch, rolled her eyes, as if she was late for a business meeting, not on time to grocery shop with a friend. When she arrived, Bea stood a few dozen feet from the Coop's entrance, carefully scanning the mass of crossing guard uniforms worn by delivery people—who were also lawyers, CEOs, doctors, actors--and the cloud of wired shopping carts. There was the person checking ID cards and the line of jean jacket wearers leading up to him.

After her mother disappeared inside, Bea's eyes settled on the door where a commotion was unfolding: a member was attempting to bring a nonmember in, "Not to buy anything, just to keep me company." Their voices echoed off the brownstones and Bea could hear everything perfectly from where she stood. The hopeful shopper was denied repeatedly, since the nonmember had left her New York State ID card at home. Eventually, they gave up and left, heads hanging. Less than a minute later, another person was trying to get in using someone else's ID and a similar scene unfolded.

Here, Bea felt especially exposed. This was where everyone in Park Slope pooled. She recognized many faces: siblings of former classmates, parents of former classmates, Sandra Cruz—who was a former classmate. Branches creaked in the wind. She kept her cool: chin down, hood conservatively positioned like Rosalie's. She felt like a character in a video game. To win, she must remain unseen in a place filled with people she knew.

She scanned the Coop windows, unable to make anything out through them. But they were in there, Patricia and Vera, and they were talking about her. She'd wanted more information about the yellow house without having to ask, had hoped to read it off their reactions, but clearly wouldn't have the opportunity. When she checked, her phone read 6:54 p.m. She and Dennis had planned to meet at 7:00 p.m.

Despite her lateness, she was still leaning against the tree when Mary Sweeney emerged from inside wearing a Coop-branded apron—Mary Sweeney, mother of Dennis Sweeney. Startled, Bea darted off down the block. She walked quickly, wondering if Mary and Patricia had already run into each other, or if they would. It was clear that Mary had only stepped out for a moment, as she was hugging a collapsed cardboard box and heading for the recycling bins.

Bea pulled out her phone as she walked, and typed, Made you a grilled cheese and a plate of steamed broccoli. You can heat both up in the microwave. Be home later. And I have something to tell you. <333

"<333" was how she'd always signed off on texts to Audrey. Having Rosalie at the yellow house would not fill the Audrey-shaped void, but what Bea couldn't tell her mother, couldn't tell anyone, was how alike they were, because she'd made them that way.

16

Inside the park Slope Food Coop, two women stood over the cheese fridge. They'd been there for almost two hours. One clutched a hunk of Jarlsberg as tightly as she might a floatation device after a shipwreck, the other smiled easily. The white-knuckled one wore a heavy jacket, a thick cashmere scarf knotted around her neck, and a woolen skirt that ended a few inches above her ankles. The smiling one wore thick pink glasses, loose cargo pants, and cracked leather loafers.

"Vera, I swear, she's supposed to be here," said one to the other. "Right here, right now."

"Relax," said Vera. Her voice was silky and full, like the narrator of a meditation app. "If Nancy isn't here today, then she isn't." She adjusted her glasses. "There's nothing we can do about it."

"If she isn't here today, that means we won't be able to do this again for two more weeks. It isn't easy for me to get here from Westchester, and suddenly the kids are going to the yellow house, and—"

Vera interrupted, "It'll be okay. If it's in two weeks, then it's in two weeks. If they go to the yellow house before we're able to see her, so what?" She touched her friend's shoulder. "Patricia, breathe."

Patricia gasped, grateful for the reminder. "I don't understand. Is she just allowed to skip shifts now that she's Nancy-fucking-Bernard?

Is that what the Coop has become? The system said she'd be restocking cheese today during the closing shift."

Working in the membership office placed Patricia in the hub of neighborhood gossip and gave her the power to find out when other members were working. Over the years, she'd typed Nancy's name into the computer before, though earlier that week marked the first time she'd done so in the hope of finding her rather than avoiding her.

This was their last resort; both she and Vera had tried texting and calling the updated phone number the Coop had on file, to no avail. They were determined to make contact, though they had no set outcome in mind. Just to see her and be seen and feel something and say something, whatever seemed right in the moment. Maybe they could laugh together again—just once more would be enough.

"Come on," said Vera, stroking Patricia's knuckles to relax her grip on the Jarlsberg. "Are you going to buy this, or shall we put it back?"

Patricia blinked. "We should put it back."

Vera struggled to remove it from Patricia's rigid fingers. Once she'd managed to, she said, "Shall we move away from the fridge, too?"

Patricia was shivering. She was always cold.

Vera guided her to the produce. Nancy wouldn't be difficult to spot from there. She was large—tall and thick—and pretty, with blond hair.

Unable to help herself, Vera began inspecting the apples. For her Coop shift, she was stationed in the composting department, combing through fruits and vegetables, searching for rottens. She likened it to city gardening.

"No good," said Vera, lifting a particularly bruised apple, handing it to a woman passing by whose son had been in Tatum's peewee gymnastics class—his name was Donald or Dennis or something like that. Donald/Dennis's mother was wearing a Coop apron, her short blond hair gelled into little points. Vera smiled to show recognition. Her name was Mary, Vera was seventy percent sure.

"Hi there," said Mary. "Thanks for that," and she dropped the apple into her apron pocket to be composted.

Patricia's gaze was still locked on the cheese fridge. The store was beginning to empty.

"This is futile," she said.

Vera was disappointed, too. She'd wanted this to work as much as Patricia; the difference was that disappointment hurt Patricia more. The fact that her daughter had died, well, it was always relevant. No matter how much pain Vera witnessed, or how much pain she herself had felt over the loss of Audrey, whom she'd considered family, she still couldn't imagine—couldn't bring herself to even try.

"Shall we call it, then?" asked Vera, extending a hand to her old friend. Patricia was the only person, aside from Tatum and her husband, she held hands with. Theirs, despite everything—all they'd been through and all the years they'd spent alive—was still a girlish relationship in certain cherished ways.

Patricia laid her fingers across Vera's palm and Vera began tugging her along.

"Should you tell someone she didn't show up for her shift?" Vera asked, jokingly. "That's your job up there in the office, after all, you snitch."

"That's just what we need," said Patricia. "For me to get her in trouble."

They were laughing when Patricia's shoulder collided with someone, sending hunks of cheese rolling across the floor.

Immediately, Vera knelt to help.

"So sorry," she said to the pair of velvet Chanel-emblazoned flats in front of her. "Give me a hand here, Pat." She tugged on the hem of Patricia's skirt. But Patricia didn't move.

Vera looked up as Patricia whispered, "Hey, Nan."

Immediately, Vera stood, leaving the cheese on the floor. Her face broke into the widest version of her smile. "Nan," she practically sang. "Can I hug you?" A few cheeses were still wedged in the crook of Nancy's arm. Her face was plump and smoothed the way most New York City women's were by a certain age, at least among lofty circles.

"Oh my god," said Nancy, ignoring Vera's outstretched arms. Either her face lacked the ability to emote due to injectables, or she was in shock. Her hair was dyed golden blond, a shade or two lighter than it used to be, and cut into a flattering, layered shape. At least her fingers had aged like theirs, though hers wore diamonds. Her husky voice was the same, which was minorly comforting, and very similar to her daughter's adult voice.

Vera and Patricia realized, in that moment, their expectations of this reunion had been sky-high, despite promising each other they had none; nothing more than a shared moment in time, they'd said. But no matter what transpired—warm embraces, declarations of love even—it wouldn't be enough. They'd never find anything close to what was lost, and that's what they'd come looking for if they were honest. And so, as Nancy stepped awkwardly into Vera's open arms, they both felt empty and jealous of their daughters, who'd folded easily back into each other's lives.

Instead of speaking, the three of them silently gathered the spilled yellow wedges and soft Brie wheels, and walked with them to the fridge. When it was all arranged, Nancy said, "Thanks." Her lipstick was crimson—vibrant and carefully drawn.

Was she still angry? Or was she so altered by success, she didn't know how to make the word "thanks" sound genuine anymore?

Unconvincingly, Patricia said, "What a surprise to see you here."

"Yes," said Nancy. Her fingernails had French tips. In the old days, she'd been the talker of their group. The life of their party of three.

They'd met in a prenatal yoga class. Out of all the swollen bellies, Nancy had invited Vera's and Patricia's over for tea. At first it had seemed random, but they quickly learned that was Nancy. She acted on impulse and instinct. She was also the first to suggest renting a summer house together.

Vera touched her shoulder. "Really good to see you."

Were they still angry at her?

Nancy said, "You too."

"Can you believe our girls are friends again?" Vera wanted to clap her hands, snap her fingers, wake Nancy up, but Nancy's eyes were trained on the space between them, as if she was mapping her escape.

Did she feel guilty?

She hadn't even called Patricia when Audrey died, instead sent a printed card and an extravagant flower arrangement that was more difficult to dispose of than it was beautiful.

And before that, she'd purchased the yellow house. When they'd left it, that last-last day of August, none of them had known it was the end. But a month later, Nancy secretly offered the Jeans well over asking for the house, beating out Patricia's comparatively modest offer of full ask. Though this had taken place before *Tammy Rose*, before Nancy was ultra-mega-rich, she'd always done well for herself, and had family money, too.

After a summer filled with Patricia's excited whispers about the yellow house traditions she'd start once she owned it, always careful she was out of earshot of the children, like inviting everyone to celebrate Thanksgiving and Christmas there, Nancy had swooped in behind her back, like a coward, and ruined it all. Patricia hadn't wanted her kids to know she was devastated, or anything about their financials, or what their family had just missed out on: the yellow house as their country home. They were only twelve, then fourteen, then seventeen, then nineteen, at which point it didn't matter anymore, as they'd stopped asking what happened—where Nancy and Layla had gone.

Once the initial shock had worn off, about a month after the house would've—should've—been hers, Patricia had confronted Nancy, who'd explained that, at the last second, she'd realized she wanted it and could afford it.

"It's really that simple," she said. "I hope you can understand."

That she hadn't come clean until after papers were signed, though, indicated she knew just how un-simple her decision really was. Usually, Patricia felt endeared by Nancy's impulsivity, her happy-go-lucky way, but this time Nancy had impulsively fucked her over. Nothing "Oh, that's just typical Nancy" about it.

"The yellow house is where I write my best work," she'd insisted, in response to Patricia saying she couldn't understand. "I need to keep working there."

Nancy had spent the early hours of many summer days locked away in her bedroom, at the desk by the window that overlooked the lake, crafting what would become the first season of her big hit, *Tammy Rose*. Sometimes she'd bring pages downstairs for Patricia and Vera to read and critique. Patricia could remember thinking, *Maybe we're the key to your best work, not the yellow house.*

Instead, through tears she'd said, "But if I owned it, you could've gone and worked there whenever you wanted, of course. That was my whole point. It would've been our shared place."

"Yes, but I feel the same. You can use it whenever you want, so what's the difference if you own it or I own it?"

"The difference is you lied." There were other differences, too, which neither admitted to the other.

Now here they stood, fifteen years and the death of a child later, by the cheese fridge. If their summer tradition had continued, if they hadn't fallen out, if Patricia's family had had that house to run off to whenever they needed time away, maybe things would've been different. Maybe it would have remained a refuge, and maybe Audrey would— Patricia swallowed hard. She wanted it to be true, wanted someone else to blame.

"No," said Nancy, "I can't," and Patricia couldn't even remember what she was responding to.

The three of them were quiet.

If Nancy was still angry, then why? Because of what Patricia had called her more than a decade earlier in the heat of anger: "narcissist," "selfish," "asshole"?

Their fight had escalated quickly after Patricia accused Nancy of lying, but Nancy was the one to start it with her actions and end it by saying, "Never contact me again. I want nothing to do with either of you."

Her words were especially unfair to Vera, who wasn't even directly involved but had taken Patricia's side.

"Are you doing something after this?" Vera tried. Nancy was still avoiding eye contact. "We could get a glass of wine somewhere. For old times' sake? Or you're welcome to come to my place, though it's what it always was: small and stuffy."

Nancy said nothing.

"I only offer that because I know you've"—Vera glanced at Patricia—"I know you're pretty recognizable these days."

"Uh," said Nancy, "this is all a bit sudden, and I do have a late dinner to get to."

"Did you know they're going back?" Patricia blurted. Her voice shook, which happened when she was nervous or angry or crying or almost crying.

Nancy said, "Yes, of course I do. It's my—" She stopped. "It's a cute idea, don't you think?"

It occurred to Vera that the polite thing would be to thank Nancy for helping their daughters with the kennel: for financing it through Layla. But doing so would anger Patricia, who was still so against it.

The Coop was empty of shoppers now; everyone working their shifts was busy closing for the night. Vera was glad they had some privacy. She said, "I've asked Tatum to take pictures while they're there."

Patricia's eyes narrowed. She hated any lack of acknowledgment of Audrey's absence, but also hated talking about her, which meant that she hated most conversations. In this case, her feelings were especially powerful. Audrey wouldn't be at the yellow house with the rest of the girls, so Patricia didn't want any pictures. They were worthless to her. Life itself was worthless. Looking at pictures of their kids' stupid smiles in front of yellow clapboard or on the dock would be like rubbing salt in the gaping wound that was her heart.

Every second she'd spent with Audrey was invaluable. Her life's work was protecting the memories she had of her daughter—that was all she cared about, why she was here, enduring this awkwardness. As time passed, no matter what she did to stop it, memories fell away like corroded land into the sea, bit by bit; if the yellow house could represent what it used to, not the anger she'd held on to for so long, it would be like making new memories. And yet, it wouldn't happen, she could see that now. Nancy couldn't even let her have that.

"Thank you," Vera said, avoiding Patricia's eyes. "For what you're doing for them. The whole kennel thing. Tatum seems excited. And Layla's a wonderful young woman."

Nancy looked confused. She said, "I'm not doing anything."

It was nothing to her, maybe. Money was nothing to her and it was everything. Vera bit her cuticle while Patricia thought of the rent checks she signed for Bea each month, the college tuition, the money she'd tried to throw at her other daughter's addiction through offers of spa-like rehabilitation centers in northern California, the memorial she'd hosted and spent thousands on catering for, which Nancy had skipped. She'd done everything she could for her children and wasn't afraid to admit it, even if she'd been unsuccessful as a mother.

"Well," said Vera. "Since you're off to dinner, we won't keep you. Great to see you again." Her voice cracked because it wasn't great at all.

On Patricia's behalf, Vera was angry now. She could remember Nancy stroking Audrey's long hair, reminding her to put on water shoes before swimming. That child, whom she'd hugged and kissed and considered her "honorary niece," or so she'd said, was dead. Was that not enough to make her warm at least? Vera wished she was home, far away from this horrible person, behind a locked door. She'd tried to let go of the past in preparation for this, tried to give Nancy the benefit of the doubt—maybe she'd grown, changed, maybe she was sorry—but now Vera's despair, her pain, her defeat, all of it came flooding back.

Nancy said, "Why don't I take down your emails so I can be in touch." And Vera and Patricia recited their emails as slowly and sadly as their children's footsteps on the way to their cars at the end of summer.

This was it. Now it was really over.

Patricia's gaze settled on a nearby shelf filled with olive jars. In the old days, she used to stop there and grab a few for Audrey before checking out. Now she hated olives. Hated that shelf. Hated the square of linoleum beneath it, where she'd stood so many times when she was a different person, a person she envied and missed almost as much as she missed her daughter.

She imagined picking up a jar and smashing it against the linoleum, how good it would feel to make it explode, even to be nicked by its glass. She imagined Vera tearing through the plastic film covering the tub of ricotta cheese Nancy had just restocked and dumping it over her perfectly coiffed hair. Her red lipstick would smear. She'd slip as she tried to leave. Choke as she called for help. Patricia imagined pushing apples onto the floor to block Nancy's escape, Vera leaping onto her back, squirting lemon juice in her eyes, sanding her skin with rough kiwis until it split. She imagined forcing a tomato into her mouth—Nancy was allergic—clubbing her with celery stalks, stabbing her with the pointed tips of carrots.

The fantasy was very Bea-like, Patricia knew, except that her daughter might act on it. For Bea's own sake, she'd wanted to fix her, mold her into a more socially acceptable person, a person less like herself in certain ways. She couldn't, though, no matter how hard she'd tried. Now she wished she was braver, like her daughter, because it would feel so good to attack and Nancy deserved it.

"Well, it's about that time, then. Look out for an email," said Nancy. She ran a sparkling hand through her hair.

"Will do," said Vera as she grabbed Patricia's clenched fist.

"Thanks for letting the girls use your house." Patricia's words were carefully chosen.

As Nancy walked away, the heels of her expensive shoes tapped out a rude rhythm. Without turning back, she thrust her arm overhead, fingers bunched in a thumbs-up. It was the very first Nancy-ish thing she'd done, as well as all the confirmation they needed that there would be no email. What she was doing for their girls was clearly charity enough.

They watched as she disappeared into a black car outside, frozen in the empty Coop, feeling more like heartbroken teenagers than they ever had.

17

From: Sachs, Anita (anita@bernard.com) April 26, 12:23 p.m.
To: Bernard, Layla (layla@bernard.com)

Subject line: touching base

Good morning,

Would you like me to set up more kennel tours for next week or have you told the girls it's not happening?

Warmly,
Anita

From: Bernard, Layla (layla@bernard.com) April 26, 12:29 p.m.
To: Sachs, Anita (anita@bernard.com)

Subject line: RE: touching base

I haven't told them yet, but no more tours. I've invited them to the yellow house for the weekend and I'll tell them there. Please have my car washed by Thursday evening and provide them with the address etc. (they may have it, but it's been a long time since they were there.)

L

From: Bernard, Layla (layla@bernard.com) April 26, 1:06 p.m.
To: Ellis, Beatrix (beatrix.ellis003@gmail.com); Kaplan, Tatum (t.kaplan@goldenpress.com)
Cc: Sachs, Anita (anita@bernard.com)

Subject line: RE: The Kennel

Migrating from text back to email. I know there's a lot going on right now between us, and I acknowledge my part in that, but as you both know, I'd like you to join me at the yellow house.

Bea, you haven't officially accepted my invitation yet, which is fine. Take your time, but I'm wondering if we can go this weekend. Let me know. If this works for all, Anita will follow up with logistics.

Thanks.
L

From: Kaplan, Tatum (t.kaplan@goldenpress.com) April 26, 1:22 p.m.
To: Ellis, Beatrix (beatrix.ellis003@gmail.com); Bernard, Layla (layla@bernard.com)
Cc: Sachs, Anita (anita@bernard.com)

Subject line: RE: The Kennel

Hey,

Yeah, sounds good. I just broke up with Ed, so this weekend would be ideal for me honestly lol. Save me from the cave that is my parents' house. Take me back to my youth, make me forget, etc. Thanks, Layla, as always.

From: Ellis, Beatrix (beatrix.ellis003@gmail.com) April 26, 7:57 p.m.
To: Kaplan, Tatum (t.kaplan@goldenpress.com); Bernard, Layla (layla@bernard.com)
Cc: Sachs, Anita (anita@bernard.com)

Subject line: RE: The Kennel

This weekend works. My roommate will come too. We will drive separately.

From: Bernard, Layla (layla@bernard.com) April 26, 8:01 p.m.
To: Kaplan, Tatum (t.kaplan@goldenpress.com)

Subject line: RE: *******PRIVATE LAYLA AND TATUM*********** The Kennel

She's gonna bring her roommate??!!? PS: I quadruple checked Bea wasn't on this email before hitting send lol OY.

From: Kaplan, Tatum (t.kaplan@goldenpress.com) April 26, 8:06 p.m.
To: Bernard, Layla (layla@bernard.com)

Subject line: RE: *******PRIVATE LAYLA AND TATUM*********** The Kennel

Ugh. Maybe she just wants some extra support.

From: Bernard, Layla (layla@bernard.com) April 26, 8:13 p.m.
To: Kaplan, Tatum (t.kaplan@goldenpress.com)

Subject line: RE: *******PRIVATE LAYLA AND TATUM*********** The Kennel

I guess?? I know I should let this go because I'm the one who fucked up, but she just gives me noooooothing . . . anyway, her roommate can come. whatever. Also, I'm a bitch because I didn't say anything about your breakup in my last email. I can't believe you didn't tell me!! Dude, I'm sorry and I'm here for you. Anita will send a lil care package so look out for that (:

From: Bernard, Layla (layla@bernard.com) April 26, 8:18 p.m.
To: Ellis, Beatrix (beatrix.ellis003@gmail.com); Kaplan, Tatum (t.kaplan@goldenpress.com)
Cc: Sachs, Anita (anita@bernard.com)

Subject line: RE: The Kennel

Bea, regarding your roommate, that's fine. Again, Anita will provide the logistics.

From: Ellis, Beatrix (beatrix.ellis003@gmail.com) April 27, 9:07 a.m.
To: Kaplan, Tatum (t.kaplan@goldenpress.com); Bernard, Layla (layla@bernard.com)
Cc: Sachs, Anita (anita@bernard.com)

Subject line: RE: The Kennel

Cool.

From: Bernard, Layla (layla@bernard.com) April 27, 11:08 a.m.
To: Sachs, Anita (anita@bernard.com)

Subject line: RE: touching base

FYI, I'm going to call you in a bit to discuss strategies for telling T and B the kennel is off because I'm honestly lost. I don't want to seem like an asshole, so I'd like to do something to show commitment to "the cause," or whatever, even if we aren't making money off it . . . I really don't want them to hate me. Especially T. I'd like to do something more personal than donating to an animal rescue. I don't know what that should be, but you always have the best ideas. Ugh. I'm so dreading this.

Also, can you arrange a care package for Tatum? Fill it with all the usuals and anything else you can think of to make it special.

L

From: Kaplan, Tatum (t.kaplan@goldenpress.com) April 27, 10:21 p.m.
To: Ellis, Beatrix (beatrix.ellis003@gmail.com)

Subject line: I'm sorry.

Hey Bea,

I wanted to reach out privately because I know things are super weird right now and I feel bad about that. I'm glad you're coming this weekend. I know it might be a lot to go back there emotionally for reasons other than the Layla-Tatum-kennel of it all, so I'm here for you despite being a mess right now myself. I do really care about you and I'm sorry I haven't been as supportive as I should've been. Actually, there's a lot I'm really sorry about dating back to my friendship with Audrey. Maybe we can find time to talk over the weekend or soon. Just wanted to say something to you now so you know how I'm feeling. I think we can have a nice time together up there.

Best,
Tatum

18

TATUM LAY ON the floor of the living room dangling a spoonful of Nutella above her open mouth, waiting for gravity to do its job. How long would it take? A millennium? Two? How long had she been lying there? A millennium? Two? No, she thought, because if she'd been there any longer than nine months, she'd remember giving birth. Her life had become a ticking clock.

She hadn't eaten yet that day; the nausea was relentless until suddenly, about thirty minutes earlier, the desperate need for Nutella had hit her like a rocket. She'd dragged herself to the deli, Mando's Mangos, of course, and purchased a tub from Armando, who asked if she was sick.

"You look bad," he said.

She sighed as she handed over her credit card.

"Yup," she said. "Sick as a dog."

Though they were on top of one another, some aspects of living with her parents were nice. When she felt lonely, she was comforted by the *click-clack* of her father's keyboard, which could be heard from practically anywhere in the apartment, the mumble of Vera's Zoom yoga classes, and the scent of her musky perfume, which clung to everything. These were the sounds and smells of her youth, which made her feel safe though they were certainly not cure-alls.

Since leaving him, Tatum hadn't heard from Ed, which made things both worse and probably better from the perspective of moving on with her life. She wondered if he was already happier without her. Had he felt unburdened the instant she was gone, the way she'd expected to? Instead, she'd felt contrite, per usual, and like a failure in so many ways. Without him, she was single, broke, pregnant, and living with her parents. When she'd called Planned Parenthood, they said she couldn't have an abortion until she was further along, so she'd have to spend two more weeks this way. She couldn't wait to just be single, broke, and living with her parents. Eventually, in the very distant future, if she crossed her fingers tightly enough and knocked on enough wooden doors, maybe she'd actually be happy: partnered, comfortable, with a home of her own, and all this would be a hazy bad dream.

When Audrey was sad—usually about boys—Tatum used to soothe her by saying, "Someday, you'll be happy and in love with someone great, and this will all be so distant and meaningless." Though, at the time, she'd put little thought into such promises about the future, now Tatum was painfully aware that nothing was certain. Maybe she'd climb out of this depressive hole and things would improve, or maybe she'd die in five minutes.

Though out of character, she hadn't told her mother what was happening—growing—inside her. Vera was accepting and wasn't a catastrophizer like Patricia, but strangely, being secretly pregnant made Tatum feel closer to Audrey.

That time when Tatum called Audrey over her lost birth control pill, after listening to Tatum cry and offering sympathy, Audrey had said, "When I was pregnant, I didn't tell anyone the test was positive. Came out of the bathroom stall at school and told my friends it was negative. They all cheered. You're the only person in the world who knows I had an abortion." Tatum had loved knowing that she was the only one. It was as if she'd been handed the key to a special box. Now Audrey held Tatum's key. She could feel it somehow.

In a few hours she'd be away from here; maybe some of her troubles would stay behind, too. But this wasn't the way she'd imagined returning to the yellow house. It was like showing up unemployed to a high school reunion. She'd imagined going back someday, somehow—even if that meant pulling up to the mouth of the driveway and peering at it from a car window—when her mind was clear, when she could truly appreciate everything it was to her, maybe even with kids of her own. Instead, her return would be clouded by regrets and tainted by morning sickness.

Vera was depressed, too. She tried to put on a good face, but her usually bright eyes were dim. She'd said, "Don't worry about it," when Tatum asked what was going on. "Just not feeling my best." Under normal circumstances, Tatum would've pressed her, but not now.

"Ed and I broke up," was all Tatum had said to her boss to get the week off.

"Oh, sweetie," she'd replied, then they'd talked about it. Tatum played up or down certain parts of the story to make herself seem wronged. Hopefully, her boss's sympathy had brought them closer. When she hung up the phone, she'd burst into tears. Not because she missed Ed, but because of the shame of loneliness and of having leveraged her own pain at work. The only pinprick of hope in her life was the dog kennel, which was still quite imaginary, especially given everything between Layla and Bea. God, Tatum might as well be twelve again, managing middle school social hierarchies, discovering first insecurities. She'd needed something to believe in then, too, and had settled for the same thing: the kennel. At both lowest, most unmoored points in her life, she'd allowed it to become her raft. It made no sense.

Together they were a trio of sad, immature adults playing the same dog kennel–themed pretend game as when they were kids. Time had moved in a circle because she'd let it.

"Hey, hun."

Tatum pressed herself onto her elbows and was surprised to find Vera sitting on the far end of the couch. She hadn't noticed her arrival though the floorboards were loud, too lost in thought.

"Hey, hun," Tatum parroted, doing her best Vera impression.

"What's up?"

"Nothing. Just rotting."

"Right," said Vera. "Well, same."

"Jesus, Mom." Tatum cracked a half smile. "Don't be so depressing."

Vera folded her legs beneath her. "I could say the same."

"Yeah," said Tatum, still clutching her Nutella-filled spoon, "but you're the mom." These words held more weight than Vera knew, more weight than Tatum had expected. Was she a mother, too? Even if just for the moment? Even if just to a cluster of rapidly dividing cells? She pretended to notice something out the window to hide her quivering lower lip.

"I guess," said Vera. Tatum could hear laughter in her voice. "I used to think like that, too: that old, and therefore 'responsible,' adult people weren't entitled to sadness the same way I was." She threw up air quotes around the word *responsible*.

Tatum bit her lip until she was certain she wouldn't cry. "That's not really what I'm saying."

"I know what you're saying," said Vera. "I was twenty-seven once. Do you want me to make you something to eat, or you're all set with that?" She gestured skeptically at Tatum's spoon.

Tatum said she was all set, thank you very much. Her stomach was churning again; the spitty, rounded Nutella-lump pressed into the spoon wasn't pleasant to look at.

When her phone buzzed, she knew it was Layla. It wouldn't be Ed. It wouldn't be anyone but Layla, since Tatum hadn't heard from her other friends in a while. She hadn't seen them since before the memorial. Layla drained her social battery. Her other friends didn't even know about the breakup yet.

Can't fucking wait. The place is
different now so just prepare
yourself. I'll scoop you at 3pm. We'll
prob get there at like 6. It's already
stocked w food and booze so don't

bring anything. EEEEK! I'M
EXCITED!!!

Tatum sent back a flurry of emojis and effusive thank-yous and I-can't-wait-toos.

"Who's that?" Vera asked. She'd moved to the kitchen, which was part of the living room—or vice versa, depending on whether Tatum was cooking or lounging.

"Layla," said Tatum. "She's scooping me soon-ish."

"When?"

"At three."

"Okay." Vera sounded, not sad exactly, but heavy.

"Will you be all right here this weekend?" Tatum had never asked her mother a question like this before, had never really worried about her.

"Yeah, I'll be fine," said Vera. "It'll be easier if I don't tell you exactly what's going on in my brain. Just know that I'm okay. A little sad, but a lot okay."

Tatum, standing now and even more concerned than before, said, "Oh god." Was *child of divorce* about to be added to her list of troubles? "Stuff with Dad?" she asked nervously.

Vera shook her head. "God, no. No worries there. We're just as happily numb to each other as always after thirty years." She set down the knife she'd been using to slice a zucchini. "Really. Trust me, everything's okay. I'm here for you, just like always, and love you more than anyone and anything."

"Yeah, yeah," said Tatum, but it was good to hear. "Bea still hasn't responded to me." She picked up her phone and navigated to the apology email she'd sent a few days earlier. This was—or should've been—the very least of her concerns. It was like the splinter in her finger, compared to the two punctured lungs, twenty-four snapped ribs, and burst brain that was the rest of her life.

Vera sighed. "I don't know what to tell you." The way she said it made Tatum feel worse. She sounded defeated. Usually, her advice was the best.

"Okay," said Tatum. She stood, trying to look like she was not about to throw up. "On that note, I'll go pack."

"Love you," Vera called as Tatum jogged off to the bathroom.

"You too," Tatum called back through her fingers; her hand was clamped over her mouth.

By three p.m. she was standing outside with her bag hiked up on her shoulder and her mother's tearstains on her shirt. As they'd said goodbye, they cried together, setting everything aside that wasn't bittersweet nostalgia.

Vera gently smoothed Tatum's forehead with her thumb and said, "I can't believe you still haven't asked me what happened."

They were nose to nose, inhaling each other's breath.

"What happened with what?"

"The yellow house, way back in the day. I'd tell you now, you know. You used to ask me so often, and I would've told you, but Patricia . . ." Vera shrugged.

Tatum shrugged back. She was too tired, too full, couldn't fit any more depressing information inside her.

"There's just a lot of other stuff going on in my head," she said.

Vera nodded and zipped her lips, then tossed an imaginary key over her shoulder. "In that case, I'll see you on Sunday."

"Sorry you're saddled with me again."

Vera scoffed. "Are you kidding? I'm so glad to be saddled with you. Such a blessing. Ed's loss is my gain." She kissed Tatum's cheek and Tatum felt her lungs expand for the first time in days. Air. This was her mom. She was okay.

"Go through the breakup care package Layla sent and use whatever you want. It's pretty crazy," she said. Designer moisturizers, clay face masks, nail polish, gorgeous chocolates that were also impressively delicious, gift cards with subscriptions to streaming services Tatum realized she could use now that Ed's accounts weren't available to her, a luxurious pair of slippers, the most beautiful and soft bathrobe she'd ever worn, soaps, aromatherapy vials, crystals, candles.

Cars swished past through light rain, and Tatum slid her phone out of her back pocket. She was feeling slightly better thanks to nausea meds and her mother, but the rain was unseasonably cold, like needles poking her cheeks.

Running late, Layla had texted the usual five minutes after she already was. Stopped to get us coffees and it took forev. See you soon.

So, Tatum stood under her umbrella, pretending to care about what was on her phone. Nodding at the neighbors she accidentally made eye contact with, trying not to think they were judging her for being back at her childhood home.

Layla was twenty-five minutes late by the time she pulled up to the curb in a different black car than last time. Tatum could've waited inside but didn't, out of fear that Layla might take the opportunity to get out and ring the bell. Layla, tiny yet brilliant as a diamond, in Tatum's parents' dusty, dark mine of a living room.

As the car came to a stop, a hand shot out the wide sunroof and a tinted window lowered enough to reveal Layla's forehead and the upper rims of reflective sunglasses. Tatum steeled herself, smiling weakly.

"I have a surprise," Layla called as Tatum hobbled to the car, thrown off-balance by the weight of her bag. Today there was no Stanley, just Layla and Tatum, which was somehow more social pressure, even though Stanley never spoke when he was there.

The trunk of Layla's car swung open without being touched. Then, once Tatum had carefully positioned her bag and umbrella in the tight space between different-sized pieces of Louis Vuitton luggage, the trunk closed itself. Tatum shuffled over to her door, still smiling hard, but there was no handle to grab. She stood helplessly on the curb, getting rained on, waiting for Layla to finish checking her phone or whatever she was doing behind the dark glass. There was something moving inside the car. Something bouncing just beyond her window. What was it? Eventually Layla reopened the window a crack and taught Tatum where to press to make the handle appear, in an *Oh, sweetie* tone.

The door flew up, like a giant wing, almost taking Tatum's jawbone with it. But the even bigger surprise was curled into the passenger seat: a gorgeous, panting dog wearing a studded collar. Tatum gasped. The dog's tongue was what she'd noticed bouncing behind the glass. Its eyes were a deep ocean blue, ears pointed and wolfish, pelt the color of the overcast sky above.

"Oh my god," she said.

"This," said Layla, "as you might remember, is Willow." She reached over and rumpled the dog's head with a heavy hand, pressing its neck deeper into its uncomfortable-looking collar.

It was the dog Tatum had first seen at the park, then again at the kennel. Staring into those wide, hopeful eyes, Tatum felt her lungs relax and expand to full capacity, the way they had when she was wrapped in her mother's arms just before leaving. The dog's tongue passed over its nose, leaving it even shinier than before, then it continued panting.

"Oh my god," said Tatum again. Tears welled in her eyes—why? The dog seemed to be smiling at her. There was something familiar about its—what? About its smile? About a dog's smile? What could possibly be familiar about this animal, beyond their two brief encounters? The way it was staring at her made her feel, well, protected. Less alone than she had all week, all year, ever since Audrey— Tatum bit her lip. She was losing it. And yet, it was a specific type of love at first sight, or third sight, that she was experiencing, standing half inside Layla's car in the sprinkling rain, the way a new mother might view her adopted baby; in this scenario, who was the mother and who was the baby? Tatum wanted to gather Willow to her chest, bury her face in her fluffy back, and tell her everything was all right now, that she was safe. The strength of her emotion reminded her of that ridiculous thing that happened in Stephenie Meyer's *Twilight* books, which she'd pumped straight into her veins as a twelve-year-old: *imprinting*. It occurred when werewolves found their true loves, whom they could view either romantically or not. In Tatum's case, of course, not.

"Hi there, sweetie," she said, and tears rushed down her cheeks as she extended a hand toward the dog's velveteen muzzle. Willow leaned into her touch and was so soft.

Layla laughed. "Jeez," she said. "I knew you'd be happy to see her. I just didn't realize how happy."

Tatum recoiled quickly and wiped her tears away. "Sorry, sorry," she said, forcing a laugh. "I'm just so worn down right now by everything."

"Okay. C'mon, girl," said Layla. "Take a deep breath and get in the car. We'll have a great weekend, and you'll forget all your troubles."

Get in the car? How was she supposed to do that when it was a two-seater and this mammoth was seated where, presumably, Tatum belonged, too?

"Right," said Layla sheepishly, as if she was only just remembering Tatum's body required space. "Like, this is my favorite car to drive, and I thought you'd get a kick out of it, but there isn't a lot of room. She'll have to sit on your lap. I hope that's okay."

Admittedly, the car was cool, but how much did this darling dog weigh? Tatum had wanted to hold her close, but for three whole hours?

"Oh, sure," said Tatum. "Okay."

A few effortful seconds later, Tatum was sitting with a bear-sized dog in her lap, its toenails digging into her thighs. Willow tried to lie down, and Tatum groaned beneath her.

"Great," Layla chirped. "Ready?"

It took the better part of another minute for Tatum to locate the seat belt and click it into the buckle.

"All set," she said then, voice slightly strained. She stroked the dog's coat as they pulled into traffic, narrowly missing a biker, the windshield spattered with rain. Willow was warm against her, like a weighted, heated blanket.

"So, how did this happen?" Each time the dog inhaled, Tatum was pinned against the seat.

"Well," said Layla as she flicked on the turn signal. Even its ticking sounded lux. "So, yeah. Um, I guess, what happened is basically that—" Was she stalling? She seemed less assured than usual somehow. Typically, she got right to the point, was almost robotically controlled. Perhaps she was nervous about driving, or was it something else? "Anita said, 'Why don't you foster a dog?' and I thought it was a great idea because, like, a) what if we hate taking care of dogs in the end? Maybe we will. And if we do, we should know that now." She sounded almost hopeful, like she wanted them to hate it. Tatum considered pointing out, based on everything Layla had said until this point, it was her understanding that they would not be responsible for actual day-to-day dog care once the kennel was up and running. They'd be doing, well, whatever it was founders did, in sleek corner offices with big windows, but she kept her mouth shut. Layla continued, "And b) helping dogs is the ultimate point here, and I guess it seems right to, like, put my money where my mouth is a little bit. Anyway, Anita called Ella at Bestest Friends because, when she suggested fostering, I instantly thought of her." Layla gestured at Willow with her elbow. "You really responded to her at the kennel, and I thought she'd be a nice addition to the weekend since you're going through a lot." She paused. "Plus, like, in the end, as long as we've helped one dog, we've accomplished our goal, you know?"

Layla was rambling, which was odd, but Tatum was moved by her thoughtfulness, her sudden, precious humanity. Flawed as she was, and as AI-generated as she often seemed, beneath it all, Layla was bighearted. "That's so sweet," said Tatum, and she meant it. "Thank you. I'm really so glad Willow is joining us."

With one hand, Layla pressed her mirrored sunglasses up her nose, and with the other, she gave Tatum's knee a quick squeeze—her only accessible body part beneath Willow's impressive mass—leaving the steering wheel momentarily unsupervised. When the car swerved slightly, Tatum resisted the urge to grab it. Thankfully, Layla turned her attention back to the road. "I really hoped you'd feel that way," she said softly.

They were quiet as Layla merged into a congested highway lane. Anxiously, Tatum pushed the dog's fur back and forth, noticing the roots were bright white while the tips of each strand were a shade or two darker. Willow raised her snout and licked the air in Tatum's direction. The show of affection made Tatum emotional again. She turned away from Layla, watching the world lurch by as they stopped and started in step with the rest of the traffic.

Layla turned on her typical thudding music with the slip of her finger across a large screen.

Soon after they cut off a Mack truck that was exiting the highway, Tatum learned that Layla had failed her driving test four times before finally managing to pass. That was how she put it, too: *finally managing to pass*. So, Tatum and Willow sat, straining against sharp turns and sharper car horns as Layla maneuvered through space and time. The curves in the road held a distant nostalgia, whether imposed or real. She thought she recognized certain trees, exit signs, and rest stops. Whenever she started to doze, which was her typical uncontrollable reaction to long drives, Willow's coarse fur brought her back to consciousness as it swept across her face or poked through her shirt. The sensation was much like a phantom tingle, what Vera called angel wings. *Willow's angel wings*, she thought, and it seemed right.

They pulled over often, saying to each other, "Better safe than sorry," about Willow's unknown bathroom needs. People at the gas stations stared when the mechanical car-wings opened—nothing angelic or delicate about them. Outside the city, Layla's ostentatious wealth and appearance embarrassed Tatum. She ushered Willow quickly away from the car, toward the nearest tree, while Layla hung back, engrossed in her phone.

As soon as they turned off the highway for the final time, Tatum was wide awake. Now, she was certain she recognized their surroundings. Though she couldn't name the towns they drove through, the shapes and colors were familiar: the church with scalloped trim, the big red heart statue by the extra-long traffic light, even the tree trunks wrapped in dirty yarn beside the house with mobiles flashing and spinning on the porch. "Quirk central," her father had always said when they drove past it. She buried her face in Willow's coat. Embarrassingly, the tears were returning yet again.

When she lifted her head, Tatum watched the house with the year-round Halloween decorations streak by, tattered ghosts hanging from branches, plastic tombstones protruding from the lawn like rotten teeth. It was still there. They used to pass this house on the way to the grocery store. Oh, the sweet country grocery store—there it was, too. She remembered bouncing out of the car, the shock of air-conditioning, placing items in her parents' cart, then bursting into tears when they denied her Milano cookies. Next, she spotted the parking lot where they'd all learned to ride the same wobbly two-wheeler, then the ice-cream shack they visited after dinner most nights—with a line that wrapped around the corner. There was the gravel road labeled PUBLIC BEACH, which led to a pile of sand mixed with dirt and the lake. The lake. She could just make it out through the trees, winking in the evening sunlight that had finally broken through the clouds.

"We're really almost there," Tatum whispered.

"Huh?" Layla lowered the music as she flicked on the turn signal for the final time, but Tatum did not repeat herself. How often did Layla come here? It hurt to think this house had belonged to her all along. That it ever sat empty while Layla and Nancy were in the city or vacationing elsewhere, at other bigger family homes. All the while, Tatum would've done anything to be here again—to be here again with Audrey. It was too late for that now.

Willow raised her head at the sudden rumbling of pebbles under their wheels.

"Okay," said Layla. "Here we are." She said it cheerfully, easily. Tatum was silent, just looking, trying to take it all in. Where was the crack of thunder, flash of lightning, the DeLorean to officially turn back the clock? She looked at her hands, the hands of a twenty-seven-year-old, not of a child. She was there, it was real, and yet so was everything else.

The house was stately as ever, painted a brighter shade of yellow than she remembered. Notoriously, the Jeans hadn't been diligent about maintenance the way Nancy clearly was. Tatum had listened to their parents complain about it often. These gardens, Nancy's gardens, were well-manicured. The shrubs were pruned into perfect orbs, with spring flowers planted in alternating color patterns between them. When Willow sat up, her tail wagged in Tatum's face, swiping against her nose. The old brick path that connected the end of the driveway to the porch had been replaced by a patchwork of jagged bluestone, in a much snakier shape than the original straight line she'd rolled her pink suitcase along summer after summer.

When the car stopped, Layla consolidated their empty coffee cups. Then she pressed a button and a little mirror descended from the ceiling. Willow barked, a loud, masculine sound, and began fidgeting painfully. Layla, after drawing on some milky lip gloss, grabbed the leash and led Willow out, leaving Tatum's thighs cold and tingling. The car was quiet without them.

There was the yellow house. There was Layla, checking the mail, dog leash looped onto her wrist.

Staring through the window, as if it was a portal, Tatum saw herself bounding up the steps, three feet tall, tripping, scraping her knee, as she always had when they first arrived, too eager for summer—which officially began when she hugged her friends. The yellow house sparkled before her like a mirage, like a memory, like it had for so many years, but this time, it was real. She could reach out and touch it.

"Tatum," Layla called, and waved. "Come on!"

19

THE CAR GROANED, old and rickety. Smiling bobbleheads cluttered the dashboard and dust bunnies blew across them when Bea exhaled.

"Not my doing," Rosalie had said of the bobbleheads at the start of their journey. "The car used to be my grandma's."

Bea was glad Rosalie had been so easily convinced to join them for the weekend, especially since, over the past days, something had shifted within her, the sort of shift that would've worried close friends or parents, but Bea was the only witness to it. The change had been mostly energetic, until Rosalie suddenly cut off her long hair. The evening she'd done it, Bea had returned home from work to find dark clippings sprinkled across the bathroom vanity and Rosalie in her room, lying diagonally on the bed, facedown, her hair cut in a blunt line at the base of her skull. Upon first seeing her that way, Bea was alarmed, thinking she might be dead, but then Rosalie grunted, "Hi."

"Always good to get a second opinion about this kind of spontaneous urge," Bea had said, kneeling next to her, lifting a lock of hair off her cheek. "For your own safety. Spontaneous urges can be dangerous."

She'd said something similar to Audrey once, after catching her slowly crafting a text to Tatum expressing that she'd be "seeking treatment soon," and inviting her over for dinner: "Talk to me first next time," Bea had said after snatching the phone away. "And appreciate what you have here or else you won't be getting anything else from me."

The language she'd used with her sister was less careful than what she'd said to Rosalie, but the circumstances were different. Audrey hadn't really been aware, whereas Rosalie was.

Then, while helping Rosalie pack for the weekend away, in the interest of making light, friendly conversation, Bea had asked, "How's work going?" Though it seemed impossible given everything, Rosalie was employed full time by a video game distributor. Her job required sending many emails each day but was remote, so she never had to leave the house.

"Bad," said Rosalie. "They fired me, actually."

"Really?" *That explains the uptick in depression*. Bea had worried it had to do with their confrontation a few nights prior, but no. She'd felt relief until a new question occurred to her: Without a job, could Rosalie afford to stay in the apartment? Where would she go, if not? Back to her old town, where she'd be forced to live with her parents, who didn't know what was good for her? Who'd try to send her off somewhere once they realized how bad things were, like everyone had tried to do with Audrey? The other night, when Bea had told Rosalie she could leave, she'd only meant it as an empty warning.

Rosalie nodded. "I haven't been working as much as I should, and I missed a bunch of important emails. My boss gave me a few chances to get my shit together, but I couldn't, so they fired me two days ago."

Bea did her best to remain composed. Why hadn't she been told immediately? Why hadn't she been asked for help before it came to this? She continued folding Rosalie's clothing, arranging everything in careful piles. "So," she said. "Will you be able to live here if you don't have a job?"

Rosalie shrugged. "I don't know. I've got some savings."

That didn't sound promising.

Now they were driving in silence, the radio softly crackling.

Bea flipped through conversation topics in her mind, wanting to make the most of every second they had to bond since time was suddenly so precious. Finally, she blurted: "I had sex the other night." It seemed almost inappropriate to share such information, like it violated an unspoken rule in their relationship. Despite their roles, though, they weren't actually mother and child, doctor and patient; anyway, the rules—their roles—were whatever Bea made them. She loved that about their relationship, that it could be whatever she wanted, and would do anything to keep it that way for as long as possible.

The dotted yellow highway line flashed in her eyes as Rosalie said, "That's nice. Who with?"

"An old classmate from middle school. I found him on Tinder. He's the same boy whose house I visited a while ago, as you might remember."

"Was it fun?"

Was it? Dennis had been waiting at Seedy Dan's when she arrived. He smiled when he saw her, gave her the booth side of the table, and was wearing a shirt much too big for him—the shoulder seams were nearly at his elbows. Maybe it was his father's. True to his Tinder picture, a thickly drawn, tattooed snake encircled his neck—its body slightly resembled a rope; Bea had only found its head, positioned lower on his chest, later when they were naked. It had blood-dipped fangs and looked remarkably like one of her own serpent drawings. Another thing they had in common.

After sex, they lay in her bed and talked easily. He told her about his family: Rod Sweeney now lived in Miami with Gertie, his new thirty-five-year-old wife; Mary Sweeney was dating but would never remarry. According to Dennis, she'd stay in that old, too-big brownstone until she couldn't make it up the stairs anymore, which made Bea think of her mother's comment at the memorial: *At least this house is all on one level. No stairs for me to break my hip on when I'm eighty.*

His brother, age twenty-two, already had a book about climate change under contract with a major publisher. After graduating from Yale at twenty, he'd immediately started a PhD program at Harvard, studying the global impact of algae's absorption of microplastics, or something.

"Whereas I dropped out of Binghamton at nineteen," said Dennis, "have about thirteen thousand dollars in credit card debt, and no job to speak of."

Bea was using his arm as a pillow. "Rough," she said. Before he could draw any of his own comparisons, she added, "I obviously know what that's like."

"Right," he said. "I mean, I suppose."

"Yeah," said Bea, flipping onto her side to face the window; her back was pressed against his ribs and her hand against her forehead, soothing her gash, which still burned when she sweated. "Audrey's career was really picking up steam before everything happened. Like, she was in magazines. My parents always paid for my portion of the rent, but she could afford hers. Plus, she was so goddamn fucking beautiful, as everyone was always telling me."

"Yeah, well," said Dennis. "That's how it goes."

"Kinda lucky she died, huh?" said Bea, laughing. "I mean, don't you kinda wish your brother would just—" Bea jerked her hand across her neck and stuck out her tongue, playing dead.

Next to her, Dennis was quiet. But he must get the joke; his experiences—insecurities—so closely mirrored her own.

"I'm obviously kidding," she said, adjusting so his arm fit tighter around her. It was nice to be held. "Gotta have a sense of humor about these things. But, I mean, really. I spent my whole life playing second fiddle. Then that suddenly changed."

Dennis retracted his arm. Now they were lying side by side, not touching.

"I guess," he said.

"You just never know what'll happen or how dynamics might shift."

Dennis sat up. "It's not like I want something bad to happen to my brother."

"Of course not," said Bea. "I'm just saying you never know. By the time my sister died, she really needed me, not the other way around, and I don't think it's fucked up of me to feel like that part of it was nice."

"I guess."

She couldn't quite make out Dennis's expression in the dark.

"I mean," she continued. "I can't change what happened. And since I can't, I've found the positive in it, and I've learned a lot from the whole thing. It's shitty to always be the ugly duckling." She rolled her eyes, embarrassed to admit that was what she'd been, especially to someone she'd just fucked. "Now I'm the only one left, which means I'm not the ugly one. Not that you're ugly, that's obviously not what I'm saying." She was getting nervous. What was he thinking? If only she could explain herself the right way, he'd understand. "I worked at a camel rescue after she died to get away from New York, and I learned a lot about pain because I was basically watching these massive animals either heal or not all day, and I learned that there's something really beautiful about the circularity of life, which, again, isn't to say that I'm glad she died, but death honestly seems sort of pleasant. Better than being alive and hurting all the time." She gestured at her sketches, which surrounded them. "That's what I'm always trying to capture in my drawings, I guess. We're all the same. And I believe everything is alive, even dead people and animals, except in some ways they're the lucky ones because they're not in any pain. We all exist, either painfully or not." As if on cue, a breeze curled in through the open window and rustled the papers on the walls. All of them, creatures she'd dreamed up. Mixes of things. Skeletons with faces. Bodies with bare skulls.

"Hm," was his response. Then, "How do you know that?"

"I just do."

"Right."

"My parents wanted to send her away for treatment."

"You didn't?"

"At first I did, but then—" Bea paused. "I don't know. It was good for both of us that she stayed. I took care of her."

When he suddenly climbed out of bed, Bea grabbed his hand. "Hey, wait. Sorry if I said something weird." She'd allowed herself to be honest because she thought he might understand, but now he was leaving. Couldn't he see where she was coming from?

"Actually, can you let go?"

She didn't want to.

"I'm sorry," she said again. "I miss Audrey all the time. Every day."

"Can you let go?" he repeated.

Her grip tightened as he tried to yank his hand free with more force than before.

"Hey," he said, louder, and then she released him, not wanting Rosalie to hear.

He staggered back, cradling his fingers against his chest.

"Jesus," he said. "That really hurt."

Bea didn't apologize.

"I mean, shit. I guess you're entitled to feeling the way you do, it's just not how I feel." His voice cracked. "And I would've done whatever I could to get Audrey into treatment if she was my sister."

Bea shook her head. "But you can't know how you'd feel. I gave her everything she needed. She was my entire life."

"Uh." He filled the doorway. "Yeah, I can know. I'd feel sad. I'd be devastated. I'd do whatever I could to keep her alive."

Bea crossed her legs, leaning against the bed. "My guess," she said, "is that your feelings would be more complicated than you think. And feelings are just feelings. Complicated feelings are allowed if you don't act on them." She was quoting a therapist she'd seen at the psych ward.

"You don't know me," he said.

Didn't she though?

She opened her legs, slowly. He was standing by the door. A shaft of yellow light fell across him. She saw his eyes flick down to her vagina, then back up to her face. Indeed, she knew him, as well as she knew herself.

"Will I see you again?" She did her best sexy pout.

"Sure, sure." But she heard the "no" in his voice. As he dressed quickly, he said, "I'll show myself out."

"Yeah, it was fun," Bea answered Rosalie over the radio static. She'd watched her shape move in the window as they fucked, back arched, breasts bouncing just above his face, her features blurred to anonymity. She liked it best when she could watch herself and forget who she was at the same time.

Rosalie said, "Cool," but her voice shook.

"You okay?" asked Bea. It was strange to be driven at full speed down a highway by someone so unstable, but Bea had never gotten her driver's license.

"Just makes me wonder if I'll ever have sex again. And makes me miss sex with Travis. And makes me think about how I'd rather never have sex again if it can't be with him. And makes me think, *What's the point of living if I'll never have sex again?*"

Bea looked out her window at the emerald wall of evergreen trees. "I'm sorry," she said. "I understand."

Rosalie punched the steering wheel, then smacked her thigh before Bea blocked her hand. The silver ring almost flew off her finger, but she caught it just in time.

"Stop," Bea commanded.

Rosalie nodded with tears in her eyes and turned into the exit lane.

By the time they arrived, the sky was velvet black. Their headlights cut through the mist. The rain had stopped hours earlier, but everything still glistened from it.

"Whoa," breathed Rosalie as their car slid in behind Layla's, which looked like a gigantic, wheeled stingray. "Shit."

Bea was glad it was dark so she couldn't see the house. She was also grateful to have spent the drive distracted by Rosalie and Dennis, which had prevented her from thinking too much about where they were going, how it would feel to arrive there. Now, suddenly and almost surprisingly, here they were.

Rosalie turned off the car, released the key, and opened the door. To her, this place meant nothing, it was just damp grass, sky, lake, house.

While Bea was alone, for the short amount of time it took Rosalie to reach the trunk, she dropped her hand into her tote and pressed the center of the aluminum olive jar lid in and out, which made a comforting little *dink*.

"We're back," she whispered.

No city sounds. Nothing except for the rusty trunk creaking open behind her and the whistling crickets, so consistent their song created its own silence.

Before she left the car, she checked her reflection in the mirror above her seat, arranged her bangs to cover her forehead scab, and ran her fingers through her hair—who was she primping for? She'd eaten a Fruit Roll-Up before they left, and her lips were still green from it. With her freckles, thin hair, dyed lips, and wide, scared eyes, she reminded herself of a little girl. Like the little girl she wished she could've been. A little girl who was allowed to be herself. Finally, she climbed out.

Bea trudged up the steps to the front door with Rosalie just behind, their weight eliciting the hollow, offbeat rhythm she remembered her parents' making. It was very different from the quick, excited slaps of her much younger—usually bare—feet.

As they faced the front door, Bea was already noticing changes. Tatum had texted earlier to warn her the house was different. Through beveled glass, she could see the entryway was painted blood red. In the old days, it was covered in pastel floral wallpaper and antique dream catchers.

They stood motionless on the top step until Rosalie said, "You wanna ring the bell or . . ."

Using her free hand, Bea pounded the doorframe with her fist, hard and loud, startling Rosalie. There didn't used to be a bell. This was how her parents had always done it at the start of summer if theirs wasn't the first family to arrive. Now there was a surveillance-type video of them on a small blue monitor above the button Rosalie had gestured to and Bea had ignored.

A minute later, she tried again. Still nothing. Eventually, she was forced to ring. A cacophony of wind chimes erupted from inside and Tatum came galloping down the hall, Bea could see through the glass in the door. She was laughing. Something hunched and large followed her. Definitely not Layla.

"Coming," shrieked Tatum. "Sorry!"

When the door finally opened, what had been only the faintest whisper from inside revealed itself as big, buzzing music. Tatum was struggling to keep the door mostly shut against what Bea could now tell was a dog. She waved. "Come in, come in."

Bea didn't have a moment to process what stepping over the threshold meant. She did so quickly and unceremoniously.

"Is that them?" Layla yelled from the kitchen. The lights were on in every room they passed but not in the hallway, which ran down the center of the house like the midrib of a leaf, connecting everything. They dropped their bags by the stairs. The very same staircase as always that widened and curved where it met the floor, though now it was lacquered black instead of worn, blond wood.

"Yes, it's them," Tatum called back. "She's making dinner," she said more quietly to Bea and Rosalie. "With her family's chef on FaceTime."

Bea felt as though she was traveling through the belly of a ghost as they walked toward the light at the end of the hall. The new Bernard aesthetic was indeed very different from the Jeans'. She liked it: the colors they'd chosen were bold, the furniture sleek and architectural. It was the kind of interior decorating that required money and not much else, but it was honest—told a clear story—and it was clean.

The hallway grew brighter as they neared the end. She could see the kitchen floor, which used to be made of ancient stone slabs and was often blamed for mangled toes, had been replaced by gleaming marble tiles. The cabinets were black.

"Whoa," said Rosalie again. "Shit, this is—" She couldn't finish her thought before they stepped into the dazzling room. Bea must've kicked off her shoes by the door, the way they used to, though she couldn't remember doing it. The tiles were cold against her bare feet. Layla raced over, wearing a pink silk apron—not a stain in sight—and hugged them.

"Hey, babes," she said. Her voice was sloppy like Tatum's. They'd been drinking, it was clear. "So glad you made it." To Rosalie, she said, "I'm Layla."

For an instant, Bea felt very small in this grand space, which Layla, slight as she was, fit snuggly into.

"Can I pour each of you a glass of champagne, or would you like some filtered ice water, or water with lemon, or sparkling water, or berry-infused water"—Layla paused for a breath—"or lemonade, or an Arnold Palmer, or celery juice, or anything else?"

Bea was hardly listening. Instead, she was trying to believe that this was the yellow house; that she was standing in the same kitchen where she used to beg for organic chocolate chips, which her mother had used as treats for completed chores and general good behavior. The same kitchen where Audrey used to sing because the acoustics were so good. It really wasn't the same kitchen. But also, it was.

"Water sounds good," she said. Tonight, she wouldn't drink. She wasn't sure when the emotion would hit. Whenever it did, she'd need her wits. Rosalie asked for champagne.

Tatum retrieved two glasses from a cabinet as Layla said, "There's drinkable water here now," then laughed. "What a revelation. No more plastic jugs taking up space in the refrigerator." She was being overly talkative and friendly, Bea could tell, trying to sweeten her up.

In the old days, they'd driven to the grocery store for water because what flowed from the tap was brownish. What used to be a regular fridge, old, white, and tiled by word magnets, was now the size of a powder room—a term Bea had learned recently from Patricia—and made entirely of glass. Inside, there were vibrant bushy leaves, plump unblemished vegetables in wooden bowls on shelves, every condiment under the sun arranged by color, and fat-marbled slabs of pink meat displayed like art on ceramic dishes.

"Pretty epic, huh?" said Layla, following Bea's eyes. "It's, like, apparently a one-of-a-kind fridge. When it was built, it was the biggest ever made or something. And then Nancy built an even bigger one for our house in Ojai, so"—she shrugged—"now, I guess, it's two-of-a-kind and not so special anymore. Hey, what happened?" She gestured at Bea's forehead.

Bea was silent. Her cut tingled against the bright lights and Layla's stare. She'd had the wound the last time they'd seen each other, though maybe it looked worse now. Probably it did since she'd been relentlessly picking at it. She tugged her bangs back into place.

"Anyway, we're making filet mignon," said Layla, moving on as if she'd never wanted an answer, only to point out something wrong with Bea. "Banking on the fact that no one's a vegetarian here?"

Both Bea and Rosalie shook their heads and Layla pretended to wipe sweat from her paralyzed brow.

"Great. There will also be French fries, though I won't be having any." Then she whispered: "They're frozen, don't tell Tatum."

Tatum giggled but looked confused. "Oh, stop. I love frozen fries." She handed Bea a glass of water and said softly, "It's good to see you."

Bea hadn't responded to Tatum's apology email because it was easier that way. She wasn't one to lie. Not really. Not for someone else's benefit. *Thank you for saying this, but I can never forgive you*, was all she could've written, which was worse than saying nothing.

Still, even if she couldn't forgive, it was nice to have received Tatum's email, in a way, to feel like someone had known—had seen it—all along: *Actually, there's a lot I'm really sorry about dating back to my friendship with Audrey*, Tatum had written. But when it was happening, she hadn't done anything. Inclusion wasn't hard. It was as easy as saying, "You should join us!" What good was an apology now?

"You really fucking freaked her out," Audrey had yelled at Bea the day after she'd been caught following them around.

Twenty hours earlier, in her typical strategy for avoiding boredom and loneliness, Bea had pulled on dark clothes and trailed Audrey and Tatum down the street, from bar to bar, as she did often. But then she'd messed up. She'd been watching them hug and laugh on the street at the end of the night and lost herself for a moment, approached them as if they were expecting her, as if they would open their arms and welcome her in.

That night, Audrey hadn't been so enraged, if anything she'd been pitying, but talking about it with Tatum had clearly riled her up. "Doing that to me is one thing," she'd said the following afternoon. "I don't really care what you do to me. Doing it to Tatum isn't cool. Generally, people don't like being stalked, Trix. It's insane I have to spell that out for you."

Bea was seated on the couch in their living room, her fists balled, head bowed.

"What do you have to say for yourself?" Audrey demanded, stooping to catch her eye, misting her with saliva.

When it came to Audrey, for some reason Bea's rage never erupted into violence. It burbled inside, like a dormant volcano, and depressed her.

"I don't know," Bea said eventually. "Sorry, I guess."

"Never do it again," said Audrey. "You hear me?" Her finger pointed at Bea's nose.

Bea nodded, wishing she could explain how hurtful it was to be ignored by Tatum, which wasn't exactly the reason she followed them but wasn't not. Despite her hunched position on the couch at that moment, Bea had always wanted to seem capable to Audrey. She did her best never to cry in front of her or complain, though some of this was inevitable. It was as if she'd always had a premonition of what was to come, not that Audrey would become addicted to heroin and die so young, but of how their dynamic would change over time. How important it was for her to be seen as strong despite everything.

The water glass was cold in Bea's hand. She imagined dropping it, using a shard to slit everyone's throat in the stunning kitchen: Layla's,

Tatum's, Rosalie's, then her own—the way their blood would trickle across marble and pool in the thin grout lines.

"And here's your champagne," Tatum said to Rosalie, as if she was the host. As if all this was hers.

You're not, Bea wanted to say. *You're nothing and you have nothing.*

"Everyone just relax. Let me feed you," Layla said, though she made no move to get back to cooking or to her chef, whose face was displayed dumbly on her phone screen by the oven.

"How was the drive?" asked Tatum. She knelt and wrapped her arms around the broad, shaggy shoulders of a dog with blue eyes. Its coat was like that of a sooty polar bear.

"Layla, shall we continue?" the chef called, and finally Layla pranced back to her phone.

Tatum blanketed the dog's face in noisy kisses. When she finally came up for air, she said, "Bea, do you recognize her? From the kennel? Layla's fostering her."

Bea did, but not from the kennel. Was Audrey sending her a message, or was it nothing at all? She reached a hand toward the dog, which craned its neck to lick her fingers.

"Why this one? What—"

Tatum was stroking the dog's head.

"Layla said she noticed my reaction to her at the kennel and thought it would be nice to bring her here." So, this was the dog Bea had never actually seen in the washroom. The one that had sent Tatum into a strange panic.

Bea nodded, trying to maintain her composure. The dog's breath was warm against her hand.

Tatum went on: "I recognized her from the dog run. She sat with me there for a bit before you guys arrived and was really sweet." Tatum paused. "It was just weird to see her again at the kennel, suddenly alone and helpless. It really got to me. I'm sure I seemed insane."

"And you don't recognize her from anywhere else?" Bea asked. It wasn't nothing, she'd decided. Years ago, perhaps Audrey had sent Tatum a picture of the puppy she'd almost adopted and, even if Tatum didn't seem to remember now, her connection to the animal subconsciously had to do with that, too? The fact that this dog looked exactly like Audrey's puppy meant something. Bea couldn't believe it was a total coincidence. The resemblance was too uncanny; this dog was frosty and majestic, and those eyes—Bea knew those eyes.

"No," said Tatum. "I don't think so. Why?"

But if it wasn't a coincidence, what was it?

Bea looked over at Rosalie, who was already refilling her glass with bubbles. She had to escape, to breathe and collect herself apart from everyone.

"Nothing. Never mind. I'm gonna take my stuff upstairs."

"Do you need help with your bags?" Tatum called as Bea left the room.

"I'm getting *this* one," Audrey had slurred the night her adoption application was approved, then handed Bea her phone. "I'll pick her up a week from today."

"And why are you getting a dog again?" Bea had asked. She'd always humored Audrey when they'd spoken about it prior, because she wasn't entirely opposed to the idea of having a dog around. In the abstract, taking care of a dog was in line with the kind of responsibility she enjoyed. But she'd never expected the rescue agency to approve Audrey's application after they'd spoken to her. That had come as a shock.

Audrey's smile was sleepy. "Because I've always wanted one. Ever since we were little. They make me so happy." Her eyelids fluttered, then closed. *They make me so happy*. The same words she'd spoken when they were young, which had started the dog kennel fixation in the first place. It had all always been to make Audrey happy.

"Okay," Bea remembered saying. "And I'm supposed to take care of your dog?" She hadn't been trying to dissuade her. It was just meant as a reminder.

"No," said Audrey as her head fell forward. "I'll take care of my own dog."

There were moments when Audrey seemed aware of what was happening to her, who she'd become, and others when she'd been completely disconnected from reality—this was one of those. It angered Bea because it meant Audrey didn't understand everything she did for her.

"No," Bea said coolly. "You can't take care of a dog. You can't even take care of yourself." Then she added, for the sake of it, *"It's insane I have to spell this out for you."*

Audrey said, "You suck," before adding, "Someday, I'll be able to. You can do it until then. Like I took care of you until you could do it yourself."

"Yeah, right," said Bea as she placed a jar of olives on the coffee table. Most of the time, she ignored it when Audrey made comments like these, understanding they were part of a coping mechanism. "Want some more before you eat?"

"Yes," said Audrey. She stretched out her arm, and Bea tied a stretchy blue band around it. After expertly administering the drugs, Bea said, "Don't forget to chew when you eat." As she stood up, Audrey fell back against the couch.

"Danny will be downstairs in an hour," Audrey mumbled. Bea knew what that meant. She'd meet him at the door and they'd walk into the little enclave where the building's trash bins were. They'd duck behind one, he'd open his tattered backpack and pass her a baggie wrapped in tinfoil, and she'd hand him cash withdrawn from her sister's dwindling account. He'd say, "Pleasure doing business," and she'd say nothing.

Her very last fight with Audrey had occurred just after returning upstairs with the little drug parcel in her pocket later that night. Audrey had been caught on a loop about taking care of the dog, repeating, "I can do it. I can do it. I can do it," until Bea yelled, "No, you can't." Then suddenly Audrey was talking about leaving, about "getting treatment." All Bea wanted was acknowledgment of the care she tirelessly provided day in and day out.

Footsteps from behind. Bea accelerated, suddenly afraid of being caught.

"Hey." It was Rosalie's voice, and Bea slowed and remembered where she was. Audrey was dead. This was all in the past.

Get a grip, Bea thought as she lifted both her bag and Rosalie's off the floor and slung them over her shoulders.

"Give me mine," said Rosalie, reaching for the strap, but Bea jerked away.

Upstairs was less changed than downstairs, which Bea found soothing. She could feel her heart rate returning to normal. As she moved along the hall, Bea poked her head into each room, noting whether Tatum or Layla had already claimed it with a bag, and providing a brief introduction for Rosalie's sake: "This is where Nancy, Layla's mom, used to sleep."

Nancy's room was the biggest, though she was only one person, not part of a married couple. Bea realized she must've won it by covering more of the rental costs even back then, when she'd had less than she did now, but still more than anyone else. The room had a balcony overlooking the lake, which, from the doorway, Bea could see pulsing under the moonlight, and the same big desk beneath the window that Bea remembered; the Jeans must have sold Nancy at least some of their furniture with the house. She couldn't enter the room, could only lean in through the doorway, arm hooked around the wall. This was another unspoken rule—one between the girls when they were young: the other parents' rooms were off-limits, only Layla could enter her mother's, and so on. What Bea felt certain was Layla's leather suitcase rested on the bench at the foot of Nancy's sprawling bed.

The room that had belonged to Bea and Audrey's parents was the second biggest. The bed in there was a four-poster, with gauzy curtains looped over dark wood to create a princess-y effect, which used to delight Bea and Audrey. It was a relief to see that it was still there. No bags inside yet; Bea imagined staking her claim, dropping into that bed beneath the breezy, lake-facing window. She willed her bag off her arm, herself into the room, but no. She turned to Rosalie. "You can take this one if you want. It's where my parents used to sleep."

Rosalie said, "You don't want it?"

Bea responded by shrugging off Rosalie's bag and leaving it by the door.

They continued past Tatum's parents' old room, which was more modest than the other two—the bed in there was queen-sized. A large mirrored dresser faced it, which Bea didn't recognize, beneath a window with a view of the driveway. This bedroom was the most different from what Bea remembered, so far. Nancy, or her decorator, had clearly tried to make it luxurious, with long curtains and a thick, blush-colored rug, but Bea saw it for what it was: less nice than the others. Tatum's bag, an oversized canvas tote, was slumped on the floor.

"Tatum's parents'," said Bea, gesturing at it as they passed.

The door to the next room was open, too, and inside were what appeared to be the very same twin beds as always, dressed in the same pink quilts, separated by the same little table.

"Layla and Tatum's," said Bea. Rosalie nodded.

"And this one was ours." The door was closed; Tatum had clearly inspected each of the other rooms first but had left this one for her. She hesitated before touching the knob, as if she was afraid the metal would burn her, though when she touched it, nothing happened. No spark, or whoosh of invisible energy, or reincarnated Audrey. The door responded to her gentle push with a creak, and there it was, as picture-perfect as the day they'd left for the last time, both beds wearing blue quilts to match Bea's back home, only these were the originals. Silver light moved across the walls in a watery pattern: moonlight through the trees.

With a thud and muted splash, her bag landed on the floor as if it had a mind of its own. She'd wrapped the glass part of the olive jar in a sweater, so she wasn't worried about it breaking. She was, however, worried about breaking down in front of Rosalie, so she kicked the bag into the room and started back toward the stairs, pointing over her shoulder at the very last door.

"And that's the bathroom," she said.

"Cool." Rosalie shuffled after her.

Bea's armpits were swamps. How would she get through a whole weekend here?

Downstairs, they found Tatum in the dining room. The table was new—it used to be ovular, with a thick base in the center that the girls had crawled around, avoiding their parents' legs, once their plates were clean. This one was glossy black like a coffin, an endless rectangle that reflected the backs of the gilded plates Tatum was arranging, and the glittering chandelier. From the doorway, Bea could see the tip of the dog's feathery tail following her.

"Did you take your parents' room?" Tatum asked when she noticed Bea and Rosalie. "That bed." She pressed a hand to her heart and clucked her tongue.

"I took my old room," said Bea. "It felt right."

Tatum nodded, placing a cloth napkin beneath a fork. Then she walked around the long table toward Bea with open arms. As they embraced, Bea could feel the booze through the warmth of Tatum's body. It was nice to be wrapped in for a moment, familiar.

Behind them, Rosalie was quiet.

Then, "Dinner's ready," singsonged Layla from the kitchen.

20

SO," SAID LAYLA when everyone was seated. "I'd like to toast to us being here. Together." She paused to look meaningfully at Tatum first, then at Bea. "To following our dreams and, of course, to Audrey, who we miss."

Tatum was too drunk for this—to talk or think about Audrey—yet the only solution was to drink more, to further poison herself, her thoughts, and her baby. Her fetus. The fetus inside her. She stole a glance at Bea, who was still and expressionless.

"So, cheers," Layla said.

Tatum gulped down her drink, then replenished it, watching champagne foam rise to the lip of her glass, then disappear, tiny bubble by tiny bubble.

"Tatum, would you do the honors?" Layla mimed serving the steaks. She was seated at the head of the table, far from the platter. The way the serving utensil was positioned, its handle pointed directly at Tatum, as if it was magnetized to her. Of the people in the room, effort was magnetized to her.

Layla spoke to her sometimes—especially tonight—as if she was the dumb husband of their married couple; then again, that was how Tatum acted. She leapt up and self-consciously did as she was asked.

There was nothing to eat but steak, Tatum realized upon settling into her seat. No side dishes or vegetables. It was the kind of tiny food one might be disappointed to receive at an expensive restaurant; though the steaks were thick, the circumference of each one was about the size of a silver dollar. She glanced at Layla, who was bent low, shoulder blades visible through the skin on her back, slicing off strips of meat, nibbling on the browned edges. Her posture, the care with which she approached her food, it was as if she was eating for the very first time. This was nothing like what Tatum remembered from their first dinner together at La Olivia. She found the sight disturbing. It was clear now that Layla was so deluded by her own fear of food, she didn't realize others might want—need—more than this. Weren't there supposed to be frozen fries? Was anyone going to ask what had happened to them?

No one did, not even Bea, which Tatum would've expected from her. Tonight, though, Bea wasn't quite herself. She seemed even more detached than usual. If it was strange for Tatum to be back, she couldn't imagine how Bea must feel.

They ate until everyone's plate, but Layla's, was empty of all but brown juice, which didn't take long.

"That was great," said Tatum. "Thank you."

Layla smiled and said, "Glad you enjoyed. Felt good to cook a little."

Rosalie, who'd hardly spoken since arriving, guzzled the rest of her champagne, then finally asked, "Is there anything else to eat?"

"Oh," said Layla, raising her eyebrows in a look of surprise. "Um, right. There are some fries on top of the stove. I just started what's called the carnivorous diet, so I can't try them, but I think they're cooked through—sorry, forgot to bring them out, I guess. Help yourself if you want." Why had she made them if she was going to judge people for eating them? Because waste didn't matter to rich people and because most women's relationship with food didn't make sense. *Whatever*, Tatum thought. *I don't care.*

Rosalie said, "Cool, thanks," and walked away with her plate.

"So," said Layla, placing her elbows on the table, "how're we all feeling?"

Bea fiddled with the ends of her hair. She eyed the doorway Rosalie had disappeared through, suddenly on high alert. It was sweet, Tatum thought, how attuned she was to Rosalie. She hadn't seen anything like this from Bea before. Were they in love? Bea visibly relaxed when Rosalie returned, her plate piled high with twiggy fries, and Tatum knew just how she felt: the utter peace which could only be attained through proximity to a single person in the world. She wished Audrey could witness this: it seemed that Bea had finally found a meaningful connection.

Tatum said, "I'm good. Tipsy."

Layla lifted her own glass. "Same, girl, same."

Bea said nothing. Rosalie sank back into her seat.

Under the table, Tatum's feet rested on Willow's back, her toes nesting comfortably in the thick fur.

"So, I was thinking we'd just hang around here tomorrow," Layla said. "As you know, there's not much happening in town this time of year."

Tatum didn't know, and she assumed neither did Bea—they had never been to the yellow house at this time of year before, had never been invited. Was Tatum allowed to be angry about that? Whatever had separated their mothers, she assumed, wasn't Layla's fault. Still, the longer Tatum was there, the worse she felt about it; the more she drank, the easier it was to laugh through the pain. Champagne bubbles tickled her throat as she took a long sip.

"Sure," she said, once she'd swallowed. "Whatever you want."

The room was fuzzy.

"Or we could go for a hike with Willow, or something," said Layla.

No one responded.

"Or we could just sit silently around the dining table all day."

Tatum forced a laugh, which sent a pink glob of steak into the middle of the table from the recesses of her mouth. This made Layla laugh, too, and Tatum blush. She wiped it away with her napkin.

"Ew," she said. "Sorry."

Beneath the table, Willow stirred.

Tatum was smitten. It was unexpected, especially since she was such a massive dog, the kind Tatum normally found terrifying. Willow was like Audrey, whose features were intimidating, but who was actually warm and safe. All Tatum wanted from the dog was gentle company, which was all she'd wanted from Audrey, too, not money or clout or anything else, in the end, and which Audrey had always provided.

Smiling, Tatum peered under the table. Layla said, "She's a real sweetheart, isn't she?"

Tatum nodded.

"Okay, so we're still undecided about tomorrow, then," Layla said.

Rosalie's munching filled the silence.

If Tatum wasn't so drunk, she never would've allowed such awkward quiet. She took another slug from her glass and smiled. It felt good to do nothing. To care less.

Her eyes shifted back to Bea, who was still watching Rosalie. From time to time, she leaned over and whispered, and Rosalie nodded and adjusted something: pulled her hair out of her face, wiped her oily fingers on her napkin; at one point, she seemed to slow her chewing, then glance at Bea as if asking for permission to swallow. Suddenly, their dynamic resembled that of Patricia and her daughters. She wondered if Rosalie felt stifled at all. Audrey had always found their mother oppressive, controlling, and at times even scary, the way her fear-driven anger could swirl up out of nothing, make her do irrational things. If Tatum thought about it, Bea's only living example of how to care for another person was her mother. Her overbearing, paranoid, unstable mother. If Audrey were still around, perhaps she would've helped Bea regulate, but Tatum couldn't—it just wasn't their relationship. Though she worried Bea would ruin things with Rosalie if she kept up this way, there was nothing to be done.

More champagne, less thinking. She reached for the bottle.

"I'm gonna put on some music again," said Layla, already scrolling through Spotify on her phone. "Let's get out of here." She pushed her chair back and cast a lingering look over her shoulder at Tatum before disappearing down the hall.

Tatum hesitated.

"Come dance," Layla called.

A deep bassline started up again from the next room. Booze and music—the combination was dangerous. Being here, vulnerable, with Layla, was dangerous.

It didn't matter. Nothing did.

Tatum poured herself another glass, spilled it down her throat, and said, "Let's go," mostly to herself.

In the living room, she watched a large disco ball descend from the ceiling, moonlike in both its position and power. She'd noticed the mysterious trapdoor overhead earlier when she'd first explored the room. This remote-controlled disco ball was the first respectable change to the house she'd seen. Everything else she found pointlessly ostentatious .

"Fuck yeah," she said, snaking her arms through the air, twisting, braiding them, closing her eyes as she danced, swinging her hips left to right. She didn't recognize the song but loved it.

"We're heading upstairs," she heard Bea say from the door.

"G'night," Tatum replied. God, it felt good to flail. To feel her body moving unself-consciously through space. She ran her fingers through her hair, massaging her own scalp, feeling the bass in the back of her throat. At first, she hardly noticed when Layla's hands found her thighs, but soon they were pressed against each other, Layla's chest to Tatum's sweaty back. Her head fell onto Layla's shoulder and her mouth opened. Their bodies moved in sweeping circles, Layla's power flowing directly into her like heat.

She opened her eyes enough to see Layla's shimmering upper lip. Dancing had freed her dark hair, and her cheeks were pink. Tatum was thirsty for her sweat.

Before she could make a move, Layla did. They kissed gently at first, then harder, until Tatum's lower lip was clamped between Layla's teeth.

Layla's fingers wound themselves into her hair, tugging her head back. It was violent, passionate. It was what she needed to forget. She was nerve endings. She was an aching hole.

Their two bodies fit together perfectly, despite all the incestuous reasons why they shouldn't. Suddenly, they were on the floor, somehow both on top of each other, faces wet, underwear, too. When Tatum's fingers hooked onto Layla's skirt, she nodded excitedly.

"Yes," breathed Layla. "Fuck me."

So, Tatum went to work yanking off Layla's vinyl skirt, which was tight around her slender hips, tugging it down an inch at a time. It was awkward and a little ridiculous, and Tatum wished she could laugh. Suddenly, she realized, she was afraid again, to be free.

When Layla said, "That's Valentino, so please be careful," Tatum's brain shuddered back to life completely, raking her out of her blind pleasure. These were Layla's legs, thin and fuzzed by hair. This was Layla's skirt—her Valentino skirt—which she must not harm. This was Layla, who was beautiful and could be generous, but who was also annoying sometimes and selfish; this was Layla, Tatum's oldest friend, whom she used to consider her sister; this was Layla, who, if Tatum was going to do this with an oldest friend, wasn't the one she'd always wanted.

She looked up, through the wild tangles of her own blond hair; her left breast was untucked from her shirt. "Of course," said Tatum. "I'll be careful." Layla's thighs were sewn together by her skirt. Tatum didn't know what to do, whether to keep going or to stop and run away, out into the night, back to Park Slope or somewhere else, or throw herself off the cliffs that surrounded the lake. Layla's fingers were still kneading Tatum's breast, her lips were still parted and wet, and she was still whimpering though Tatum was hardly touching her.

Layla said, "Don't stop."

But Tatum couldn't move. What was she doing?

Layla started tugging on her skirt herself. "C'mon," she said urgently.

Tatum jerked back into gear like an unoiled machine. Though she was attracted to Layla in the abstract, she didn't want this. And yet, with Layla's skirt off, her head dipped down.

At the sound of nails on wood, Tatum's eyes flicked back up. Willow crossed the room, stepping around Layla's convulsing body. When the dog slid to the floor next to Tatum, her company helped a bit.

What if Bea and Rosalie could hear Layla's theatrical moans? Her hand clawed at the back of Tatum's head, pressing it down, her toes curled—it was about to end. Just a few more seconds, and then—suddenly, she bolted upright. Bile was filling her mouth. She pressed a hand to her lips, stood, and sprinted out of the room, tripping over Willow, who yelped.

"What the fuck," she heard Layla exclaim just before Tatum vomited into the kitchen sink, all over the dishes Layla had left as she'd cooked. Then she vomited again. And again.

"Jesus," Layla said from behind her. "Fuck." She pinched her nostrils and passed Tatum a roll of paper towels. She was naked. Tatum vomited a fourth time as Layla left the room.

When she was finally confident it was over, she cleaned the sink, washed out her mouth, and staggered back to the living room, where she found Layla on the couch in her thong. Tatum was ashamed, embarrassed, and grateful the nausea, whether from pregnancy or booze, had cut their sex short.

She was also more sober now, but still stupid and clumsy, and didn't know what to do or say. The music was loud, vibrating through her skull. These walls that had comforted her as a child were closing in now, crushing her.

"You okay?" Layla asked.

"I think I need to go to bed." It was hard to catch her breath.

"Right," said Layla, standing.

The disco ball rained teardrops across them.

"I'd kiss you," said Layla, "but, you know."

Tatum blinked. "No," she said. "I mean, yeah, I just puked."

"You're really great," said Layla. "Like, obviously. I just mean I've wanted to do that for a long time. I wasn't sure if you felt the same."

What did *wanted to do that for a long time* mean between lifelong friends?

"Like, even when we were kids." Layla seemed to read Tatum's mind. "I mean, not like I was dying to have sex with you when we were little babies, but like, the crush was always there, I think."

Tatum was nodding, heard herself say, "Me too." She wanted to cry. This wasn't supposed to happen. It never had with Audrey, and Tatum had been full-on in love with her; the fact that Audrey hadn't felt the same didn't matter, because Tatum had always known that crossing this line would overwrite their history, alter their futures, and nothing was worth that. Romantic love was fickle, especially when it came to Audrey, who'd moved swiftly from person to person. Though Tatum was not in love with Layla—not at all—and the two adult friendships were not comparable, it was still painful to think of the innocence they'd just destroyed together, and her own displeasure as it was happening, to which she'd been a bystander.

Layla was pulling on her top.

I'm pregnant, Tatum imagined saying. Maybe she should keep the baby after all. Maybe she should get back together with Ed, get married. She could avoid this unhappiness by opting for that unhappiness. Was unhappiness just life?

Layla looked nervous, which was a first. "Cool," she said. "Well, I guess I'll see you tomorrow." She walked to the door as Tatum tried not to stare at her ass.

"See you tomorrow," Tatum repeated. Willow lumbered over then. Tatum pressed her face into her fur, inhaling the leathery smell of her skin.

The music stopped as if it had sensed Layla was gone, though the disco ball kept spinning.

21

INITIALLY, BEA HAD wanted to help Rosalie settle into her room but was finding it hard to be in there. As Rosalie changed into her pajamas, Bea ran her fingers along the top of the bureau where vials of her mother's homeopathic potions used to be arranged. Her heart ached for things she hadn't thought about in so long: the scent of Patricia's Weleda cream—specifically the way it smelled on her; the way her father cleared his throat when he was ready to shut off the light and sleep—the kids' sign to leave the room for the night; the toes of her mother's silk slippers poking out from beneath the bed, and even her mother's smile, the way it used to look. She hadn't felt this kind of homesickness, hadn't thought anything good about her mother, in a long time, but being back here reminded her of when things were different. When she was young, she'd felt protected and loved by Patricia. But that woman, the one she'd known in early childhood, might as well be dead, just as this house might as well be a tomb.

"Are you tired?" she asked.

Rosalie nodded.

Bea could tell she was drunk by how long it took her to find the leg holes in her pajama pants.

She sighed and walked around the bed to help. "You really shouldn't drink so much."

Rosalie said, "I'm fine," as she almost fell over. Bea caught and held her shoulder as she guided the stretchy pants over the cuts on her thighs.

"You really shouldn't, though."

Pulling the hood of her sweatshirt down, Rosalie said weakly, "Okay."

Bea squeezed her shoulder. "Good."

Alcohol would only confuse things, she thought. It emboldened and deluded. It could make Rosalie think she was better, even just for the evening, and that wasn't safe. When Audrey had been drinking, she hadn't been as open to Bea's help. In contrast, the substance she'd eventually relied on above all others—heroin—had made her totally dependent.

Bea accompanied Rosalie to the bathroom, where they brushed their teeth together, spitting into the sink one after the other.

When they opened the door, each having peed and washed their faces, Layla was coming up the stairs. She was dressed in a sheer thong and her tight corset top from earlier, carrying her skirt. Her makeup was smudged, pink lip gloss all but rubbed off her mouth and onto her cheeks and chin. Bea blinked and for a moment, there she was, four feet tall in this same hallway, hair a matted web down her back, dirt packed under her toenails, Paul Frank T-shirt over loose shorts, no fake boobs or lips or lashes or Brazilian bikini wax.

"Oh," said Layla. "Hey, there."

Bea nodded.

"Do you have everything you need?" Layla asked brightly, as if nothing about her appearance was strange.

"Yep," Bea replied.

"Great," said Layla. "Well, then. I'll see you in the morning."

When her door was shut, Rosalie said, "Um, did they just—"

Quickly, Bea said, "I have no idea." And she didn't care.

"Is that something they do?"

Bea shrugged. The kennel was nothing to her anymore, and neither were they.

"Wow, that's crazy." Rosalie appeared to have been enlivened, somewhat, by this potential development. "I know you said you guys are super old friends, so that must be weird."

"It really isn't," said Bea. "They're both shitheads."

Rosalie didn't respond.

"Well, good night," said Bea.

"Night."

As soon as possible, Bea was in bed, the bed that had felt the most "hers" out of any throughout her life. Her shirt was pulled up, hands folded over her soft stomach. She glanced at the olive jar, tucked under Audrey's quilt like a person, then at her phone, useless on the nightstand. There was hardly any service here and she'd forgotten to ask Layla for the Wi-Fi password. The window was open a few inches, which hadn't been easy to do—her fingers, against her stomach, were still stinging from the ordeal. Chilled forest air swirled through the room, wet and spiced.

From what she could tell, she hadn't gotten any texts, not even the green kind, which specifically meant she hadn't heard from Dennis. She wouldn't hear from him, she knew. Still, she'd wait.

A tree branch scratched the window.

"Hey, thanks for all that, by the way."

Bea's eyes, which had begun to close, snapped open. She scanned the small room. There wasn't so much as a closet. Just a low dresser, long curtains, a hanging light fixture. She was alone.

"Really, Trix. Great to know there was a positive side to my death."

"Hello?" Bea whispered. It was unmistakably Audrey's voice: the smoker's rasp, the nickname. Though her words often played in Bea's mind, this was different. This was no echo. It was an enormous shock, a hallucination, an impossible dream come true, but she absorbed it quickly. Somehow, she'd known this would happen if she kept the olive jar safe, ever since returning from Arizona and finding it in the otherwise empty refrigerator, like a totem in Audrey's honor. The jar was, after all, a more fitting urn than their mother's dull, impersonal selection.

For a moment, she debated switching on the light before deciding it wasn't worth it. She didn't need to see her to know Audrey was there. Of course this was finally happening at the yellow house. She hadn't thought of it before, but maybe she should've—maybe she should've prepared. Or she could've been afraid: of Audrey, who was dead, of herself if she was losing her mind, of this dream—if it was a dream—which could easily become a nightmare. But she wasn't. She was only relieved, especially since she was certain this wouldn't be happening at all if she'd kept swallowing pills every day to appease Patricia. Pills that had dulled her instincts and unique sense of the world.

"Just stopped by to say I hope Dennis never texts you again." Audrey's tone was playful.

"Am I dreaming?" Bea asked pointlessly. "Are you really here?"

Silence.

"Aw, babe. Stop crying."

Bea realized then that her cheeks were wet, that she could hardly breathe. "Can you see me?" She gasped.

"Something like that." Audrey laughed. It had been so long since Bea had heard that sound.

"I've been waiting for you to speak to me," said Bea, between hiccups. "I've felt you with me."

"You think I'm the olive jar you've been carrying around."

"Aren't you?"

Nothing. Okay, so, maybe she'd been wrong about that.

"Are you the dog downstairs, then?"

Nothing.

"That is the dog you wanted, though, right? You must have had something to do with it being here, at least?"

"Trix," said Audrey, and the way she said it told Bea to stop asking questions. There was a long pause, then Audrey said, "The whole kennel thing's pretty cute. The Bennel Kennel is a truly terrible name, though."

"Thought you'd like it—the idea, not the name." Bea wiped her nose with her shirt. "Then I thought you'd hate it. The name is bad, I know, but whatever. I don't care about any of that now."

"Of course you don't," said Audrey, "that's what I'm here to discuss."

"What?"

"Rosalie."

"Rosalie?"

"You're really good at taking care of people."

Bea inhaled sharply. She felt a press of warmth against her cheek—real or imagined?—and eyed the olive jar, which was as motionless as ever.

"You're proud of me?"

"I am."

"You aren't mad at me for anything?"

"I'm not."

"I did the right thing?"

Silence.

"And the olive—"

"No," said Audrey. "Throw the fucking olive jar away."

"It's the one you were eating from when—"

"I know what it is. Throw it away."

Bea fell quiet. She felt panicky, sweaty, short of breath, but happy, too. Happier than she'd been in so long. The air was thick, as if each oxygen molecule held a bit of Audrey in it.

"I love you," Audrey said, and it was what Bea needed to hear most. Euphoria. Such gratitude for Audrey, and for herself—Bea—exactly as she was. This, she realized, was what Audrey had once said heroin gave her: "It makes me love myself. Turns down all the noise: bad thoughts, fear, and self-doubt." At the time, Bea hadn't understood. Audrey shouldn't have needed drugs to love herself. She was the most lovable person alive—everyone thought so. And she loved Bea, even now, which had made Bea love herself; it still did.

"I love you, too," Bea whispered. "I forgive you and I'm sorry." She couldn't help but apologize, despite what Audrey was saying. Even as she thought about Audrey's selfish choices, Bea was the one who felt guilty for what she'd chosen to do in the end without knowing if it was right or wrong.

"Trust," said Audrey. "You know what to do."

"You're not angry at me?"

"Trust," Audrey repeated. "She needs you like I did."

Bea understood exactly what she was saying. Her head fell back against the pillow, as if she was a marionette and the string that held it had suddenly snapped. She was weightless, immobile. She hoped this was death, that Audrey was showing it to her, for it was wonderful. It was relief from bad thoughts. It was only the here and now. Maybe it was how children felt at the very best of times, in the very best of conditions. No sense of foreboding or guilt, only the pleasant darkness of their bedroom, the knowledge that they were safe and loved, the belief that things unequivocally were, and always would be, okay. Maybe death was safety, and in that way, the essence of youth itself—at least the way youth should be for all children—only it was infinite. Maybe it really was the escape—the reversion to an even better past—she'd always imagined it to be. Or maybe this was heroin.

Again, Audrey said, "Just trust. You'll do what's right."

And with that, the room relaxed, and Bea could breathe deeply and move again.

"Audrey?" she said. "Hello? What was that? What did you just show me?"

Silence.

"Hello?" Nothing. It was over, whatever *it* was.

The whispering breeze, the push of distant water against rock, the thrum of crickets; the same sounds as before, and yet everything was different now.

There was so much Bea hadn't known for sure about their relationship. Since, by the end, Audrey's one real love was drugs, there hadn't been space for Bea inside her heart anymore. She'd never said, "Thank you." But Bea had done her best, for both of them, never knowing for certain if she was right. Now that she did, she could do the same for

Rosalie with new confidence. Whether Bea was awake or trapped in a lucid dream, Audrey's visit was real enough, and she'd confirmed that Bea was doing the right thing now, with Rosalie, and that she'd been right all along.

Bea, or maybe her dream self, got out of bed. She pried open the window screen, grabbed the olive jar from Audrey's bed, and threw it as hard and as far as she could into the forest. She heard it shatter, a sudden, shocking sound, then all was peaceful. Now she could focus entirely on Rosalie. Audrey had given her permission—encouraged her to do so.

After muscling the screen back into place, she lay down and eventually the world faded away.

22

WHEN TATUM OPENED her eyes, she didn't know where she was. Her vision was blurry. Her head killed. She was on a couch, though not the one in her parents' apartment, upholstered in worn, scratched leather; also, not the one in her apartment with Ed. No, this fabric was itchy, thick brocade. She shifted onto her back and stretched, and as she did, her eyes found a revolving disco ball casting splinters of light across the ceiling in steady circles. It was mesmerizing, and the subtle *click, click* of its motor the perfect soothing white noise. Her eyelids were so heavy. She was almost asleep again, when someone spoke.

"Hey."

Tatum lifted her head and squinted in the direction of her feet, where the voice had come from.

Sure enough, someone was there, hunched and shrouded in dark fabric. The Grim Reaper? *Take me*, Tatum thought. *Please.*

When the figure moved, exposing the pale sliver of a cheek, Tatum knew that it was Rosalie, and remembered where she was and what had happened earlier that night.

"Hey," she croaked, and suddenly Willow's large head was all she could see, the fractal pattern on her glossy black nose. "Oh, and hey to you, too," she said, petting the dog, ducking to avoid her smelly tongue. "Okay, yes. Hi there. Good girl. Very good girl. Okay, give me some room. I need air. Stop licking me, please. Hi, yes, I love you, too." She was being smothered and was too weak to fight it. "Sit," she tried, and Willow obeyed.

At the far end of the couch, Rosalie's legs were tucked inside her sweatshirt. She was facing Tatum, whose mouth tasted terrible, like rot.

"What time is it?" Tatum asked, reaching under herself in search of her phone.

"A little after three in the morning," Rosalie whispered.

Tatum rubbed her eyes. Everything hurt.

"You okay?"

Tatum nodded. "Just have to get some water, I think."

She'd begun the long, painful journey to standing by bending her knees, when Rosalie said, "I got you some already. It's behind you."

When Tatum turned, she found a frosted glass on the side table. "Wow," she said. "Thank you so much, that's really nice."

Was this the first nice thing anyone had ever done for her? At that moment, it felt like it.

Rosalie said, "Figured you could use it."

Apart from her upper cheek, Tatum could hardly see her face through her hair, which moved in little puffs when she spoke.

Tatum sucked down the contents of the glass, wetting her chin and the front of her shirt, while Rosalie sat quietly.

"Can't sleep?" she asked once she'd swallowed, placing the glass back on the table, adding a coaster beneath it.

Rosalie shook her head. "Mostly I don't. Then sometimes it's all I can do."

Tatum tried to get comfortable. It seemed like Rosalie wanted to talk. She was still in the clothes she'd tugged on that morning in her childhood bedroom in Park Slope, which might as well have been decades ago: jeans and the tight boatneck shirt that restricted her shoulder and arm movements but highlighted her clavicle. Her clavicle. Layla's mouth. She wanted to forget she had a clavicle. Would certainly never be highlighting it again.

Though more than anything Tatum wanted to retreat to bed, she asked, "At home, what do you do at night if you can't sleep?"

Rosalie tucked a section of hair behind her ear, revealing half her face. Veins drew a hazy map through milky skin.

She said, "Nothing really. I think, or I pretend to be asleep."

Tatum said, "Right."

Silence.

"How's living with Bea going?"

Rosalie looked away. "It's fine."

Tatum smoothed her curls, probably to no avail since they were always wild after she slept, and Willow sighed adorably as she curled herself into a spiral on the floor, resting her long snout across her paws.

"Good," said Tatum. She wasn't going to probe.

"It's also really weird sometimes, though," said Rosalie.

Tatum nodded. "Okay, I can't say I'm entirely surprised to hear that."

Rosalie, still facing away, didn't respond.

"So, where are you from?"

Rosalie mumbled something.

"Pardon?"

"I said, 'It's more than weird, actually.' Living with Bea, that is. Oh, and I'm from Long Island. Not the fancy part, though."

Tatum frowned. "I thought you two were close."

Rosalie was looking at her now. "I don't know what we are."

It was the sort of thing people said about romantic flings. So, maybe that was it after all. Tatum understood these thoughts often swirled up, in their most potent form, late at night, and Rosalie was an insomniac in need of romantic advice who'd stumbled across another person at the perfect moment. Sadly, when it came to Bea, Tatum had little advice to give. Plus, her throbbing head made thinking hard.

She tried: "Well, there's no rush to figure things out, you know. You can take your time and see where it goes."

Rosalie was still. "Honestly, I get the sense I don't have that much."

Tatum asked, "That much what?"

"Time."

Tatum crossed her arms. What was Rosalie talking about? "You're young," she said. "You've got heaps of time." Was she sick or something?

Rosalie shrugged. "I'm just not sure I do." She mumbled something else that Tatum couldn't quite make out. It almost sounded like she'd said, "And I'm not even sure I want it."

This was all cause for concern, which, at that moment, Tatum was incapable of. She said quickly, "Let's talk about it more in the morning. Are you planning to stay down here all night?"

"She watches me sleep," said Rosalie, almost inaudibly. Tatum cupped her ear and leaned forward. "I mean, she thinks she's watching me sleep, but I'm actually awake." So, Tatum surmised, at home they spent nights in the same bed. Maybe Bea wanted to keep their romance under wraps, which could explain why they weren't sharing a room that night. It was very Bea to keep secrets, and it wasn't surprising to hear that she watched her partner sleep. Though it made sense that Rosalie found it unsettling, that was Bea: unsettling. Any partner of hers would have to embrace it somehow.

Tatum yawned. She was uncomfortable in all ways. Her joints ached. Her swollen brain pressed against her skull. "She watches people—that's always been a thing. I never liked it, but Audrey didn't really care. You could bring it up with her, if you want." It was difficult to talk. Her jaw was stiff. Tatum needed real sleep, was probably still drunk.

"She also controls what I eat," Rosalie said. "Insists on making me everything. Won't let me cook for myself or eat what I want."

Tatum nodded. "Well, that definitely sounds a lot like her mother."

"I just thought you might be able to explain," said Rosalie, "since you've known her so long and you're doing that whole business thing together. I don't know what she wants from me or what I should do."

"Please," Tatum scoffed. "I've known her all my life, but I don't know her at all."

Rosalie looked confused.

"I mean, we've just never been on the same wavelength. I think she's a special person, and the way she took care of Audrey was really . . ." Tatum shook her head. "I mean, from what I could tell, it was amazing. I mean, there were weird things about it, too. Do I wish Audrey had been in a program? Yes. But it seemed like she was unwilling to go." Tatum paused. "The point is, I can't figure Bea out, either. Not at all. She's sort of unknowable to me. Has been since we were young. I got the sense even Audrey didn't really understand her. She was always saying things about how Bea was, how she thought, but I could tell it was mostly guesswork." The inside of Tatum's mouth was putty. Disgusting.

Rosalie was quiet, then said, "What do you mean, she 'took care of Audrey'?"

She shouldn't have brought Audrey up. It was opening a can of worms when all she wanted to do was sleep. Rosalie was looking for answers, though Tatum couldn't figure out what her real question, or worry, was.

"I never really saw her in action. It was the pandemic and stuff, so I wasn't over there much. What I know is what Audrey sometimes texted me, things like 'Bea's making me soup,' and what Patricia—their mom—told my mom, though Patricia is insane, so I take everything she says with a grain of salt. It seems like Bea did just about everything for Audrey. Made her food, helped her bathe, kept their apartment—your apartment, I guess—in order." Tatum scratched her head. "Once, I tried to get Audrey actual help." She frowned. "Did I *really* try?" All she'd done was ask a high-out-of-her-mind Audrey if she'd like to go to rehab. "Maybe I didn't *really* try, but I did try. I don't know, the whole thing was just so upsetting and confusing, and Bea was right there over my shoulder, and she was taking such good care of her, and—" Tatum sucked in a breath. "Anyway, it doesn't matter now."

"And then Audrey died from an overdose?"

"Her addiction killed her." Tatum's physical discomfort allowed her to detach and speak relatively numbly about this. "But she didn't die from an overdose, no. She actually choked to death." Tatum looked down at Willow for comfort, who was motionless except for the metronomic rise and fall of her side.

Rosalie's face was completely exposed now. Hair hooked behind both ears, she was staring at Tatum, eyes very round. "What exactly did she choke on, do you know?"

It was an odd question, Tatum thought, bordering on insensitive. Why did it matter? At this point it seemed like Rosalie was probing for the sake of it. Still, sleep-deprived, she said, "Audrey really liked olives. Ever since we were kids. And she was very high while eating them one night, and—" That was enough said. It was time to disappear now. When Tatum stood, clutching the couch arm for support, so did Willow. "I really need to go to bed."

As she passed, Rosalie grabbed her hand. Her fingers were ice cold. Tatum fought the urge to recoil.

"Did you hear that sound, earlier?" she asked.

Tatum shook her head. "I don't know what you're talking about, I'm sorry. I'm not in the best state of mind."

Rosalie nodded and released her.

"It came from outside. Sounded like breaking glass."

Again, Tatum shook her head—this time, it threw her off-balance. She stumbled, then caught herself.

"I just want to know where this is all going," said Rosalie. "I hate my life in general, so I don't care what happens—what she does to me—I just want to know what to expect, because it can't stay like this. It won't." Her lips hardly moved as she spoke; she was frozen except for her thumb, which rubbed the thick silver band on her pointer finger in quick strokes. She was staring past Tatum, as if she didn't exist at all. Tatum fought the urge to snap her fingers, to wake Rosalie from whatever unblinking, insomnia-induced trance she was in.

Even snapping her fingers would be too difficult, though. Tatum had to get to bed before she passed out.

"All is well," she said. "You'll work it out with Bea. It takes time to learn a person and build a healthy relationship, or whatever, and it's hard to relax your first night in a new place. Don't worry, though.

You're safe here, and whatever that sound was, just don't think about it. I'll see you tomorrow."

The next day, Tatum's head was a block of cement, and she had only the vaguest memory of their conversation. A mirror faced the bed, and she could see herself in it, curls felted into one big thing. She groaned, throwing her arms over her face against the sun glaring in through the window. The skin on the back of her neck was gummy. She was disgusting, naked, smelly, bloated, hungover. It was going to be a long day, she knew, filled with weirdness. The thought of all the complicated dynamics made her want to close her eyes and sleep for as long as she could, but she had to pee.

Willow's position across the foot of the bed had required Tatum to bend her legs all night, but the company, her protection, was worth it. The rhythm of Willow's breath had nursed her to sleep after she'd jolted awake, a few hours after finally making it to bed, from a dream she mostly couldn't remember, except that it had ended with Audrey, ghostly in translucence and a long, white dress, leaning over her face in the dark.

"Fuck," she said, wiping sweat from her upper lip, squinting against the sun. Willow opened her eyes. "Hi, sweetie." Tatum rumpled the fur on her back.

When she stood, her bladder felt even more full. Cradling her lower stomach, she moaned. What time was it? Maybe it was very early and no one else was up. As far as she could tell, the house was quiet.

Willow leapt off the bed and trotted brightly to the door, tail wagging.

"Okay," said Tatum. "Okay, okay." She pulled on a sweater and a comfortable pair of shorts.

The knob squeaked when it turned and she winced, then poked her head into the hall. No one was there, and all the other doors were closed. She'd use the bathroom downstairs since Willow had to be walked anyway, and it would be quieter.

Outside was beautiful. A swath of the garden was visible from the bathroom window. Trellises had been added, and enormous, flowering bushes. There was the wooden door that led to the enclosed vegetable area. There were the black-eyed Susans, and bobbing, multicolor hydrangeas, like clouds painted by sunset. Though these flowers were not in season anywhere else in the state, nothing could be put past Nancy, it seemed.

Willow leaned against the bathroom door, her black-splotched tongue evoking Brooklyn pavement as she panted.

After washing her hands and swallowing a nausea pill, Tatum led Willow to where her stained, green leash was conspicuously coiled on an expensive-looking marble table in the kitchen. She fastened it to her collar and shivered—the house was drafty; when she went to open the back door, she realized why. It was already ajar. Had it been left this way all night, or was someone else awake? Was it Layla? Was she on the porch, waiting to bombard Tatum with unrequited love before she'd even had a sip of coffee? Willow whimpered. She had to go out, which meant Tatum did, too. So, she squared her shoulders, sucked in a deep breath, and stepped into the sunlight.

Wedged into the overstuffed cushions of a broad, wicker porch chair was Bea. Tatum exhaled.

"Oh, hey," she said while being pulled down the steps by Willow, who peed the instant her paws touched grass.

"Morning," Bea replied. "Sleep well?"

Tatum noticed the sketchbook against her knee.

"I'm pretty hungover," she said. "And fell asleep on the couch for a while last night, so, not great." She thought of mentioning her conversation with Rosalie, but didn't. What had they talked about? Bea?

Bea nodded, then asked, "Did you and Layla fuck?"

Tatum laughed out of surprise, then stammered, "Uh, I mean, sort of?"

Bea took a long sip from a mug. After she'd swallowed, she said, "Cool. Is Rosalie up yet?"

Tatum, still recovering, said, "I don't think so."

"Cool," Bea repeated, then looked away and began sketching furiously.

Willow sniffed a row of flowers, lumbering across the lawn and taking Tatum along with her.

"Beautiful morning," said Tatum, hoping to ease some of the tension she always felt with Bea. Wanting to offer her something—friendship? Conversation? Interest?

Birds were chirping, and though the air was cool, the sun was warm, and here she was, on sacred ground, yet her heart was so heavy. Willow's gentle tugs on her wrist helped keep Tatum present, but when they reached a patch of mulch, she chose to poop. "Shit," said Tatum, watching Willow's hindquarters quiver. "Don't have a bag. Would you mind looking for one in the kitchen?" Tatum hated asking Bea for anything. "Or you could hold her leash for a second while I get a bag?"

Slowly, Bea looked up from her work.

"So sorry," Tatum said, wincing.

Bea rubbed her forehead, which looked very painful—yellow in places, brown in others—cracked her wrists and each of her fingers before rising and disappearing inside. Her sketchbook lay open on the chair. A photorealistic, black-and-white drawing of Audrey stared out, her beautiful face hollowed the way it had been more toward the end of her life, when her thinness looked like sickness. Tatum yanked Willow closer. She reached up and through the porch railing, lifting the drawing for a better view. Bea had etched a few spindly branches reaching across Audrey's face, as if she was staring out through a young tree or a bush. She'd always known that Bea was good but hadn't realized how good. She'd perfectly captured the light behind Audrey's eyes but also the secrets, and the branches, slender and forked, were even reflected in them. Tatum realized then that she'd forgotten so much about her friend's face, as she'd avoided pictures of her over the past few years. Now there was Audrey, looking somehow even more herself than she had in real life.

"Will this work?" Bea asked from the open doorway. Tatum staggered back, almost tripping over Willow.

"Jesus," she said. "Yeah, I mean, I think so. Sorry." She struggled to drag Willow through the grass, away from the flowers she was so interested in, to where Bea was holding a large ziplock bag.

Tatum thanked her and took the bag, then said, "You're so talented. Like, really. That drawing is beyond incredible."

Bea stared at Tatum as if she could see through her clothes, there was something so violating about it, and Tatum crossed her arms over her chest as she made her way back to Willow's poop.

As Tatum squared off against it, wrinkling her nose at the smell, she could still feel Bea's eyes. Willow was teaching her exactly how much she didn't know about dogs, and now she was teaching Bea the same thing, and it was embarrassing, because, though it all felt so far away now, they were still supposedly founding a dog kennel company together.

After fumbling with the bag, steeling herself, then chickening out a few times, Tatum glanced helplessly at Bea.

"I—"

"Give it," said Bea as she clomped down the porch steps. She stuck her hand inside the bag, then closed it around the poop, and with a flourish turned the bag in on itself. "Voilà. Learned from watching the neighbor at my parents' old house, who had a dog."

"Thanks," said Tatum. *Watching the neighbor.* What did she mean by that?

Bea zipped it shut and tossed it near the porch, then returned to her chair. The sight of it there was enough to make Tatum gag. She averted her eyes and guided Willow up the stairs to a love seat. She thought of going inside, retreating to her room, but it was dim in there, and the outdoors was what she'd always loved most about this place. Plus, she'd need to face everyone eventually. If she went back to her room now, she'd have to summon the courage to leave it all over again.

The instant Tatum sat, Willow collapsed at her feet, as if exhausted.

Silence. Wind. Birds. Insects. The scrape of Bea's pencil tip.

"Can you believe we're actually here?" Tatum said eventually.

"I guess not," said Bea, still sketching.

"Yeah," said Tatum. "Pretty insane."

Silence. Wind. Birds. Insects. The scrape of Bea's pencil tip.

"Rosalie seems nice," Tatum tried.

"She is."

"And a bit sad," said Tatum. "I hope she's okay."

At this, Bea dropped her pencil and looked up. "She is," she said. "She's got me."

Tatum felt like raising her hands in surrender. "She's lucky," she said. "Very lucky to have you."

Bea went back to drawing.

Silence. Wind. Birds. Insects. The scrape of Bea's pencil tip.

Tatum wanted to address the email fiasco. She felt many things about her hook-up with Layla, but what she cared about most at that moment was that Bea knew she saw Layla's flaws. She wanted to apologize, in person this time, wanted to hear from Bea that it was okay. That it was all okay.

"I'm sorry again about—"

"So, why'd you break up with Ed?"

Tatum was taken aback. "Oh," she said. "Uh, it's kind of complicated."

Bea glanced up, waiting, so Tatum continued—not because she particularly wanted to. "We're just really different, and I've known it would happen for a while."

"Why didn't you end it sooner, then?"

"It was hard because we were living together and stuff." This was, of course, an oversimplification. The real reason was embarrassing: she didn't think she could make it on her own. The way Bea was looking at her, it was clear she knew there was more to the story.

"My mom always told me you were so in love," said Bea, her tone mocking.

"Yeah, well," said Tatum. "I guess I loved him at one point, but I haven't felt that way in a while, honestly." More quietly, she said, "Maybe I never did. Who knows?"

Bea was quiet.

"Are you and Rosalie—" Tatum started to ask, before Bea interrupted her again.

"Are you sad? Or angry? Or do you feel bad about it?"

Tatum bit her lip, thinking. "Hm," she said. How much should she divulge? But it was nice to be asked these questions, actually—to be pressed to explore her feelings. "Probably all three."

"Why?"

Tatum leaned back. "I suppose I'm sad because it didn't work out, and change is hard; I'm angry because I wish he'd been different in certain ways, like played video games less often and been more motivated or something; and I feel bad because I'm the one who ended it." *Immediately after telling him I'm pregnant*, she added in her head. "And I should've done it a lot sooner." *Especially because then I wouldn't be pregnant right now.*

"Interesting," said Bea. "And now you're going to be with Layla?"

"No," Tatum said immediately. "I mean, I don't know, but no. I guess I should talk to her about it before saying anything definitive, but I don't want to be with her like that."

Bea smirked. Could she read Tatum's mind? It sure seemed like it. Speaking to Bea was the opposite of speaking to Audrey; it was like being laughed at while stark naked.

"So, then the answer is no."

Tatum was staring at the hem of her sweater, fiddling with the knit fibers. "I really don't know what's going to happen. But yes, no. I mean, yes, the answer is no, I don't think so."

Bea was smiling. "Do you think the kennel is going to happen?"

Tatum rolled her eyes. "No." She just didn't—no caveats this time. For all of Layla's capability, the tours of spaces and kennels, Anita's thumbnails diligently clicking against her phone as she took notes, and the fact that Tatum had nothing else hopeful in her life, it was still so murky and impossible, like trying to imagine the faces of book characters, which couldn't be done—not really. The kennel wasn't supposed to exist. She knew this and always had. If she softened her thoughts, kept her eyes up—didn't look down or to the side—she could think about it as if it was real, and that had made her feel better about her life, especially over the past week. And it had brought her Willow, too, who was suddenly so important. But no. The answer was no. It felt good to say so with such certainty, to let go of the façade for a moment.

Bea raised her eyebrows in what seemed like a look of approval. "Ah," she said. "A straight answer from you."

"Do you?" Tatum asked.

Bea said, "So, what if Layla wants to be with you, then?"

The bit was getting old now. Tatum straightened in her seat; below, on the floor, Willow lifted her head. "So, what about you and Rosalie?" said Tatum, ignoring Bea's question. "Are you two together?" She raised an eyebrow, matching Bea's expression.

The corners of Bea's mouth twitched. "Why?"

Tatum didn't reply, just pursed her lips.

Bea looked amused. "It's more complicated than that. Rosalie needs me."

Tatum leaned back, folded her hands across her stomach, and sat quietly as Bea returned to sketching, only it wasn't awkward this time. The quiet was actually sort of nice. They were just being together, and that did remind her of time spent with Audrey. Tatum yawned, and at the sound, Willow rose and rested her head against Tatum's knee.

When Bea sneezed, Tatum said, "Bless you," then smiled. "You know, it's funny, a few weeks ago, I could've sworn I heard your sneeze."

Bea did not look up from her work. "Oh?"

Tatum nodded, stroking Willow's soft muzzle. "Yeah. I paid your old house a visit, actually. I was a little emotional, and had a really weird, intense reaction to being there—I'm just full of *weird, intense* reactions these days, apparently. Anyway, I thought I heard you sneeze." She laughed, because it was ridiculous. When they were young, it had always been a joke that Audrey and Bea sneezed exactly the same way—sharp, sudden, and loud.

"Maybe it was Audrey," Bea said.

"That's honestly what I thought at first. Then I thought it might be you, somewhere. Then I knew I was insane because I was clearly alone." Tatum frowned. "Like, to be clear, I'm not accusing you of anything here." She really wasn't.

More quiet sketching.

"Does Audrey ever visit you?"

Bea's eyes flicked up.

"I mean, not really, but like, energetically or whatever?"

"No." Bea sounded stern. Defensive, almost.

There was a noise from inside. So, someone else was awake. Tatum was feeling better now—something about her time with Bea, and Willow, too. It was as if they'd given her a coat of arms. Bea's approval, or at least the small amount of respect she'd just earned, had made her stronger. She was ready to face Layla. To be herself—be honest and protective—like Bea was. Why not finally relax? Why not admit that she knew what she wanted, what was real and what wasn't? Would this feeling hold?

"Hey." It was Layla's deep voice. Tatum turned to find her wearing a black silk negligée, her dark hair twisted into a claw clip. Layers of foundation coated her face, visible even from where Tatum sat, with two bubble-gum-pink wells pressed into the apples of her cheeks—no makeup artist around to fix it. How long had she spent getting ready before coming downstairs? The perfection Tatum was usually awed and intimidated by was gone. Now she found it all so annoying: Layla's thick, clumpy lashes, glossed lips, hair extensions—the tracks were visible with her hair pulled onto her head as it was—and the ease with which she glided through life, her finger-snappy, surreal existence, where things just appeared, and help abounded, except for this weekend. It was like a filter had been removed from Tatum's retinae, and she could see clearly, and she was angry.

Neither of them responded verbally to Layla's greeting.

"Anyone want breakfast?"

Tatum wasn't hungry. Bea said, "I helped myself earlier."

Layla nodded.

"Is Rosalie up?" asked Bea.

Again, Layla nodded.

Bea stood. "I'll make her something, then."

"Tatum?" Layla asked.

Tatum said, "I'm good," and turned away. She could feel Layla hovering over her shoulder for a few seconds longer, then she was gone.

Again, Bea's sketchbook was left open on her seat, but the image of Audrey was much changed. Over her delicately rendered face, Bea had added harsh, dark lines: teeth over her lips, holes over her eyes and nose, the skull beneath her sister's skin. The image was so upsetting, so heartbreaking, Tatum gasped.

At the sound, Willow leapt onto the love seat next to her and started licking her face. So compassionate and intuitive. At that moment, it was impossible not to think of Willow's own loss—of her previous owner, the woman Tatum had seen at the dog run who reminded her of Audrey. The coincidence was so close to magic, she was embarrassed to give it any credence, but she'd thought it at the time, and now that woman was dead. There was some intangible thing about her that Tatum had noticed, as she hadn't even seen her face, just her arms, her floaty gait as she'd walked away, her thick, brown hair. It was a feeling that had come over her when the girl appeared, then disappeared so quickly. Tatum hadn't wanted to see her face, because she'd wanted her to be Audrey. Somehow, they were connected—she was certain—Willow and Audrey, and now Tatum and Audrey. It didn't make sense, and for once, it didn't have to.

23

BEA COULD TELL something was different about Layla the instant she came in from the porch that morning. The muscles in her back reconfigured as she strained to reach an upper cabinet knob, and Bea had the foreign urge to help her. Of course, she didn't act on it, but when Layla came down from her tiptoes with a box of oats in hand, Bea was reminded just how small she was. Layla usually wore platforms or spindly stilettos, and now she was barefoot, but it wasn't just that. Today, Layla's size made her seem weak. Before, it had been more like a superpower.

Bea shrugged the observation off. She turned her attention to Rosalie, and with the contents of the box Layla had fetched, made her a gray lump of oatmeal topped with brown sugar crumbles she found in a chrome tin on the counter, and maple syrup from the fridge. Rosalie accepted the bowl, said, "Thanks," and shuffled with it to the breakfast nook, where she ate with her back facing the rest of the kitchen.

Tatum stayed outside for a while after Bea left, but when she eventually came in, she beelined for the table where Rosalie was, without any food of her own and or even a glance in Layla's direction. Frizzy blond springs bounced around her face, which seemed to annoy her—

she kept swatting at them; her pale legs, speckled by beauty marks, were bruised in random places, and there was green crust in her eyes. As she had on the porch, inside, Willow remained close to Tatum's shins, settling beneath her chair and sighing as she did, as if the marble floor was a soft bed. They'd bonded quickly. It was like they belonged to each other already. Everyone, except Bea, was automatically drawn to Tatum, as if her heart was a magnet with a near-universal polarization: the dog, Layla, Audrey, Ed, if he still counted.

Today, Tatum was visibly exhausted; her eyes were bloodshot and puffy, her movements seemed labored, a far cry from her usual put-togetherness. Now her appeal had less to do with admiration and envy, and more to do with pity—also true of Layla. Bea liked them better this way—stripped down to what was real.

As she dusted the top of her own oatmeal with cinnamon, she looked over to find Rosalie pushing her bowl toward Tatum.

Tatum nodded and smiled, then helped herself to a spoonful of what Bea had made specially for Rosalie. Their heads were angled toward each other, and they were speaking softly. What were they saying? When Tatum touched Rosalie's shoulder, Bea tucked her bowl into the crook of her arm and hurried over to join them. Maybe she should've been clearer with Tatum before everyone else was awake, explained more explicitly that she needn't worry nor interfere.

As Bea settled into the seat on Rosalie's other side, Tatum said, "That's delicious," pointing at Rosalie's bowl. "You're an oatmeal artist, Bea. What did you put in that?"

Bea took a bite from her own bowl. Without looking up, she said, "Sugar and syrup."

"It's great, as usual," said Rosalie.

"Do you often make her breakfast at home?"

Bea didn't like being questioned, especially not in front of Rosalie. Questions, she'd always found, led to judgments, confusion, suspicion, if answered honestly, so she smiled, hoping Tatum would see the warning in her eyes.

"She does," said Rosalie, and Bea's eyes jerked toward her, squinting to impart a different message: *Be quiet*. "She makes me every meal."

"Oh, right," said Tatum, tapping her temple. "Right, right. It's all coming back to me."

What did that mean? When had they spoken about this before? Or was Tatum thinking about what Bea had done for Audrey?

She wanted to ask what Tatum meant, what she knew, tell her to back off, and tell Rosalie to shut up, but she couldn't. She must appear unbothered and calm, like the ideal mother: the perfect, doting caretaker without needs of her own. Rosalie stood and crossed the room to place her dish in the open dishwasher, passing Layla, who was watching two shriveled, frozen sausages circulate in the microwave.

When everyone was finished eating and cleaning, Layla asked, "What now?" and no one answered.

The only activities that occurred to Bea were the childish things they used to do, like playing tag on the lawn or hide-and-seek throughout the house, which had once been cluttered with dusty oddities, making it tantalizingly easy to hide and hard to seek.

What did Layla do at the yellow house as an adult? Or was she ever even here?

"Nothing?" Layla pressed sarcastically. She glanced at Tatum. "We could sit outside, and, like, I don't know. Or we could watch a movie. Or we could—"

"I'd like to see the water, I guess," said Tatum. Bea felt the same, though it was too cold to swim.

"Great," said Layla. "Let's do that," She sounded desperate.

It was decided that Willow wouldn't join them, as the steps down to the little beach were narrow, with a steep drop-off on one side and a rough cliff face on the other.

Tatum knocked Rosalie with her shoulder and said, "You'll be fine, though," as Layla explained the situation, noting the importance of sneakers. Once again, Bea felt her face grow hot. What was Tatum trying to do? And Rosalie was letting her—smiling, brushing the hair from her eyes, thanking her for the reassurance.

"Oh, totally," Layla said. "You'll be fine, I just think it's better to leave Willow."

Once Layla had changed into leggings, they walked in a single file line through the fragrant gardens to the very edge of the cliff, where the ground fell away all at once. The chiseled staircase down to the water was long. Bea gripped the steel railing attached to the rock. Her stomach swooped as she took the first step. "Careful," she said over her shoulder to Rosalie, who'd even hooked her hair behind her ears for the perilous occasion.

Far below, lake waters shifted between miniature peaks and valleys. There was the pebble beach, where they'd skipped stones every day of summer, and dozed, coated in layers upon layers of sunscreen. There was the dock, which jutted into the lake like a tongue.

"Whoa," said Tatum, and Bea turned as Rosalie was recovering from a stumble. She was nearly crouched on the step above, gripping the railing with all her might, taking short, sharp breaths. "Steady there," said Tatum. "Go slow."

Without a second thought, Bea said, "Tatum, switch with me."

Timidly, Rosalie straightened out. "Hey," she said. "It's okay, I'll be more careful."

Again, Bea said, "Switch."

They were halfway down the stairs. Layla was far ahead, almost to the beach. She turned back, hand over her eyes in a salute against the sun.

"You okay?" she yelled up.

As had become the day's norm, no one answered her.

"Tatum," said Bea, and the sharpness of her tone surprised even her. But she must be the one to spot Rosalie from behind, to advise her, to offer comfort.

Tatum said, pleadingly, "Bea, I don't know how to do that without either Rosalie falling or myself."

When she looked down, Bea realized it was true, that it would be nearly impossible for Tatum to step around Rosalie safely. So, she said, "Rosalie, hold on to my shoulders."

"I think I'll feel safer if I'm holding on to the railing," she said.

Bea glared up at her. *This is for your own good,* she tried to convey through her eyes.

"Rosalie," she said. "Hold on to my shoulders." *How many meals have I made for you?* She hoped Rosalie could hear her thoughts the way twins sometimes could. *You can trust me.*

Seconds passed.

Hold on to my shoulders. Don't embarrass me. Don't make me force you.

How would Bea even do that? If she tried, she'd fall, but it felt good to threaten, even just mentally. It reminded her of Patricia; she'd often said things like, "Don't make me come up there," or "I'll count to five," which had always been effective.

With shaking hands, Rosalie released the railing and gripped Bea's shoulders. When Bea took a step down, Rosalie gasped. "Bea, I'm going to fall if we do this."

"Fine." One at a time, Rosalie's hands left her shoulders.

They descended the rest of the way in tense silence. Bea dug her teeth into her lower lip to keep calm.

When they finally reached the bottom, Tatum said, "It's insane we were allowed to do that as little children."

It really was the least Patricia thing about Patricia that she'd allowed them to use those stairs when they were young. There was no rhyme or reason to it, just the deepest trust, shared by all, that this place would not harm them, that it would only heal them, and it only ever had.

Layla was kneeling by the water's edge, running her fingers through the pebbles, facing the sun with closed eyes. "Fuck, it's nice here," she said, as if only just remembering that it was.

"It's the best place on earth," said Tatum.

From the cliff far above, one could see the lake's distant green-fringe border, but from where they stood now, it was an endless ocean. A perfect mirror for the sky. As expansive as existence itself.

Rosalie was removing her shoes and socks. When her bare feet touched water, she shrieked.

Quickly, delightedly, Tatum followed suit.

"Oh my god," she said as water lapped at her toes. Goose bumps sprouted across her bare thighs. "My feet are numb."

Rosalie nodded and actually laughed, which was a sound Bea had never heard before.

She glowered at their backs as Tatum wrapped an arm around Rosalie, and they huddled together for warmth. Bea could tell Layla was trying to catch her eye, searching for comradery, but she wouldn't oblige.

Rosalie's face was pink, her smile wide, when she turned around. "Bea," she said, beckoning her. "Come!"

But Bea shook her head. "No, you come. Put your shoes on."

Tatum chorused, "Bea, come here! It's so cold but nice!"

Again, Bea shook her head. "Rosalie."

Delicate, depressed, slashed and bloodied, with a permanently broken heart; as Rosalie stepped away from the water, gone was any trace of smile. She stumbled back toward Bea, wincing when she stepped on sharp stones. Her hair untucked itself from behind her ears and she was gone, like a snuffed candle flame releasing a whisp of sadness into the air above her. She pulled on her socks and shoes, then stood beside Bea, facing the water, arms crossed. Tatum looked concerned, but Bea didn't care; though she'd craved it at times, she didn't need her approval now.

"Don't cozy up to Tatum," she whispered to Rosalie. She could see the very corner of Rosalie's eye, the straight set of her mouth through her hair. "Don't forget how much I've done for you."

Though she wasn't sure this was the right approach, something had to be said, and she didn't have time to think hard about what. Rage filled her lungs. To her, ingratitude was the worst sin, and Rosalie's behavior felt like that. She sighed out hot air. Rosalie sniffed. Was she crying?

Awkwardly, Bea attempted to wrap an arm around her the way she'd seen Tatum do, but Rosalie did not step into her like she had Tatum. Rather they stood, side by side, like rigid planks that did not fit together, like an unhappily married couple on the brink of divorce.

Tatum was slowly making her way back from the water's edge now, toward her shoes, and Layla sat quietly on the dock steps; she looked even smaller than before, hands wrapped around her thin biceps. Her lips were purple. Was she crying, too? Her eyes were glassy. No one had paid attention to her in minutes. It was a shift so obvious, Bea felt compassion for Layla, though not acutely enough to do anything about it, which she supposed was the problem with most of humanity. It wasn't that people didn't feel bad for others in need, it was that most people didn't care enough to help.

When Tatum's shoes were back on, she asked, "Does anyone want to skip stones?"

Layla shrugged, then stood.

The four of them faced the water. For a moment, they were silent as their losses washed over them, crystal-clear memories, cleansing them of everything that didn't matter and Bea of her rage momentarily.

She closed her eyes and could feel her sister again. When the wind picked up, swirling around her face, she smiled. It lifted her hair, exposed her wounded forehead, and kissed the back of her neck; it was the closest thing to embracing Audrey one more time. Bea whispered, "I'm trying." She knew this wind was a gentle reminder of what they'd discussed.

Only when she opened her eyes did she realize Layla was holding her hand. She looked over and saw that Tatum and Rosalie were hand in hand, too. They were connected in grief and longing. All Bea had wanted from Audrey was her company, to be the most important person to her, and to make her comfortable and happy. Releasing her from her demons, into the wind—letting her go—was the hardest thing she'd ever done, and the most selfless.

When it first happened, Bea had thought Audrey's death represented the ultimate personal failure. But her time in Arizona with the camels had taught her that death could be freedom. Maybe she'd always known this deep down, and rather than being *stunted*, as her mother had often said, she was enlightened. Humanity's closed-minded fear of death was worse than death itself; Audrey had confirmed as much just last night.

Still, she'd never forget her sister's face, gray as the clouds, her empty eyes and open mouth, frozen in its hunger for oxygen. Bea remembered the silence that had followed the gulps and gasps and thumps of Audrey's fist against the coffee table, and the confusion in her eyes as Bea stood over her motionless, watching, then retreated to the kitchen to watch from there. In her final moments, she was the liveliest she'd been in so long, thrashing and flailing, then suddenly all was still and she was gone. Eventually, Bea called 911, or the shell of her did. And when they questioned her, she'd said she was in the other room and didn't know what happened. Audrey had been high at the time of death—had nodded off with an olive in her mouth—and it was clear she'd been incapable of running down the long hall to Bea's room.

Red and blue lights flashed against the walls. Bea remembered her mother's face, gaunt and anguished, her thin frame keeled over by the window, her shrieks and sobs. It had taken everything not to scream, "This is your fault," into her face. Not because Bea believed that it was, but because it would've felt good to blame someone else. And when Patricia approached her later that terrible evening, after the police had gone, and said, her knobby finger wagging, "Why didn't you help me get her into rehab? Why didn't you let her go?" she realized her mother felt the same way.

Tatum cleared her throat. The sound snapped Bea back to the present. She watched Tatum kneel and search the ground for stones. When she found one, she handed it to Rosalie, who handed it to Bea, who handed it to Layla. They did this until each of them held a smooth, flat stone, then walked together to the water.

"We always used to skip stones with Audrey," Tatum explained to Rosalie. "Do you know how?"

Rosalie nodded. "Sort of."

Bea said, "None of us were good at it. Audrey was the best, by far."

"What if we all skip on the count of three, and we make wishes on our stones?" Tatum asked.

Everyone nodded.

"Okay, who wants to count us down?"

Weakly, Layla said, "I can."

"Sure," said Tatum. "Everyone, don't forget to make a wish."

"Three," said Layla. "Two." Bea looked at Rosalie. Rosalie stared straight ahead. "One." Their four stones went flying. Layla's sank immediately, Bea's made two arcs across the water, Tatum's three, and Rosalie's six.

And in the moment of silence after all four had disappeared below the surface, Bea thought, *I wish Rosalie the freedom of the wind.*

24

When they arrived back at the house, Tatum lay on the widest couch in the largest of the three living rooms, which they used to call "the sitting room"—deliberately avoiding the one in which she and Layla had danced together and so much more—hugging a large bag of pretzel sticks. Willow settled in protectively at her feet.

She stayed there all afternoon, as it was hard to move. Other than the constant nausea, she experienced shocking pain whenever her nipples were brushed, and terrible bloat. The day dragged on, and as it did, these discomforts, on top of everything, made her irritable. She could barely look at Layla, let alone speak to her, and was aggravated by Bea, too. Though she'd enjoyed their time on the porch earlier, now she found Bea's attitude toward Rosalie annoying.

Whenever Tatum interacted with Rosalie, there was Bea, inserting herself. What was she so worried about? Tatum was just being nice. If she wanted to talk to Rosalie, she would. And if Bea had a problem with it, she did. Rosalie was there, she was sweet, and she seemed to like chatting. It was harmless, and Tatum was too overwhelmed to think any harder about it than that.

Rosalie spent the day in a chair by the windows, across the room from Tatum, reading a book she'd plucked from the shelf. Behind her, outside, tree branches bowed in the wind. The sunlight, which had slanted over Tatum's bare legs all afternoon, was warm and soothing and had drifted down slowly as the hours passed. Now it heated only her toes.

Bea had chosen to sit on a small, uncomfortable-looking ottoman in the center of the room between them, her back facing Tatum.

Layla was elsewhere in the house—maybe in her room, licking her wounds. Tatum didn't care where she was, what she was doing, how she was feeling.

God, who was this version of herself? This heartless, resentful person? At least she was strong. Tatum rarely viewed herself that way.

After turning it over and over in her mind, she'd decided that what happened last night was inappropriate. She'd been wasted. Didn't feel like, given that and Layla's position of power when it came to the kennel and life in general, what had happened was completely consensual. Their flirtation was one thing—playful, light, detached. This was another. And here, of all places.

The hours Tatum hadn't spent stewing on Layla, she'd spent mostly napping, or something like that; drifting in and out of near sleep, her eyes opening whenever Rosalie or Bea spoke, which wasn't often.

"Rosalie, are you hungry?" Bea had asked at one point.

"No."

"Do you want me to show you how to work the shower?"

"I'm okay."

But now Tatum was sick of drifting—too achy to sleep, too bored of trying. She sat up to scratch Willow behind the ears, as trees glittered outside, and asked, "Rosalie, what do you do for work?"

Bea whipped around and Tatum almost laughed at her expression, which was so pinched and angry. Totally ridiculous. She could tell Bea's strange reactivity was driving Rosalie away. Each time she was possessive, Rosalie grew stiff and quiet, whereas when Tatum spoke, she opened up.

"I was recently fired," Rosalie said. "From a video game distributor called Gumball. It sucks but whatever."

Tatum respected her lack of excuses.

"Shit," she said. "Sorry that happened."

"It's been a bummer. Money's pretty tight right now."

"That sucks," said Tatum. "For what it's worth, I think I'll be living with my parents indefinitely since I don't have a rich boyfriend whose parents pay most of our rent anymore." The words flowed easily from her, though she'd never said anything like this aloud before. "He would've had a million questions about what it's like to work at a video game distributor, by the way."

Rosalie said, "Yeah, well." She glanced at Bea, who was still swiveled toward Tatum, staring menacingly. "As long as your parents are okay people, it's fine to live at home."

"Was that where you were before you moved in with Bea?"

At the sound of her name, Bea turned back to face Rosalie, who nodded. "Yeah, out in Long Island. I'll probably end up back there soon if I don't get another job."

Tatum glanced at Bea.

"And how does Bea feel about that?"

"Bea," said Bea, "didn't know about it."

Rosalie shook her head. "I told you."

Bea said, "You made me think it wasn't imminent."

Rosalie folded her arms over her chest. "It's not that I want it to be," she said.

"That's beside the point."

Rosalie's eyes, behind her veil of hair, begged Tatum for help. What exactly was going on here?

"Are your parents nice?" Tatum said quickly, hoping to deescalate.

"Yeah," said Rosalie. "It's the town that isn't. It all just reminds me of—" She stopped and scratched her head. "Things." Tatum wouldn't pry. Not in front of Bea.

"Hometowns are weird," said Tatum.

Outside, the light was beginning to purple. In minutes, the sunshine had matured to deep orange. Now it touched only the very tops of the trees. She'd wanted to watch the sunset over the water like they used to but was missing it, which was okay. The magic of this place, she'd realized, lived in the people they'd been here. It wasn't mixed into the plaster coating the walls or the soil feeding the trees and flowers outside. *They* were the magic. Their childhood love for one another was, when there was no earning or losing approval, or questions of compatibility, or insecurities.

There was no denying the place was still beautiful, but it felt empty now, too, and that was disappointing. The house, devoid of their magic love, and of their mothers' inspiring, tight-knit friendship, was just a house. The same was true of Park Slope.

Rosalie said, "Well, you two still live in your hometown."

"Yes," said Tatum. "But I've been thinking, maybe I should move away for a bit." She hadn't been thinking this. Not at all. But the instant she said it, she realized it was exactly right. She should go where no one knew her, where she could create the life she really wanted. Where she could be her real self, whoever that was. Also, somewhere cheaper, where she could afford a backyard for Willow. Where she could escape the bone-crushing pressure of New York City to do big things, make big money. Maybe then she'd find the time, the will, the strength, to take a real stab at writing. See if she was any good. Or maybe she'd find happiness doing something else entirely.

Rosalie asked, "Where would you go?"

Tatum shrugged. "I honestly have no idea. Somewhere far away. Another country, maybe."

"So, this kennel thing is dead in the water, then."

Tatum turned to find Layla standing in the doorway.

"I don't know what it is," said Tatum.

It was hard to speak normally. She wanted to shout her words.

Layla strode into the room and dropped into the armchair matching Rosalie's on the other side of the fireplace. She'd changed back into the black silk negligée she'd worn to breakfast. Her hair was mussed and sleepy. Mascara was smudged into the skin beneath her eyes, making them look dark—maybe from tears.

"Well, I think we should talk about it."

Bea's foot had begun to tap. She seemed impatient for this conversation to end. So, she truly didn't care about the kennel at all. Had she ever? Tatum didn't understand and knew she probably never would.

Layla's directness was clearly a challenge, but Tatum was strong enough to take it now. She met her gaze for the first time that day. "Sure," she said. "You're the one who's in charge, so why don't you kick us off?"

Layla blinked, ran her tongue over her teeth, then said, "Right, well, I think it's over. I don't want to do it anymore with two people who aren't committed. I'm the only one who's done anything. I'm not just talking about monetary stuff, I'm talking about starting conversations, planning meetings between the three of us, showing any amount of enthusiasm. Even fostering this goddamn dog."

It wasn't just the kennel that was over, Tatum knew. Layla was saying they were, too.

Instead of protesting, making excuses for herself such as pointing out that she'd taken care of Willow since they'd arrived without help, Tatum said simply, "I think that's for the best."

Bea was quiet. Her focus was still on Rosalie, who seemed uncomfortable. She was shifting in her seat, and whenever she moved, so did Bea's head, like the jerky second hand of a clock, little ticks.

Layla's eyes narrowed. Tatum wasn't giving her the reaction she wanted. Perhaps she'd expected her to beg.

The sky outside was navy now, cracked in one giant place by the sun's last gasp. It was dramatic; the sort of sky that made one feel unimportant. Tonight, though, Tatum absorbed its power. She imagined that orange crack piercing her heart. The sun pouring directly into her, filling her with fire.

"Tatum, do you want to talk in the other room for a second?" Layla asked.

Tatum stood and squared her shoulders. "Sure." Why not? Now she had nothing to lose.

Stepping over the pretzel bag Tatum had placed on the floor, Layla said, "Also, in the future, no eating anywhere but the kitchen and dining."

Usually, Tatum would've asked if it was okay to eat in the living room before doing so, and if it was okay to eat the pretzels in the first place since they weren't hers. Not today.

They walked in silence to what they used to call "the front room": the smaller living room to the left of the entryway with a large bay window overlooking the cars. Layla flicked on the light and practically stomped to a set of chairs tucked inside the curved glass nook. On the far wall hung a glossy *Tammy Rose* poster that was taller than Tatum.

When they were young, they used to stand in this four-paned window making faces at their mothers as they returned home from errands. Now Layla glowered at Tatum. It was like only her skeleton was there, like she'd been dropped in a tub of acid and everything soft and pretty had burned away. Suddenly and finally, Tatum felt a twinge of sympathy.

"What the fuck is up?" asked Layla. "I don't understand what changed today."

Tatum sighed and leaned back in her chair, shifting her eyes to the ceiling. "You just stated that you feel I've been uncommitted all along," she said. "So, I'm not sure what you mean by 'today.'" It was childish, because of course she knew exactly what she meant.

"Right," said Layla. "I'm pretty sure you do know, though."

"I just—" Tatum paused. The detached façade wasn't easy to maintain anymore. Big, strong feelings churned inside her, but she couldn't say everything at once. She had to start somewhere.

"C'mon," said Layla. "Talk to me."

"Be patient," Tatum said sharply, and Layla gasped. She was afraid it seemed. Of what? Tatum didn't want to scare her. More gently she said, "I'm collecting my thoughts."

When she was ready, she said, "I don't feel good about what

happened last night. I wasn't in my right mind, and it was all a little out of my control, I guess."

Layla stammered, "But we were both drunk, and we've been dancing around it for weeks. Now you're single, and I guess I thought it was what you wanted." She closed her eyes. "What we both wanted."

Tatum could understand this, of course, and probably would've made the same assumption if the situation were reversed. And, in fact, part of her had wanted it. It had taken being with Layla to know it wasn't right. She'd felt the same way about Ed at first, gone back and forth before eventually deciding she did want him because she should want him, which had led to nine years of dissatisfaction. Whatever it was: pregnancy hormones, hangover, yellow house magic, or the disappointment of there being no yellow house magic after all, she felt strong enough, clear enough now, to not make the same mistake again.

"I get it," said Tatum. "I do. It's not just that. Today, I feel different somehow. I'm not totally sure why. I guess it's a confluence of things, I don't know. I just feel like our relationship is so weird." She stared directly into Layla's eyes. "I've felt like I can't be myself with you. Like I have to appease you, and make you like me, because you have so much money and stuff that I want. And you're making the kennel thing happen—or you were—and I was going to do it, too, but I don't know why, because I never wanted to. I mean, I do know why." Tatum shook her head. "But my heart was never in it."

Layla broke eye contact.

Tatum went on: "I mean, you have this house. Did you think it wouldn't be weird for us to be here? I didn't even know it was yours until a week ago. Before now, you never reached out or invited us. And, whatever, maybe your mom's name is on the deed, but this place was always shared. It was all of ours. And I know our parents suddenly hated each other and probably still do, but you could've done it anyway." Tatum waved her arms to indicate she was talking about the house. "Or about Audrey." She was crying. She wasn't sure who she was talking to or for—herself or Layla? She wished Willow was with her, but she'd stayed in the other room, fast asleep. And as always, she wished Audrey was there, too; she would be proud of her. She used to say, "Tell me how you really feel. I'll still like you no matter what," whenever Tatum was upset: about Ed, her parents, a silly misunderstanding with a college friend. Though Tatum had tried, she'd never done it. Not really. She'd been honest about those things, sure, but when it came to her true feelings for Audrey, never. And that sat like a rock in her stomach and would forever. Even if she'd never wanted to date her or even kiss her, she still wished she'd said, "I love you," the kind of love she'd actually felt.

Layla said, "Well, you didn't reach out to me, either. Why is it my responsibility? Because I'm rich? You think that because my life is easier in some ways I owe you more than you owe me? I don't."

"That's not what I'm saying at all," Tatum sobbed. "I'm saying I was trying to be someone I'm not to make you like me, and want to keep me around, and help me. And as of today, I just can't anymore."

"Do you know how manipulative and fake that makes you seem?"

"Yes," Tatum practically screamed. She was standing now, palms pressing into the table between their chairs, leaning over Layla. "Of course I do. I'm not an idiot."

Layla sank deeper into her seat. "I never said you were," she yelled back.

"Yeah, well," said Tatum as she turned away. "I'm just saying it's been really fucking weird to be here. And I'm just supposed to pretend it's not. And last night we fucked, and I'm pregnant, and I just can't hold it all inside as if I'm not losing my fucking mind anymore." She turned back to face Layla, who was standing now, too. "I'm losing my fucking mind," Tatum screamed. "I'm losing it!" She grabbed fistfuls of her hair and started to pull. It felt good. So good. "I'm losing it."

Layla reached for her arm. "Hey, stop." She tried to pry open Tatum's fingers. "Hey, let go." Reluctantly, Tatum did. "You're okay," said Layla. "You're okay."

Tatum closed her eyes.

"You're pregnant?"

Tatum nodded.

"Are you—"

"Yes," said Tatum.

"You're keeping it?"

"Oh, no. I'm getting an abortion. But they can't do it yet because it's too early."

"Shit," said Layla. "I mean, obviously I had no idea. I don't even know what to say."

Tatum dropped to the floor as suddenly as if she'd fainted. She could hardly think. She was the rawest version of herself, and here was Layla, witnessing it.

"Hey," said Layla. "You're okay." She took a pillow from one of the chairs and offered it, but Tatum shook her head.

"I can't move."

"Okay," said Layla. "We'll just sit here, then." She joined Tatum on the floor and tossed the pillow aside.

Slumped against the windowpane, Tatum blinked slowly. She was so tired. Hadn't eaten anything but pretzels all day and hadn't wanted to. The nausea was always there, tugging at the edges of her consciousness, despite the helpful drugs.

"There's something I have to tell you," Layla said.

"What's up?"

She could say anything, anything at all—confess that she'd murdered Audrey herself, shoved that damn olive down her throat—and Tatum wouldn't have the energy to react.

"The whole kennel thing was already off the table before this weekend." Layla was picking at her nails, avoiding Tatum's eyes. "My mom's people advised against investing in it, and there's a clause in my trust that prohibits me from putting money into anything that isn't approved by her business manager." Layla grimaced. "Fucking Jeb."

Tatum was confused. "Wait, really? When did you find out?"

Layla hid behind her hands. "Before we even toured the kennel," she said, voice muffled.

"So, why did we tour it?"

Layla shook her head, still covering her face. "I don't know. I'm embarrassed."

Now it was Tatum's turn to reach for Layla, and in an instant, it was the old days, when they would huddle together in this very room, giving and receiving comfort. Tatum was hit by memories of the darker times—a different shade of dark, perhaps, than what she'd classify as darkness now as an adult, but dark to her very young, innocent mind. Like when she'd stubbed her toe, screamed and sobbed and insisted it was broken, only for her mother to assure her it was fine. "Either way, at the hospital they'll just tell you to bandage it to another toe," Vera had said, leaving Tatum afraid and helpless, like if she couldn't convince her mother to take her to the hospital, she'd be in agony forever. Eventually they did go, and, after a three-hour wait in the ER, it was pronounced "fractured." The doctor's recommendation was exactly as Vera had promised and Tatum's toe remained in the very same bandage configuration as when she'd entered. On the plus side, a prescription for 500mg ibuprofen capsules had effectively numbed the pain.

She didn't tend to think about her childhood this way, but helplessness was real and intrinsic to those years, and she was lucky she'd only been affected in such non-traumatic ways. Still, even her little struggles had felt so big at the time because she'd relied on others to solve them, to take her pain seriously, and because Park Slope had always knocked things out of perspective.

Helplessness was paralyzing. Terrifying. As an adult, she still felt it often, about her life but also about bloodthirsty, power-hungry governments around the world. Yet even when faced with those irreparable slashes to the fabric of humanity, there were things she'd done and should do more of to take a stand. In the past, she'd protested alongside friends, held up cardboard signs, screamed and chanted and marched until her feet ached. She'd phone banked for politicians she believed in. She'd called her representatives, waited for the *beep*, and spoken passionately to their answering machines.

She should do the same with her own life now because she could. She wasn't a little kid anymore. Rather than succumb to endless hemming and hawing, to imagined helplessness, she should take a stand. Take a risk. She wasn't helpless—not at all. And it was an immense privilege that she wasn't.

Of course, she'd known all this in theory, but somehow, as she sat wrapped around Layla, she felt lucky in a way she hadn't ever before. So, unbelievably, sickeningly, unfairly lucky to be who she was. To have had the peaceful childhood she did, and to have left it behind.

"I never really wanted to do the whole kennel thing, anyway, even when we were kids," she said.

"Really?" Layla spoke into Tatum's shoulder. Her breath was hot and damp. "I wish you'd said so sooner."

"Me too. Now *I'm* embarrassed."

"Maybe we can both be more honest going forward," said Layla. "You know, you can always just ask me for help."

When she blinked, more tears poured down Tatum's cheek. "Really?"

"Tate, I love you." The first time she'd used that nickname since they were kids. Layla quickly added, "Not in a weird way, but in an 'I've known you forever and despite my weirdo crush, and the fact that last night happened, we'll always be family' way."

Tatum buried her face in Layla's shoulder, which smelled a bit like BO, and said, "You don't even seem like a real person to me sometimes."

Layla laughed—the sound was harsh, not joyful. "I feel like no one sees me as a real person. I wanted to do the kennel thing because—honestly, I guess there were a few reasons, but the biggest was probably that I'm so fucking lonely."

Tatum rubbed her back.

"Like, Tate, I don't have a lot of friends. Really, I don't. And the ones I do have don't seem like real people *to me*, you know. So, I just wanted to be in your life. And thought I should do something to make you want to be in mine, especially since I never reached out after Audrey. I don't know why I didn't, I just couldn't. It was like talking to you would make it real or something. I'm so sad I wasn't around when she was alive, and that I missed so much of your life, too. I'll never know her, and I wish I could've, and I wish I could've known your friendship and been part of it. I hope I haven't fucked up knowing you, too. I think I've fucked it up with Bea, but—"

"You're real to me," Tatum interjected; Layla's voice was elevated, and she didn't want Bea to overhear anything inadvertently mean. "Or, at least, I'll work harder to see you that way despite all the stuff." She gestured at the expensive-looking furniture. "In terms of Audrey, I get it. I've done a lot of weird, probably unhealthy things to cope. It's just nice to know you cared. And you can officially stop pretending to be financing a dog kennel to keep me around. I love you. I always have and I always will." In that moment, she knew it was true.

This time, Layla's laugh was genuine. "Cool, cool, cool," she said. "Well, love you, too."

They dried their faces and disentangled from each other.

"Can we forget about what happened yesterday?" Layla wiped her nose. "I'd really like that. I'm so sorry."

Tatum nodded.

"Okay," said Layla. "Thanks."

"And maybe we should make a pact that this is the last time we try to start a dog kennel together? Two times is more than enough."

"Well, what if in ten years—"

Tatum shook her head. "Time for new dreams."

They sat in silence, as memories passed between them, smiling.

"Can I come back here sometime?" asked Tatum. "I'd like to when I can really appreciate it."

Layla nodded. "Of course. Let's come back in the summer when we can swim. As long as you haven't moved far away or something."

Unfallen tears tickled Tatum's eyes. When she blinked, they fell, though they were irrelevant now. The release of emotional tension felt like she'd unbuttoned tight jeans, like the body-high after a strenuous workout. "I don't know where I'll be, exactly," she said, "but I'd really like that."

"Should we watch a movie tonight?" Layla asked. "I'm exhausted."

"Yeah, what should we watch?"

"I don't know."

Suddenly, it was easy. To think, talk, be together.

Eventually Tatum said, "I guess we should consult Rosalie and Bea, too. Something scary could be fun. Transportive."

"Sure," said Layla. "Let's find them."

"And we should feed Willow."

They helped each other stand. "I really think you should adopt her," Layla said. "You guys are so fucking cute together."

Tatum sighed. "I have to. There's no other way. I, like, can't be without her. Wherever I go in the future, she's coming with me."

They left the room, arms linked. Tatum was much taller than Layla barefoot, so their gait was awkward.

As they entered the sitting room, Tatum was just beginning to say, "So, what movie should we watch tonight?" But when they turned the corner, they found the room was empty, and the ottoman where Bea had been sitting lay on its side.

"I wonder where they went," said Layla. "And where's Willow?"

At that moment, a bark erupted from somewhere. They gasped and clutched their hearts, then burst into nervous laughter.

"Jesus," said Layla. "That almost gave me a heart attack."

The two of them stumbled, still laughing, toward the sound. Another bark, which inexplicably fed an even stronger stream of giggles.

When they made it to the kitchen, there was Willow, standing by the back door. She seemed agitated, stamping her paws, yelping.

"Hey, there," said Tatum. "C'mere." But Willow didn't move. She jumped against the door, pawing at the frame.

"No," bellowed Layla. When Tatum looked at her, surprised that her voice could sound so terrifying, she said, "What? My mom will kill me if she scratches anything."

Tatum turned back to Willow. "Sweetie girl, what's up?" She knelt beside the dog, whose wet nose was pressed so hard against the crack between the door and wall, the soft skin around it bunched. "I guess I should take her out."

Layla said, "Sure, and we can feed her after."

Willow's tail began wagging furiously when Tatum picked up the leash.

Layla flicked on the porch light.

The moment the door opened, Willow was pulling.

Tatum could barely contain her, could barely keep herself upright. "Shit," she said. "Willow, chill." She practically fell down the stairs after the dog, but unlike that morning, Willow did not squat in the grass. Instead, she ran hard against her leash, her big, shaggy shoulders pumping, toward the garden path that led to the cliff and the lake beyond.

"Hey," Tatum cried. "Willow, no. Stop. No." Rain was gently falling, making everything glisten.

"Bad girl," Layla chimed in.

All Tatum could do was hang on; suddenly, she was as helpless as a child once more.

"If she gets close to the cliff," Layla called from a few feet behind, "you have to let go."

"Willow," Tatum shrieked. "No!" She pulled with all her might, to no avail. There was no stopping her.

25

Just after Tatum and Layla left the sitting room, Rosalie announced, "I'm going for a walk."

Bea was rigid, trying to contain herself, though she could feel her rage bubbling up again. She watched Rosalie stand, pull her pants out of her butt crack, and walk toward the door. On the ottoman, Bea turned slowly, keeping Rosalie in her eyeline as she crossed the room. And when Rosalie left, she rose, knocking the ottoman over behind her, and followed.

The back door *thwapped* shut just as Bea entered the hall. From the shadows, she could see Rosalie through the screen, tugging on her shoes, squatting to knot her laces. She didn't look up, even when Bea was practically standing over her on the other side of the screen. When her shoes were secured, she jogged off the porch, then turned on her phone's flashlight.

The grass was frigid against Bea's bare feet. Frozen numbness shot up her legs in little zings. The wind blew strong through the trees, shushing her—a reminder she didn't need. Rosalie's flashlight bobbed across the lawn in a jagged line. Sometimes it stopped, sometimes it dipped down. Slowly, it approached the garden.

Bea followed from the shelter of the woods. Her bare feet made it possible to step quietly over dried leaves and uneven terrain. She matched Rosalie's leisurely pace, though inside, her heart was leaping.

When Rosalie stopped short to inspect the tightly wrapped bud of a rhododendron, Bea's foot came down hard on what felt like the tip of a knife. It entered her flesh with ease, slicing through her calloused skin. She yelped—couldn't help it—then bit down on her arm to keep from screaming. Rosalie whipped around. Her face was a black void inside her hood.

Tears pricked Bea's eyes as she staggered toward a nearby tree. It was big, gnarled, and beautiful, with branches stretching wide across the cloudy sky. Even through her pain, Bea could appreciate its grandeur. It made her feel insignificant in a familiar, comfortable way. She wrapped an arm around its trunk, then lifted her foot and found a thick, curved shard of glass embedded in the pad just beneath her toes. Dark blood oozed out. To keep walking, she'd have to remove it. She gripped the shard, closed her eyes, and pulled. The pain was excruciating but exhilarating, too. It was like the full moon to a werewolf. It made her powerful. Primal. She held the glass piece up and when she angled it the right way, the light from the house behind her illuminated the letters M-A-T-A. It was part of the olive jar she'd thrown out the window, a reminder from Audrey that she wasn't alone, a spur in her side—it had to be.

She glanced back in Rosalie's direction to find her gone. Without another thought, Bea dropped the glass. *Where is she?* Less afraid now of remaining undetected, Bea hobbled blindly over branches and pine needles, using the smaller trees she passed as supports. Still no Rosalie. She needed more visibility. The forest tugged at her hair. She was sweating, arms bleeding, scratched by brambles. *Where is she?*

Bea limped into the garden. Now only imperfect darkness concealed her. As quickly as she could on her punctured foot, she stumbled down the path, leaving bloody prints on stone. She was all but calling out for Rosalie. *Where? Where? Where?*

She'd never lost someone before. Not Audrey, when she used to follow her. Not Audrey's friends, including Tatum. No one. *Where?*

As she neared the cliff's edge, a shape rose up, as if from nothing. As if it had materialized, like a ghost.

Before her, the figure was still. Bea lurched toward it. "Audrey," she whispered. "Is that you?"

The figure did not reply. When Bea was close enough, she reached out, and it reached back.

When she felt chapped, rough fingers, as cold as the stone beneath her feet, she knew it was Rosalie and was relieved, and disappointed.

"You followed me," Rosalie said. "I knew you would."

Bea was out of breath. She said, shakily, "I wanted to make sure you were okay."

Their fingers were still interlaced. The way Rosalie was standing, Bea realized, her heels hung off the cliff's edge. Her toes and Bea's body were her only anchors to the ground.

"You're leaving," said Bea. "You said so to Tatum."

Rosalie said, "I know that hurts you."

"It's not about me," Bea snapped.

Rosalie's phone was on the ground now, its flashlight facing up. It must've been tucked into her body when Bea couldn't find her. She'd been hiding, which meant that Bea was enacting *her* plan, not the other way around.

"I've been very grateful for everything," Rosalie said.

"You can't leave. I can keep helping you."

"Like you did with Audrey?"

"Yes," said Bea. How did Rosalie know about that? She'd always been careful not to say too much about her relationship with her sister.

"Only, you didn't help Audrey."

"What?"

"You killed her."

"What?" Bea shrieked. "She choked to death because she was on drugs."

Rosalie said, "It's okay, it's okay. You don't need to say that." She leaned back slightly, and their arms, still joined, straightened. She was angled over the water. Bea could feel her weight. It made her foot hurt more but she pressed her toes flat, as if they were little suction cups. A drop of rain—two—on her forehead. The stone would grow slippery if it kept falling. Then, if Rosalie didn't let go, they'd both go over the edge. Or maybe Rosalie wasn't holding on to her at all.

Bea looked at their hands and found that Rosalie's fingers were relaxed. Her silver ring had slipped off and was pinned between their palms.

"I didn't kill her." More quietly, Bea added, "She was killing herself in slow motion over a long period of time." She adjusted slightly, causing Rosalie's body to tilt back even more, enough that her hood came off, and allowing her to slip the ring onto her own finger for safekeeping. It fit perfectly. Snuggly. Like it was supposed to be there and stay there.

"Was it because she wanted to leave? To get professional help for her addiction? Is that why you finally let it happen?"

"Stop," said Bea. At any moment, she could send Rosalie spiraling backward, down, down, down, until she smacked into the pebbles far below. "I was helping her. I did everything for her for over a year."

Rosalie nodded.

Bea was crying, her tears mixing with the rain, which was falling more consistently now. She said: "I just want to be needed. I just want company." Her nose was running. She couldn't stop it. "I didn't do anything to her. I wouldn't."

Bea hadn't done anything but support her sister, and she'd treated Rosalie like a sister, too, which was more than she deserved.

Rosalie smiled. "I've been so curious how this would end." She was perfectly calm as rain fell on her face, though every so often Bea's wet hands slipped. "Nothing in this fucking world comes free. And the more I got to know you, the more I could see there was something lurking beneath it all, but I didn't really care. I still don't. I mean, look at me." Bea was looking. Rosalie went on: "Then, this weekend, I guess I realized I don't have to just sit around and wait for it to find me. I can be like Travis."

Bea's muscles were growing tired.

"I remember that conversation we had after I ate the fucking olive, or whatever."

Bea frowned.

"You mentioned you took that class."

"Which?"

"The babysitting class."

"So?"

"Specifically, you mentioned you know how to administer the Heimlich maneuver. I know Audrey choked to death."

Bea's lips parted in agony. *Just say you were in the other room. Explain that Audrey couldn't move because she was high. You can fix this.*

The truth was, though, Bea had been there. Right there. Sitting next to her sister, then standing, then watching her die from the kitchen.

Audrey was going to leave. Bea knew she couldn't keep her forever against her will, and she'd been talking about it more and more.

"I can't go on like this," she'd slurred, "I've gotta get help."

Bea had shouted the word "ungrateful" just as Audrey placed the shiny brined fruit on her tongue. Seconds later, she was clutching her throat.

Bea could've saved her, Rosalie was right of course. Knew exactly how: one hand over the other, and the upward J-shaped motion required to do it. She could've, but she didn't. She'd watched as her sister's life ended, and so did her suffering. The days and weeks that followed were hollow and terrible. Bea had missed tending to her. The sound of her voice. The warmth of her breath. But from the start, before the ambulance had even arrived to take her body away, she'd felt Audrey all around and known she'd always be there, invisible, silent, yet permanently close, which, she'd come to realize, was what she'd always wanted.

"Death can be relief," she whispered. Her vocal cords were shot. Everything was. Her feet were totally numb now, her arms shaking.

Her fingers, wrapped around Rosalie's hands, were seconds from giving out.

"Do you regret it? What you did?"

"I didn't do anything."

"What you let happen?"

"I don't regret anything." It was true. Finally. *I have no regrets and love myself more today than ever for having done all I could*, she thought. Perhaps, when this was all over, she would find that Reddit post again. Maybe she would respond to it. Thank whoever had written it for making her feel understood.

"But you ended her."

Suddenly, one of Patricia's favorite words to describe Bea rang in her ears: *stunted*. Had she stunted Audrey's life? Drugs had turned her from success to disappointment, but Bea had played a role in that, too. And then she'd let her die. Out of a desire to even the score? Was Rosalie right? Was it possible they both were?

No. She'd given Audrey everything; it wasn't any more complicated than that. No regrets. None. "You don't know what you're talking about."

"If you want to do it now, then do it. I don't care if I live or die, but something has to change. Put me out of my fucking misery. I can't go on like this"—Audrey's exact words, and suddenly Bea was suspended between then and now. When she looked down, Rosalie's hands were Audrey's, long and delicate, then they were Rosalie's, stocky and pink, then Audrey's, then Rosalie's, then Audrey's; all the while, Rosalie's ring on Bea's finger glinted in the faded white phone light. *I'll keep you safe with me forever*, she thought, staring at the thick silver band. *I'll always protect you.*

Rosalie was still talking. "If you don't, I'm moving out—like you suggested once. You'll never see me again. If you do . . ." She paused. "You can tell everyone I slipped. Just make the fucking decision for me."

"Do what?" asked Bea, as if she was a different kind of person, as if she didn't already know what was about to happen.

Rosalie closed her eyes. "Let go."

As Tatum was being dragged down the wet path toward the cliff's edge, she pulled back with all her might, arching against the leash, which burned her hands. Cold rain pelted her eyes and skin. She was slipping on the smooth stones, closer and closer to the drop-off, yet despite Layla's advice to let go, she wouldn't. Couldn't. She trusted the dog not to hurt her. There was a light up ahead. A prick of white through the rainy haze. Tatum thought she could see someone standing—hovering—over the water through the dark, but her eyes were playing tricks. They had to be. When she held up her phone, it illuminated only the slanting raindrops, big as marbles.

"Hello?" she cried, through the deluge. "Get back. It's not safe."

No one answered. But someone was there. The closer she was pulled, the better she could see. Either Bea or Rosalie was peering over the edge as if they'd dropped something.

When Willow stopped short a few feet from the figure, Tatum nearly ran her over. Now she could tell it was Bea up ahead.

"Where's Rosalie?" Tatum called.

Below her, Willow was still, head bowed, prayerlike against the storm. Tatum patted her and cooed, "You're okay. Everything's—" But when she looked up again, Bea's expression stopped her mid-sentence, and for a moment all was quiet. Though she'd never say so to anyone, in the split second before Bea fell to her knees screaming, Tatum could've sworn she was smiling.

ACKNOWLEDGMENTS

I'm here because of the people in my life. Could write a book's worth of acknowledgments but will strive for brevity . . . Here goes!

I'm so lucky the brilliant Sabrina Taitz is my agent. I'll never forget the sticky summer morning when you changed my life forever. You've embraced me exactly as I am and encouraged me to do the same—the most wonderful gift. Cashen Conroy, your help and excitement are so appreciated. Thank you.

Pilar Garcia-Brown, my incomparable editor, your compassion, intuition, patience, and steadfast support have carried me through this wild process. Above all, thank you for understanding; this book would not have reached its full potential without you. Ella Kurki, thank you for the encouragement, for fielding my questions and providing such excellent feedback on *Harmless*.

Ana Inciardi, you're the most generous soul. Thank you for collaborating on my first book cover with the amazing Dutton designers, Jason Booher and Vi-An Nguyen. So thrilled to showcase your art and have your support.

I'm so grateful to everyone at Dutton. Thank you, Janice Barral, Lara Robbins, Melissa Solis, Lauren Morrow, Isabel DaSilva, Gaelyn Galbreath, and Nancy Resnick for all you've done in service of

Harmless and my career. I know what goes into this firsthand. Without you, there is no book. You are all my heroes.

My whole BookEnds fellowship family, thank you, thank you! Jennifer Yeh, Rachael Warecki, Katie Kalahan, Katie Aspell, Stefani Nellen, Bobby Crace, Giano Cromley, Vanessa Cuti, Daisy Florin, and many more.

Extra-special thanks to the following:

Craig Holt, for enthusiastically reading draft after draft of *Harmless* and sharing your immense talent with me—you're one of my favorite writers. Also, for always seeing what I'm "trying to do," for inspiring me with your incredible work ethic, and for your resilience. Suzanne LaFetra, for your sharp insights and steadfast friendship. Fae Engstrom, for the many hours of helpful conversations. JP Solheim, for making BookEnds go—we're so lucky—and for always being there to listen and soothe. Karen Bender, for reminding me to trust myself! Susie Merrell, for your warmth and generosity, and for your faith in me.

Thank you to all my former teachers, but especially: Yabome Kabia, Vanessa Prescott, John Schwartz, Jenna Alden, Sean Mills, and Laura Hymson—without you, who knows! Thank you for taking me seriously. Sean Mills presented me with the Creative Writing Award at my high school graduation. When I think about that moment, I'm still so proud.

To my colleagues Lisa Schwartz, Vanessa Robles, Amy White, Amanda Cranney, and the rest of the PYR Production Department, thank you for being hardworking, bighearted people, and for always answering my urgent questions about POs . . .

Thank you, family:

Mom, for forming the Mother's Group just before I was born, which inspired this novel and gave me my first friends; for letting us adopt a dog, Winnie, who inspired my own childhood dog kennel dream . . . which (obviously) *also* inspired this novel; for being a safety net; for always trying to accommodate; for your art; for watching the cats as needed; for the fruit-plate faces you made on dreary school mornings; for so much more than I can even remember. I love you.

Dad, for reading my essays in high school; for copyediting every piece of writing I've ever cared about; for letting Charlie and me live with you during COVID in Kinderhook; for the hours we spent playing games, watching movies, and for that tranquil setting, amidst all the uncertainty and grief, that served as the perfect creative retreat; also, for leading by example when it comes to writing; for believing I've had a knack for storytelling ever since I was small. I love you.

Holly, for always being there. Sisterhood is so complicated; I love you and am proud of how far we've come. Also, for bringing Susie Brustin into my life!

Aunts, uncles, cousins, for your love and excitement, all the laughs and years.

I don't have any living grandparents. I miss them and think of them often; of the sacrifices they made for me and their interesting quirks . . .

Thank you, newer family:

Meg, for everything. I am so lucky to learn from you, laugh with you, and watch your star shine so bright. Richard, for listening; for loving movies; for playing Codenames online; for your sense of humor. Gabriel, Devon, and Luca, for making delicious pizza; for teaching me about dinosaurs; for welcoming me into your lives. Margot, for being so precious. Hilma, for telling the best stories; for inspiring me in every way.

Thank you, family friends: Nellie Hartzell, Dick Hartzell, Valerie Berk, Phyllis Berk, Amy Mintzer, Bill Sweeney, Judy Londa, Bruce Londa, Aoife Henchy, and Niamh Henchy. I love you. (Side note: Aoife, Niamh, and my sister, Holly, shared in my childhood dog kennel dream.)

Bowen Fernie, thank you for taking my author photo. Charlotte Bravin Lee, thank you for doing my makeup for said author photo.

Thank you, writing friends: Alison Fairbrother, Maya Moverman, Jeffery Chin, Sophie Green, Julia Pike, Meriç Ateşalp, Benny Peterson, and Amber Hunter. I cannot wait to be first in line at each of your book signings. I cherish you. Our relationships transcend the label of "writing friends," but for organizational purposes . . .

Thank you so much to my amazing blurbers. Your generosity astounds!

Thank you, beloved nonwriting friends, who compose another family of mine and know me better than anyone. Deep breath. To Zoe Rohrich, Amy Chabassier, Nora Cady, Maddie Assarson, Sage Elder, Stella Frank, Séverine Kaufman, Gabe Karon, Madeleine MacGillivray, Jasper Hartnett, and Marshall Bone, thank you for planning parties to mark each publishing milestone and, in general, for filling my life with so much love. Ella Geismar and Olivia Cucinotta, thank you for speed-reading drafts on multiple occasions—my two lifelong best friends, without whom I'd be lost. We were so little, now we're not! There are many other names I want to include but don't have space for. My heart itches as I think of your beautiful faces. At its core, this novel is about the strength of friendship. Thank you for teaching me all about that.

And thank you, Charlie Panek, my deepest, most special love. You take the best care of me. I've loved you for more than one third of my life—can't remember what I did before loving you, but I'm sure it sucked.

And thank you, readers. It's such an honor. Such an immense honor.

ABOUT THE AUTHOR

Miranda Shulman attended Bard College, where she majored in human rights. Before pursuing a career in publishing, she worked at Planned Parenthood. She grew up in Brooklyn, New York, and still lives there. *Harmless* is her first novel.